THE TRIANGULUM FOLD

THE FOLD SERIES BOOK 8

NICK ADAMS

Elliptical
Publishing

PROLOGUE

GERINTH CIVRAY JEP stiffened in her seat. Something anomalous had registered on the attentiveness display. A slow pulsing warning of a problem on the outer confines of the vessel's porcelate dermis. Returning her attention to the ship's current profile, she saw a sudden and continuing sharp temperature reduction in area seventeen.

'That's got to be a hull breach,' she said to herself. 'How can that be? I haven't impacted anything since the stretch.' She activated the dermis regeneration rig, programmed it with the breach location and continued on with the scan of this previously unexplored and unnamed system.

Civray was a Wellasian surveyor. A native of the planet Wellas, some one thousand eight hundred light spins distant in the near centre of the galaxy. After the introduction of stretch drives only twenty-seven spins ago, a cadre of thirty-six surveyors were dispatched out into the unknown to discover habitable worlds and useful resources to supplement their planet's dwindling reserves. The single-occupant ships were designed to be away for up to four spins at a time and almost completely automated. Hence the reason Civray was a little perturbed at how the latest sophisticated Xantion array had missed something that had potentially punctured the dermis.

Letting the automated system get to work with the leak, she watched as the results of the scan revealed more detail of the strange return she'd received while many light spins away: exotic metals, masses of them congregating around and near the fourth planet in the system. There was just so much, it couldn't possibly be a natural phenomenon, which made her suspicious and just a little bit nervous.

She could stretch there in a few seconds, but something told her to be cautious. As the stretch drive took a while to charge, she decided to travel there utilising the standard Bairdon drive and keep the stretch drive charged just in case a quick exit was required. The returns hadn't shown any life signs at all, but her fur bristled and she shivered uncontrollably, which was usually a sign of trouble.

The hull breach warning went out and she emitted a sigh of relief, at least that was one thing less to worry about. She slept fitfully as the ship powered its way across the empty void, waking constantly with a start, her eyes darting across the readouts. As the vessel clawed its way closer, more detail began to appear. The planet seemed uninhabited, but it was evident by the gasses in the atmosphere, a life form of oxygen breathers had existed there at some point in its distant past. Strangely, it had three moons that orbited in a close-knit group, forming an almost perfect equilateral triangle, which was peculiar in itself.

But it was the lumps of exotic metals, all of which were in some form of permanent orbit around the planet. There were thousands, tens of thousands in all shapes and sizes. She concentrated the array on one specific large piece and sat back violently in her seat as the computer put an image together and she realised what it was.

'It was a ship,' she exclaimed and suddenly feeling hot she began to pant, her breaths coming fast and short.

The Wellasian's hadn't had first contact, so this was the first evidence Civray had ever seen that proved they were not alone, hence her state of shock.

It soon became evident that all the exotic metal returns were vessels, or at least parts of vessels. She almost hit the emergency stretch command, but something stopped her. It was the fact that everything was so cold, no life signs, no power readings, and the closer she got the more detail became available.

'There must've been hundreds of ships,' she whispered, as if she was scared of waking the dead. 'What the hell happened here?'

Before too long, she was able to get detailed images of some of the other wrecks. It was obvious by the way the hulls were twisted and holed, there had been the mother of all space battles here. The evidence of weapon damage was unmistakable. The ships had been torn apart as ordnance or their own magazines had exploded within. The sheer density of the shrapnel was a worry, so Civray slowed her approach and decided to circle the planet from a distance.

She looked on with awe, until suddenly the slow pulsing alarm from before caught her attention again.

'Not another one,' she moaned, glancing at the display.

Sure enough, another small dermis breach. This time in area twelve and just as she was reprogramming the dermis regeneration rig again, there was another breach in area twenty.

'How can this be?' she gasped out loud this time, a tremor evident in her voice.

Then a second alarm, this one slightly more critical as it had an audible alert too. It warbled away indicating a cooling problem with the main power node.

'What on Wellas is going on?' she cried, diverting some of the cooling fluid from the Bairdon drive over to the node.

It made no difference, the cell's temperature continued to climb. She flinched as a third and then a fourth alarm joined in, turning the cockpit into a cacophony of warnings. Both environmental and propulsion were now showing critical errors and shutting down.

'No, don't do that,' she wailed, frantically stabbing at the touch display to absolutely no avail.

She nearly vomited when the power node master alarm sounded.

'No, no, no...this is madness,' she screamed, knowing she would very soon be vaporised as the node indicated it was rapidly approaching a critical and irreversible temperature.

She swore out loud as she glanced at the lifeboat hatch and at the planet below, knowing that was now most likely her only chance of survival. Her belts were off and because the artificial gravity had also failed, she floated across to the access hatch. She ejected the ship's memory core as she went and slid it into her flight suit pocket. The lifeboat hatches both opened quickly, she dived inside, closed both, before strapping herself in, uncovering the launch toggle and hitting it hard. For a moment, her heart missed a beat as nothing happened. But because the ship's drives had failed, the vessel had begun to tumble and the lifeboat had paused slightly until it was facing the planet. Finally, after what seemed like an age but was only a split second, she was crushed into her seat padding as a heavy weight hit her in the chest and the little pod blasted clear of the surveyor vessel.

Civray gritted her teeth and prayed the lifeboat wasn't affected by all the sudden critical errors the main ship had suffered. She was just stretching up and peering out the tiny window in the door hatch, when she was suddenly blinded by a flash.

'Goodbye, little ship,' she whispered, watching her home of the last two spins vaporise and bracing herself for the concussion wave.

It arrived with a vengeance and slammed her into her seat for a second time, but what she didn't know was the pressure wave was also clearing the worst of the old debris out of the way and as the little pod struggled to stay on course it was able to approach the upper atmosphere without the risk of a major and lethal collision.

Civray knew survival was out of her hands now. She folded her arms across her chest and closed her eyes. In the next few minutes her fate would be decided.

1

Castle Virr, Somerset coast, England, Earth

'IT DOESN'T LOOK any bloody different. It's still an old shit box,' said Andrew Faux, watching as an ancient Spilaio class, Pallion-designed freighter landed in the courtyard of the castle. 'How much did you say you spent on it? Cuz you've been robbed.'

Edward Virr grinned at his friend and shook his head slowly.

'Oh ye of little faith,' he replied.

'But there are broken bits still hanging off it and it's covered in rust.'

'The supposed broken bits are disguised antenna and the rusty bits are fake.'

Andy shrugged as they both approached the ugly vessel. The dust settled and a set of steps whined down from underneath the cockpit area.

It'd been eighteen months since Ed had appropriated the old ship from a bunch of particularly unfriendly pirates. Since then, it had been having a clandestine no-expense-spared refit at the Southampton shipyard, a three-year-old extension to the Armstrong station in orbit above Earth.

A short lady dressed in slightly grubby unironed mechanic's coveralls, stepped down to greet them.

'Mr Virr, a pleasure to see you again,' she said, brushing a lock of her jet-black hair out of her face.

'Hello, Fliss,' he replied, shaking her hand. 'Didn't expect you to deliver it personally.'

'Ah, gets me out of the workshop occasionally.'

'Andy, this is Fliss Zachary, co-owner of the shipyard where it's had the refit,' Ed said, waving an arm at her and up at the freighter.

'Hello,' Andy said, sheepishly. 'What exactly have you done to it over the last year and a half? It looks exactly the same.'

Fliss smirked and raised her eyebrows.

'That's excellent news, Mr Andy,' she said. 'Then we have succeeded in the first part of the remit. If you'd like to follow me, I'll show you the few modifications we've made on the inside.'

Ed chuckled as she led the two men up the steps and into the underside airlock.

'This airlock, as with the other two, have all been extensively re-engineered to the latest specifications, but remain old and worn in appearance.'

She cycled them through and they stepped out into a scruffy corridor. The walls and floor were badly stained, occasional bird's nests of wiring hung out of broken conduits, giving the ship the appearance that it was on its last legs.

'Excellent,' said Ed. 'It's perfect.'

'But it looks worse than before,' mumbled Andy, thrusting his hands into his pockets, so he didn't touch anything and get them dirty or electrocuted.

'Yes, that's the point,' said Ed. 'If the ship is boarded or we have guests, the subterfuge remains.'

Fliss opened a door on the opposite side of the passage and led them into the cargo bay.

'This is still eighty percent the same size as before and can still legitimately be used to carry goods from place to place.'

They found themselves in a space about the same size as a six-car garage. Again the space was dirty and gave the impression of being unmaintained.

'The loading ramp has been modified too,' she said, opening a box on the wall and turning a lever.

A narrow ramp powered down at the far end with a hiss, but plenty wide enough to facilitate a loaded auto trundle.

'Defences?' Ed queried, giving her a glance.

She nodded and pressed another button in the box. Two substantial-sized laser cannons appeared out of hidden compartments in the ceiling above the ramp and swung down to point outside.

'Reconditioned weapons from an aging destroyer being scrapped,' she said. 'They're old models and perfectly congruous with the freighter's age and can also be operated from here or the cockpit. Just like the other eight spread around the hull.'

'It has eight more of those things?' Andy marvelled. 'I didn't see them.'

'That's just the point,' Ed replied.

Fliss smiled again and turned to Andy.

'Along with two rail guns, one forward firing and one rear, an astrapi lamp and two multi-directional six-rack kataligo missile launchers. It can achieve point-nine light in twenty-eight seconds, jump up to five hundred light years, has a reconditioned katadromiko cruiser shield generator and the latest Theo-designed cloak.'

'And a partridge in a bloody pear tree,' Andy mumbled, giving Ed a sideways eye roll. 'Now I'm beginning to understand where all the cash went.'

'Come and see the two cockpits,' she said, turning for the door, her long black hair swishing to and fro as she walked.

'Two cockpits...really?' Andy sighed, as he fell into step behind Fliss and Ed. 'Yeah...of course it does...I mean, why would you only have one?'

She led them back past the airlock where they entered and forward to a staircase that led upwards. It went up four short flights and came out on a small landing with a door on the right that she led them through. It was the original cockpit, still just as filthy, with grubby oil-stained seats and dusty, coffee ringed control surfaces.

'Still fully operational if you need the keep up the ruse while in flight,' she said.

'Smells like a sumo wrestler's jockstrap in "ere,' Andy complained, wrinkling his nose.

'Excellent,' said Ed, nodding enthusiastically. 'No one would want to hang around on this ship. Show me the other one.'

Back out on the small landing, she stopped them and pointed at a small pin-hole up in the top left-hand corner of one wall.

'Place a finger over the hole,' she said, stepping back.

Ed did as requested. Both he and Andy jumped as the entire wall facing the stairs zipped down into the floor, revealing a narrow airlock.

'It operates fast, just in case you're being pursued,' she said, pulling them both in and tight against the far side. 'So be extra careful once you're in here.'

She mashed the cycle button and the wall/door snapped up and slammed shut.

'Cuz you don't want to meet that on the way up.'

'No shit,' said Andy, giving Ed a worried glance.

There was a slight hiss and the inner door motored open quickly, but not like the outer guillotine door.

'Wow,' exclaimed Ed, turning and peering into a small room lit by low green shadow lighting.

'Welcome to your concealed internal command bridge,' she said proudly. 'It's set up for two, but there are two more seats if needs dictate.'

'Oh, shit the bed,' said Andy, stepping inside to run his hand over one of the raised leather command couches before gazing up at the multi-coloured holo display of Earth slowly rotating above. 'This is the bollocks this is...'

Fliss turned to Ed, a bemused expression replacing the proud confident one from before.

'Sorry about my colleague's rather crass turn of phrase,' Ed sighed, noticing her disquiet. 'It means he likes it.'

'Oh...good,' she said, brightening again. 'There are

also two small self-contained cabins behind and a small galley.'

'I don't see a lifeboat?' queried Ed.

'That's where it gets really interesting,' she said, moving over to the couches and pointing to a small box built into the side of the chairs. 'Under that is a red button, only to be pressed in extreme circumstances...'

'Why? Is it an ejector seat?' Andy quipped, unable to stop himself glancing up at the ceiling.

'Andrew, try and say something sensible just occasionally,' Ed said, giving Fliss an apologetic eye roll.

'Actually, he's not far off,' said Fliss.

Andy turned to give Ed a smug grin as she continued.

'It actually jumps this entire unit away from the ship a few light years and into a safe area.'

'Ah...that explains an internal airlock coming in here,' said Ed, nodding back at the door.

'It's an embedded jump too...so whoever it is you're escaping from might not even know you've gone, let alone where.'

'Is it automated from then on, like an ordinary lifeboat?' Andy asked.

'No, you can fly it just as before, but with a restricted range and of course you have no weaponry,' she said. 'Another thing to note is when utilised, the main ship will auto self-destruct sixty seconds later, so no one gets their hands on all the weapons.'

'Cool bananas,' Andy quipped, sliding into one of the couches and waving the holo console up into his eye line.

'Don't you be getting my nice new seats grubby with those scruffy old jeans,' Ed complained, pointing at the pristine cream leather.

'There's another ship coming in to land,' Andy said, glancing over at Fliss.

'That's my ride back,' she said, handing Ed a data node. 'Everything you'll need is on there. Oh and by the way, did you know your weapons-instal authorisation came direct from the Admiral of the Fleet's office?'

'Friends in high places,' replied Ed.

Fliss raised her eyebrows but didn't pursue the point.

'Got a name for the ship yet?' Andy asked.

'The *Secchio*,' he said.

'The what?'

'*Secchio*, it's an Italian word for bucket.'

'Oh.'

'You don't like it?'

'Not the *Cartella II*?'

'No…there was only one *Cartella* and she's gone forever.'

2

Starboard hangar, the *Gabriel*, orbiting Earth

ED SQUEEZED the newly delivered *Secchio* into the *Gabriel*'s starbcard hangar. It was tight and had caused the moving of two of the shuttles across to the port hangar. He had to concentrate hard as he turned it slowly around and sat it down on its six struts.

'Made to measure,' he said, shutting everything down.

'Blind bloody luck, more like,' Andy replied. 'What would you' have done if it was too big to go in here?'

'Got Cleo to enlarge the hangar.'

'That's on the assumption she would've wanted this rusty shit box in her pristine hangar.'

'Correct assumption,' said Cleo, appearing suddenly and sporting an expression of displeasure. 'Although…it's quite smart in here isn't it?' she added, peering around, her face brightening somewhat.

'It's wonderful, Cleo,' said Ed. 'Just ignore the outside…it's designed so it doesn't get a second glance.'

'Are we planning going on a trip somewhere?' she asked, with a hopeful inflection in her voice.

'We are,' Ed replied. 'It's been a while and from what I can gather, everybody's getting a bit restless and wanting a bit of adventure. Andy suggested we travel to the galactic gate and explore another galaxy. There's certainly plenty of them.'

'Oh cool,' she said. 'I thought something might be in the wind when Linda turned up yesterday with Callon and a shuttle full of wine.'

'She brought wine?' asked Andy. 'But you can produce any wine we want.'

Cleo looked awkward for a moment.

'She has a surprise for you and I'm not allowed to tell you what it is.'

Half an hour later, Ed and Andy arrived up in the blister lounge on the topmost deck of the *Gabriel*. The entire ceiling in this room was carbon glass and provided a spectacular view of a beautiful blue Earth turning slowly below.

Phil, Linda and Callon were already there, all sporting wide grins and after the hugs were completed, Andy was unable to contain his curiosity.

'What's the big surprise then?' he asked, excitedly.

Linda exchanged a glance with Callon, before pouring glasses of sparkling wine and handing them around.

'I take it we're celebrating something?' said Ed.

'Yes,' said Linda, holding up her glass. 'Callon and I bought a vineyard last year and this is our first vintage.'

'Awesome,' blurted Andy.

'Congratulations,' said Ed, as they all chinked glasses and took a sip.

'It's delicious isn't it?' Phil admitted, getting positive nods from the boys.

'Top drawer,' said Ed.

'Just as well you like it,' said Callon, glancing over at the bar. 'Cuz we've brought a dozen cases.'

'The Gabriel Vineyard is now fully operational, but it does involve a lot of work, so is it okay if Callon stays behind to oversee this year's harvest?' Linda asked.

'Of course,' said Ed. 'We're only going exploring for a few weeks this time and not intending to get involved in any wars.'

'Famous last words,' chuckled Phil.

'When are the girls due up here?' Linda asked.

'Tomorrow morning,' Andy replied. 'They're doing a bit of retail therapy before we go.'

'Shall I wait until they're back and return on the same shuttle?' said Callon.

'No need...use one of the Lambo ships,' said Ed. 'They don't get much use.'

'They're smaller too and will fit in one of the vineyard barns,' said Linda.

'Wow...but they're beautiful, and cost you a fortune,' Callon said, her eyes wide. 'Linda told me they're the only two in existence and you don't use them very often.'

'They should get used more,' said Ed. 'Sitting in the bridge hangar gathering dust isn't good for them. I've had Cleo instal cloaking on them too. Probably best not to use that round here, you'll just get an idiot fly into you,' he added, eyeing the busy space traffic outside.

'Sorry to change the subject, but have you let Bache know of our plans?' Phil asked.

'Yeah,' said Andy. 'He was a bit pissed off he couldn't come with us.'

'He does miss the cut and thrust doesn't he,' said Ed. 'I think he has to spend the majority of his time in his office on Dasos shuffling paperwork.'

'Brrr.' Linda shivered. 'He can keep that freezing, heavy-gravity shit hole. If I had to work from an office, it would be on Panemorfi, with a sun lounger and a cocktail bar only metres away.'

'I like your thinking,' said Ed, then turned to face Andy. 'Did Bache say what ship he has patrolling the gate at present?'

'It's one of the older cruisers, The *Lytrotis* under a Captain Tzooums apparently. Sounds like a fast captain to me.'

Ed rolled his eyes and turned to the others.

'We'll leave at lunch time tomorrow, once the girls are here and settled.'

The next morning Ed sat on a bench under a palm tree in the *Gabriel*'s huge atrium. His eyes were shut as he used his DOVI to inspect the hull of the six-hundred-metre-long and a hundred and fifty-metre-wide starship. With all the weapons pods retracted he reckoned it resembled a Blackbird, an old American stealth bomber from the last century. His dad, an aircraft fanatic, had once had a model of the plane on a shelf in his office and Ed always thought how it looked like it was doing Mach 3 when stationary.

He grinned inwardly and marvelled at the fact this beautiful vessel was his. He didn't really need to do an inspection at all as Cleo, the sentient computer that ran the ship, would soon let him know if anything was awry. Opening his eyes again he watched as a rainbow parakeet squawked at him from the palm tree above and flew off, joining the small flock circling in the tropical-themed atrium.

'Good morning, lover,' said a familiar voice, as a tall, beautiful young woman joined him on the bench and slid up close.

'Hello, pretty girl,' he said, enveloping Pol in his arms and kissing her on the cheek. 'Did you buy lots of nice things?'

'Yes…but not as much as Rayl. I think she bought a new outfit for every day of the year. I'm sure the shuttle was overloaded on the way up.'

'Sounds like Cleo's going to need to increase the size of her dressing room again. She's already done it twice.'

They both turned as Phil came trotting over sporting his trademark anxious expression.

'Oh dear, somethings afoot,' Ed whispered in her ear.

'I think we need to leave as soon as possible,' Phil muttered, his brow furrowed and wringing his hands nervously.

'What's up, mate?' said Pol, getting raised eyebrows from Ed at her sudden and unusual use of an Aussie accent.

'Message from the Admiral,' he said. 'They haven't received their regular update from the *Lytrotis* out at the gate. He's still desperately short of operational vessels and as we're due to go there and one of the fastest ships in the region, can we investigate the lack of communication?'

'Absolutely,' said Ed. 'Send a message back that we're on our way at flank speed.'

'Okay, boss.' He turned on his heel and sped off again towards the nearest elevator portal, his face remaining a picture of disquiet.

Ed stood and held a hand out to Pol.

'Come on, I think we're needed on the bridge before Captain Worry has a coronary. And Cleo,' he called, glancing up, 'can you plot the jump sequence to get us there? And make them long. We need to get there yesterday.'

'Already done and dusted, Edward,' Cleo's voice boomed around the atrium. 'ETA around three days.'

'Is that fast?' Pol asked, as they walked purposely towards the same elevator portal that Phil had used.

'It took over five days with the old less efficient drives. It's next to a planet called Pyli in sector ninety-seven, right on the far edge of the galaxy. It would be quicker but we have to skirt around Klatt space to get there.'

Pol pulled a face, remembering their last altercation with those rather antagonistic reptilian warmongers.

3

Flex Du domicile, Calistromal locale

TYME DU GRIPPED his knapsack tightly and followed his twin brother Jaccin onto the grey-green trollicar. He slid onto his usual worn seat next to his brother, not bothering to glance around as he knew who would be sat in every other seat. The vehicle hummed off with a slight rattle, that Tyme knew was a worn tallis shaft in the front divv. It'd been like that for a while now as maintenance on human transportation was low on Repp priorities. He glanced down where he knew it was located beneath the floor and hoped it hung in there and didn't decide to fail while he was sitting directly above.

'It's not going to break today,' Jaccin said, noticing his concerned expression. 'They let them get a lot worse before they change them out.'

Tyme rummaged in his knapsack, locating and slipping

on his pair of goggs as the trollicar exited the relative twilight of Calistromal and emerged into the bright surface light of the Pessawinn locale. His brother had his perched on his head and just flicked them down to avoid the sudden glare. He turned to watch the brown barren landscape of the uplight, stretching away in all directions, only broken up by the growing slag piles that he thought encroached on their locale more and more each day.

'Be careful out there today,' Jaccin said, without turning his head. 'Haslyin lost a spade man yesterday. They sent him for a blade extraction in punishment, along with the boy's two brothers.'

Tyme shivered, his knees involuntarily clamping together at the thought. Having a large needle inserted into his testicles was not something he ever wanted to experience. His regular summons to the milking salon could be painful enough.

He could smell the refinery long before they got there and knew by the taste of the sickly cough-inducing gasses, that it was haklion plate being refined here.

The automated vehicle turned sharply through the security scanners, almost causing Tyme to slide off the shiny plastekine seat. His brother caught him and slid him back into place. It shot into the arrival tunnel and braked hard to align the side exit door with the safety scanner. Everybody immediately disembarked, holding their arms up in the air as they passed through the scanners.

Tyme nodded at his brother as they separated to join their respective work crews. A short tunnel led to a platform where a trollie was waiting to take them to the melting stacks. He boarded quickly along with his usual crew to avoid the chance of a stinger. One of the older men

stumbled and went down on one knee. He bellowed as a
stinger bolt hit him on his right shoulder. Two hands
reached out, grabbed his collar and hauled him inside the
trollie just as the door snapped shut.

He could smell the man's singed clothing and felt a
bit sorry for him as he must be getting close to thirty
now. Not long before his transition into the vassalage
duration which would be up on the Lamination.
Allegedly, according to the rumours, it was much easier
work than this and well worth putting in the effort to get
there.

The trollie lurched forward, jostling Tyme against the
metal bulkhead. He steadied himself, watching the older
man rub his shoulder where the stinger had hit. The burn
mark on his jumpsuit was still smoking slightly and Tyme
could see the reddened skin beneath the torn fabric.

'You all right, Merrin?' someone called.

The man nodded grimly, his weathered face tightening.

'Not my first stinger. Won't be my last either.'

Tyme looked away, not wanting to stare. He knew the
Repps used the stingers more frequently on the older
workers, almost as if they were testing their reflexes,
seeing who was still worth keeping around. It made his
stomach knot.

The trollie whined as it navigated the twisting tunnel
towards the melting stacks. The air grew thicker, hotter
with each passing second. Sweat began to bead on Tyme's
forehead, and he adjusted his goggs to keep them from
slipping down his nose.

'Station four today,' announced the crew leader, a
gaunt man named Pell. 'They're processing the haklion in
batches of three hundred units per cycle. Keep your

helmets sealed tight, the particulate levels are running unusually high today.'

Tyme's chest tightened. Station four meant working directly beneath the primary discharge vents where the processed haklion particles rained down like toxic snow. Even with the protective gear, he could taste the metallic bite in the air through his respirator's worn seals.

The trollie shuddered to a halt and the doors hissed open. Heat slammed into him like a physical wall, making his eyes water behind his goggs. The familiar roar of the melting stacks filled his ears, a constant grinding, bubbling cacophony that would leave his head pounding by day's end.

He shuffled out with the others, his boots clanging against the metal grating. The work platform stretched before them, a maze of pipes, conveyor belts, and collection bins. Steam hissed from various joints, and the floor vibrated with the rhythm of massive machinery hidden somewhere below.

Tyme grabbed his assigned tool pack from the rack, a collection of scrapers, brushes, and suction hoses that felt heavier each day. His shoulders already ached just from lifting it. He wondered if Jaccin's job today was any easier. His twin had been assigned to the cooling tanks, which wasn't as hot but came with its own hazards, sudden temperature drops that could freeze skin on contact if protective gear failed.

'Du... Stop daydreaming,' Pell barked. 'Take position three with Merrin.'

Tyme nodded quickly and hurried to his station. Position three meant working the collection troughs where the refined haklion pooled before being channelled into the setting trays. He clipped his safety tether to the overhead rail and adjusted his respirator one last time.

Merrin shuffled beside him, still rubbing his stinger-burned shoulder. 'Stay alert today, boy,' he muttered through his mask. 'The Repps changed the flow rate again. Makes the stuff splash more.'

The warning bell sounded, three harsh clangs that echoed through the chamber. Tyme braced himself as the massive valves overhead creaked open. A moment later, the first molten stream of haklion plate poured down into the collection system, glowing a sickly yellow-green. The heat intensified immediately, and Tyme could feel sweat running down his back, soaking into his jumpsuit. The acrid smell of the molten material cut through his respirator's filters, coating the back of his throat with a metallic tang that made him want to gag.

He positioned his collection scraper at the edge of the first trough and began guiding the flowing haklion towards the main channel. The substance moved like liquid fire, casting dancing shadows on the walls around him. Each time a droplet splashed up from the trough, he flinched back, remembering the permanent scars he'd seen on some of the longer-term workers.

The rhythm of the work was hypnotic, scrape, guide, clear the blockages, repeat. His muscles fell into the familiar pattern, but his mind wandered to what Jaccin had said about Haslyin's crew. A blade extraction. He'd heard whispers about the procedure but never wanted to know the details. The thought of those needles made his hands shake slightly as he worked.

A loud clang from somewhere above made him look up. One of the discharge pipes had shifted, and now the

haklion was pouring at a different angle, splashing danger-
ously close to where he stood. He stepped back quickly,
bumping into Merrin. The older man grunted and pushed
him forward again.

'Watch yourself,' Merrin growled, steadying his own
scraper. 'Can't afford to get knocked off balance by the
flow.'

Tyme's heart hammered against his ribs. He'd seen
what happened when someone fell into the collection
troughs, there wasn't enough left to send home to their
families. He repositioned himself carefully, giving the
erratic stream more room while still being able to reach his
work area.

The haklion continued pouring, and Tyme fell back
into his rhythm, though his nerves remained on edge. The
heat seemed to be getting worse, or maybe it was just his
imagination. His heat suit clung to his skin, soaked on the
inside with sweat that also stung his eyes despite the
goggs.

A sudden new sound joined the constant roar of the
heavy machinery, a clunking that Tyme didn't recognise.
He glanced up, trying to locate the source. The noise
seemed to be coming from the shifted discharge pipe. As
he watched, it shifted again and discharged a lump of
something that landed with a splat in the collection trough
right in front of him. Dodging the droplets of haklion, he
instinctively scooped it out and slid it onto the metal grid
platform he and Merrin were working from.

Merrin stumbled back, a look of horror on his face.
Tyme couldn't see what it was through his steamed-up
goggs, though he quickly continued guiding the white-hot
haklion while Merrin was temporarily distracted. The

smell hit him first. A foul, rotten odour rising through his respirator's filters. When he managed to wipe his goggs clear with his forearm, he froze. There on the grid was what appeared to be a severed human arm, charred and partially melted.

'Keep working,' Pell shouted from across the platform, either not seeing or choosing to ignore what had just landed. 'Maintain flow.'

Tyme's stomach lurched. He glanced at Merrin, whose eyes had gone wide behind his goggs. The older man gave a slight shake of his head, a warning not to react, not to draw attention.

With trembling hands, Tyme turned back to his scraper, guiding the haklion while trying not to look at the grisly object just feet away. He kept peeking at it though, he couldn't help himself and then he recognised something. A slightly melted ring on one of the fingers and the remnants of a distinctive tattoo. His eyes went wide and all the hairs on the back of his neck stood up, as he suddenly realised he knew 'whose arm it was. How had he ended up in the furnace and discharge pipe? The questions made him feel quite sick, or maybe it was the heat, the fumes, the shock.

'Flow stop in ten,' called Pell's voice over the intercom. 'Then prepare for transition of the plates.'

Ten minutes. Ten minutes of pretending he didn't have his dead friend's arm on the floor next to him.

4

The bridge, the *Gabriel*, en route to Pyli

SIXTY- THREE HOURS AFTER LEAVING EARTH, Linda, who was on late-night bridge duty, summoned Ed from his bed.

'What is it?' he asked, yawning and running a hand through his bed hair.

She pointed up at the holomap.

'The remains of a GDA communication drone,' she said.

'Is it from the *Lytrotis*?'

'We're not sure,' said Cleo. 'It's pretty messed up and only two jumps out from Pyli.'

'So, you're saying it only got this far before being fired on?'

'No, there's no conventional weapon damage at all,' Cleo continued. 'It's almost as if something was eating it.

It looks like a lump of Swiss cheese, there's random-sized holes all over it.'

'How far away is it?'

'A hundred thousand kilometres and travelling at point two light in the direction of the next jump point towards Dasos. We've turned and are matching its velocity.'

Ed rubbed his chin and thought hard, trying to wipe the fogginess of sleep from his brain and decide what to do about it. He reclined on his couch and surveyed the holomap.

'Nothing around?' he asked.

'Nothing uncloaked, no,' Cleo admitted.

'Hmm,' he grunted. 'Do we risk going closer?'

'You think it might be a trap?' Linda asked.

'We've had a few before haven't we?'

'Yeah.'

'And we are near Klatt space here. That thing could explode suddenly, take down our shields and twenty cloaked Klatt warships suddenly invite themselves for tea and muffins.'

'I have an embedded jump all ready to rock, if it's any help,' said Cleo.

Ed nodded and raised his eyes at Linda.

'Is it shielded? |Is that why we can't scan its electronics?'

'It's as if it doesn't have any electronics,' said Linda. 'But we all know they have to be there. They can't just dissolve.'

'Unless...' muttered Cleo.

'Unless what?' Ed asked, looking up at the ceiling.

'Shit,' said Cleo. 'Emergency jump.'

The holomap suddenly realigned and Ed heard the two asteri beams thrumming away, causing the lighting to dim with the massive amount of power they required.

'Who are we firing at?' Ed called in confusion, staring up at an empty holomap, knowing full well Cleo was a pacifist programme and her software absolutely forbade her from taking a life.

'It's some sort of weaponised nano technology,' Cleo replied. 'It's attacking our shields.'

'Are the beams neutralising them?' Linda shouted, above the racket of the beams.

'I believe so,' she replied, sounding a little concerned. 'Give me a minute.'

'That must've been what happened to the drone,' Linda said, turning to Ed. 'Is this some new Klatt thing?'

The din of the beams ceased suddenly, the eerie silence that followed had both Ed and Linda holding their breath.

'Is that it, Cleo?' Ed asked at last, looking up hopefully.

Before she could answer, Andy, his hair dishevelled and pillow creases across his face, shot up on the tube lift wearing nothing but his underpants.

'Are we at war or something?' he stammered, wiping the sleep from his eyes.

'We were for a while it seems,' said Ed.

'With who?'

'We're not entirely sure,' said Linda. 'Have you got any more answers, Cleo?'

'Self-replicating nanos that dismantle electronic componentry at an alarming rate, using it to multiply rapidly.'

A rotating holographic image popped up of what at first glance looked like a mosquito, but on further examination turned out to have miniature teeth like a tiny chainsaw.

'Bloody hell,' said Linda. 'You think the mossies can bite in Florida.'

'These are the size of a pin head,' added Cleo. 'Trillions and trillions of them, they're extreme cold resistant, which is why they're able to survive in space, and it takes the ultimate heat of an asteri beam to neutralise them.'

'Where the fuck have they come from?' asked Andy. 'If they were to get inside a ship it'd be doomed.'

'I estimate they would render a ship the *Gabriel*'s size completely dead in less than an hour,' Cleo said.

'You're absolutely sure none got through?' Ed asked.

'Yes,' she replied. 'I was able to study their attack profile against our shield harmonics and build a fluctuating and random sequencer that thwarts them. I'm currently working on a predator nano, that will hunt and kill them, but it's going to take a little while to perfect.'

'Let me know as soon as you've done it,' said Ed. 'Can you imagine the absolute disaster if a swarm of those reached GDA space?'

'It'd be the end of everything,' said Linda.

'They're definitely not a natural phenomenon then?' Ed asked.

'Completely impossible,' Cleo answered. 'They've been engineered at some point by an intelligent race.'

'But wouldn't they turn against their masters too?' Andy asked.

'That's the weirdness of the thing,' agreed Cleo.

'Either they escaped while being developed or they've mutated since deployment.'

'Or the creators had an antidote that made their vessels immune,' said Linda.

'I've just thought,' said Ed, his eyes opening wide with fear. 'If that drone came from the *Lytrotis*—'

'Oh, shit,' Linda interrupted. 'It's one of the older cruisers. They wouldn't have had shields anywhere near as good as ours.'

'Or Cleo to analyse the threat,' Andy added.

They all looked at each other. A cold shiver went down Ed's back.

'Cleo...are you completely sure we would be safe in an environment containing those bastard things if we continue on to Pyli?' he asked.

'If you give me an hour or so, I'll have the anti-nanos that'll attack and neutralise them,' she said, appearing in the centre of the room.

'This happened days ago,' said Linda. 'If that cruiser was attacked by these things...well...you know what Cleo said about how long it would take to render a big ship helpless. Another hour won't make a jot of difference to them, but it could ensure our safety.'

Cleo, Ed and Andy all turned to stare at her.

'Just saying,' she said. 'If you don't agree, we'll go now...we're only a couple of jumps away after all.'

Ed was still groggy from being woken in the middle of his REM sleep. He chewed on his lip for a moment and turned to Andy.

'What do you think? Go now, or wait a short while until we know we're completely safe?'

'We should wait,' Andy replied. 'If we go down...

there'll be nothing to stop the little bastards reaching GDA space.'

Ed nodded and turned to Cleo.

'Cleo, as soon as you have that anti-nano thing in the arsenal, take us to Pyli.'

'Understood...I'll be as quick as I can,' she said and promptly disappeared.

5

The bridge, the *Gabriel*, en route to Pyli

SIXTY-NINE MINUTES after the decision was made to wait for the antidote, the *Gabriel* winked into the outer edge of the Metafora system. Pyli, the planet where the three moons that made up the triangular galactic gateway orbited, was still many millions of kilometres away. Phil, piloting at the time, had deliberately done this so they could scan the system for evidence of the aggressive nanos.

'Oh, no,' grunted Linda, staring at her screen as the holomap updated with a detailed picture of Pyli and the surrounding area.

'Have you found the *Lytrotis*?' Ed asked.

'Yeah.'

'What's the problem?'

'No life signs.'

'Ah, shit,' Andy mumbled. 'Are the lifeboats still attached?'

'Actually, most are gone,' Linda said, looking over, a little more enthusiasm returning to her tone.

'Scan the planet's surface,' said Ed. 'Especially where the underground control room is.'

A close-up image of the *Lytrotis* appeared. Parts of the hull were missing along its entire two-kilometre length, gasses spewed from multiple fractures, and it hung at a strange angle in relation to the planet.

'I have intact lifeboats on the surface,' said Pol. 'Most are still transmitting their distress signals.'

'And a few dead ones in orbit I'm afraid,' added Linda.

'A few made it down then,' said Ed. 'Life signs?'

'No,' said Linda. 'But we know that doesn't mean anything, they could be underground like last time.'

'Very true, they have all landed together in close proximity to the control facility,' said Andy.

'What facility?' asked Pol.

'It's where the ancients sited the control room and constructed the hardware for the gateway,' said Linda.

'What, like the one where we found Pyriaeus a couple of years ago?'

'Yes, almost identical,' said Andy. 'We'd better get over there and see how many survived.'

'Is the drone ready to go?' Ed asked, glancing across at Cleo. She was sat on one of the guest seats painting her nails. 'Cleo…we are in the middle of an operation here!'

'You do know I can undertake a million tasks at any given time without raising a sweat, darling,' she said, without looking up. 'And yes, the drone is all prepped and ready to rock and roll. D'you want me to send my babies over to play?'

Ed took a deep breath, rolled his eyes at the others and nodded.

'Yes, please…if you'd be so kind.'

A heavily modified and shielded GDA drone popped out of the port hangar and jumped the relatively short distance across to Pyli. Everyone on the bridge went quiet as it gradually deployed its canisters of anti-nanos into space adjacent to the *Lytrotis* and around the planet.

'Is anything going to happen?' Andy huffed impatiently after a couple of minutes.

Cleo smiled and crossed her arms.

'Let them disseminate and the show will commence,' she said, spreading her fingers and admiring her handiwork.

Almost as she finished talking a bright sparkling near the wreck of the *Lytrotis* caught everyone's attention. As they watched, it spread outwards in all directions rapidly, almost like a grass fire in a drought. The display of shimmering miniature multi-coloured explosions grew and grew. They all sat mesmerised, watching as the kaleidoscopic spectacle extended expeditiously and began encircling the planet.

'Wow,' said Andy. 'It's like New Year's Eve on Sydney Harbour.'

'You could almost call it pretty,' said Linda. 'Except for the fact that those bastard little things have killed hundreds of people.'

'It's quite safe to jump over to the *Lytrotis* now,' said Cleo.

All eyes swept to the wreck, where internal flashes, some big, some small, were non-stop.

'The paparazzi are already there,' said Andy, but no one laughed.

Phil jumped the *Gabriel* five kilometres away from the *Lytrotis* and matched its orbital speed.

Linda shook her head at Ed, when she'd completed her close-up scan of the wreck – just in-case there were any small pockets of survivors anywhere, however unlikely.

'As soon as it's safe, we need to get down to the surface,' said Ed, turning to Cleo. 'Can you put a load of supplies for the survivors in the *Secchio* please?' he asked.

'Anything specific, boss?' she asked, blowing on her fingernails.

'Food, water, comfortable bedding, anything they might need for a few days,' said Ed. 'We're not their rescue party. Bache will have to organise that. Pol, can you send a drone to the Admiral with the details of what's happened here and Cleo, include some of your anti-nano stuff to disperse around the *Lytrotis*'s drone back at the last jump point. I don't want anyone else coming this way bumping into that crap.'

A reply of nods was confirmation they understood and got busy.

'The wreck's orbit is slowly decaying,' said Linda. 'Do you want me to try and tractor it back into a stable one?'

Ed turned and peered up at the holomap, pursing his lips for a moment.

'It's a really old ship,' he said, finally making a decision. 'But knowing how desperately short of vessels Bache is, he might want to refit it. So, yes, give it a go.'

While everyone was busy doing their various jobs, Ed

and Andy went down to the starboard hangar and prepped the *Secchio* for the trip down to the surface of Pyli. Cleo had been busy, a dozen loaded-up pallets sat next to an auto-trundle down near the ramp.

'How many of them are down there?' Andy asked, eyeing the heavily loaded pallets.

'Not sure, but Linda's counted seventeen intact lifeboats, each one can take a maximum of twenty crew, so we're looking at around three hundred odd. Cleo's provided enough food and water for four hundred people to last a month.'

'They shouldn't have to wait that long.'

'No, but you know how strapped Bache is for logistics even now. He might not have a ship available straight away.'

They made their way up to the cockpit and settled on their couches.

'Linda,' Ed called. 'We're going down with this stuff now, has there been any contact with anyone down there yet?'

'Not a peep,' she answered. 'The distress beacons are still singing out, but you have to remember, it's over a hundred degrees down there during the daylight hours and they're most likely sheltering underground. No one's going to be sitting in a lifeboat sauna during the daylight hours.'

'Okay, can you watch over us while we're down there?' I don't want a repeat of the last time.'

'Are you going to wear your PFJ's?' she asked. 'Then that can't happen.'

'Ah, yeah, good idea,' said Andy, standing again and dragging two out of a recharging storage locker.

Personal fold jackets were new and introduced to them

by Menka, the insect queen on their last mission some eighteen months ago. Cleo had taken the design and improved it, making them lighter and less conspicuous. They had the *Gabriel*'s logo emblazoned on the front and now resembled a professional ship's uniform, making them a little less conspicuous. Although the range had been slightly reduced, they could still reach a ship a few light minutes away.

They both slipped one on and sat back down. Ed closed his eyes and manoeuvred the ship carefully out into space.

6

Pessawinn Refinery, Pessawinn locale

TYME'S HANDS MOVED MECHANICALLY, scraping and guiding the molten stream while his mind reeled. The arm belonged to Kestrel, one of the older men who'd recently undergone transition into his vassalage duration. The tattoo of interlocked circles on the forearm was unmistakable, even half-melted as it was. Kestrel had been so proud of that marking when he'd gotten it done in secret using smuggled ink and a pointed stylus. He should have been up on the Lamination several days now. Tyme's mind reeled with confusion – why was he still down here? How had he ended up in the furnace system? Had he fallen? Been pushed? The questions hammered at Tyme's skull as he continued working, the scraper feeling impossibly heavy in his grip.

He risked another glance at Merrin, whose face had

gone pale beneath the grime. The older man caught his eye and mouthed a single word.

'Later.'

The haklion kept flowing, its yellow-green glow casting sick shadows across the grid platform. Tyme could taste bile rising in his throat, mixing with the metallic tang of the processed ore. His goggs fogged again from his rapid breathing, and he had to force himself to slow down before he hyperventilated.

The minutes crawled by like hours. Tyme counted them down, watching the flow gradually weaken until it became a trickle, then stopped entirely. The sudden quiet felt wrong after the constant roar, broken only by the hiss of cooling metal and the distant rumble of machinery from other sections.

Pell's boots clanged across the grid towards them. Tyme's heart hammered against his ribs as he watched the crew leader approach, certain the man would notice the charred remains. But Pell only glanced at their collection trough, nodding at the pooled haklion.

'Good flow management. Prep for plate extraction.'

Tyme waited until Pell moved on before daring to look at the arm again. The flesh had cooled and darkened, making the melted ring more visible. He remembered Kestrel showing it off just weeks ago, claiming it had belonged to his father before the Repps took him for final processing. Now both father and son were gone.

Merrin shuffled closer, keeping his voice low. 'Don't stare at it. You'll attract the Repp. Act normal.'

Normal? Tyme almost laughed at the word, but it came out as a strangled cough instead. Nothing about this place was ever normal.

'Do we get rid of it?' Tyme whispered, giving Merrin a quick sideways glance.

Merrin quickly took a peek over to where the Repp overseer loomed.

'I'll let you know when it's not looking this way,' he said. 'Kick it off and it'll drop down into the slag truck.'

Tyme positioned himself slightly to block the view, his scraper clattering against the metal grid as he pretended to clean it. The acrid smell of the charred flesh mixed with the lingering haklion fumes made his stomach churn again. He kept his breathing shallow, trying not to gag.

The Repp overseer's heavy footsteps echoed across the platform as it moved between stations. Tyme had never been up close to one, none of the human workers were allowed near, but he could hear the mechanical whir of its joints and the soft hiss of its breathing apparatus. The sound always made his skin crawl.

'Now,' Merrin whispered.

Tyme used his boot to nudge the severed arm towards the edge of the grid. It moved slowly, the melted flesh sticking slightly to the metal surface. He had to push harder than he'd expected, and when it finally broke free, it tumbled down into the slag truck below with a dull wet thud.

His hands were shaking as he gripped his scraper again. Kestrel had been kind to him, one of the few older workers who didn't treat the younger ones like burdens. He'd even shared extra ration cubes with Tyme occasionally and nobody else ever did that.

The image of Kestrel's face kept flashing through Tyme's mind as he prepared his extraction tools as if on autopilot. The man had always worn this crooked grin when he talked about his transition, how he'd finally made it through the worst years and earned his place up on the Lamination. The stories he'd told about the better quarters, the cleaner air, the lighter work, they'd given Tyme something to hope for during the hardest shifts. Now those stories felt like lies, or worse, like bait.

The extraction bell chimed, and Tyme positioned his thermal tongs over the first cooled haklion plate. The metal had hardened into a dull grey sheet, still radiating heat that he could feel through his gloves. He lifted it carefully, transferring it to the collection rack where it would be sorted and weighed.

His movements felt mechanical, disconnected. Part of him wondered if he was in shock. The rest of him just wanted to get through the next few hours without ending up in the furnace like Kestrel.

'Transition's not what they tell us, is it?' he whispered to Merrin during a brief lull between extractions.

The older man's jaw tightened, his eyes darting towards the Repp above them before focusing back on his work. 'Keep your voice down,' he muttered through gritted teeth. 'And stop asking questions you don't want answered.'

The warning hit Tyme like a physical blow. He fumbled with his thermal tongs, nearly dropping the haklion plate he was lifting. The metal clanged against the collection rack, sending a sharp ring across the platform. Several workers turned to look, and Tyme felt heat rush to his face that had nothing to do with the furnaces.

He forced himself to focus on the extraction process, but his mind kept circling back to Kestrel's arm, to that melted ring, to the way Merrin had looked at him with something that might have been pity. The older man knew something. They all knew something, all the workers who'd been here long enough to see others disappear.

The haklion plates felt heavier with each extraction, or maybe his arms were just getting tired from the trembling that he couldn't seem to stop. It was at this moment Tyme decided he was not going to end up like Kestrel and if the transition up to the Lamination was all a fabricated lie to keep the human workers in line, then he must escape. Where to was another question, and one that he needed an answer to quickly.

The rest of the shift dragged on interminably. Tyme's muscles burned from the repetitive lifting of haklion plates, and his mind raced with fragmented thoughts about Kestrel, about escape, about survival. He kept glancing over at Merrin, hoping for some sign, some explanation, but the older man remained focused on his work, deliberately avoiding eye contact.

When the final extraction bell rang, his knees nearly buckled with relief. After carefully stowing his tools in their designated slots, he followed the others towards the exit trollie. The platform seemed longer now, each step requiring conscious effort as exhaustion settled deep into his bones.

He squeezed into the trollie beside Merrin, their shoulders pressed together in the cramped space. The doors hissed shut, and the vehicle lurched forward, carrying them away from the melting stacks. Only then did Tyme dare to breathe normally, the filtered air in the trollie tasting almost sweet compared to the toxic fumes of the refinery.

'Don't say anything about what you saw,' Merrin muttered into his ear, his voice barely audible above the whine of the trollie's engine. 'They listen to us everywhere.'

Tyme nodded slightly, his determination to escape this madness even more resolute.

As the trollie wound its way back through the tunnels towards the security scanners, Tyme's mind churned with possibilities. He needed to find Jaccin, needed to warn him, but how could he do it without being overheard? The Repps were always listening and they had spies among the workers, everybody knew that, even if nobody talked about it openly.

The trollie shuddered to a halt at the arrival platform, and Tyme filed out with the others, his legs a little wobbly beneath him. The familiar routine of passing through the scanners felt different now, more sinister. He raised his arms automatically, but his skin prickled as the beams swept over him. He wondered what else they might be looking for besides contraband and stolen tools. Tyme hoped it couldn't detect the suspicion and determination growing inside him.

On the other side of the security checkpoint, he spotted Jaccin's distinctive walk before he could make out his brother's face in the crowd of workers. Even exhausted, Jaccin moved with that slight bounce in his step that Kestrel used to tease him about. The memory hit Tyme unexpectedly, a sharp pang of loss that made his chest tighten.

He pushed through the crowd, trying to reach his brother before they boarded the trollicar back to the Calistromal locale.

7

The *Secchio*, upper atmosphere, Pyli, Metafora system

'ARE you not using the antigrav to slow our descent?' Andy asked nervously, as he eyed the high insertion speed.

'Don't need to,' Ed replied, his eyes shut as he used his DOVI to maintain a forty-degree angle of attack. 'I had them instal the latest military heat-resistant coating on the underside. It's the same stuff they use on their marine fast-attack gunships.'

'I hope they tested it properly,' Andy replied, bringing up the hull temperatures on his screen and inspecting them closely.

'Don't worry, I did,' said Cleo, appearing in the corner of the cockpit. 'I check everything the GDA designs. With them the cheapest quote normally gets the gig, not necessarily the best.'

'I think Bache is trying to address that policy,' said Andy.

The roar of the atmosphere passing by at many times the speed of sound outside was suddenly joined by the scream of the antigravs as Ed fired them up to begin the deceleration phase.

Andy switched the holomap to show the surface below. It presented the desert-like terrain approaching at what seemed like a reckless momentum. The engine note reached a high-pitched howl, hauling the ship back incredibly quickly to a slightly more sensible rate of descent. Without the standard one G gravity plating in the ship, they'd both've been squished into the floor.

'Bloody hell,' grunted Andy. 'That never ceases to amaze me.'

'Still makes you grunt though doesn't it?' said Ed. 'Even without the physical sensation.'

He levelled the *Secchio* out at around a thousand metres and skirted around the landing site. Andy scanned for any life signs or movement. All the lifeboats had settled within roughly a square kilometre on the edge of the mountainous area where the underground facility was located.

'Nothing?' Ed asked.

'Nothing…apart from seventeen powered-down lifeboats,' Andy confirmed. 'And the wreck of the *Vrachos* still sticking up out of the desert two hundred kilometres away.'

Ed didn't answer, he just commanded the landing struts to lower and brought the ship in as close as possible to where the facility was located, but still on flattish ground.

'Give it a minute or two and see if anything occurs,'

said Ed, finally opening his eyes, as the antigravs powered down.

The *Secchio* settled into the terrain as they waited, finally deciding on a slight six-degree tilt. They watched for five minutes, but apart from the tall indigenous grasses swaying in the light breeze, nothing moved.

'Shall we go and knock on the door?' Andy asked.

'Be rude to come all this way,' said Ed, shrugging.

Both grabbing a laser rifle from the rack, they exited the internal cockpit through the inner airlock and made their way down to the loading bay. While Andy walked over to the ramp, Ed closed his eyes and did a final check on the outside cameras. Powering the ramp down, he joined his friend and they both stepped out onto Pyli for the first time in several years.

'Hasn't changed a bit,' Andy muttered, glancing around. 'All this real estate, lovely climate, not one house built.'

'Be my guest,' Ed replied. "I think I'll stick to Somerset.'

They both strolled across to the depression in the hillside where they knew the underground door was located. Ed concentrated with his DOVI and as before they heard the whining of the hydraulic rams and the twenty-metre door rumbled open upwards.

Andy, rifle in the shoulder, stepped into the shadow of the door and peered down the corridor he'd investigated once before.

'Clear,' he said, as Ed followed him and they made their way fifty metres down the circular tunnel to the right-hand bend and the metal iris door that this time they knew was there. 'D'you want me to open it this time?' he asked, as they approached it.

'Be my guest.'

While Andy closed his eyes and set about the lock mechanism, Ed remembered the greeting they received last time and crouched down on one side, training his rifle on the centre of the door.

'In your own time,' he said, with a sigh.

'I seem to remember it took you a while too,' Andy countered.

Ed didn't have time to hit back as a click sounded and the iris began sliding open. Andy jumped to the opposite side to Ed and also trained his weapon on the expanding circle of the iris. This time, however, there were no black-clad soldiers pointing rifles at their heads. It was clear and as they peered inside, flashing their weapon lights around the cavern, they were surprised to find the large space completely empty.

'Where the hell are they?' Andy griped. 'There's nowhere else here that several hundred people can hide.'

'There's something at the far end,' said Ed, as they entered and trotted across the large space. 'Tents,' he added, as they approached. 'So they were here.'

'Hang about,' Andy called, staring at the collapsed inflatable tents. 'Look at the dust on them. These are the old emergency tents from the *Vrachos*'s lifeboats, not the *Lytrotis*.'

'Shit, you're right,' Ed answered, wiping some of the dust away with his boot.

They both looked up at the doorway behind that they knew led to the gate room and the stairway down to the control room. They both turned, their eyes meeting for a second.

'Are you thinking what I'm thinking?' Andy asked.

'Why would they go through the gate?' Ed countered.

'Well, they must have if there's as many of them as we think there are. You might cram thirty people in there, but not three or four hundred.'

They made their way over and found the gate room also empty and exactly as they remembered.

'The lifeboats are here, the crew aren't on the surface, they must've gone through the gate then, there's no other answer,' Ed muttered, shaking his head.

'But where to?' Andy asked, glancing over at the control room door, still sitting open. 'I seem to remember there being over five hundred and seventy-odd destinations.'

'It'll be the one it's set on now.'

'Can you tell which one it is from down there?' he asked, nodding at the open stairwell.

'They've sent drones through to every destination and logged and recognised the galaxies they go to. It should have the current destination logged in.'

Quickly descending the stairs, they entered the small control room. The main panel was illuminated, a peculiar-shaped character or rune was slowly flashing.

'What's that thing relate to?' Andy asked.

Ed pointed to a large board that had been fixed to the wall, showing all five hundred and seventy-two destinations. There was a number given to each one.

'Hang on,' said Ed, pulling out his tablet. 'Give me the number next to the rune that's flashing.'

Andy scanned the lines of characters until he found the identical one.

'Four, nine, one,' he said, turning back to Ed.

Ed scanned down the list of numbers he'd been sent by the Admiral.

'Four, nine, one is the Triangulum Galaxy, just over two point seven million light years away in the Triangulum Constellation.'

'If I remember rightly, that's quite local in the grand scheme of things, shall we go there then?' Andy said, turning back to the door.

'Woah there, just a minute,' called Ed. 'We need to let the others know and it'd be best to have the *Gabriel* go through too. That can now be the destination for all of us. If that's where the weaponised nanos came from, we need to go there and clean up.'

'Yeah, okay, you're right. It looks as though our choice of galaxy to explore has been made for us.'

'Let's unload the supplies into the cavern and when we find the *Lytrotis*'s crew we can send them back here to await the rescue party.'

8

The bridge, the *Gabriel*, Pyli, Metafora system

FOUR HOURS LATER, with the supplies unloaded and the *Secchio* back in the starboard hangar, Ed and Andy returned to the bridge and informed the others of the plan.

'So, Cleo, can you ensure we have a substantial stock-pile of the anti-nanos,' said Ed, glancing up.

Cleo appeared sitting cross-legged on a seat at the side of the bridge. She was sporting long straight blonde hair and her black ninja outfit today in complete contrast to her newly painted bright red nails.

'Wow,' said Rayl. 'I want that outfit too.'

Andy coughed and sighed theatrically, glancing at Ed with a pained look.

'She's going to need one of our hangars for a wardrobe before long,' he moaned.

'Shut up, you,' she said. 'A girl's gotta have something to wear for every occasion.'

'Absolutely,' said Linda.

'Quite right,' said Pol.

Both of them looked at Andy with smug expressions.

He turned to both Ed and Phil for a little backup, but received none. They both kept their eyes firmly on the holomap for safety.

'Everyone ready to go?' Ed asked, quickly changing the subject.

A circle of nodding heads was the reply.

'Linda, if you could do the honours and take us across to the gate, let's go and pay the Triangulum Galaxy a visit.'

Thirty-eight seconds later the *Gabriel* vanished from the Milky Way and in the blink of an eye travelled two point seven-two million light years.

As the holomap began resetting, Linda cloaked the *Gabriel* and put her into a high orbit around the planet they'd appeared adjacent to.

'Holy moly,' said Pol, as the full scale of what was out there became apparent.

'Bloody hell,' said Ed. 'How many ships are there?'

'Jeez,' mumbled Andy. 'Hundreds, maybe thousands.

'It's hard to tell,' said Phil. 'A lot of them are just bits of ships and they're all full of holes, just like the *Lytrotis*.'

'Are we looking at the weaponised nanos out there, Cleo?' Ed asked.

'Oh yes. It's like a blizzard of them,' she said. 'I'm

about to dispense a vast quantity of the antis, so be warned this could get quite bright.'

They didn't hear the launch on the bridge, but they soon saw the results. Everywhere around them began lighting up with the miniature detonations. This time it wasn't like a firework display, more an expanding explosion, with the *Gabriel* smack bang in the centre.

Ed shielded his eyes with his hand, it was so intense.

'Some of these wrecks have been here a very long time,' said Phil, examining his scan results.

'So it hasn't just happened then?' Ed asked.

'No, judging by the decomposition of the metals in some of them, this began over eight thousand years ago.'

'What about the planet?'

'Goldilocks,' said Pol.

Linda groaned and gave Ed a glare.

Pol didn't react and continued with her scan result.

'Seven and a half percent smaller than Earth, gravity point nine-two Earth. Five main continents, all absolutely littered with ship debris.'

'Life signs?'

'Abundant animal life, still attempting to separate animal from human, but it's safe to say there was a whole bunch of intelligent life as I'm getting some quite large settlements, but they appear to be in ruins and badly overgrown.'

'Look for modern technology,' said Andy. 'Cuz our GDA crew will have tablets and weapons and so forth.'

'They'll be near the gate control room here too,' said Ed. 'So I'm hoping they haven't travelled too far.'

'Found "em,' said Pol. 'Patching in to their communications. Do you want to talk to them?' she asked, looking across at Ed.

'Yeah,' he said, nodding enthusiastically.

She held up a hand, tapped a couple of icons with her other hand, nodded and pointed at him.

'This is Captain Edward Virr of the starship *Gabriel*. Crew of the *Lytrotis*, do you copy?'

'*Who the fuck is that? If that's you, Lieutenant Sifferen, you're on a fucking charge and half rations for a week.*'

Andy sniggered and Ed held his hand up to quieten him.

'Whoever you are, you're getting the wrong idea. This really is the starship *Gabriel*. We have traversed the gate to find you. We will travel down in a shuttle shortly when the region is clear of the weaponised nanos. Do you understand?'

This time there was a pause before the reply came.

'*Who sent you?*'

'Admiral Loftt. We have placed twelve pallets of food and supplies in the cavern back on Pyli. How many survivors are you?'

'*Seventy-four.*'

'Seventy-four? But the *Lytrotis* had a crew of five hundred and twenty-eight and seventeen lifeboats made it safely down.'

'*It happened too quickly for most to get near a lifeboat station. In four minutes almost the entire ship was open to space. Three of those lifeboats came down empty, several others only had one or two crew in them.*'

'What's your name by the way?'

'*Chief Engineer Lings.*'

'Why did you all come through the pedestrian gate, Chief?'

'The emergency rations in the lifeboats hadn't been replaced in decades and were all ancient and inedible. We were starving and realised the planet the gate was connected to had abundant plants and wildlife. We've collected a load of food and are on our way back now. I sent a distress message to Dasos, so a rescue vessel will arrive in a day or so.'

'I'm afraid your drone didn't make it. We found it dead two jumps away, it was infected with the nanos. We sent another one earlier today, so your rescue ship is still a couple of weeks away. But you have plenty of food now.'

'Why isn't your ship affected by the nano weapon?'

'We have Theo-designed shields and an anti-nano virus. We're gradually wiping out the weaponised nanos. Did they originally come from this galaxy?'

'We think so, yes. They must have hitched a ride back on one of our exploratory drones. Have you managed to avoid all the wrecks up there?'

'We have, Chief. Did Captain Tzooums survive?'

'No one from the bridge is here, I'm the only surviving senior officer. In fact, the majority of us are from the stern of the vessel as the exploratory drones were housed in the smaller bridge hangar up front and that's where they attacked. They seemed to know to take out the emergency systems first, which prevented me from closing all the internal bulkhead doors and compartmentalising the ship and allowing the crew time to get to their lifeboat stations.'

'Good luck, Chief. Our condolences on the loss of your colleagues. We're going to stay here for a while and ensure this virus is completely wiped out. We'll be coming back through in a couple of weeks, so we'll check you've been picked up. *Gabriel* out.'

'*Thank you for the supplies,* Gabriel, *and good luck with the hunt.* Lytrotis *out.*'

'Well, he was a bit more professional than the last one wasn't he?' said Linda.

'He's an engineer like Bache,' said Ed. 'He knows what side his bread's buttered on.'

'Good people, engineers,' said Andy, smugly.

'Yeah, some of "em,' said Rayl, winking at Linda.

9

Pessawinn Refinery, Pessawinn locale

JACCIN WAS ALREADY at the trollicar, saving a seat as he always did. When Tyme approached, he immediately noticed something was wrong. His brother's face was one of suspicion, the skin around his eyes tight with unease.

'You look like slag,' Jaccin murmured, as Tyme slid onto the worn seat beside him. 'Bad shift?'

He wanted to blurt everything out, about Kestrel's arm, about his suspicions, about the growing certainty that transition was a lie, but Merrin's warning echoed in his mind. *"They listen to us everywhere."* He glanced around the trollicar, noting the small black sensors in the corners of the ceiling. Recording devices, he'd always assumed, but had never given much thought to before.

'Just tired,' he said, instead, keeping his voice neutral. 'Station four today.'

Jaccin winced sympathetically.

'The heat must have been brutal.'

'Brutal doesn't begin to cover it,' Tyme said, leaning closer to his brother. He wanted to say more but stopped himself, conscious of the recording devices. Instead, he pressed his knee against Jaccin's, applying just enough pressure to signal something was wrong.

Jaccin's eyebrows rose slightly, a subtle acknowledgment of the silent communication they'd perfected over years of shared hardship. He shifted in his seat, angling his body towards Tyme while appearing to simply adjust his position.

'We have a little job to do at home,' Jaccin said, his voice casual but his eyes saying otherwise.

'Oh, yes?'

'We need to clean out that storage compartment under the floor.'

Tyme understood immediately. The hidden space beneath their living quarters was where they sometimes spoke when they needed privacy from prying ears. Their father had discovered years ago that the dense composite material somehow interfered with the Repps' monitoring equipment.

The trollicar hummed along the track, the familiar rattle of the worn tallis shaft now sounding ominous rather than merely annoying. Tyme stared out the grimy window, watching the slag piles grow smaller as they retreated from the refinery. The scorched-metal smell of burning haklion still lingered in his nostrils even though they were getting farther away from the refinery. His thoughts kept returning to Kestrel's arm, the melted ring, the implications too horrible to fully process.

The trollicar slowed as it entered the twilight of Calistromal. Tyme felt the familiar shift in temperature, the cooler air and dimmer lighting a small relief after the inferno and stark brightness of station four. He waited until they were off the trollicar and walking the final stretch to their living quarters before speaking again.

'Did you see Haslyin today?' he asked, keeping his voice casual.

Jaccin shook his head.

'His whole crew was reassigned. Something about efficiency restructuring.'

Tyme's stomach clenched. Reassigned. Just like Kestrel had been "reassigned" to the Lamination. He quickened his pace slightly, eager to reach the safety of their hidden space.

Their living quarters were spartan, identical to every other worker unit in the locale. A single room with two sleep platforms, a hygiene cubicle, and a small food preparation area. The floor was covered with large worn composite tiles, one of which, near the far wall, could be lifted to reveal the cramped space beneath.

Tyme moved towards it without hesitation, prying up the tile with his fingernails while Jaccin checked the door seal. The hidden compartment was barely large enough for both of them to crouch inside, but it had served them well over the years when they needed to speak freely.

They squeezed into the space, pulling the tile back over their heads. The darkness was complete, and the air smelled of dust and old composite materials. Tyme waited a moment, listening for any sounds from above, before speaking in the barest whisper.

'Kestrel's dead.'

He heard Jaccin's sharp intake of breath beside him.

'What? How do you know?'

Tyme's hands shook as he described what had fallen from the discharge pipe, the melted ring, the distinctive tattoo. Even in whispers, the words felt dangerous, like speaking them aloud might somehow summon the Repps' attention.

'His arm came down with the haklion. He should have been on the Lamination by now, but instead...'

Tyme's voice trailed off, unable to finish the thought.

'He was in the furnace?' Jaccin whispered, his voice tight with horror.

'That's where they really send them,' said Tyme. 'I think Merrin knows something but is too terrified to say.'

Tyme felt the walls of the small compartment becoming claustrophobic. The darkness suddenly seemed suffocating rather than protective.

'But why? Why lie about the Lamination?' he said. 'Why tell us we'll get better conditions when they just...' He couldn't finish the sentence.

Jaccin shifted beside him, his shoulder brushing against Tyme's in the confined space.

'Control. Hope keeps us working. Keeps us compliant,' whispered Jaccin.

Hearing it from someone else struck Tyme like a physical weight. All those years of enduring the refinery, the heat, the fumes, the stingers, all for the promise of something better that never actually existed. His whole future, the one thing that had kept him going through the worst shifts, had been a complete lie, fabrication, bullshit.

'We have to get out,' Tyme said, the words feeling both terrifying and liberating. 'Before they decide it's our turn.'

'And go where?' Jaccin's voice was barely audible. 'The Repps control everything. The locale, the uplight, all of it.'

Tyme had been wondering the same thing, but now the urgency made his chest tight with panic. There had to be somewhere, some place the Repps didn't monitor. His father had mentioned rumours once, whispered stories about settlements beyond the slag zones, but Tyme had dismissed them as children's fantasy stories.

'The outer reaches, the water oceans,' he whispered, remembering fragments of those half-heard conversations. The Repps didn't like water. 'Past the mining operations. Dad said there might be people living rough out there.'

'Might be?' Jaccin repeated, scepticism clear even in his hushed tone. 'That's not much of a plan.'

Tyme's knees began to ache from crouching in the cramped space, but he couldn't bring himself to leave yet. Up there, in their regular quarters, he'd have to pretend everything was normal. He'd have to wake up tomorrow and board the trollicar and go back to station four, knowing that Kestrel's remains might still be flowing through the discharge pipes.

'We'll need supplies,' he said, his mind starting to work through the logistics. 'Water containers, food rations, protective gear for the uplight. And we'd have to leave during the night period, when the work crews are sleeping.'

'Yeah, but remember, the Repps don't have to sleep. They'll be wide awake and so will all their detection equipment.'

Tyme's heart sank. The Repps never needed rest, never needed food, never seemed to need anything except to keep the humans working until they were no longer useful. He pressed his palms against the rough composite walls of their hiding space, feeling trapped between the certainty of death if they stayed and the near impossibility of escape.

'The maintenance tunnels,' he said suddenly, remembering something from his early days at the refinery. 'There are old passages that run beneath the transport lines. Dad mentioned them once when he was talking about the original construction.'

Jaccin was quiet for a long moment. Tyme could hear his brother's breathing, shallow and quick in the stale air of the compartment.

'Those tunnels probably haven't been used in hundreds of years,' Jaccin finally whispered. 'They could be collapsed by now, flooded, lined with stingers, anything.'

'Or they could be our way out.' Tyme felt a desperate kind of hope building in his chest, the first real possibility he'd felt since Kestrel's arm had landed at his feet. 'The Repps might not monitor them if they're abandoned. According to them no one alive would know of their existence.'

Jaccin was silent again for a moment.

'I might know of a way in,' he whispered.

10

The bridge, the *Gabriel*, unknown system, Triangulum Galaxy

IT WAS TAKING LONGER than expected to clear the whole system of the weaponised nanos. Everybody got some sleep while Cleo got on with the job.

Andy was on bridge duty when Ed staggered off the tube lift, wiping the sleep from his eyes early the following morning.

'Bloody hell,' Andy said, making a big deal of looking at his watch. 'Did you shit the bed?'

'I'm surprised I didn't with the amount of that curry I had last night,' Ed replied, grimacing. 'That's gotta be the hottest jalfrezi Cleo's ever made.'

'I agree. As you are aware I like a hot one too, but it seems as I get older my body's starting to disagree with my taste.'

'We'll both be on birianis like Linda before long. Anyway, what's occurring?' he asked, sliding onto his couch.

'Cleo's almost finished tidying up now, there's just a few hidden away in some of the wrecks. She's having to be thorough, cuz if you miss just one, it'll replicate so fast you're back to square one in a matter of hours.'

Ed watched the holomap for a while. The occasional flash here and there from inside the multitude of wreckage was all too evident of the task at hand.

'Any timescale, Cleo?' he asked.

'Not yet, boss,' she said, suddenly materialising lying on the couch next to him with her hands behind her head. 'I had to do a little redesign last night and produce a rummaging variety of anti-nano. The originals were fine out in space and in larger areas, but tended to miss a few hiding in the tighter spots within the wreckage.'

'Is it just me, or is there less shrapnel flying around today?'

'I've been nudging the smaller bits into the atmosphere to burn up. It saves having to search them and guarantees the nasties within are destroyed.'

'What about using the two asteri beams to cut the bigger lumps into burnable sizes? We could clear the whole area then and make it safe for navigation again.'

'I can do that,' said Andy, grinning and bringing the beams online. 'A bit of wanton vandalism is always fun.'

'I'll indicate the ones for you to chop,' said Cleo. 'I don't want you waving those things around willy nilly.'

Ed chuckled at Cleo's use of the old English phrase.

'Oh...now that's new,' she said suddenly, sitting up and staring at the holomap.

'What is?' asked Ed, his eyebrows raised.

'We've just been scanned.'

'Is it our friends from the *Lytrotis*?'

'No, they went back through the pedestrian gate hours ago and anyway, this emanated from over eight and a half thousand kilometres away on another continent.'

'Put us above the spot and get our biggest camera zoomed in,' Ed ordered.

'It seems to be some sort of lifeboat,' she said. 'It's pulsing a distress beacon now.'

'One thing I haven't asked is whether these wrecks were flown by humans, or are they alien in design?' Ed queried.

'Definitely human, taking into consideration the designs of corridors and rooms in the wrecks,' Cleo answered. 'The gateway is here in this galaxy, so it's safe to assume the ancients seeded this place with human life-forms many thousands of years ago too.'

They arrived over the lifeboat's position and the camera panned down.

'That looks a lot more recent than anything else we've found,' said Andy. 'It looks almost brand new.'

'We haven't found any newish wreckage up here...so where's the ship it came from?' asked Cleo.

'And if it is recent, where are the survivors?' added Ed.

Almost as he finished speaking, a figure wandered out into view and climbed into the lifeboat.

'Can you pan in on that airlock, Cleo? Let's see who we've got,' Andy asked, sitting bolt upright excitedly.

They didn't have to wait long, as the figure popped straight back out again and began staring around upwards.

'He knows we're here now,' said Andy.

Ed squinted as the image became larger and three dimensional, the array technology giving it depth and more clarity, clearly showing a dark fur-covered face gazing up.

'Bugger me, it's a Wookie,' exclaimed Andy.

'A very small one,' said Cleo. 'I estimate its height to be around four and a half feet.'

'Doesn't that make it more of an Ewok?' Ed asked, giving Andy a smug glance.

'Are you lot wittering on about those silly ancient movies again?' said Linda, appearing on the tube lift.

They all pointed at the holomap image as she approached.

'Oh…wow…is that an Ewok?' she said.

'Told you,' said Ed, nodding and pointing at Andy very self-satisfactorily.

'For heaven's sake, you two, you're grown-ups, you're not twelve anymore,' Linda grumbled, giving Cleo a roll of her eyes. 'Anyway…where did he or she come from?'

'Must've been in a cave or something,' said Cleo. 'Somewhere our scans can't penetrate. It's quite mountainous around there.'

'Is that a new lifeboat?' Linda asked.

'Yeah,' Andy answered.

'Where's the ship it's from then?'

'That's what we were wondering,' said Ed, turning to Cleo. 'Is it safe to go down there yet?'

'Yes, but take a small ship,' she said. 'There's nowhere to land your freighter in amongst that rockery.'

'We are the knights who say—'

'No we're not,' snapped Ed, interrupting him. 'That's a shrubbery.'

'Oh, yeah, right.'

'For fuck's sake,' sighed Linda, her head in her hands. 'Someone please save me.'

———————

Once the rest of the crew had been roused. Ed and Andy had taken one of the shuttles and were currently dropping into the planet's lower atmosphere.

'I'm going to name this planet Endor,' said Andy.

'No you're bloody not.'

'Why not?'

'Because Linda would nail our bollocks to the nearest bulkhead.'

'Hmm…yeah, there is that I suppose,' Andy answered, pulling a pained expression. 'Have you any ideas for a name then?'

'How about Scalene?'

'Where the hell's that come from?'

'Type of triangle.'

'Oh…right…okay…I should know that shouldn't I?'

Cleo was piloting the shuttle remotely and began the standard wide turns to scrub off speed. They both stretched up in their seats to peer downwards at the blue oceans and green continents, interspersed with tall sheer mountain ranges jagging up abruptly from wide flat valleys.

'Hmm…it seems to be a planet of opposites,' said Ed. 'There's no small hills or anything. The land is either flat as a witch's tit, or the north face of Everest.'

'I wonder what happened to the societies that were once here?' Andy said, as they passed above the overgrown grid of a long-gone metropolis.

'Perhaps whoever's down here can shed some light on that.'

The antigravs shrieked out as Cleo slowed their descent dramatically and turned them in towards the foot of one of the mountain ranges where the lifeboat had settled.

'Have we got a translator in here?' Andy asked, glancing behind at the storage lockers.

'Got one here,' said Ed, removing it from a pocket and clipping it to his jacket.

They cleared a copse of spindly trees and the lifeboat came into view. It had landed in the centre of a reasonably flat area, the ground littered with low brown, dry-looking shrubs. There was no sign of the small hairy human.

'Where is he?' Andy wondered.

'He doesn't know who we are, I'd hide too until I knew it was safe.'

'I'll circle a couple of times before landing,' said Cleo, appearing in one of the back seats.

They both peered out the front screen, looking for any indication of where their elusive castaway was hiding. Several cave openings were apparent in the nearby rock formations and Cleo settled the shuttle facing these and just to the side of the lifeboat.

'See anything?' Ed asked.

'Nope...do we go out armed?'

Ed chewed on his lip for a moment, trying to make his mind up.

'Just have them slung across your back,' said Cleo. 'At least that way your personal shields are there as a backup just in case. He could be the gentlest race around, or alternatively the Triangulum Galaxy's version of the moguls.'

'What she said,' said Ed, pulling two rifles from the rack and handing one to Andy.

They both made sure the shield activator was live and slung them across their backs.

'Right,' said Ed. 'Let's go find out who we've got.'

11

Lifeboat landing site, the planet Scalene, Triangulum
Galaxy

THEY EMERGED from the shuttle nice and slowly, giving
the alien a good view of the fact they didn't have any
weapons in their hands. Cleo remained hidden with a rifle
set to a medium stun as backup.

'Have you farted?' Andy asked, wrinkling his nose and
looking at Ed accusingly.

'It's sulphur in the air,' Ed replied. 'There must be
some volcanic activity in the area.'

Approaching the lifeboat, they both peered inside,
before walking into clear space and calling out.

'Hello,' they both shouted.

'You're quite safe,' added Ed, holding his hands out
wide.

Nothing happened, no movement at all.

'Sit down,' said Ed. 'I'm going to try something else.'

They both sat cross-legged and Ed retrieved three energy bars from a pocket, gave one to Andy, stood up to place one on a small log a few metres away and returned to sit with Andy. He waved and pointed at the bar on the log, slowly unwrapping his, taking a bite and emitting a loud '*mmmm*' noise.

Andy did the same, only he went '*mmm... mmm...mmm.*'

'Are you overacting or what?' Ed whispered.

'Could've been a movie star, me,' he whispered back.

'Third-rate porn star more like.'

Movement just to their left curtailed the conversation, as the short hairy alien stepped out of the shadows of a cave. He stood expressionless and observed them for a few moments. His head twitched every few seconds as if he had some sort of nervous tic.

Ed and Andy both smiled and indicated the energy bar on the log again. His expression didn't change, but he obviously decided to accept the invitation and moved slowly across and sat next to the log. Ed noticed he was dressed in some sort of red uniform. It was grubby and a little damaged in places, but had obviously been quite smart at some time in the not-too-distant past.

Their new friend decided to take their offer of a free meal and picked the bar off the log, sniffing it suspiciously. Ed ripped a bit more of the paper off his bar, demonstrating he should do the same and he did. He sniffed it again and took a tentative bite. He raised his eyebrows and his expression softened.

'Mmm...*tokag*,' he said, in a slightly high-pitched voice and nodding slightly. '*Gallow tokag.*'

'I think he likes it,' said Andy.

Ed pointed at himself.

'Edward,' he said, then indicated Andy. 'Andrew,' he continued, saying it slowly, before pointing back at the alien adopting a questioning expression.

The alien nodded and swallowed his mouthful of energy bar.

'Civray,' he said, prodding himself in the chest. 'Gerinth Civray Jep,' he continued, grinning for the first time.

They both smiled back as Ed indicated the universal translator clipped to his lapel and made a talking gesture with his hand next to it.

Civray stared back nonplussed, seemingly not understanding the gesticulation, his head tic returning with a vengeance.

'Talk to us,' said Andy, making the same talking gesture with his hand next to the translator and then pointing at his ear.

Civray seemed to have a eureka moment.

'*Gus trine haveer singortripe*,' he or she said, nodding, the tic disappearing again.

Ed unclipped and held the translator out like a microphone as Civray began chatting away. It wasn't long before the amazingly versatile machine began picking out conjunctions, shortly before the occasional nouns, verbs and adjectives began creeping in. A few minutes later, they could make out the gist of the conversation, but not every detail.

'The machine is learning your language,' said Ed.

It translated it and Civray sat up straight, staring at the machine in almost reverence.

'Ah, clever machine,' he or she said.

'Where are you from?' Andy asked.

'Wellas planet,' was the reply. 'Gort system.'

'How far away?' Ed asked.

'Stretch long,' came the reply, which puzzled them a bit.

'Stretch could mean jump,' said Andy. 'So it means a long jump away.'

'Yes,' said Civray, nodding. 'Jump long.'

An hour later they had ascertained Civray was a female of her species, a Wellasian from the planet Wellas and one of thirty-six explorers or surveyors sent out into the galaxy to find habitable planets and resources to ensure their future survival.

'Was your ship completely destroyed?' Ed asked.

She nodded slowly, ticking a couple of times.

'We can take you home,' said Andy, ignoring the glance from Ed.

'Where in galaxy you from?' she asked.

'We're not from this galaxy,' Ed stated. 'We come from a nearby galaxy called the Milky Way.'

She stared at them weirdly.

'I…impossible,' she stammered, ticking heavily. 'Millions of light rotations distant.'

'A galactic gateway is here,' said Andy, pointing upwards. 'Built by an ancient race hundreds of thousands of years ago.'

She stared, her eyes flicking between the two of them.

'I did not see it,' she said eventually.

'The three moons,' said Ed. 'Did you see them?'

She glanced upwards for a moment.

'I remember…yes.'

They didn't say anything, but both nodded.

'They are gate?' she asked, not able to hide her astonishment.

'Come and we'll show you,' Ed replied, standing up and holding out a hand.

She didn't move.

'You are first contact for us...for me,' she said, remaining seated. 'How I know to trust?' Her tic returned as she waited for a reply.

Ed sighed, adopted a rueful expression and tilted his head to one side.

'I suppose you don't have to,' he said, shrugging. 'But your alternative is to remain here and eventually die alone.'

Civray sat and thought that over for a moment.

'Do you have more of these?' she asked, holding up the energy bar wrapper.

'As many as you want and lots more better things too,' Andy assured her, strolling off towards the shuttle.

She stood, sighed and, glancing over at her lifeboat, she seemed to make a decision.

'I need to get thing,' she said, pointing towards the little ship.

'Take all the time you need,' said Ed. 'Grab all your belongings and we'll be waiting for you.' He turned to follow Andy.

'She has a serious nervous twitch doesn't she?' Andy said, once they were back on board the shuttle and out of ear shot.

'She does, but don't ever comment on it,' said Ed. 'She could be a bit sensitive about it, unless it's a trait of her species.'

'Hey, I'm not that inconsiderate.'

Ed just gave him a knowing glance as he stowed the rifles.

'What's that look for?'

'Sometimes things come out of your mouth that should really stay in there.'

'That's just my sense of humour.'

'Some races don't get sarcasm.'

'More fool them.'

'Hello,' said Civray, standing awkwardly on the steps outside the airlock. She stared nervously down at her feet, seemingly trying to work out how each free-floating step was supported.

Ed smiled and beckoned to her.

'Come aboard, Civray, have a seat here.' He indicated the co-pilot's seat. Cleo had made herself scarce so as to not completely freak their new guest out quite so soon.

Civray peered around the cockpit and its control surfaces with eyes like dinner plates.

'It's very different to my ship,' she said. 'Your starship is much bigger, you have more space and my starship couldn't land on a planet.'

'Ah…this isn't our starship,' said Andy. 'This is just one of its shuttles.'

'Your starship is bigger than this?' she asked, sitting tentatively on the edge of the seat as if she was about to make a bolt for the door.

'Some of the human races in our galaxy have been spacefaring for tens of thousands of rotations,' said Ed, quickly, as he could see she was struggling with the comprehension of it all.

'So this ship docks with an even bigger ship?'

'No,' said Andy. 'This ship flies inside the bigger ship and lands in one of its hangars.'

She ticked badly for a moment, her gaze flicking between them again, as she tried to comprehend what Andy had just said and probably debating if they were telling the truth.

'Your starship has hangars inside it?...Then how big is it?'

'Best way is to show you,' said Ed, sliding into the pilot's seat and closing the airlock doors.

12

Flex Du domicile, Calistromal locale

TYME'S PULSE QUICKENED, a sharp spike of hope cutting through his exhaustion. He turned towards where he knew his brother's face would be in the darkness, wishing he could see Jaccin's expression.

'What do you mean, you might know a way in?' he breathed.

'The cooling tank section has these old grates,' Jaccin whispered, his voice barely audible even in their hidden space. 'Most of them are sealed, but there's one near the emergency overflow that's loose. I noticed it weeks ago when I was cleaning the filters. It drops down into some kind of passage.'

Tyme felt his hands clench involuntarily. The possibility seemed almost too good to be true, which made him immediately suspicious. In his experience, things that seemed too convenient usually were.

'You've seen it? This passage?'

'Just the opening. It's maybe a couple of metres down from under the grate, and I could see it continues in both directions. The air coming up smelled different, stale, but not toxic like the refinery air.'

Tyme's mind raced, trying to picture the layout of the facility. The cooling tanks were on the opposite side of the complex from the melting stacks, which meant the tunnel might run under a significant portion of the refinery complex. If they could access it from Jaccin's cooling tank area, they might be able to travel underground all the way to the outer perimeters without being detected.

'How long would it take to get to this grate?' Tyme whispered.

'From the main platform? Maybe fifteen minutes if I move fast. But I'd have to time it right, when the Repp overseer is doing rounds on the other side of the tanks.'

Tyme's chest tightened with a mixture of excitement and terror. This could actually work. Or it could get them both killed, or worse, subjected to blade extraction like Haslyin and his brothers. He pressed his back against the composite wall, feeling the rough texture through his clothing.

'We'd need to coordinate it,' he said. 'I'd have to find a way to get from the melting stacks to the cooling tanks without being seen.'

'The shift change,' Jaccin said immediately. 'When the day crews are switching with the night crews, there's always confusion. Workers moving in different directions, trollies running extra routes. If you could time it right…'

An idea was forming in Tyme's mind, but it felt fragile, like it might shatter if he examined it too closely. The shift change only lasted about ten minutes, and he'd have to move through several secured sections to reach the cooling tanks. One wrong turn, one unexpected Repp patrol, and it would all be over.

'We'd only get one chance,' he whispered. 'If we're caught...'

He didn't need to finish. They both knew the consequences of what happened to workers who tried to escape. The stories were whispered sometimes in the darker corners of the locale, tales of executions meant to discourage others from similar attempts.

Tyme's legs were cramping badly now, and the stale air in the compartment was making him lightheaded. But leaving meant returning to the pretence that everything was normal, that he hadn't seen his friend's remains fall from a discharge pipe.

'Tomorrow,' Jaccin whispered suddenly. 'If we're going to do this, it has to be tomorrow. I heard some of the cooling tank crew talking about maintenance inspections coming up. If they find that loose grate...'

Tyme's stomach dropped. The timeline was accelerating beyond his comfort zone, but Jaccin was right. They couldn't afford to wait, couldn't risk losing their one chance at escape. Tyme took a deep breath, trying to steady his heart rate.

'Tomorrow then,' he agreed. 'During shift change. I'll need to find a way to get to your section without being noticed.'

'The emergency notification system,' Jaccin said, his voice quickening with inspiration. 'If someone triggered an alert in one of the sectors between us, it would create enough confusion. Workers would be evacuating, running in all directions.'

Tyme considered this. It might work, but triggering a false alarm carried its own risks. The Repps punished infractions of that nature severely.

'What about Merrin?' he asked. 'He seemed to know something about what happened to Kestrel. Maybe he could help.'

'Can you trust him?' Jaccin's voice was sceptical. 'Fitter men than him have been sent to transition.'

Tyme thought about the older man's warning, the fear in his eyes when they'd found Kestrel's arm. 'I don't know. Maybe not. He has been here longer than most, and you're right, it is surprising he hasn't been taken for transition yet. You're thinking he might be a Repp spy?'

'That might be why,' Jaccin said grimly. 'Perhaps that arm was supposed to land in front of him.'

'What, like a little reminder?'

'You said he seemed really rattled by it.'

'Yeah, but so was I. I still am. I need to think about Merrin,' Tyme whispered. 'There's something not right about him still being here at his age.'

The cramped space was making Tyme's muscles scream in protest now. He shifted slightly, trying to find a more comfortable position without making too much noise.

'We should get out of here before we suffocate,' Jaccin said. 'We'll need to rest if we're going to attempt this tomorrow.'

Tyme nodded in the darkness, then felt silly as he realised his brother couldn't see him.

'Yeah. Let's go.'

They carefully pushed the tile up and climbed out, their joints cracking from being in the confined position for so long. Tyme squinted and stretched, feeling the tension in his back and shoulders. The dim lighting of their quarters seemed bright after the complete darkness beneath the floor.

Jaccin moved to the food preparation area and activated their daily ration dispenser. The machine hummed and clicked before delivering two identical grey nutrient blocks.

'Eat,' he said, handing one to Tyme. 'Then get some sleep, we'll need the all the energy we possess tomorrow.'

Tyme took the block, though his stomach was still knotted with anxiety. The bland, gritty texture of the nutrient ration stuck in his throat as he forced himself to swallow. He needed the sustenance, but his mind kept flashing back to the arm, the melted ring, the charred flesh. Each bite became more difficult than the last.

'I'm going to check the corridor schedule,' Jaccin said, moving to the small data terminal near the door. 'See if there's anything unusual about tomorrow's shift patterns.'

Tyme nodded, watching his brother's fingers dance across the scratched screen. The soft blue glow illuminated his face from below, casting strange shadows that made him look older, more haggard. Or maybe it wasn't just the lighting. Maybe the knowledge of what really happened during "transition" had aged them both in the space of a single day.

The sleep platform felt unusually hard as Tyme lowered himself onto it. His muscles ached from the long shift at station four, but his mind refused to quieten down.

He stared at the ceiling, counting the familiar cracks in the composite panels while trying to piece together tomorrow's race though the refinery.

The terminal chimed softly, and Jaccin turned back towards him. 'Standard shift rotation tomorrow. Nothing unusual scheduled until the maintenance inspection at the end of the cycle.'

Tyme rolled onto his side, facing the wall. The composite was cold against his cheek, a small relief from the lingering heat that seemed permanently trapped in his skin after working station four. He closed his eyes and tried to imagine the maintenance tunnels Jaccin had described, dark passages running beneath the refinery like arteries taking him to a new life. The thought should have been comforting, a promise of escape, but instead it made his chest tighten with claustrophobia.

Sleep came in fragments. He'd drift off for what felt like minutes before jolting awake, his heart hammering as he remembered where he was, what they were planning. During one of these half-conscious moments, he heard movement from Jaccin's platform, the soft rustle of fabric, the creak of composite under shifting weight. His brother was having just as much trouble sleeping.

When the wake cycle chimed through the quarters, Tyme felt like he'd barely closed his eyes. The artificial lighting flickered on, harsh and immediate, making his head pound. He sat up slowly and took a deep breath. Today was going to be a big day

13

Shuttle cockpit, entering orbit above Scalene, Triangulum
Galaxy

ED HAD, for appearance only, flown the shuttle up from the
surface, but in reality Cleo had. He'd just randomly
pressed a few icons here and there to avoid their guest
freaking out.

'That was very quick,' said Civray, as the antigravs
died away and the AVF drive's quiet hum took over. She
stared out at the planet below and out into space. 'Where
all the wreckage gone?' the translator repeated.

'We cleaned it up,' said Ed. 'It was an extreme navigation hazard as you emerged from the gate.'

'How did you…what is that?' she said suddenly, sitting
up straight and pointing out the front screen.

'Our ship, the *Gabriel*,' said Andy.

She went quiet for a moment and just stared, her mouth

hanging open, as the sleek six-hundred metre starship grew larger and began to fill the whole screen.

'I had no idea a vessel could be made so huge,' she said eventually.

'Actually, ours is quite compact compared to some,' said Ed.

'You wait till you see a katadromiko,' chuckled Andy. 'A floating city, with forty-seven thousand crew.'

Civray turned to stare at Andy, then turned to point at the translator clipped to Ed's jacket.

'Are you sure that thing is translating properly?' she asked. 'Forty-seven thousand crew can't be correct.'

She leant forward, craning her neck to peer up and down the *Gabriel*'s hull, her eyes nearly popping out of her head as the hangar door opened and she saw the size of it.

'It must take an age to re-pressurise a hangar of that size,' she said, just before the shuttle buzzed through the atmosphere shield. 'What was that?' she asked, as the shuttle spun around and clunked down next to the two other identical vessels. She cried out, pushed herself back hard into her seat and grabbed the armrests as Ed opened both airlock doors.

'Oops, sorry,' he said, holding his hands up, realising he'd just frightened her to death. 'It's okay, there's a shield.'

Andy, who'd been sitting behind her, moved over to the door and beckoned her to follow.

'Civray, come with me,' he said, holding out a hand.

She peeled her hands off the armrests, took his hand nervously and followed as he led her outside into the hangar. Then down to the atmosphere shield. He prodded it with a finger and demonstrated how although it was completely clear, when you touched it, it flexed and buzzed.

Tentatively, she did the same. Snatching her hand back when it tingled, causing Andy to chuckle. She glared at him for a moment, before a slight smile creased her features and she giggled too.

'See, quite safe,' he said, quickly realising he didn't have the translator, so she wouldn't understand.

'That's a big weird,' she said, in almost perfect English.

Andy looked at her in astonishment, checking over his shoulder to ensure Ed and the translator were not nearby.

'You can speak our language?' he said, taking a pace backwards and raising an eyebrow.

'Our species are language experts,' she said. 'We can be word-perfect in a big short period in time.'

Andy smiled.

'In a very short period of time,' he corrected her.

'Thank you, yes.'

'Come and show Ed,' he said, beckoning her to follow again. 'Then we'll introduce you to the rest of the crew.'

On the way, she marvelled at the opulent wood-panelled corridors and the lighting that brightened as you passed through each section. She seemed to find the transparent tube lift a bit disconcerting but grinned nervously as it traversed the ship all the same.

'Everyone, this is Civray,' said Ed, as they arrived on the bridge deck.

She was greeted by smiles and waves from everyone as they were introduced.

'She's from a planet called Wellas and that's our first

destination. Her ship was destroyed by the weaponised nanos and we're going to take her home.'

'I'm going to need some navigational input,' said Linda, turning to Civray expectantly.

Civray's convivial expression wilted somewhat.

'Er…all my navigational waypoints were on the ship,' she said, as she rummaged in a tunic pocket. 'I have a data node that it was all recorded on,' she added, holding it up. 'But it won't be compatible with your ship's systems.'

'Ah…now that's where Cleo comes in,' said Andy.

'Who is Cleo?' she asked.

'I am,' said Cleo, appearing a few metres away, dressed today in her regal finery.

Civray yelped, jumped back and hid behind Andy.

'It's okay,' said Ed, reassuringly. 'She's our ship's computer and an indispensable member of our crew.'

Cleo smiled, walked over and gave a very nervous Civray a hug.

'Now, shall I have a look at this?' she said, taking the small data node out of Civray's hand and studying it.

'Any use?' Linda asked.

'Yes,' Cleo replied. 'It's fairly rudimentary, I can interface with it, no problem.'

'How long will that take?' Ed asked.

'Done,' said Cleo, waving an arm at the holomap above.

A route appeared from their present location and traversed a zigzag course back to a star system some eighteen hundred light years away.

'It's designated the Gort system,' said Cleo, turning to Civray. 'Is that correct?'

Civray nodded, her ticking making her nods a little exaggerated.

Linda plotted a direct route and gave Ed a thumbs up.

'ETA?' Ed asked.

'Six hours,' she said. 'Seven embedded.'

'Okay, take us there with embedded jumps, we don't want to leave a trail.'

'Six hours?' repeated Civray, gazing up at the holomap in wonder. 'That journey would take sixty days in my ship.'

'Technology marches on,' said Ed. 'You're newcomers to deep space travel. In a couple of thousand years your race will be in starships like this, or maybe sooner now you've met us.'

Phil approached and smiled at Civray.

'I couldn't help but notice you have a nervous twitch,' he said.

Ed cringed and an obviously embarrassed Civray just nodded.

'I should be able to cure that for you, if you like?' he continued.

She glanced at Ed questioningly. He shrugged and returned a warm smile.

'Medical technology has equally improved,' he said. 'Phil is a very good ship's doctor, if I were you I'd give it a go.'

'Will you come with me?' Civray asked.

'Of course,' Ed replied, pointing. 'Phil, lead the way.'

14

The *Gabriel*, approaching the Gort system, Triangulum Galaxy

LINDA CALLED everyone to the bridge as she was programming the final jump. Civray had spent a couple of hours with Phil and Ed in the medical suite had received a full check over in an autonurse. It'd found a slight deficiency of vitamin C and D and administered a small cluster of advanced neuroleptic nanos to hopefully eliminate the nervous twitch.

As everyone arrived and took their seats, the lighting dimmed slightly as Linda jumped them in just on the outskirts of the Gort system and cloaked the ship.

'Okay,' she said. 'Which planet is yours?' as the system panned into view above them.

'The only inhabited one, fourth out from the star,' said Civray. 'You'll need me to talk to orbital management before you approach. As you can imagine, your arrival will cause quite some chaos.'

As the *Gabriel* moved out from behind the star, Phil sat up suddenly and stared first up at the holomap and with a confused expression back down at his display.

'Hold your horses,' he said. 'You said the fourth planet didn't you?'

'Yes...it'll be the one with the most space traffic,' answered Civray. 'And we're mining on two others, so you'll see a bit of traffic around those too.'

Phil glanced across at Ed, a scared look in his eyes.

'What is it?'

'Erm...I've got no traffic, an uninhabited space station, and a very quiet planet.'

'That's impossible,' said Civray. 'I've only been away two rotations. Are you sure you've come to the right system?'

'Check for the weaponised nanos,' said Ed.

'Negative.'

'Are we scanning the entire system?' Ed asked.

'Yes,' said Pol.

'No hidden ships anywhere?'

'Not that we can see.'

Civray stood up from her seat at one side of the bridge and stepped over to examine the holomap closely. Phil panned in as best he could from this range on the space station.

'That is yours I take it?' Ed asked.

'Yes,' said a subdued Civray. 'It's normally the busiest area of space traffic. Those docking positions are normally full and you have to book well in advance.'

'There's only five ships attached,' said Phil. 'Seventeen empty docks.'

'This is very unusual...can I call them?' Civray asked.

'Phil, open up a multi-channel transmission for her,' said Ed.

He tapped away for a moment and nodded at Civray. She called out in her own language, using her, what should've been recognised, call sign. There was no response. She tried again...and as before the only reply was a hiss of static.

Turning to Ed, she shook her head and held her hands out wide.

'This is extremely worrying,' she said. 'Three hundred lived and worked on that station and over four billion on Wellas...can we get over there straight away?'

Ed nodded and turned to Linda.

'The planet has two moons. Can you jump in close behind the largest, recloak and then get over to the station as quickly as possible?'

'Give me a minute,' she said. 'What's that big moon called, Civray?'

'Jatt,' she said. 'The small one is Felline and the station is called Queffer.'

Andy sniggered.

'Sounds like a twentieth-century hairdo,' he said.

No one laughed with him. Luckily, Civray didn't understand it, so wasn't offended.

'Jumping,' said Linda, as the lights dimmed slightly.

Everyone glanced up as the *Gabriel* emerged behind the grey-coloured moon and the holomap updated with hugely improved clarity.

'No human life-signs on the station or the planet,' said Phil, softly, looking at Ed with a wide-eyed expression.

'Shit,' mumbled Ed, giving Civray an apologetic glance.

'The power's down on the station too,' added Phil. 'So we can't piggy-back into the cameras.'

'Put us in an orbit next to the station please, Linda,' Ed said.

'Do we go in there and have a recce?' Andy asked.

'Look at this,' said Pol, as they approached and passed the station. She had aimed a camera at the row of five docked ships and panned in on the cockpit window of one of them.

'Oh, shit,' said Ed, as he saw the partly mummified body of a Wellasian slumped in the pilot's seat.

'Whatever happened here happened a while back,' said Phil. 'He seems to have been dead some time.'

Civray, who'd remained quiet for a few moments, spoke softly.

'I've only been gone two rotations,' she said.

'Working on the speed of this planet around its star, I have estimated that two rotations here equates to twenty-nine months and three-hundred and thirty-six days Earth time,' said Cleo.

'Two and a half years, give or take,' said Andy. 'I revert to my previous question…do we go over there?'

'Not without a lot of precautions,' said Linda. It could've been a particularly nasty virus, or another weaponised nano thing. Until we know what we're dealing with, no one goes anywhere near that station, is that clear?'

'What the lady said,' said Ed, giving everyone a wide-eyed look and pointing at Linda.

'I can go in there,' said Cleo.

'No power, no holo-emitters,' said Phil.

'I can send a smaller seeding drone in first,' she said. 'It'll eject emitters everywhere it goes and then I can follow.'

'Just make sure you have an emergency jump for the *Gabriel* ready to go,' said Ed.

'I have now and at all times,' she said. 'Even the slightest power fluctuation from anything but me and we're all a light year away.'

Ed glanced around at the six faces staring at him expectantly.

'Unless anyone has a better idea, I think we have a plan,' he said.

No one said anything, so he sat back on his couch and stuck both thumbs up.

'Cleo, let's go with that then.'

15

The *Gabriel*, orbiting Wellas, the Gort system, Triangulum
Galaxy

WITH CIVRAY'S GUIDANCE, Cleo had opened one of the
airlocks on the smaller upper control level of the station
and floated inside with the drone. She manually stuck a
couple of emitters on the ceiling inside and closed the
outer door. It went immediately pitch black as the starlight
was shut out and she activated the drone's powerful lights.
There was no gravity plating activated either, so she had to
remain on the float. Opening the inner door, she waited
while emitters were distributed inside the corridor by the
small drone.

'Which way do I go for the main control room?' she
asked, turning her head left and right, witnessing walls
glistening with ice.

'I seem to remember it being in the centre somewhere,'

answered Civray. 'Sorry, I only went there once and it was a long time ago.'

'My scan of that level shows a six-metre circular room, smack bang in the middle,' said Phil. 'It doesn't really matter which way you go. That corridor circles around the outside of the whole level.'

'That'll be it in the middle,' Civray said, watching the images transmitted back from the station. 'I remember it being small, central and round.'

Cleo didn't need to walk or float forward, just flick to the next group of emitters as the drone ejected them. She'd decided on going right and as soon as a left turn towards the middle was available she sent the drone that way, flicking along behind.

She passed closed doors on either side, but ignored them, until a set of double doors appeared out of the icy gloom at the end of the passage.

'That's it,' Civray called, pointing up at the holo image.

'What are those red lumps in front of the doors?' Linda asked.

The drone halted as it reached the doors and Cleo was able to materialise up close and what she saw on the floor made grim viewing.

'Ah, shit,' said Ed, turning to Civray. 'Bodies,' he said, grimly. 'Wearing a similar-coloured uniform to you.'

'They were Planetary Guards,' she said dejectedly, staring at the frozen, mummified remains. 'They never left their post all the time whatever it was happened. That's definitely the control room then.'

Cleo pushed the right-hand door, which swung inwards easily.

'The locks were electronic,' she said. 'Everything unlocked when the station's power went out.'

The drone hummed past her, illuminating the small room and went about distributing its emitters. Cleo didn't flick inside, instead she floated slowly in, expecting the worst and finding it. Out of the fourteen control positions, four were manned with similar corpses to the guards outside. They sat slumped and frozen on their control stations. A fifth body floated strangely near an open cabinet on the far side of the room. Again, it was frozen, but weirdly in a sideways fetal position.

Inside the cabinet, there were seven sizeable bright blue handles, one of them larger than the other six and all in the same position with writing above.

'Go over there,' said Civray. 'I want to see what they are.'

Cleo floated over, gently pushed the corpse to one side and gazed at the blue handles.

'Well?' Ed asked.

'Power shutoff switches,' said Civray. 'The big one is main power, then there's lighting, security, plating, docks, habitation, and positioning. They're all in the off position.'

'Do I turn them back on?' Cleo asked, her eyes dropping to the body below.

'Wait,' said Ed. 'We don't know whether that person had just turned them off, or was attempting to turn them back on.'

The drone's lights made eerie shadows dance and flicker around as it bobbed and weaved around in the small room.

'Can't you get the drone to be still, Cleo?' said Pol. 'All that movement is making me seasick.'

'If they had just been turned off, that would mean he or she had a really serious reason to do that, as anyone alive on the station would almost certainly die,' stated Andy, looking up to glance around at the others.

'He's right,' said Ed, standing up and pacing around and through the holomap. 'I think he'd just turned them off and curled into that position, knowing he was going to die.'

'But why hadn't the other bodies floated up like he had?' Linda asked.

'Mag-boots,' said Cleo, pointing at the other four corpses. 'They're wearing them and he isn't.'

'Which suggests the gravity plating was off before everything else,' said Ed.

'Why would they do that?' Pol asked. 'It would make moving around a lot more difficult.'

'Perhaps it wasn't meant to hinder them, but whatever was attacking them?' said Andy.

'Are you able to detect anything out of the ordinary, Cleo?' Ed asked. 'What about the corpses, anything there?'

'I would need to put one in an autonurse,' she said. 'Apart from that, the air quality in here is very stale, almost breathable, but obviously it's way too cold for you without a suit.'

'Would bringing a body back here be safe?' Linda asked.

'With your permission, I will move an autonurse into the room I use as the birthing chamber. I'll bring the body over completely contained in a body bag and seal the autonurse and the room as soon as it's in. It'll be frozen too, which could help.'

'Do it,' said Ed. 'But be ready to eject it if there's any sign of danger to us.'

'While I'm here, d'you want me to test reactivating any of the station's systems?'

Ed looked around at the others.

'What d'you all think?' he asked. 'Shall we start with lighting and see what happens?'

'Cleo has a reaction time so much quicker than ours, the emergency jump is on a millisecond delay,' said Phil. 'So I think we're okay to fire up the station.'

'I agree,' said Andy.

Linda, always being the health and safety advocate, sucked on her bottom lip for a moment, before nodding at Ed.

'If anything so much as coughs, I want us to be a light year away. Is that clear, Cleo?' she said.

'Crystal,' said Cleo, her avatar stepping up to the cabinet and firstly grabbing the main power lever. 'Here goes,' she said, turning it sharply to the on position. She spun around as a few clicks and hums sounded behind her. 'It's okay,' she said. 'It's just the control surfaces booting up.'

Screens on the consoles and around the walls sprang to life, lighting the room a little bit brighter.

'Okay, try the lighting switch first,' said Ed.

She turned that lever on with a clunk. Immediately the whole station began illuminating like a Christmas tree. Cleo, in the station's control room was bathed in a bright white light from flush-mounted ceiling panels. A few of them continued winking for a while and either eventually came on like the others, or died completely.

'Bloody hell,' mumbled Linda. 'It's like the Fourth of July suddenly.'

Hundreds of floodlights around the entire station came on illuminating every side, corner and especially the docking bays.

'The cameras are coming online too,' said Rayl. 'D'you want me to see if I can hack into them?'

'Go ahead,' said Ed. 'What d'you recommend next, Cleo?'

'Positioning,' she said. 'Its orbit has been gradually decaying over the last couple of years. It's not in any immediate danger, but will drop into the atmosphere within a few more weeks.'

Ed glanced over at Linda.

'Get ready to move with it,' he said. 'I imagine it'll want to go higher and reposition as quickly as possible.'

He turned back to the holomap.

'Okay, Cleo…do it.'

She did with another clunk and as expected, a wailing alarm sounded in the control room. Cleo was also able to hear the roaring of the positioning jets immediately beginning to push the station into a higher orbit. It was slow going and Linda was easily able to duplicate the movement in the *Gabriel*.

'What about environmental or habitation as they call it?' said Rayl.

'I would leave that for a while,' said Linda. 'There's a lot of bodies on that station and they'll begin to decompose if they were to thaw out.'

'Good point,' said Ed. 'Perhaps try the plating next, Cleo. It'll make it easier for us to move around if we need to come aboard.'

Before she did that, she pushed the floating body down onto the ground and glanced above her just in case. Andy laughed as she did it.

'You're a hologram, Cleo...you can't be hurt by anything falling on you.'

'I know,' she said. 'Weird eh? It just seemed the logical thing to do.'

'You're becoming more human all the time,' said Ed, with a momentary smirk.

Cleo shrugged and turned the plating lever. She heard a few clunks and bangs from nearby on the station and hoped no serious damage had been done as gravity returned.

16

Flex Du domicile, Calistromal locale

JACCIN WAS ALREADY UP, standing outside their small hygiene cubicle with his back to Tyme. His shoulders looked tense, rigid in a way that made Tyme's stomach turn with fresh anxiety.

'You ready for this?' Jaccin asked without turning around.

Tyme swung his legs over the edge of his sleep platform, his bare feet hitting the cold composite floor. The chill shot up through his legs, a sharp reminder that this might be the last morning they'd wake up in these quarters. If they were caught, there wouldn't be any more mornings at all.

'As ready as I can be,' he said, though his voice came out rougher than he'd intended.

They went through their usual morning routine with

mechanical precision: hygiene, rations, work gear. But everything felt different now, with a little more significance. Tyme found himself memorising small details, the way the water recycler hummed in the cubicle, the scratched surface of their food dispenser, the faint chemical smell that always lingered in their quarters. He might never experience any of it again.

The walk to the trollicar felt endless. Each step brought them closer to either freedom or death, and his legs felt like dead weight beneath him. He kept his eyes down, focusing on the worn path that countless workers had trodden before him, wondering how many had harboured similar thoughts of escape. How many had failed?

The morning crowds at the trollicar station moved with the same listless energy they always did, shuffling forward in a daze of exhaustion and resignation. Tyme scanned the faces, looking for Merrin. He spotted the older man near the back of the queue, his burned shoulder causing him to stand slightly lopsided. Their eyes met briefly, and Tyme felt a chill run through him. There was something in Merrin's gaze, knowledge, warning, or perhaps complicity. He couldn't tell.

'Remember,' Jaccin murmured in his ear as they boarded the trollicar. 'Act normal. Don't draw attention.'

Tyme nodded slightly and slid into his usual seat, the worn plastekine smooth beneath him. The familiar hum of the trollicar's engine vibrated through the floor, and he could feel as well as hear the tallis shaft rattle. Today it almost felt comforting, like a familiar companion that had been with him through countless journeys to the place that might kill him today.

The refinery's acrid smell hit his nose as they

approached, but today it carried an additional weight of dread. He pulled on his goggs as they entered the bright surface light, the automatic gesture feeling strange when he knew it might be the last time. The brown wasteland stretched endlessly beyond the window, broken only by those encroaching slag piles that seemed to sneer at him. Tyme shivered as he realised they were actually graveyards for thousands of workers over many centuries.

'Remember what I said about being careful,' Jaccin said quietly, his voice steady but carrying an undertone that made Tyme's chest tighten further and did nothing to stop his hands shaking in his gloves.

The trollicar shuddered through the security scanners, and Tyme gripped the edge of his seat as they were thrown sideways. His knapsack was heavier today, weighted down with extra water and clothing.

When they disembarked and passed through the scanners with arms raised, he wondered if the machines could somehow detect his racing pulse and the sweat gathering under his work suit.

He caught Jaccin's eye as they separated towards their respective work crews. His brother's face looked pale under the harsh lighting, but the wink he received steadied Tyme's resolve. This was it. The last time they would see each other until the shift change.

As Tyme boarded the trollie to the melting stacks, he noticed Merrin climbing in behind him. The older man said nothing, just nodded slightly. Tyme turned away, unsure what to make of Merrin's closeness. Was he an ally? A spy? Someone desperate to survive like the rest of them? He couldn't afford to trust anyone today except Jaccin.

The trollie lurched forward, carrying them deeper into the facility. Tyme's heart hammered against his ribs as they approached the melting stacks. The familiar roar grew louder, and heat warmed his face even before the doors opened. When they did, the blast of superheated air hit him like a hammer.

'Station two today,' Pell announced, his voice cutting through the cacophony of machinery. 'Regular extraction pattern, watch the flow rates.'

Station two. Tyme felt a small surge of relief. Station two was closer to the central corridor that connected to the cooling tanks. It would make his journey during shift change marginally shorter and gave him an extra boost of confidence.

He grabbed his tool pack from the rack, the familiar weight of scrapers and collection hoses somehow reassuring. His hands had stopped shaking, replaced by a strange calm that surprised him. Maybe this was what people felt before they did something that would forever change their lives.

The work platform stretched before him, pipes and conveyor belts creating their usual maze of industrial complexity. Steam hissed from joints, and the floor vibrated with that deep mechanical rhythm he'd grown to hate. But today he looked at it differently, noting the positions of the Repp overseers, the timing of their patrols, the sight lines between work stations.

Merrin took position beside him at station two, just as he had the day before. The older man's burned shoulder seemed to be bothering him more today, his movements careful and measured.

'Flow starts in two minutes,' Pell called out over the intercom.

Tyme clipped his safety tether to the overhead rail and adjusted his respirator. The familiar ritual felt different now, like he was putting on armour for battle rather than just another shift. He glanced at the huge clock on the wall behind him, calculating. Six hours until shift change. Six hours to act normal while his mind raced through every scenario.

The warning bell sounded, and Tyme braced himself as the molten haklion began to pour from the overhead valves. Even after years at the refinery, the initial surge always made his stomach clench.

'Keep your head down today,' Merrin muttered above the noise, positioning his scraper at the edge of the trough. 'Pretend you never saw anything yesterday.'

Tyme nodded slightly, focusing on guiding the flow into the collection channel. The haklion moved like liquid fire, its heat penetrating his protective gloves. He settled into the familiar rhythm, scrape, guide, clear, repeat, while his mind went over escape plans.

The hours crawled by. Tyme's arms burned from the repetitive motions, and sweat trickled down his spine, soaking his jumpsuit. He kept glancing at the massive clock on the wall, watching the minutes tick away with excruciating slowness. Five hours until shift change. Four and a half. Four.

The Repp overseer moved slowly along the upper walkway, its metallic joints clicking with each step. Tyme counted the seconds between its movements, trying to establish a pattern. Twenty seconds at each observation point, then forty-five to traverse to the next. If he timed it right during shift change, he could slip into the service corridor while the overseer's back was turned.

Two hours left. The haklion flow ebbed momentarily, allowing Tyme to stretch his aching shoulders. His throat felt raw despite the respirator, and his eyes stung from the constant heat. He risked a glance at Merrin, who was working with the same mechanical precision he always did, but there was a tightness around his eyes that hadn't been there yesterday.

'You've been quiet today,' Merrin said, his voice barely audible over the roar of the furnaces.

Tyme shrugged, turning back to the haklion trough. 'Just focused on the work,' he said, as confidently as he could.

'Smart,' Merrin murmured. 'Very smart.'

One hour left. Tyme's arms felt like lead, but adrenaline kept him moving. The knowledge that he might never have to stand at a haklion station again made every scrape of metal feel like a countdown to freedom.

Thirty minutes. The shift change bell would sound soon, and the corridors would fill with workers moving between sectors. Tyme's pulse quickened as he visualised the route he'd memorised...through the service corridor, past the filtration units, down two levels to the cooling tank section where Jaccin would be waiting.

The Repp overseer paused directly above his station, its breathing apparatus hissing softly. Tyme forced himself to maintain his steady rhythm, guiding the molten haklion while his skin crawled under the machine's observation. Twenty seconds. He counted silently, watching the flow while listening to the mechanical clicks of the overseer's joints. Finally, it moved on, heading towards the far end of the platform.

'Flow stop in five,' Pell's voice crackled over the intercom.

Tyme's hands began trembling again as he prepared for the final extraction. The haklion stream weakened to a trickle, then stopped entirely. Around him, other workers began the familiar process of lifting cooled plates with their thermal tongs. He moved mechanically, transferring the grey metal plates from the cooling trough to the collection rack. Five minutes until shift change. He placed the last plate carefully, making sure it was properly aligned. The slightest deviation from routine might draw attention.

When the shift change bell finally rang, its harsh clang echoed through the melting stacks. Tyme's heart leapt into his throat as workers began moving towards the exits, their tools clattering as they returned them to the racks.

'Move quickly,' Merrin muttered, suddenly close beside him. 'I'll create a distraction near the main corridor in two minutes. Don't waste it and take this for luck.'

Before Tyme could respond, the older man had stuffed a rare halite stone into his hand and was shuffling away, disappearing into the crowd of tired workers. Tyme stood frozen for a moment, confusion mingling with hope. Merrin was helping him? He hadn't expected that, how the hell did he know?

He quickly stuffed the stone into his pocket, returned his tools to the rack with practised movements, before joining the stream of workers heading towards the exit trollies. The platform was crowded now, day shift workers leaving as night shift arrived. Perfect cover for what he needed to do.

He moved with the flow until he reached the junction where the main corridor branched towards the cooling tank section. Instead of following the crowd towards the trollies, he veered left into the service corridor. The shift in direction made his stomach lurch with fear, but the corridor was empty, just as he'd hoped.

His boots echoed against the metal flooring as he sprinted through the narrow passage. Emergency lighting cast strange shadows on the walls, and the air tasted different here, less processed, with an underlying metallic tang. He could hear the distant rumble of machinery through the composite walls, but it felt muffled, separated from him by layers of industrial infrastructure.

A sudden commotion erupted from somewhere behind him…shouting voices, the clatter of dropped equipment. Merrin's distraction. Tyme's pace quickened, his breath coming in short gasps that fogged his goggs. The older man was risking everything to help him escape; he hoped he wasn't running into a trap.

The service corridor branched ahead, and he paused, trying to remember the facility layout. Left towards the filtration units, then down two levels. His hands were sweaty inside his gloves as he gripped the stair rail, taking the steps two, sometimes three at a time. The metal rang beneath his boots, echoing through the stairwell like alarm bells. Each footfall felt too loud, too obvious, but he couldn't slow down now.

Two levels down, the air grew cooler and carried the distinct chemical smell of the cooling tanks. Tyme could hear the hum of circulation pumps and the periodic hiss of pressure valves. He was close now, maybe three minutes from where Jaccin would be waiting.

17

The *Gabriel*, orbiting Wellas, the Gort system, Triangulum Galaxy

CLEO HAD RETURNED to the *Gabriel* with her corpse and had safely sealed it up in the autonurse. Everyone on the bridge watched the holographic image as the machine began thawing the body and evaluating what had taken this male Wellasian's life.

Earlier the space station had ceased moving, seemingly having reached its designated high orbit. Civray was in a state of shock and had wanted to spend some time alone. She lay on one of the sofas up in the blister, staring out at her dead planet below. Apart from the other thirty-five surveyors, she was the last of her species. They were all out there somewhere discovering worlds and resources for a race that no longer existed.

Ed realised Civray was going to need a lot of looking

after. Coming to terms with the loss of your entire civilisation was no small feat. She'd agreed that the bodies on the space station should be ejected planet-side, so as to be claimed by the gravity well and cremated in the upper atmosphere of their own planet.

They were all at a loss to decide what to do about the planet itself. The *Gabriel*'s high-powered cameras had picked out thousands of bodies lying in the city streets below. Even all the animals and birds had perished too. It would obviously be logistically impossible to safely cremate over four billion corpses. So for now, until they knew what they were dealing with, all they could do was muse on the situation and wait for Cleo to find some answers.

'Should I go up there?' Pol asked, glancing at the camera feed from the blister.

'Let her have some time,' Ed replied. 'She'll let us know when she's ready.'

'I can't believe what she's having to go through,' said Linda. 'Can you imagine us going home and finding Earth completely dead? It's inconceivable.'

'It does bring it into perspective when you put it like that,' said Ed.

'Scary shit,' said Andy.

Cleo appeared dressed in a white lab coat and sat on one of the guest seats set along the bulkhead wall. Her expression was grim as she looked up and stared around at six expectant faces.

'I take it from your demeanour the news isn't good,' said Ed, before she had a chance to speak.

She nodded slowly and took a deep breath.

'It's basically what was known as the Bubonic Plague

or Black Death on Earth,' she said. 'Based on a virulent virus called Yersinia pestis.'

'Ah…right,' said Andy. 'Not such bad news then… we've had a vaccine for that for well over a hundred years.'

'Not so fast,' said Cleo, holding up a hand. 'I said based on.'

'So it's evolved into something even nastier?' Ed asked.

'That's where we have a problem,' she continued. 'The odds of this evolving naturally are billions to one against.'

'So you're saying this was deliberate?' said Linda, waving a hand up at the holographic image of Wellas turning slowly above them.

'Whether it was deliberate or an accident, I don't know,' admitted Cleo. 'What I'm pretty damn sure of…is the virus down there and in the space station was purposely manufactured.'

'Or weaponised,' said Andy. 'This has killed every living thing on the planet.'

'Hmm,' grunted Ed. 'Well…we can hope it was just a terrible accident, but after the weaponised nanos over at the gate system and now this, I kinda think otherwise.'

'Are you able to produce an antidote for this variant?' Linda asked.

'In time.'

'How much time?'

'I estimate around twenty-three years.'

'Fuck's sake,' Andy mumbled, shaking his head. 'That's just ridiculous.'

'Unless…' Cleo adopted a resigned expression.

'Unless what?' Pol asked.

'I had a live patient,' she said.

'Well, there's no chance of that is there?' said Andy. 'They've all been well dead for a good couple of years,' he added, pointing up at the holomap.

Cleo folded her arms across her chest.

'In the thirteen hundreds, about half the population of Europe survived. Some because they were lucky and didn't contract the virus and others for whatever reason managed to recover and then it seemed they were immune from recontracting.'

'So...reading between the lines here, Cleo,' said Ed, 'you're saying, if we can find just one survivor down there...'

'I can use a sample of his or her blood to formulate a vaccine very quickly...yes.'

'A lot quicker than twenty-three years then?' said Andy.

'Twenty-three minutes, probably,' Cleo admitted, rubbing her chin thoughtfully.

Ed turned to the others.

'Out of four-odd billion, there has to be someone who managed to pull through,' he said.

'We're getting nothing on the scans,' said Pol.

'We've all seen the disaster movies,' said Andy. 'There's always a small group of survivors hiding somewhere.'

'Yeah...that's just Hollywood,' said Linda. 'If there wasn't, they wouldn't have a film.'

'Our scans can't penetrate certain rock layers, remember,' said Andy. 'A remote cave is the first place I'd go in the circumstances.'

'Right,' said Ed. 'Operation Caveman is in full operation. For the sake of Civray and her colleagues being able to return to their home planet and start again safely, find Cleo a live Wellasian.'

They'd had all three shuttles out doing low-level scans for two days. Ed had the *Secchio* down into the atmosphere too to cover some of the multitude of mountain ranges, especially in the Southern Hemisphere. Civray had accompanied him on the second day and sat quietly in the co-pilot's seat of the old tatty cockpit glumly watching the readout from the array showing nothing for hours on end.

'I don't know whether the others would want to resettle down here after what's happened,' she said, glancing over at Ed after being silent for several hours.

'Whether you decide to or not, we have a moral responsibility to eradicate that virus,' said Ed, not taking his eyes off the rather grubby screens. 'Travellers could come here unknowingly at some point in the future and take it back home or to other civilisations on their travels. We simply can't take that risk.'

'Andy was telling me there's over sixteen hundred human races in your galaxy. Are they all as conscientious as you?' she asked.

'Unfortunately not, Civray,' he replied, giving her a fleeting apologetic glance. 'Think yourself lucky you weren't found by the Klatt.'

'Ah...not as benevolent eh?'

'You could say that.'

Ed looked at the time and was about to call it a day, when Phil called.

'Ed…I…er…I've just had a ping a few kilometres away from my position,' he said, sounding a little unsure. 'I turned around and it'd gone and the contact hasn't returned. What should I do?'

'Pinpoint the position as best you can and wait for me,' Ed sent back, before turning his ship around, taking it up high and gunning it north.

He arrived an hour later to find Andy already there in his shuttle. Both he and Phil were criss-crossing the area slowly and thoroughly.

'Anything?' he asked.

'Not a sausage,' replied Andy.

'Sorry, guys,' said Phil. 'It must've been just a glitch or something.'

'Not necessarily,' said Ed. 'There are a lot of caves here… How about we land in front of them and see if anyone peeks out at us. I know if it was me the suspense would be too much, I'd have to know what was going on.'

The two small shuttles and the *Secchio* settled one at a time on a slightly sloping piece of ground around eighty metres away from the two largest cave entrances. They were at the base of a low rocky escarpment and appeared quite natural, all except for a series of steps cut into the hillside leading up to them. The other three caves were much smaller, higher up, and you'd likely need climbing gear to reach them.

'Those steps look ancient,' said Andy. 'You can see how worn they are.'

'Our early ancestors would've lived in them,' said Civray. 'Not a bad place to hide if you're scared of human contact.'

'Are we suiting up?' Andy asked.

'Not yet,' Ed replied. 'Let's just wait and watch for a while. Switch your front screens to privacy.'

For several minutes nothing happened, then suddenly, Phil piped up excitedly.

'Movement in the left-hand one,' he blurted. 'A small heat signature bobbed up and disappeared again.'

'Oh cool,' said Andy. 'Everyone concentrate your shit on the left cave.'

A couple of minutes later the heat signature returned and this time they all saw it and it remained there, most likely watching them.

'Is anyone having any luck with their image intensifiers?' Phil asked.

'No,' said Ed. 'It's too bright out here for the night vision stuff as well.'

The little crimson blob on their screens moved right, grew slightly and hid behind another rock.

'He's getting braver,' said Ed. 'Nobody move…I want to make sure it's definitely human before we get too excited.'

'My screen is saying it's human,' said Andy.

'It's quite small though and those detectors have made mistakes before,' Ed reminded him.

More movement shut everyone up again. The blob moved forward quickly this time and took up residence behind a boulder right in the entrance. Ed smiled as his camera finally got a sharp image of a Wellasian face peering nervously over the rock.

'Well, that confirms it,' said Andy. 'He's very small though.'

'It's a child,' said Civray, glancing over at Ed. 'Female, no more than three or four rotations.'

'D'you think there's a family in there?'

'Possible…but unlikely,' Civray said, holding her arms out in surrender. 'Considering the potency of this virus.'

'Indeed,' said Ed. 'But how the hell has she survived this long and what's she eaten?'

'Plenty of fruit and berries around here.'

'Okay, everyone, we need to make a decision on how to approach this.'

18

Hillside caves, Wellas, the Gort system, Triangulum
Galaxy

ED, Civray, Andy and Phil had debated the best, safest and less traumatic way of capturing the child. They'd eliminated chasing her as they would all have to be wearing the black Theo-designed space suits which would make them look quite menacing. They finally, and not without some concern from Civray, came to the conclusion a single low-powered stun shot was probably the safest option.

Civray was to clear the front screen of Ed's ship and move around a lot inside the cockpit to get the child's attention, while Ed, all suited up, quietly lowered himself down from the concealed underside airlock, that at this angle was hidden behind one of the freighter's struts.

Ed had chosen a Makrys sniper rifle as it would be more accurate over the distance and would interface into his suit's systems. Once the peculiar liquid suit had formed around him he gave Civray the nod up in the cockpit. He'd double-checked he'd set his weapon at its lowest stun setting and ensured it was talking to his suit.

Andy and Phil, similarly suited, watched the child on their helmet displays while loitering in their airlocks for the retrieval.

'Go, Ed,' said Andy. 'She's staring up at the cockpit now.'

He slowly lowered himself down, rested the rifle on the strut and armed it. He listened to the low whine of its targeting system in his ears and watched the weapon search for, identify and lock the target. He checked the weapon's settings for a third time and, although he knew the shot wouldn't cause any lasting harm to the child, he still felt a sick feeling in his stomach targeting a young girl with a weapon of war.

'Stand by,' he said to the others and waited until the red circle around the child turned green. 'Sorry, little one,' he whispered, before gently caressing the trigger.

The bolt hit the girl firmly on her left shoulder, she spun around and dropped out of sight behind the boulder.

'Go, go,' shouted Ed.

Andy and Phil didn't need to be told twice. They both leapt down from their shuttles and ran as fast as they could in the suits, over to the girl. Phil got there first, picked her up and then, with her over his shoulder, trotted back to Ed's freighter and straight up the lowering rear ramp, placing the small body in an autonurse that Cleo had earlier transferred into the cargo bay.

It quickly sealed up and began its scanning of the girl.

They all jumped as Linda began shouting in their ears from the *Gabriel* above.

'Guys, guys, you've got company,' she screamed.

They barely had time to turn around when two rather scruffy, adult Wellasians sprinted up the ramp and attacked them with two-metre-long wooden staffs. Although the Theo suits would protect them from a vicious clubbing swing, they wouldn't absorb the kinetic energy of a staff followed by a two-hundred-pound adult slamming into them. Phil and Ed went clattering down like nine pins, rolling into the far wall and desperately trying to parry the jabbing, swinging staffs.

Andy dodged around the autonurse and slammed into one of the assailants from behind, pushing him forward hard, to crash into a protruding bulkhead stanchion. The intruder dropped his spear and turning, he growled at his attacker just as Civray burst in the side door and began shouting in their own language.

'*Balaen...balaen,*' he hollered. '*Tagaa se valesoleen wu.*'

'*Filten baack scheelden, fanderay caaaar,*' replied the one facing Andy and stabbing a finger at him. '*Gaad se caaaar.*'

'Civray, no,' shouted Ed, as he struggled to his feet. 'You're not wearing a suit.'

'Sorry, Ed...they think you're going to kill the child and you're to blame for this virus,' she said.

The other Wellasian glowered at Phil and went to raise his spear again.

'*Gaad se caaaar,*' he snarled.

Civray stepped towards him and grabbed his arm.

'*Balaen…balaen,*' she said, softer this time. '*Tagaa se valesoleen wu. Geety wu.*'

Cleo appeared suddenly, holding a rifle. The two uninvited Wellasians shrank back in complete shock.

'*Gee te alhoos helpun,*' one of them shouted, pointing at Phil who was nearest.

'They want to know why you have naked faces,' said Civray, turning to the Wellasians and talking to them in their own language again.

Their eyes widened and they shrank back towards the ramp.

'The girl has immunity, I've taken blood samples and she will wake any moment,' said Cleo. 'I'm working on the vaccine right now. As soon as the girl is out of the autonurse, Civray, you must get straight in.'

Ed had now managed to find his suit's translator menu and activated it.

'We mean you no harm,' he said, the translator repeating it in Wellasian. 'We needed a blood sample from a virus survivor to formulate a vaccine.'

The girl stirred in the autonurse, and she sat up as the field sealing her in vanished. She stared around nervously at everyone as Civray lifted her out and placed her down on the deck. She burst into tears and ran to one of the newcomers, grabbing him and clinging on.

The Wellasians had at first seemed quite shocked that they could suddenly converse with the aliens, but as with everything else they came to terms with it quickly enough.

'You should've asked first instead of shooting a baby,' one of the Wellasians grumbled, eying Ed accusingly.

'We had no idea there were more of you,' said Civray. 'We thought she was alone.'

'How many of you are there?' Phil asked, climbing to his feet.

'Just the three of us,' he said, turning and eyeing Civray suspiciously. 'How did you survive?'

'I'm one of the surveyors, my ship was destroyed and these hairless human aliens rescued me, they're from another galaxy.'

'How d'you know this virus wasn't from them?' one of them asked.

'How do we know it wasn't from you, for that matter?' Civray asked. 'After all, billions are dead and you three seem to be the only survivors.'

'It wasn't any of you,' said Cleo. 'The technology involved in formulating this strain was far in advance of anything you had even at your civilisation's peak.'

'But not you though,' said the other Wellasian, glowering.

'Can everyone stop pointing the finger?' said Ed, sighing. 'The only reason we're here is to try and save your civilisation from extinction and prevent any others from contracting this virus and going the same way.'

Cleo walked over to the autonurse and pointed inside.

'Civray, in,' she said. 'The longer you spend out here gassing, the more chance you have of contracting it.'

Civray wrinkled her nose and reluctantly clambered in. The containment field resealed over her and the machine began humming away to itself. Ed could see her eyes flicking left and right.

'Cleo, are you able to provide some supplies for these three?' Ed asked, nodding at the newcomers.

'What do you need?' Cleo asked sternly, all the while studying the readout screen of the autonurse.

'Anything and everything,' one of the Wellasians said. 'We live in a cave…what do you think?'

'Are we the only survivors you've found?' the other asked.

'Yes,' said Ed. 'Our scans don't penetrate underground here. The rock is too dense. We only found you because the girl popped out into the open for a few seconds.'

They both gave the girl a stern stare.

'The percentage of those, like yourselves, who've developed a natural immunity will be infinitely small,' said Cleo, turning to face them. But I'm sure there will be more in hiding and staying underground or in caves just like you and well away from areas of civilisation.'

'How long ago did it happen?' Andy asked.

'Two rotations,' said one.

'Just after the vessel drop,' said the other.

They all froze and turned to stare at him.

'The what?' Cleo asked.

The two Wellasians looked at each other in puzzlement.

'You don't know about that?' the first one asked.

'We've only just arrived,' answered Ed.

'Yes…right,' said one.

'I lived in one of the larger cities,' began the other. 'It was early one evening, there were loud booms from above, followed shortly after by a shower of small fragile containers falling and bursting everywhere.'

'Then within hours everyone started getting sick,' said the other. 'It was really quick. People were falling in the streets, vehicles crashing, aircraft falling from the sky, panic, looting. I lived on the outskirts and fled here into the mountainous region. I was sick for weeks, but woke one day, weak but alive. The virus had gone.'

'Pretty much the same for me and the girl,' said the other.

'Do you still have any of those containers?' Cleo asked.

'No…they just dissolved away after a few minutes.'

'The booms must've been larger insertion units dropping in from space at over the speed of sound,' said Ed. 'Some of those units could've survived.'

'I know where one of those could be,' one Wellasian said. 'I thought at the time it was a crashed satellite or something.'

'Take us there,' said Cleo.

19

Pessawinn Refinery, Pessawinn locale

TYME PUSHED through a heavy door marked with warning signs and found himself in a maintenance corridor that ran parallel to the cooling tank section. Through the thick composite walls, he could hear the muffled sounds of workers finishing their shift routines. His heart was working overtime as he tried to orientate himself in the maze of pipes and conduits.

A soft whistle reached his ears…three short notes, then two long ones. Jaccin's signal. He followed the sound and squeezed through a gap between two massive cooling units. The metal surfaces were freezing cold, causing his sweat-soaked jumpsuit to cling uncomfortably and chill his skin.

He found his brother crouched beside a partially loosened access grid, his hands working fervently to remove the remaining three bolts. Below the grid, a square opening in the floor dropped away into darkness.

'Hurry,' Jaccin hissed, as Tyme helped with one of the remaining bolts, his voice tight with urgency. 'The night shift supervisor will be along here any minute for his routine inspection.'

Tyme's fingers felt clumsy with adrenaline, slipping on the cold metal. The bolt finally gave way with a reluctant snap, and Jaccin pulled the grid completely free.

'Let's go,' he whispered, pointing into the darkness below. 'You go first and I'll close the grid over me.'

Tyme peered into the opening. A drop of about two metres led to what appeared to be an ancient service tunnel. The air wafting up from below carried a musty, forgotten smell that made his nose wrinkle. No trace of haklion or the other chemicals that permeated every corner of the refinery, just dust and decades of neglect.

Jaccin lowered himself into the hole. Bracing his feet against the walls, he dragged the grid with him before pulling it into place and dropping next to his brother with a soft thud. Tyme glanced up nervously, listening for approaching footsteps. The sounds of the shift change continued above, but seemed much more distant now.

Jaccin pulled a small light from his pocket, illuminating the tunnel stretching in both directions. The beam revealed cracked composite walls covered with dust and ancient markings. The ceiling hung low, forcing them both to stoop slightly.

'It must be that way?' Tyme whispered, pointing right, his voice sounding echoey in the dead air of the tunnel.

Jaccin nodded. 'It should lead away from the refinery, towards the outer perimeter.'

They moved cautiously, their boots making soft crunching sounds on the debris-strewn floor. The tunnel smelled of age and abandonment, nothing like the acrid chemical stench they'd lived with for years. Tyme found himself taking deeper breaths, savouring the absence of haklion fumes despite the musty odour.

'How long do you think this goes?' Tyme asked, keeping his voice low although it was unlikely anyone would hear them now.

'No idea. But it has to lead somewhere. These tunnels were built before the Repps took over completely. They must connect to the ancient human settlements.'

Jaccin's light bobbed as they walked, casting elongated shadows that made Tyme's heart miss a beat every once in a while, when he thought they were being followed. The tunnel stretched endlessly ahead, and Tyme wondered if they were walking towards freedom or just a different kind of trap. His legs already ached from crouching, and the musty air made his throat feel scratchy despite the relief from the refinery's toxic atmosphere.

'Wait,' Jaccin whispered, stopping abruptly.

Tyme nearly collided with his brother's back. The light revealed a junction ahead where three tunnels branched off in different directions. Ancient symbols were carved into the walls above each opening, but the markings meant nothing to him.

'Which way?' Tyme asked, though he suspected Jaccin wouldn't have a clue either.

Jaccin moved the light between the three options. The left tunnel angled upward slightly, while the centre passage continued straight. The rightmost opening seemed to descend deeper.

'The lower one,' Tyme said, hopefully, pointing at the rightmost tunnel. 'If we go down, we're less likely to run into Repps or any workers. The Repps like to stay above ground.'

Jaccin hesitated, sweeping his light once more across the three options. 'You sure? It might flood down there. Or be a dead end.'

Tyme felt a chill creep up his spine at the thought, but he nodded firmly. 'Better to face water than stingers. Or blade extraction.'

His brother couldn't argue with that one. They ducked into the descending passage, the ceiling dropping even lower so they had to crouch uncomfortably. The air gradually grew colder and damper as they moved downward, and Tyme could feel wetness seeping through the knees of his jumpsuit where it occasionally brushed against the tunnel floor.

After what felt like hours of painful crouching and careful steps, the tunnel suddenly widened out into a larger chamber. Jaccin's light couldn't reach the far walls, but the beam reflected off small puddles scattered across the floor. The air smelled different here, less dusty, more organic, with hints of something sweet Tyme couldn't identify.

'What is that smell?' he asked.

'That could be vegetation,' Jaccin whispered, his voice tinged with wonder. 'I think it's plants...you know, green stuff.'

Tyme inhaled deeply, trying to place the unfamiliar scent. He'd only ever smelt the synthetic nutrition blocks, slag piles and the acrid fumes of the refinery. This was different...earthy and alive.

The light beam swept across the chamber floor, revealing small green shoots pushing up through cracks in the ancient composite. Tyme crouched down, reaching out with trembling fingers to touch one. The delicate stem bent slightly under his touch, springing back when he released it.

'How is this even possible?' he murmured, in astonishment. 'There's no light down here and nothing grows on this planet anymore.'

His brother moved the beam upward, illuminating a network of thin cracks in the ceiling. A faint glow filtered through them...not the harsh white of the uplight, but something softer.

'Look,' Jaccin said, pointing to where the small plants clustered most densely. 'They're growing towards that light source.'

Tyme stood slowly, wincing as his muscles cramped with the effort. The chamber was larger than he'd first thought, stretching perhaps fifty metres in each direction. Along the far wall, he could make out what looked like another tunnel entrance, this one with a more regular shape, as if it had been deliberately constructed rather than carved out of necessity.

'There,' he called, excitedly and pointing towards the opening. 'That looks more promising.'

They picked their way carefully across the chamber, stepping around the scattered puddles and trying not to disturb the fragile green shoots. Tyme found himself fascinated by the tiny plants, their alien beauty a stark contrast to the industrial wasteland he'd known his entire life. He wanted to stop and examine them more closely, but Jaccin was already moving more quickly now towards the far tunnel.

The new passage was indeed very different from the maintenance tunnels they'd been following. The walls were smoother, more deliberately shaped, and the ceiling two metres high, high enough that they could walk upright. Carved symbols decorated the walls at regular intervals, but these weren't the crude markings they'd seen earlier. These looked purposeful, artistic even, as if someone had spent a lot of time and effort over them.

'This is old,' Jaccin whispered, running his fingers along one of the carved symbols. 'I mean, really old. From before the Repps.'

Tyme nodded, though his attention was caught by something else. The air itself was moving. A gentle current flowed through the tunnel, carrying with it smells he'd never experienced before...this time it was floral, almost sweet, mixed with the earthy smell of wet soil. His skin tingled as the moving air brushed against his face and the hairs on his arms stood up, so different from the stagnant, recycled atmosphere of the refinery.

'Do you feel that?' he said to Jaccin, not bothering to lower his voice this time.

His brother nodded, lowering the light slightly. 'Wind. Real wind.'

Tyme smiled and laughed out loud, something he hadn't done since their father had been taken. He'd heard about wind in the old stories their father used to whisper, but he'd never imagined it would feel so alive against his skin. The smell of freedom, it pulled them forward, faster now and deeper into the tunnel.

They trotted in silence for several minutes, the carved symbols flowing past in the wavering light beam. The tunnel curved gradually to the right, and with each step, the air grew fresher, the mysterious scents stronger. Tyme's jumpsuit, still damp with sweat from the refinery, began to feel cold in the moving air and for the first time in as long as he could remember, he shivered.

20

Shuttle cockpit, Wellas, the Gort system, Triangulum
Galaxy

PHIL CRUISED the shuttle along at five hundred metres, being directed by the Wellasian. The man sat in the co-pilot's seat, having been absolutely amazed at the technology around him, was now staring out at the topography and trying to find his bearings back to where he'd seen the satellite crash site. It had been two rotations ago and everything had become very overgrown since then making it much harder.

The other Wellasian had taken the frightened girl back to their cave and a rather disgruntled Civray had to stay in the autonurse until Cleo had the vaccine prepared. Ed and Andy had secured their ships and come along, sitting in the rear seats and craning their necks to see where they were going.

'Over there by the river,' he said, pointing. 'I stopped along here somewhere for the night and topped up with water.'

'I'm getting several returns for metallic objects in the next kilometre or so,' said Phil.

'It was at the side of that roadway,' he said. 'Well, the crater had actually blown out a chunk of the road.'

'Found it,' said Phil, turning the shuttle sharply and descending. 'Down there, next to that copse of trees.'

There were several pine-type trees with extremely long ferny leaves sitting in a group. The once smooth road surface was more like a farm track now, with cracks, weeds and long grasses sticking up right across it. They swayed gently in the breeze, but suddenly flattened themselves against the ground as the screaming antigravs came in above. Even the copse of trees flapped their disapproval as Phil landed on the old roadway next to the rather over-grown crater.

Ed was the first out and under supervision from Cleo, talking to him from the *Gabriel* above, he took samples from the crater. Soil, metal fragments and anything else he felt would prove useful to Cleo, all went in a sealable box.

Andy grabbed hold of the main metallic piece sticking up out of the weeds and wrenched it up and turned it over.

'There you go,' he said, indicating part of a scarred and pock-marked concave disc. 'The remains of a heat shield. This was no satellite…it's the remnants of a delivery system.'

The Wellasian stood and watched, his face a picture of apprehension.

'You think the virus was delivered from space then?' he asked.

'That's becoming a fair bet,' said Ed. 'The question now is…was this self-inflicted, or sent from an as yet unknown player?'

'My money's on somewhere else,' said Andy. 'If it was local, then it was a suicide bid.'

'Stranger things have occurred before,' Phil said. 'A deliberate self-inflicted act of genocide can't be ruled out.'

'If you get me those samples up here, I might be able to give you an answer to that,' called Cleo.

'Okay, we're on our way,' Ed answered.

They all turned and were strolling back to the shuttle when Pol called.

'You might want to hold fire with that,' she said, the edge of concern in her tone didn't go unnoticed by Ed.

'What's up, sweet pea?' he asked.

'A vessel with a very noisy jump signature just arrived in a system only four light years away and it's continuing in this direction.'

Phil, hearing the message too, turned and gave both Ed and Andy a nervous glance.

'That might be who did this,' he said, jumping up into the shuttle.

'Or another of their surveyors returning home,' said Ed. 'Cloak the ship, Pol…and Linda, move the *Gabriel* away from the station, it might be expecting to dock there. We'll cloak and loiter down here till we know who we're dealing with.'

'We need to get back to our ships and cloak them quickly, Phil,' said Andy, patting him on the back as he sat down behind.

The Wellasian took one of the rear seats this time and

after hearing the exchange looked between the three of them nervously.

'Has something happened?' he asked, having to raise his voice as Phil had already gunned the antigravs back to fever pitch and was quickly raising the ship.

'Another ship coming in this direction,' shouted Ed.

'It's not one of yours?'

'No, definitely not.'

'We're going to hide until we know who they are,' Andy said.

'How are you going to hide three spacecraft?' he asked. 'There are no caves big enough.'

'Actually, it's four,' said Andy. 'Our starship is in orbit close to your space station. And trust me, none of them will show up on their scans.'

'You have an even bigger ship?' he asked, seemingly surprised.

'Are you ready, guys?' Phil interrupted, reducing height and speed dramatically.

A few minutes later the Wellasian looked on from his cave entrance in complete astonishment as the three spacecraft, one at a time, vanished in front of his eyes. Shortly after, he nearly fell over backwards when an airlock appeared hanging in thin air. Andy jumped down and walked towards him, a translator clipped to his shirt.

'You've forgotten your suit,' the Wellasian shouted, gesticulating avidly.

Andy held up his hands and smiled.

'It's okay,' he called back as he approached. 'I've had

the vaccine. The three of you must too, just to make sure it doesn't ever return.'

'You really are quite hairless aren't you?' the Wellasian said, now able to inspect Andy's helmet-less face. 'Are all the humans like you in your galaxy?'

'No, there's a complete mixture,' he replied. 'As there probably is here too. Now you have jump drive technology, I'm sure it's only a matter of time before you meet more humanoid races. Some will be friendly, some not so much.'

The other Wellasian appeared out of the cave and stared open-mouthed at the open airlock.

'What?' he mumbled, glancing at his colleague for an explanation.

'They have invisible ships,' the other replied.

A sudden shout from the freighter caught their attention.

'Need to get under cover,' Phil called from his ship. 'I have food though.'

They all gathered in Phil's shuttle cockpit, ate pizza and watched the holomap beamed down from the *Gabriel*.

'I'm embarrassed,' said Ed. 'We don't know your names.'

The older-looking greying-faced one, dressed in a shabby faded green boiler suit, answered first.

'I'm Braaj, this is Yannak and the girl's Qallik,' he said.

Ed introduced himself and the others, just as a tone sounded from the holomap.

'The unidentified ship has jumped in system,' said Phil.

Civray swayed left and right examining the holomap from different directions.

'It jumped in at a recognised zone,' she said, pointing at its emergence point.

A three-dimensional image of the vessel appeared and they all turned to look at Civray, who sighed and her shoulders visibly dropped.

'It's a surveyor ship,' she said, and the tension in the cockpit became one of relief.

'There are no internal life signs,' Linda called from above, in an obviously puzzled tone.

'Is the cockpit shielded or something?' Ed asked, turning to Civray.

'No…it's not,' she whispered.

21

The *Gabriel*, orbiting Wellas, the Gort system, Triangulum
Galaxy

THE CONSENSUS OF OPINION, when they discovered the
surveyor ship seemed to have returned home on autopilot,
was for them to get back up to the *Gabriel* as soon as
possible. Civray naturally knew her way around the ship's
systems and convinced them she should recover its flight
log and see where it had been and come from.

Cleo made sure the three locals had a dose of the
vaccine before they left and they raided the rations on all
three ships too with a promise they would be back with
more help before they went home.

Once back, the rest of the *Gabriel*'s crew were vaccinated and Linda manoeuvred the ship back up close to
the space station again. The surveyor ship had been able
to dock automatically now the power was back on and it

sat in its clamps all on its own on the end of a six-dock spur.

'How did it know which dock to go to?' Rayl asked.

'That spur is specifically designed to fit our ships,' said Civray. 'Only six can be home at any one time and they're programmed to dock at the first available.'

'Why can't we see in the front screen?' asked Pol.

'It looks like it's set to opaque, it's a privacy setting.'

'We need to get on that station now we're all vaccinated,' said Ed. 'I want to find out where that ship has come from and what's happened to the surveyor it belonged to.'

'Don't forget environmental is still off,' said Cleo. 'I didn't turn that on because the bodies would thaw and begin to fester.'

'I don't particularly want to put a suit on again,' said Andy.

'Nor me,' admitted Ed. 'Cleo, if you turn it on, how long until it'd be safe for us?'

'Overnight probably,' she said. 'You'll need to get the bodies out and cremated within a day or two if you do that.'

'That shouldn't be a problem...are you okay with us doing that, Civray?'

'As far as I can see, it's the only way to make the station habitable again,' she said. 'I'll probably know some of them, so I should help you with giving them a respectful send-off.'

The following morning, Cleo materialised on the station once more and tested the atmosphere. Overnight she'd scanned one of the docking points and constructed an adapter to allow one of their shuttles to hard dock.

She acknowledged that the temperature was still a bit cold but acceptable and the atmosphere was a little stale but breathable.

Ed was the first out of the airlock after the shuttle docked, closely followed by Rayl, Andy, Civray and Linda. He sniffed the air and wrinkled his nose.

'Bloody hell, it's cold on here,' moaned Andy, zipping his jacket up under his chin. 'Smells like a fucking sewer too.'

'It'll smell a lot worse if we don't get the bodies despatched quickly,' said Linda, giving Civray an apologetic glance.

'You don't need to tiptoe around me, they've been dead a long time,' Civray said, striding past everyone. 'Come along, I'll lead you to the surveyor ship.'

They passed several bodies in the corridors. Stepping around and over them with unnecessary care, Civray decided to use the emergency stairs instead of the elevators just in case. Apparently, they'd been a running joke since the station was new as being out of service more often than not.

'This is the airlock leading to the surveyor's spur,' she said a few minutes later, indicating a double sliding door with a small porthole in each half. She peeked through one of them, before opening a panel on the wall to the left. Bright green lights inside reflected off the passage walls as she entered a code to an internal keypad and the two doors swished apart, completely disappearing into the bulkhead wall on either side.

'Everyone do your coats up tight,' she said, stepping

forward and inspecting a small screen on the wall inside. 'It's always a bit colder in this spur.'

'Oh good,' said Andy, earning him a punch on the arm from Rayl.

It was indeed noticeably colder as the internal doors disappeared either side. The passageway here was narrower and forced them to walk in single file. The ship was docked at the far end on the right. Civray again operated the first airlock door that opened directly to the surveyor ship's hull. A short umbilical had extended and sealed around the ship's outer airlock door.

Civray hesitated and faced the others.

'Seems like a lifetime ago I was entering one of these ships,' she said, pensively.

'Would you like us to go on board?' Ed asked.

'No, no,' she answered quickly. 'I'll be fine. I will need to retrieve the data node so we can see where it's been.'

The atmosphere inside the ship appeared normal, so she placed her hand over a gold protruding nodule about the size of an apple. There was a clunk and a hiss as pressures equalised, the small circular door popped inwards and slid down and away.

'It's a tiny airlock,' she said. 'Only room for two at a time.'

Even that was a squeeze, as Civray and Ed stooped down, stepped over a high threshold and crammed themselves inside.

'I'll operate it from inside to get you guys through,' she said to the other three before cycling the two of them inside.

Ed stepped out into a small galley and immediately recoiled at the smell.

'Oh dear,' said Civray, also pulling a revolted face. 'That doesn't bode well for the pilot does it?'

'No,' agreed Ed. 'Andy will be moaning for months about this. Hold fire bringing them through, let's just have a quick peek in the cockpit, you can extract the node and then someone can come back here wearing a suit.'

They both stepped across and popped their heads into the cockpit. It was as bad, if not worse than they expected. An emaciated, half decayed body lay slumped in the pilot's seat. Ed watched as something dripped from underneath the seat, adding to a dark damp stain on the flooring below. He gagged and turned away.

'Grab the node, Civray, and let's get out of here,' he said, trying not to breathe too deeply.

The others were surprised to see them still in the airlock as the outer door reopened.

'What's up?...and dear |God, what is that stink?' Andy asked, stumbling back and waving a hand in front of his face.

'Can't you guess?' Civray replied.

'I take it from that you found the pilot and he's not very alive?' said Linda, holding her nose and backing away to stand with Andy.

'What's left of him,' Ed replied, flapping his coat to get rid of some of the stink.

'Did you get the…'

Civray showed Linda the node, so she didn't have to finish the sentence.

'We'll get that to Cleo to decipher,' said Ed. 'Then come back to clean up the station, and I would advise whoever collects this body wears a hazmat suit.'

22

Ancient underground passage, unknown locale

THE FIRST HINT of outside light appeared as a faint glow ahead, barely visible beyond the reach of Jaccin's dull lamp.

'Turn off the light,' Tyme whispered urgently, grabbing his brother's wrist. 'If there are Repps out there, they'll see us coming from kilometres away.'

Jaccin clicked off the lamp, plunging them into darkness that wasn't quite complete, but it took a few moments for their eyes to adjust. The faint glow ahead seemed brighter now, and Tyme could make out the rough outline of the tunnel walls. The smell of growing things became stronger with each careful step forward.

His boots walked on smooth stone rather than the cracked composite they were used to. Someone had paved this section of tunnel, the blocks fitted together with precision that spoke of skilled craftsmanship. Tyme ran his fingers along the wall as they moved, feeling the transition from carved symbols to natural rock. The air current strengthened, carrying sounds he'd never heard before...a rhythmic whispering that might have been water gurgling over rock.

'Is that water?' Jaccin asked, beside him, echoing his thoughts.

'I hope so, brother,' Tyme said, through a grin.

The tunnel curved sharply left and suddenly the light ahead wasn't just a glow but actual illumination filtering down from above.

Tyme's heart was nearly bursting out of his chest as they approached what looked like a natural opening carved into rock. The air smelled so rich and weird that it made his nose tingle. He pressed himself against the tunnel wall and peered upward in complete awe.

Above them stretched something impossible...a cavern so vast he couldn't see its ceiling, filled with soft, greenish light that seemed to come from everywhere. The sound of moving water echoed from multiple directions, and the air carried scents that made his mouth water despite having no names for them.

'Look at that,' Jaccin breathed beside him. 'Just look at that.'

Tyme was in shock and could barely process what he was seeing. Plants...not the tiny struggling shoots from the chamber below, but massive green things that towered upward like the support columns of the refinery, only these were alive and swaying gently in the moving air. Some bore clusters of colourful objects that might have been fruits their father had described in whispered stories.

Water flowed in channels carved through the cavern floor, the liquid clearer than anything Tyme had ever seen. No chemical stains, no oily residue, just water that caught and sparkled the mysterious light around the walls. He wanted to drink it, it looked so inviting. He was suddenly very thirsty.

And then he saw the people.

Tyme blinked hard, certain his eyes were playing tricks after hours in the dim tunnels. But they were still there when he opened them…figures moving between the towering plants, tending to the flowing water channels with tools he didn't recognise. They wore clothing that looked soft and flexible, nothing like the harsh jumpsuits he'd known his entire life.

'Jaccin,' he rasped, his voice catching in his throat. 'There are people.'

One of the figures straightened and turned in their direction. Tyme pressed himself harder against the tunnel wall, his heart hammering so loudly he was sure everyone in the cavern could hear it. The person…a woman he suddenly realised, he'd never seen one before. She had skin that looked healthy, unmarked by chemical burns or stinger scars. Her hair fell loose around her shoulders instead of being cropped short for hygiene and efficiency.

She called out something in a language Tyme didn't understand, her voice carrying clearly across the water cavern. Other figures paused in their work, turning to look towards the tunnel opening. None of them seemed alarmed, more…curious.

Jaccin just emitted a grunt. He was rooted to the spot, terrified, just like his brother.

Tyme's legs felt like they might give out beneath him. These people looked nothing like the workers he was used to, but he still swept his eyes around the cavern, looking for a Repp overseer. But there wasn't a single Repp in sight. No mechanical joints clicking, no hissing breathing apparatus. Just...humans. Free humans.

The woman who had called out was approaching now, her steps unhurried as she followed the path beside one of the water channels. Tyme pressed back against the tunnel wall, unsure whether to flee or step forward. His muscles tensed, ready to take either scenario.

'It's all right,' the woman said, now close enough that Tyme could see her face clearly. He thought she was absolutely beautiful. Her words were accented strangely, but understandable. 'You're safe here,' she continued.

Tyme exchanged a glance with Jaccin, whose wide eyes reflected his own disbelief. Safe? The concept seemed, outrageous, foreign, dangerous even to believe.

'Who...who are you?' Tyme managed to stutter, his voice cracking from the dryness in his throat.

The woman smiled. Her teeth were white and even, not stained by chemical exposure like everyone he'd ever known before. 'My name is Eleni. Welcome to Tin Koilada. And you are from the surface factories, yes? The Repp prisons?'

Tyme nodded slowly, still scanning the cavern for any sign that this might be a trick, a hidden Repp, wall-mounted stingers, it all seemed too perfect. He shrank back as she rummaged in a bag, thinking a hand weapon or something was about to be produced. It was nothing more lethal than an apple.

Tyme had never seen anything so beautiful, so colourful, so delicious-looking. He'd heard rumours about fruits from his father years ago, allegedly grown on the planet's surface before the Repps came. But he'd never seen any.

'Wow...look at that,' whispered Jaccin, the first of the brothers to pluck up courage to speak.

'You are hungry?' Eleni asked, offering the red fruit to Tyme. 'Please...take it. Eat...you look exhausted.'

Tyme hesitated, his stomach knotting with equal parts hunger and suspicion. He glanced at Jaccin, who gave him a slight nod of encouragement.

With trembling fingers, Tyme reached out and took the fruit. It felt smooth and cool against his palm, nothing like the gritty texture of the nutrient blocks he'd been forced to eat his entire life. The weight of it surprised him, substantial yet somehow delicate.

'Go ahead,' Eleni said, her smile warm and patient. 'It's sweet.'

Tyme raised the fruit to his mouth and bit into it. The crisp sound of breaking skin was followed by an explosion of juice and flavour that overloaded his senses. Sweetness flooded his mouth, so intense he almost gasped. The texture was firm yet yielding, nothing like the processed uniformity of refinery ration cubes.

'This is...' he started, but couldn't find the words to describe the sensation.

Eleni giggled, her laugh and smile lighting a desire within him he hadn't felt before. It surprised him and he stopped chewing for a moment.

'Yes, I know. The first taste is always overwhelming.

Come,' she said, turning and beckoning them to follow. 'You need to meet the Gerousia.'

'Wow,' grunted Jaccin again, turning to his brother. 'Females are so beautiful.'

'Am I dreaming this?' said Tyme, handing half of the apple to Jaccin as they nervously followed Eleni.

23

The *Gabriel*, orbiting Wellas, the Gort system, Triangulum Galaxy

THE DEAD SURVEYOR'S name was Tehindor Fylan Jep. Departing a few months before Civray, he'd travelled almost directly into the centre of the galaxy. Ed, Civray and Phil were on the bridge watching the data node's play-back of his journey since leaving Wellas. The others had gone back to the station to begin the clean-up, taking trol-leys with them to move the frozen bodies into planet-side airlocks.

At first, Fylan's journey had been fairly routine. He'd visited one hundred and thirty-seven systems, inspecting and logging the planets within each one, and making special note of any that might prove potentially lucrative for future mining projects.

It wasn't until about one and a half rotations into his

journey, on his one hundred and thirty-eighth system, he stumbled upon a small moon orbiting a nondescript airless planet that his scans said already contained some sort of an abandoned mining colony. As his race had, as yet, not made first contact, he found this absolutely amazing and fascinating. The video logs showed him dancing around the cockpit with consummate glee.

He proceeded to take his ship down to one of the hollowed-out landing platforms and although his ship didn't have landing struts as such, it did still have the three underbelly pads from its construction on Wellas Station. Settling it down carefully on these he proceeded to suit up and cycle himself through the small airlock.

The gravity on this moon was slight, but enough to keep you grounded so long as you didn't get too enthusiastic or try to move overly quickly. They watched fascinated as he learnt to take long leisurely slow paces with stiff legs. If you tried to use your knees, that was enough to bounce you up a couple of metres, sometimes coming back down on your hands and knees.

His first destination was a weird-looking machine parked in a corner. It resembled a huge spider sitting on four of its back legs, with another four appendages sticking up at the front as if it was trying to defend itself. On closer inspection, it had an intricate assemblage of manoeuvring jets around its torso or hull and the raised legs contained four different machine tools.

'That's gotta be some sort of space-enabled mining machine,' said Ed. 'It's old too…look how dirty it is.'

'It must be remotely operated,' said Phil. 'I can't see any cockpit either.'

Turning, the surveyor made towards an open doorway behind the machine.

'That's a human-sized doorway,' said Civray.

'Doesn't mean they were human here though,' Ed replied. 'I want to see more evidence first.'

Continuing through the door, the surveyor was confronted by a set of tall stairs. In the light gravity they proved easy to bounce up, but he quickly discovered he had to be careful how high he bounced to avoid hitting his helmet on the ceiling. A short corridor at the top ended in a closed door with no obvious handle or controls to open it. He searched around for a few moments, but found nothing. He shouted something loud in his helmet at this point and kicked the door.

Ed and Phil both turned to Civray as the translator failed to translate for the first time.

'He swore,' she said, shaking her head. 'Very bad words.'

He'd obviously heard something as he kicked the door again and this time they all saw the door move slightly and heard a hiss of escaping gas.

'It's pressurised on the other side,' said Ed. 'Can't be very high though, or it wouldn't have moved.'

The surveyor proceeded to put his shoulder against the door and grunted as he pushed. The hissing sound returned, only this time he kept pushing and whatever pressure there was on the inside, began to reduce. A couple of minutes later it stopped and he found he could slide the door to the right. It was hard to push and he could hear a dead motor turning but without power the locking mechanism and motor were inoperative.

'It was only the pressure holding that door closed,' said Phil.

Inside was some sort of a control room. Dirty windows looked over the landing pad and as he wiped one of them with his glove, he could see the spider machine below and his ship just beyond, its outer airlock open and awaiting his return.

Turning, he flashed his suit lights over the rest of the room, immediately recoiling and emitting a shriek of surprise.

'What did he see?' Phil asked, squinting at the now rather shaky images.

'A body,' said Ed, as the camera footage stabilised.

'Two bodies,' Civray corrected, as another came into view.

They were sat at control panels, the last sinews of flesh the only thing holding the skeletal remains together. Eyeless sockets staring and hanging jaws silently screaming made it quite a macabre sight.

'Definitely human,' said Civray, raising her eyebrows at Ed.

'Indeed,' Ed replied. 'Dead a really long time too.'

'Many years,' agreed Phil, nodding. 'Well, it wasn't going to be them that killed him.'

The surveyor didn't loiter after seeing the corpses, he hurried, albeit as fast as he could in that gravity back to the ship. His camera footage showed the rough terrain beyond the landing pad for a few moments.

'Stop it there,' said Ed, suddenly. 'Back it up, slowly.'

Civray did as he asked. Ed stood up, staring at the holomap image closely.

'Stop,' he snapped, pointing. 'What does that look like?'

He was indicating something metallic sticking up from the surface just off the pad.

'Er...the back end of a large missile,' said Phil, turning his head from one side to the other.

'The fins at the back end of it look almost identical to the remains of the delivery system we found down there,' said Ed, jabbing a finger at the floor.

'That moon's several thousand light years away from here,' said Phil. 'It can't be, surely.'

'The race that have concocted that virus and delivery system are vastly superior to anything we've seen here so far. You heard what Cleo said. They could be as advanced as we are. We need to find out who did this.'

'That delivery missile wasn't destroyed because of the low gravity there,' said Phil. 'It might contain clues as to its origin.'

'I like the way you think,' Ed replied. 'That moon has to be our next port of call.'

They continued watching as the surveyor cycled himself back through the airlock, removed his suit, had something to eat and took off. No matter how far they fast forwarded, he never left the pilot's seat again.

24

Wellas Space Station, Wellas, the Gort system, Triangulum
Galaxy

ANDY HAD RETURNED to the *Gabriel* to collect Ed and
Civray. The first thing Ed noticed as they strode through
the station was the lack of bodies lying in the corridors.

'Smells a bit better on here now,' he said.

'I changed all the filters in the environmental system,'
said Andy. 'They were well buggered. Rayl found a ride-
on floor cleaner machine and every time we picked up a
body, she'd scrub up any mess.'

'How many have there been so far?' asked Civray.

'A hundred and twelve when I left to get you. We
started with the main corridors and common rooms, bridge
and so on, then started going round all the cabins. A lot of
'em died in their beds, so we're wrapping them up in the
soiled bedding and ejecting them that way.'

Ed nodded.

'Is the bridge clear?' he asked.

'Yeah.'

'I want to take Civray there to find the station data log and go through that.'

'Okay, follow me.'

When they arrived on the bridge, Rayl was humming around on the floor cleaner. She grinned as they entered and stopped the machine.

'You'll have to pay me extra now, Edward,' she said. 'I have a new skill.'

Civray wandered over to one of the main consoles and peered around with a puzzled expression.

'Where's the chair gone?' she asked.

'We had to eject most of them too,' Rayl said. 'You wouldn't have wanted to sit on one after we removed a corpse.'

'Ah, right, yeah, I didn't think of that.'

She turned and began tapping away at the console, mumbling to herself as she went. The screen in front of her lit up and she transferred its data up onto one of the much larger wall screens.

'I'm going to go back in the station's logs to when I left and fast forward from there,' she said.

Ed watched over her shoulder. It only took ten minutes to find what they were looking for. Seventy-three days after she left, there was sudden excitement on the station. An unidentified target was approaching from deep space and slowing. All attempts to contact it went unanswered and as it neared they could indeed confirm it was an alien vessel of some kind. It was big too, somewhere in the region of a kilometre in length. Opinions were mixed, it seems. Some wanted to greet it as a friend and others lobbied for it to be destroyed.

While the arguments raged, it suddenly disgorged hundreds of small torpedo-like craft, the mother ship veered away and began accelerating away again. The cluster of torpedoes continued on towards Wellas and reminded Ed of a swarm of insects.

'Well, we all know what they turned out to be,' said Rayl, staring at the big screen with her arms folded as all the torpedoes gradually spread out and encircled the planet. Finally, as one, they ejected their outer casings to reveal heat shields and began dropping into the atmosphere.

'Can we get any more information on that delivery ship?' asked Ed, turning to Civray.

She did her best with panning in on the vessel, but the camera technology wasn't as advanced as theirs and the image just got grainier the bigger she made it.

'Sorry, that's the best I've got,' Civray admitted.

'Bring the data node with you,' said Ed. 'Cleo might be able to clean it up a bit and give us a better view.'

She nodded and turned back to the console.

'Do you want me to continue with the playback?' she asked.

'No,' he said, putting a hand gently on her shoulder. 'I think we know what comes next, nobody wants to see that.'

Ed and Civray had joined the others with the grim task of collecting and ejecting the final corpses. It was particularly harrowing for Civray as she knew some of them. Ed encouraged her as they went along and tried to engage her in conversation on other topics to take her mind off the dreadful job.

'The Ancients certainly wouldn't be happy about this,' he said, as she helped him wrap a body in its bedding.

'How would you know?' she answered. 'You told me they did this pan-galactic human genome distribution thing three hundred thousand of your years ago. It's not as though they're around now to engage in conversation and ask their opinion.'

'Actually, they are around and they're still world-building now,' said Ed.

She stopped what she was doing and stared at him.

'I don't know how long one of your years is…but even I'm sure three hundred thousand is going to be a long time in my rotations too. There's no way they can still be around.'

'I've personally met two of them and Andy and Rayl have met a third.'

'How's that even possible?'

'They've kinda digitised themselves into the fabric of the universe. It's really hard to describe. Even they find it difficult to explain in such a crude language as ours. I think the nearest they get is an omnipresent dynamic plasma swarm, or something like that.'

'Are they here now?'

'No, they're not absolutely everywhere in every galaxy if that's what you mean…but the one I know the best, she can manifest herself in any shape or form and move planets with just a thought. As you can imagine, I'm always very polite.'

They loaded the body onto the autotrundle with the other two and set it off towards airlock 72b.

'Do they have individual names or anything?' she asked, as they followed the machine.

'They do...they were human like you and I once. The one I know is Neferuptah the Seventeen. Then there's her husband Pyriaeus the Fourteen and finally Menka the Nine, who we don't talk about.'

'Why's that?'

'Long story...let's just say she's lost her humanity and has been ostracised by the other two and us for that matter.'

'I thought you said it would be dangerous to annoy them.'

'Menka isn't as powerful as Neferuptah, but I must admit she is a worry.'

They arrived at the airlock where Linda was recording the names and numbers of bodies before despatch.

'I think you've got the last,' she said. 'The others are just doing a final check.'

'How many were there?' Civray asked.

'A hundred and fifty-seven with these three,' she said, almost apologetically.

Civray nodded and shrugged.

'There's normally over three hundred personnel up here at any one time,' she admitted.

'Perhaps some of them thought the virus was just restricted to the station and going back down to the planet would help them escape it,' said Andy.

'That would equate to the lack of ships docked I suppose,' she said. 'What are we going to do about the planet?'

'Nothing,' said Ed.

'Nothing?' she repeated, staring at Ed open-mouthed.

'There's nothing we can do,' he replied, regretfully. 'We have to let nature take its course down there. The bodies are already in the later stages of decomposition.'

'You would need a couple of million immunised people to clean up and even then it would take years,' said Andy.

'I'm going to prepare a permanently transmitting satellite,' said Ed. 'It'll remain in orbit and warn any visitors not to visit the surface without being suited up or vaccinated first.'

'What are we doing next?' Linda asked.

'We have a mining colony to visit.'

25

Tin Koilada settlement, unknown locale

THE CAVERN STRETCHED out before them in impossible beauty. Tyme's feet moved without direction, he was in a daze following Eleni along a path carved from smooth stone that ran alongside one of the water channels. The sound of flowing water filled his ears, a gentle murmur so different from the harsh mechanical roar of the refinery that he found himself listening to it with wonder. Each step took him deeper into this underground paradise that defied everything he'd believed about their planet.

Other people moved through the vast space, tending to plants and trees, all working with tools he'd never seen before. They glanced up as the brothers passed, offering smiles or gentle nods. No fear, no hurried avoidance of eye contact like in the workers' quarters. These people moved with an ease and contentment Tyme had never witnessed before. They were actually happy in their work.

'How many of you are there?' Jaccin asked, his voice still hushed with disbelief.

'In Tin Koilada? Err…perhaps around six hundred,' Eleni replied, pausing to think and then adjust something on a climbing plant that reached towards the cavern ceiling. 'But there are many other settlements. Other places like this.'

Six hundred. The number struck Tyme like a physical blow. Six hundred people living free while thousands toiled in the refineries, dying from chemical burns and being fed into furnaces when they outlived their usefulness.

'Other settlements?' Tyme's voice came out as barely more than a whisper.

'Oh yes. Throughout the underground river systems. Some larger than this, some smaller. We've been building them for generations, ever since the Repps took the surface.' Eleni gestured towards a group of children playing near one of the water channels, their laughter echoing off the cavern walls. 'Most of us were born here, but we get refugees from the surface regularly. People like you who find the old tunnels.'

'Isn't there some way of letting the workers know the truth?' Jaccin asked.

'We can't,' she said. 'There are millions up there. If they all suddenly descended, our world down here would be overrun and invite the Repps to destroy us.'

'Don't they ever come down here?' asked Tyme, wiping the last of the apple juice off his chin and licking it off his finger.

'The rock above us interferes with their concatenated mind-state and they can't operate as individuals.'

'Concatenated what?' said Jaccin, his face a picture of non-comprehension.

'You don't know much about them, considering you've lived with them all your lives,' she said, stopping for a moment and staring at them. 'They're a genetically enhanced human brain inside a ninety percent androidal human replicant structure...hence, Repps.'

The brothers looked at each other and then back at Eleni with renewed respect.

'You know a lot of stuff,' said Tyme.

'Basic education,' she replied. 'They make sure you remain ignorant up there,' she added, pointing at the rock ceiling high above. 'It's in their interests...otherwise why would you work?'

Tyme stared at the children, his mind struggling to process what he was hearing and seeing. They looked healthy, their skin unmarked by chemical exposure. Their clothes were clean and colourful, no grey jumpsuits in sight. One of them, a girl who couldn't have been more than six, waved at him with a bright smile.

He smiled back, as Eleni led them off again.

The path took them around an absolutely massive tree trunk, its bark worn smooth with decades of people brushing past. As they walked, Tyme caught glimpses of dwellings built into the cavern walls. Doors and windows of various shapes and sizes dotted the rock face, with light spilling from within. Some were decorated with colourful fabrics or strings of tiny glowing objects that cast multi-coloured patterns on the stone.

'The Gerousia meets in the central chamber just there,' Eleni explained, gesturing towards a larger opening ahead. 'They'll want to hear your story and help find you a settlement that's accepting Sooties.'

'Sooties?' queried Jaccin, wrinkling his nose at the word.

Eleni baulked slightly and appeared a little embarrassed.

'Ah…yeah…it's a name we have down here for anyone escaping from the refineries above,' she said, apologetically.

'Because we're always a little grubby?' asked Tyme.

'Yeah…and smell of chemicals. Sorry.'

She turned and led them towards the larger building.

Tyme's legs felt unsteady beneath him as they approached the chamber entrance. The enormity of what was happening – of what they'd discovered – had made his head spin. Just hours ago, he'd been guiding molten haklion at station two, believing his future held nothing but more of the same until he was deemed no longer useful and sent to 'transition'.

Now he was about to meet the leaders of a free human settlement that had existed right beneath the Repps' feet for multiple generations.

The central chamber was larger than he'd expected, its ceiling rising in a natural dome that had been enhanced with carved supports. Light filtered down from what looked to be crystal formations embedded in the rock above, casting a warm glow over the gathered people.

Five elderly individuals sat in a semicircle on curved wooden benches, watching Tyme and Jaccin with eyes that seemed to see right through them. Three women and two men, their faces lined with age but their postures straight and strong. Nothing like the broken, bent figures of the older workers at the refinery who shuffled along with chemical burns and failing joints.

'These are the Gerousia,' Eleni said, gesturing towards the elders. 'Our council of elders.'

Tyme tried to stand straighter, suddenly aware of his filthy jumpsuit and the lingering refinery stench that clung to him. The apple's sweetness still lingered on his tongue, a stark contrast to the acrid chemical taste in the back of his throat that he was used to.

The eldest woman leant forward, her silver hair braided in an intricate pattern that wrapped around her head. When she spoke, her voice carried a strength that sounded younger than Tyme expected.

'Welcome to Tin Koilada. I am Chresta, First Voice of the Gerousia.' She studied them with piercing blue eyes. 'You have found your way through the old tunnels. Not many manage that journey without help.'

Tyme shifted uncomfortably under Chresta's gaze, the weight of her attention making his hairs stand on end. The chemical smell rising from his jumpsuit seemed stronger in this clean air, marking him as an outsider despite the warmth in the elder's voice.

'We followed the maintenance tunnels from the refinery,' he said, his voice sounding rough and foreign in the peaceful chamber. 'My brother found a loose grate in the cooling tank section.'

Chresta nodded slowly, her eyes moving between the two brothers.

'And what drove you to seek the tunnels? Most surface

workers live their entire lives without questioning their situation.'

Tyme's throat tightened as the memory of Kestrel's severed arm flashed through his mind. The melted ring, the charred flesh, the way it had landed with that wet thud in the collection trough. His hands began to shake again, and he clenched them into fists to stop the trembling.

'We found out what really happens during transition,' Jaccin said quietly, speaking for the first time since they'd entered the chamber. 'A friend of ours...' He stumbled slightly and took a deep breath.

'Take your time,' Chresta said softly.

'We, err...we saw his remains come through the discharge pipes,' Tyme said, giving his brother time to recover.

A ripple of murmuring passed through the Gerousia members and assembled people behind the two brothers. The elders' faces tightened with familiar grief. The oldest man, his beard streaked with grey, leant forward.

'The furnaces,' he said, his voice deep and resonant. 'That is where the Repps dispose of those deemed no longer useful. We have heard this account many times from those who escape.'

'They tell us we're being promoted,' Tyme said, the words scraping his throat. 'That we're going to better conditions on the Lamination. It's all lies.'

Chresta nodded, her weathered hands folded in her lap. 'The Repps maintain control through false hope. As long as workers believe there is something to strive for, they will always remain compliant. The Repps have been doing this for a very long time.'

Jaccin shifted beside him, their shoulders brushing.

'How long have you been here? How did all this…' he gestured at the vast cavern beyond '…begin?'

The second woman of the Gerousia spoke, her voice softer than Chresta's.

'We're not here to give you a history lesson, young man. That question can be answered by others. We're here to find you somewhere to spend the rest of your lives. Although we do have to inform you that your exposure to the toxic chemicals up in the refineries will shorten your lifespan. Saying that, you're both reasonably young, so you'll do better than most.'

'How long have we got?' Jaccin blurted.

The woman's expression softened, though Tyme noticed she didn't look away or try to sugar-coat her answer. The directness felt strange after years of half-truths and lies from the Repps.

'It varies,' she said. 'Those who escape in their teens or early twenties, like yourselves, often live another thirty to forty years. The chemical damage accumulates slowly, affecting your lungs and liver primarily.'

Tyme felt his chest constrict, though whether from the mention of lung damage or the shock of the number, he couldn't tell. Forty years. It sounded impossibly long after believing he had maybe five years before transition. But it also felt impossibly short when he looked around at this underground paradise he'd never known existed.

'That's longer than we would have had up there,' Jaccin said quietly.

Chresta leant back slightly, her weathered fingers drumming against the wooden armrest of her chair. 'There are settlements that specialise in helping refugees from the refineries. Places with healers who understand chemical exposure, communities that have developed treatments to slow the damage.'

'Where?' Tyme asked, surprised by the eagerness in his own voice.

26

The *Gabriel*, entering an unnamed system, Triangulum
Galaxy

IT TOOK them two days to reach the system containing the
mined moon. As per the new standing orders on operations, Linda had the *Gabriel* cloaked and as she angled the
ship in towards the second planet with the mined moon,
Pol and Phil scanned the entire area to check they were
alone.

'Anything out there I should know about?' she asked.

Phil was rubbing his chin in thought and glanced up at
the question.

'We might want to swing by the third planet at some
point,' he said. 'It's showing returns of a civilisation
having once been there. It's a definite goldilocks, just like
Wellas, but similarly with nothing alive and a few dead
satellites.'

'I don't like the sound of that,' Andy piped up, crossing his arms and turning to Ed. 'D'you think we should go there first?'

'What's the gravity like on that planet?' Ed asked Phil.

'One point two Earth,' came the reply.

'Hmm,' he grunted. 'If this planet suffered the same fate as Wellas, then the used delivery missiles will have impacted the surface hard and been completely obliterated. Let's carry on to the moon on the second planet and inspect the one we think has survived. Then we could come back and check out that planet.'

Linda nodded and kept the *Gabriel* on its original track, arriving some thirty-seven minutes later.

'That's gotta be where he landed,' said Phil. 'There's the spider ship parked in the right place and the door behind.'

He tracked the camera around the edge of the landing platform until he found what he was looking for.

'There she be,' he said. 'Who wants to go down and grab it?'

Two hours later a small group stood in the port hangar as Ed and Pol dragged the empty delivery casing down the *Secchio*'s rear ramp. Cleo was amongst them and as soon as it clunked down onto the deck, she strode over and stared at it for a few seconds.

'Please tell me it has useful information for us,' said Ed. 'It took us an hour to dig that thing out of the regolith.'

'Fascinating,' said Cleo, striding around it and inspecting it from every angle.

Andy rolled his eyes.

'All right, Dr Spock, we'll have less of that. What's the consensus then?'

'It's design and manufacture is extraordinarily perfect,' she said. 'I've never seen anything like it. From the lack of any even slight impurities in the alloy, to the thickness of the casing being absolutely regular throughout down to a microscopic level.'

'An advanced race then?' Ed suggested.

'At first glance, more than us,' she said, looking over her shoulder at Ed. 'We need to be wary, this is...oh... fuck me.'

'What now?' Andy asked.

'There's a data node thing in here that makes Earth quantum computing look like banging rocks together and my Theo technology to mere steam power.'

'Really...can you read it?' Ed asked.

'It'll take a while for me to be able to interface with it, but eventually...yes, I reckon so.'

'Do it.'

'In the meantime we can go and take a butcher's at that dead planet,' said Andy, raising his eyebrows at Ed.

'Absolutely,' Ed agreed, nodding at the nearest camera that he knew Linda would be watching through.

In a very short period of time, they went from a very hot brown airless moon and planet to the next one out from the star, and the difference couldn't be more acute. This one was glowing with bright blues and greens, its atmosphere thick and full of cloud layers. Back on the bridge, they were all staring up at the holomap when an alarm shrilled.

'It's one of the dead satellites,' exclaimed Pol. 'It's woken up and…shit…'

'What?' Ed asked.

'It's got some kind of weapon lock on us,' she said, her concerned face glancing across at Ed.

'But we're cloaked.' He turned to Linda. 'Aren't we?'

Linda nodded, pointing to the cloak engaged signal on her console.

'How the hell is that thing tracking us?' he asked.

'I have no idea…shit, missile away,' said Andy, manning the weapons station.

'Our shields are phasing in and out,' called Pol.

'JUMP, CLEO,' Ed shouted.

The lighting dimmed slightly and the holomap immediately blinked into a new configuration.

'What the fuck just happened?' Ed snapped. 'How can that thing have tracked us, let alone neutralise our shields so bloody easily?'

'It was the same technology as the node in my hangar,' said Cleo, appearing in the middle of the bridge. 'We need to hold fire for a bit and let me get my head around this stuff. If we met an armed jump-capable ship with this tech, we'd be gone in seconds,' she said, her expression more serious than Ed could remember.

He slumped back in his seat and puffed out his cheeks as he thought.

'Do you think you can combat it?' Andy asked, before he could respond.

'Give me time,' she said. 'This is ground-breaking stuff and not some lesser alien tech I can interface with in a couple of milliseconds.'

'But you will manage it?' Linda asked.

'Watch this space,' she said and phased out of sight.

Ed looked back up at the holomap.

'Okay…where are we?'

'A light year away from the planet, just outside the system,' said Linda.

'What happened to that missile?'

'It detonated where we'd been only a second before,' said Andy.

'Is the satellite still active?'

'Hard to tell at this distance, I can't detect any electronic signatures, but you heard Cleo, it's very different to anything we've come across before.'

'Right…jump us back in half a million kilometres from the planet and be ready to bug out again if that satellite or anything else pays us attention.'

The holomap snapped to another star configuration once more and they all held their breath. Nothing happened.

'I can confirm the satellite has gone back into sleep mode,' said Andy. 'Oh…bloody hell, it's…'

'What now?' Ed demanded, before Andy had a chance to finish.

'That exploding missile dispersed a cloud of the weaponised nanos.'

'Well, that confirms all this stuff is connected doesn't it?' said Ed. 'Someone or some race is responsible for wiping out several entire civilisations in this galaxy and in this case has left measures that should ensure no one reports the crime.'

'It seems we're unable to hold whoever they are to account as well,' griped Linda.

'Let's hope Cleo finds some sort of defence against this tech then,' said Rayl.

'In the meantime, while we wait for Cleo to do her thing, can someone get rid of those nanos?' Ed asked.

'Yep, on it,' said Andy.

'And give that planet a thorough scan too. I want to know how long this one's been dead.'

27

The *Gabriel*, unnamed system, Triangulum Galaxy

IT WAS early morning ship time on the third day when Ed was woken by an excited Cleo suddenly appearing beside his bed.

'I think I might've cracked it,' she whispered, to a bleary-eyed captain, trying not to wake Pol too.

'Shit, Cleo it's five thirty in the morning,' he rasped, squinting at his watch. 'Couldn't this wait until nine or something?'

'Time is irrelevant to me, remember? I'm wide awake all the time and anyway, I thought you'd want to know as soon as possible.'

'Yes, yes, okay, well I'm awake now,' he said, sitting up and reaching for a bottle of water on the bedside table. 'Right, what you got?' he asked, after taking a swig.

A copy of the bridge holomap materialised in the

centre of the room. It zoomed in on the troublesome alien satellite.

'I now have control over it,' she said and as Ed watched, it came to life, turning left and right and opening and closing its underslung missile rack.

'Can you get it to self-destruct?' he asked.

'It doesn't have that facility...but I can blow it to bits with one of our missiles.'

'No, actually come to think of it, it's probably best not to do that. It might distribute a shit load of nanos.'

Ed rubbed the sleep from his eyes and thought for a minute.

'Can you move it out of orbit so it drops into the atmosphere?' he asked. 'That way it'll all burn up and there'll be no space debris or chance of those nanos troubling anyone again.'

She turned and looked at the satellite, and a determined expression washed across her face.

'Ed, Ed,' a rather anxious-sounding Phil called from the bridge. 'The satellite, it's doing stuff.'

'It's okay, Phil, don't panic,' he said back. 'It's Cleo, she's gained control over it.'

'Oh...thank fuck...I was about to emergency jump the ship.'

'It's okay, I'm up now, I'll be with you in a few minutes.'

He turned to Cleo, rubbing his chin.

'Are you sure you've gleaned everything from it before it finally goes?' he asked.

'Oh, yes,' she said. 'I have gleaned well. In its data bank amongst a lot of other things, were the course co-ordinates for its journey here.'

Ed's eyes opened wide as he realised what Cleo had just divulged.

'Please tell me you know where it came from?' he said, grabbing her hand.

She grinned and squeezed his hand.

'They call themselves the Khenemetneferhedjet and originate sixty thousand light years away ón the opposite side and outer fringe of Triangulum. From a planet called Aratap. The satellite has a top of the range array and took one hundred and seventy-nine years to get here.'

'Fuck, Cleo, you're amazing,' he said, standing and giving her a hug. 'I'd hate to try and spell their name though.'

'It is too long isn't it…I'll shorten it for you.'

Pol took this precise moment to wake and witness Ed standing in his boxer shorts, cuddling an incredibly beautiful woman right next to her.

'I've never considered it too long,' she said, sitting up and giving him a lop-sided grin. 'If you wanted a ménage à trois, you only had to ask.'

'Uh-oh, rumbled,' said Cleo, her face a picture of overacted horror. She promptly vanished again along with the holomap.

Ed turned and gave Pol one of his best sheepish grins.

'I take it she had news?' Pol asked, letting him off the hook.

'Err…yeah, actually she did, big news.'

———

At eight o'clock, everyone was present on the bridge. Even

Andy was there – well, in body anyway. Morning person he was not.

'I take it something has occurred for us to be here in the middle of the night?' he whinged, squinting through puffy, bloodshot eyes.

'Yes, Andrew,' Ed said. 'Things have definitely occurred.'

He explained everything that Cleo had achieved and the fact that now she'd managed to interface and learn all the wonders of the new tech, she was engineering it into their systems. Which meant they now wouldn't be detected while cloaked and their shields would do their job again. The real good news was, they now had that technology and no one else in their galaxy did.

'So, let me get this straight,' Linda piped up. 'We will be able to see cloaked ships and render their shields useless?'

'That's about the gist of it,' said Ed, grinning.

'Fucking hell,' said Andy. 'That's massive.'

'Are we going to give this to Bache?' Phil asked. 'Cuz you know what the GDA's like.'

'Yeah, a leaky boat,' said Linda. 'Within months everyone will have it, probably including the Klatt and we're all back to square one with no advantage.'

'I, for one, say we keep it to ourselves,' said Rayl.

'I agree,' said Pol. 'It gives us another level of safety.'

'Actually, I agree too,' said Ed, shrugging. 'We'll keep it under our hats for now.'

'What about this stupidly long name they have for themselves,' moaned Andy. 'Can't we just call them the twats or something?'

Rayl sat back and rolled her eyes.

Ed sighed and received a knowing look from Linda.

'No, Andrew,' he said, dejectedly. 'We won't be calling them that. I think calling them the Khen will be sufficient.'

'Are we planning on going to this Aratap planet?' Civray asked.

'We will,' answered Ed. 'I just want to gather a bit more evidence from this planet first and then we'll be on our way.'

'It's a long way,' she said. 'How long will it take?'

'Many many days,' said Linda. 'We'll have to take shorter jumps than we would normally as the galaxy may contain pitfalls we don't know about. Coming back will be quicker though.'

'Don't feel you have to come with us,' said Ed. 'It'll mean a long time away. We can drop you back on Wellas or at the station if you so wish.'

'No, I'm coming,' she said, without hesitation. 'I want to see who destroyed my world…and this one…and why.'

'Good,' Ed replied, turning to Phil. 'Can you put us into orbit please? I want to know what civilisation was here and how long ago it was destroyed.'

An hour later they all watched as the troublesome satellite finally lost its battle with the planet's gravity field and became a fireball, streaking downwards and gradually vaporising into almost nothing, the last stubborn blackened pieces dropping into one of the planets several oceans.

'Good bloody riddance,' mumbled Andy.

'Thank you, Cleo,' said Linda, glancing upwards.

'You're welcome,' came the reply, Cleo's voice echoing around the bridge. 'If it's of help, I've just dated some of the alloy shrapnel floating about up here. I don't of course know whether this was from the civilisation that existed here, or from a later visiting ship that was attacked by that satellite. But what I do know is it's around seventy-eight thousand years old.'

'That would about fit in with the timescale of what's left on the surface,' said Pol. 'The once huge cities down there are almost invisible now. They've virtually crumbled into dust. I can only detect the vague outlines of some of them and pretty much nothing of others where they've been swallowed up by shifting desert sands and sea level change. This degree of degeneration would have to take tens of thousands of years to have occurred.'

'Is it worth us going down there?' Andy asked, his tone suggesting he didn't think it was.

'No,' replied Ed. 'We could spend a month digging about in the dust down there and still not learn anything. I think our time would be much better spent cracking on towards Aratap and see if we can find any more destroyed civilisations along the way.'

He turned to Phil.

'You're in the chair, Philip…can you begin this marathon journey?' he asked. 'Take your time with each jump, there's no hurry. Scan ahead carefully and avoid jumping in system, just in case we bump into them unwittingly.'

'Cloaked?' Phil asked, glancing up.

'Yes…full tactical shields at all times and an embedded emergency jump ready to go in a split second. It seems these bastards have outwitted plenty of spacefaring communities over tens of thousands of years, let's not be next.'

28

Tin Koilada settlement, unknown locale

'DARO KOILADA,' Chresta said, her eyes softening. 'It's a settlement three days' journey from here, following the underground river system. They specialise in detoxification treatments and have developed medicines from certain fungi that grow only in the deeper caverns.'

Tyme's mind reeled with this new information. Medicines? Treatments? In the refinery, the only treatment for chemical exposure was reassignment to a slightly less toxic area until you were too damaged to work at all.

'Can we go there?' he asked, his voice insistent.

The youngest of the elders, a man with black hair, leant forward. 'Not immediately. All new arrivals spend at least two weeks here in Tin Koilada. We need to assess your skills, begin basic decontamination, and teach you our ways. The journey to Daro is challenging even for those born underground.'

'But eventually?' Jaccin pressed, hope burning in the question.

'Yes, of course,' Chresta nodded. 'If that's where you wish to go, we'll arrange passage with the next trader caravan.'

Tyme's mind was spinning as he tried to process everything. Two weeks in this miraculous underground haven, and then possibly on to a place that could help counteract the chemicals eating away at their bodies from the inside.

'Where will we stay?' he asked, suddenly aware of how filthy and out of place they must look among these clean, healthy people.

Eleni stepped forward again.

'I'll show you to the newcomers' quarters. We have spaces prepared for refugees.'

Chresta nodded her approval.

'Go with Eleni. Rest, eat real food, and begin to heal. Tomorrow, we'll start your orientation to life below ground.'

As they turned to leave the chamber, the youngest elder called out.

'Wait.'

He approached them, studying their faces with keen interest.

'Do I understand you're brothers?'

'Twins,' Jaccin replied.

The elder's eyebrows rose. 'Twins are rare here and valuable in our communities. Your genetic similarity might help our healers better understand how the refinery chemicals affect human biology.'

Tyme wasn't sure if that was good news or not. Being studied didn't sound much better than forced labour. But before he could voice his concern, Chresta, perhaps noticing his change in expression, raised a weathered hand.

'Don't worry, we don't experiment on people here,' she said, her voice firm but caring. 'We study to heal, not to satisfy curiosity. Your participation would be entirely voluntary. But it may well help you and possibly others in the future.'

The reassurance helped, though Tyme still felt uneasy about being considered unusual. All his life, he and Jaccin had tried to blend in, to avoid drawing attention from the Repps. Being notable for any reason felt dangerous, even in this safe place.

Eleni gestured towards a passage leading away from the central chamber.

'Come. You both look hungry and ready to collapse.'

She was right. The adrenaline that had carried Tyme through the escape was wearing off, leaving behind a bone-deep exhaustion that made each step feel like he was walking through thick liquid. His jumpsuit clung to his skin, caked with years of chemical residue that made him itch.

They followed Eleni through passages carved from living rock, past more dwellings that glowed with warm light from within. The sound of conversation and laughter drifted from some of them, normal human sounds that Tyme hadn't known existed.

The newcomers' quarters turned out to be a series of small chambers carved into the cavern wall, each furnished with simple but comfortable-looking furniture that made Tyme's eyes widen. A real bed with what appeared to be soft coverings, a wooden table, even a chair that looked like it might actually be comfortable to sit in. After years of sleeping on hard composite platforms, the sight made him want to lie down and sleep for ever.

'This one can be yours,' Eleni said, nodding at Tyme and gesturing to the first chamber. 'Jaccin, you're next door. There are clean clothes in the chest there, and warm water for bathing.' She pointed to a ceramic bath that steamed in the soft light. Real water, not recycled and warm too. Something he'd never had before.

Tyme glanced around the chamber, his boots clunking on the stone floor. The space felt impossibly luxurious after the cramped quarters he'd shared with his brother. He could stretch his arms without touching the walls, and the ceiling rose high enough that he didn't have to duck.

'There's food waiting in the common area when you're ready,' Eleni continued. 'Just follow that passage back in the direction of the main cavern. You can't miss it. Just follow your nose.'

She left them alone and Tyme stood in the room for a moment after she left, unable to move. The silence felt strange after the constant babble he was used to. No mechanical humming, no hissing pipes, no distant shouting and everyday hubbub. Just complete quietness, broken only occasionally by the soft murmur of voices from somewhere deeper in the settlement.

He stepped across to the table and ran his fingers along the wooden surface. The grain felt slightly rough under his fingertips, natural in a way that was alien to him. Everything in the refinery had been smooth composite or cold metal. This had texture, character, imperfections that spoke of something grown rather than manufactured.

The steaming bath drew him like a magnet. He knelt beside it and dipped his fingers into the water, gasping at the warmth. It was clean too, no chemical film on the surface, no acrid smell burning his nostrils. Just warm water that felt like silk against his skin. Incredible.

His jumpsuit peeled away from his body with a crunching sound, the fabric stiff with years of accumulated chemical residue. The smell that rose from it made him gag...how had he lived with that stench for so long? He kicked the garment away in disgust and stepped into warm water for the first time in his life.

The sensation of being completely submerged in warm water was so overwhelming that Tyme gasped, unintentionally getting a mouthful of the water. He chuckled and sank down until only his face remained above the surface, feeling years of grime begin to loosen from his skin. The water darkened almost immediately, turning a murky brown-grey as the chemical residue dissolved.

He scrubbed at his arms and legs with his hands, watching in fascination as his true skin colour emerged beneath the filth. It was paler than he'd realised, with a pinkish undertone that had been hidden beneath layers of industrial grime. The sensation of being clean, truly clean, felt weird, foreign, but wonderful.

When he finally stepped out, he dried himself with a soft cloth that had been left beside the bath, marvelling at its soft texture against his new lighter skin. The clean clothes from the chest felt impossibly luxurious compared to his stiff jumpsuit. The fabric was light and breathable, like nothing he'd ever worn before.

Dressed, and feeling strangely lighter and perhaps vulnerable without the almost armoured weight of his work clothes, Tyme ventured out to find his brother. Jaccin was already outside his door, wrapped similarly in clean clothes, his wet hair slicked back from his face. Tyme barely recognised his twin without the layers of grime that had always covered them both.

'You look completely different,' Tyme said, his mouth hanging open.

'So do you,' Jaccin replied, running a hand through his damp hair. 'I found freckles I didn't know I had.'

They did as Eleni had said, following the passage back towards the main cavern, both walking differently and lightly in bare feet. They'd seemingly both decided to do without their heavy smelly industrial boots. The smell of cooking food grew stronger with each step, something rich and savoury that made Tyme's stomach gurgle with hunger. The aroma was like nothing he'd smelled before.

The common area turned out to be a large open space with dozens of wooden tables where people sat eating and talking. Some glanced up as the brothers entered, offering smiles or nods of acknowledgment before returning to their conversations. No one stared or pointed, though Tyme felt sure they must stand out in their new clothes and freshly scrubbed skin.

Eleni waved to them from across the room, gesturing to empty spaces at her table and nodding at a man behind the servery. As they approached, the man brought out steaming bowls for them and placed them on the table. He grinned, nodded and returned to the cooking area.

Tyme stared at the bowl as he sat down, and the steam made his mouth water. Inside was a thick stew filled with chunks of vegetables and something that might have been meat, though he'd never tasted real animal protein before.

Small pieces of bread sat on a wooden plate beside it, their crusts golden brown.

'This is just the beginning meal,' Eleni said, smiling at their wide-eyed reactions. 'Wait until you try the harvest feast next week.'

Tyme couldn't help the small moan that escaped him as he tried the first mouthful.

'Good?' Eleni asked, though the answer was obvious.

'I had no idea food could taste like this,' Tyme said, already loading his spoon with another bite. Each mouthful revealed new flavours he couldn't identify but desperately wanted more of.

Jaccin was equally entranced, tearing off pieces of bread and closing his eyes as he savoured every spoonful.

'I think I'm going to enjoy two weeks of this food,' he said. 'Is it as good where we're going?' he asked Eleni.

Eleni laughed, the sound making Tyme's chest flutter in that strange way again. 'Daro Koilada has some of the finest cooks in all the settlements. They've had centuries to perfect their recipes using ingredients you've never even heard of.'

'What about the journey there?' Jaccin asked between mouthfuls. 'You said it was challenging.'

'The river passages can be tricky,' Eleni said, her expression growing more serious. 'Some sections require swimming, others involve climbing over rock falls. And there are... things that live in the deeper waters. Not dangerous exactly, but they don't like strangers.'

Tyme's spoon paused halfway to his mouth. After the paradise of Tin Koilada, the idea of facing new dangers felt almost surreal.

'What kind of things?'

29

THE *GABRIEL*, on route to Aratap, Triangulum Galaxy

Ed couldn't remember a longer and more boring journey. He spent his ten-hour shifts on the bridge scanning nearby systems and even though there were many that warranted a closer examination, stopping to do so was not an option. That was until the twenty-fourth day, when Andy, piloting at the time, called him late one evening.

'Geezer, you'd better come and look at this,' he said.

Ed noticed a change in the background hum of the ship as he made his way up to the bridge. Cleo was there too when he arrived. Stopping as he stepped off the tube lift, he followed their gaze up to the holomap.

'Bloody hell,' he muttered. 'Where on Earth is that?'

A small system, some two light years away, was highlighted. He couldn't remember seeing a busier region of space. It made the Dasos system look like an empty backstreet.

'There's tens of thousands of ships,' said Andy, shaking his head in wonder. 'How the hell is that organised?'

'I can confirm it's definitely all Khen technology,' Cleo said, raising a hand.

Ed walked over and slid onto his couch.

'Well, we definitely can't jump in there for a look around can we?' he said. 'Get as close as you can. We need to study this for a while.'

The system had a yellow dwarf star and seven planets, two of which, the third and fourth, had the biggest concentration of traffic, although everywhere was stupidly busy. Andy conducted a short jump to what seemed to be the quieter side of the system and brought the *Gabriel* to a halt just on the edge of an asteroid belt. None of the swarming Khen traffic seemed to extend outside the belt, so he felt reasonably safe setting up camp here.

'They're all automated,' said Cleo.

'What?' Ed exclaimed, tapping away on a few icons and staring at the result. 'She's right you know...no life signs whatsoever.'

'Wow,' said Andy, but not because of Ed's confirmation. He panned in on several large shapes in orbit around the fourth planet and pointed at them. 'They're ships,' he said.

'Don't be daft,' Ed replied, glancing down to find the scaling command icon. Finding and touching it, he looked back up and realised Andy was right. 'Holy crap...they're over eighteen kilometres long.'

'They're not warships though,' Andy confirmed. 'No armaments, only basic shields and full of...well...rock actually.'

'Ore carriers…that's all they are. This must be an automated mining colony, you can see the planetary ships streaming up and down from the surfaces of the planets and moons.'

'There must be someone somewhere,' said Andy. 'Maintenance engineers or something. I mean, look at all that kit…surely things wear out from time to time?'

'Yeah, you'd think so wouldn't you.'

'You'd also think they'd have some defensive capability too. I mean, we could just waltz in and destroy everything and there's not a thing they could do about it.'

'Unless they do and it's well hidden, or they're not expecting any interference because they've already destroyed every spacefaring civilisation in the region or even galaxy.'

Andy slumped back in his seat, crossed his arms and watched the organised melee for a few more moments.

'Shall I call the others?' he said, finally.

Ed glanced at the ship time and shook his head.

'It's late,' he said. 'Keep an eye on everything. Don't do anything to convey our presence and we'll reconvene in the morning and decide what to do then. Call me if anything changes during the night.'

As had Ed and Andy the previous evening, the next morning the rest of the crew all stared up at the swarming beehive of activity with a similar degree of amazement.

'They're ripping the guts out of everything,' said Phil. 'Even the moons of the planets are being stripped.'

'Do we intervene?' Linda asked.

'I've been pondering exactly that overnight,' said Ed. 'I think the best idea is to shadow one of those huge ore carriers and see where it goes.'

'Looking at the design specifications, I don't think they're particularly fast ships,' said Rayl. 'What if it takes several years to reach its destination?'

'We'll know its intended track from the first jump or three,' said Andy. 'We're already close to Aratap and I'll hazard a guess that's where they're going. They'll be easy to follow too, I've noticed their jump drives are so noisy and short-ranged, you could follow them on a bicycle.'

'Don't you find that weird?' said Linda. 'They have the most sophisticated computers we've ever come across, but their space drive technology is as bad as ours was before first contact.'

Ed pulled a face, causing Linda to give him an apologetic look and Andy to snigger.

'It's okay,' acknowledged Ed. 'She's quite right, my first Virr drive was stone age compared to what we have now and it does make this scenario all the more peculiar.'

'Perhaps these Khen haven't invented this technology at all. They've just stolen it and have no idea how it works,' said Rayl.

'They just haven't come across a race with more efficient jump drives yet,' Pol proposed.

'That theory certainly works,' Ed agreed, rubbing his chin.

Before anyone else had a chance to speak, Phil had concentrated his array on one of the enormous ore freighters that had left the orbit of one of the moons a while ago. It headed out to a slightly less busy region, then suddenly vanished.

'Want me to follow it?' Andy asked, still piloting the vessel.

'Yes...stay well clear and make sure you embed the jumps.'

Andy needed no further orders and three minutes later the lighting dimmed as he followed the cumbersome freighter about three light years nearer Aratap.

'Yeah, it's gotta be going where I thought,' Andy said, raising his eyebrows at Ed.

'Let's see one more jump, just to check.'

Six minutes later the freighter jumped again, same direction, same distance.

'If it is going to Aratap and jumping this distance every six minutes, d'you realise it'll take it nearly a year and a half,' said Phil, glancing up from his station.

'That confirms we're definitely not following it all the way,' said Linda.

'Of course we're not,' agreed Ed, turning to Andy. 'How far to Aratap?'

'Just over three and a half thousand light years,' was the reply.

'ETA?'

'Later this evening.'

'Shit,' said Rayl, suddenly getting everyone's attention, as she didn't swear very often. 'Dead system,' she added and nodded up at the holomap.

She swiped what she was looking at up above them all. It was a multi-planet system, only seven light years away from where the Khen were mining.

'Holy moly,' exclaimed Linda.

'I believe our friends have been here before,' said Ed.

'Holy is definitely the operative term here,' admitted

Andy. 'There's huge lumps missing from almost every planetary body.'

'This is what they're doing back there,' said Linda. 'Extracting everything.'

'Turning systems into Swiss cheese,' Ed muttered.

'They just dispose of any civilisations first,' said Pol.

'What the hell would they need all this ore for?' Rayl asked. 'It seems they've been doing this for thousands of years.'

'Building bloody death stars perhaps,' quipped Andy.

'We'll find out in a few hours then, won't we?' grunted Ed, ignoring Andy's silly comment. 'Take us there, only slowly and carefully.'

30

The *Gabriel*, on route to Aratap, Triangulum Galaxy

SEVERAL HOURS after Phil had taken over piloting the *Gabriel*, he called Ed and Andy to the bridge.

'Have we stopped?' Andy asked, as both he, Rayl and Ed arrived up on the bridge deck at the same time.

'I thought it might be prudent, so we didn't bump into any of those,' said Phil, nodding at the holomap.

'Holy moly,' exclaimed Ed, as the three of them stopped and stared. 'Are those mines?'

Rows of what at first glance appeared to be orbs or mines, all identical in size, filled the holomap, some of them in various stages of construction.

'No,' said Phil. 'Not mines…you're not looking at the scale.'

'Oh, fuck,' Andy mumbled, finally comprehending the actual size of the spheres.

'That can't be right…surely?' said Rayl, turning to Ed.

'No way,' Ed whispered. 'Just how big are they?'

'A diameter of just over fifty-eight kilometres and there's forty-six of them,' Phil said.

'Death Stars, I fucking told you didn't I?' Andy spluttered. 'That really was what they wanted all the mined resources for and you thought I was having a laugh.'

'Actually, they're unarmed,' said Phil. 'As far as I can make out, they're just huge mining platforms. Although, for some reason, they seem completely hollow. Those small ships buzzing around them are almost the same size as the ore carriers.'

'They don't need big weapon systems,' said Cleo, appearing for the first time. 'They have the aggressive nanos that can dismantle a ship in minutes. In tens of thousands of years they've never had anyone coming close to challenging them. It seems they don't need it, they don't bother upgrading anything. They have no scale of time. Hence the slow noisy jump drives, it's sufficient for them, so why change it?'

'Who started this though?' Ed asked. 'There must've been a life form at some point that began all this. Hugely powerful computerised systems don't just occur naturally.'

'How far are we from Aratap now?' Andy asked.

'Err…a few hundred light years,' said Phil, referring to his three-dimensional holographic display. 'Three jumps… two if I take a punt.'

'We'll come back to this,' said Ed, nodding up at the holomap. 'The answers have to be at Aratap. Take the three jumps, Phil. We don't want to be taking any chances now and don't, whatever you do, jump into the Aratap system. I want to have a good look at it from afar first.'

'Righty ho,' Phil chirped, his hands busy amongst the floating icons again.

A couple of hours later, they were all present on the bridge as Phil prepared the final jump to a location some five million kilometres outside the Aratap system.

'That's weird,' he said, a puzzled expression forming. 'I can't see inside the system.'

'He's right,' said Pol. 'I'm getting all the usual gravitational disturbances from a system being there, it's just not visible.'

'It's not some small black hole or something is it?' Andy asked.

'No,' said Ed. 'The gravitational effects would be off the scale if it was.'

'It's as if the system's cloaked,' Pol said.

'I thought we could see through cloaking now?' Linda queried.

'Not at this distance,' said Cleo. 'I recommend caution here. I'm not able to penetrate whatever it is either.'

'Okay, Phil, make the emergence point a hundred million kilometres out from the edge of the system and have that emergency jump all prepped.'

The lighting dimmed slightly as the jump took place. Ed's fingers hurt, he was gripping the couch rests so tightly. All eyes were on the holomap as the new star field phased into view. Only this time, it wasn't what they were expecting.

'What on Earth is that?' Ed was the first to ask the question they were all thinking.

'Pixelated space,' said Andy. 'It's like an LCD television when the signal is too low.'

'It's curved too,' said Cleo. 'It encapsulates the whole system about thirty-nine AU or five point nine billion kilometres out from the star.'

'Is it a natural phenomenon?' Rayl asked.

'I don't believe so,' said Cleo. 'It has a physical presence.'

'You mean, someone or something actually constructed that out of some sort of material?' Ed said.

'I'm struggling with the scale of it too,' said Cleo. 'The logistics of that thing are just massive. Whoever built this took an exorbitantly long time doing it, it must've taken tens of thousands of years at least.'

'It makes me wonder what the hell they're protecting on the inside?' said Pol.

'Is there an entrance?' Phil asked. 'Because we can't jump inside. The shield blocks any internal scans, so I can't log any emergence co-ordinates.'

'We need to get closer and loop around it a few times,' said Ed. 'If only there was some traffic to follow.'

'It'll take too long to fly around it,' Phil said. 'But I can jump to the other side.'

He did so and when the holomap reset, it was the same result. No doorways, no portals, just the same impenetrable wall of pixelation.

'I've got one of those ore carriers just under three light years out and coming in this direction,' announced Rayl.

'Follow it closely,' said Ed.

'There's another just jumped in behind it,' said Pol.

'That must be a standard route emergence zone,' said Andy. 'Let's see where they go next.'

They waited for what seemed like an age, but was in fact fifty-one minutes, when Rayl finally broke the silence.

'Mine's jumped,' she said, raising her hand.

'Emergence?' demanded Ed.

'None,' Rayl answered.

'Can it have jumped anywhere we can't detect it?'

'Their range is too short for that, so it must've jumped inside the Aratap system,' Cleo said, rejoining the conversation.

'We could use a drone,' said Andy. 'When that second carrier jumps in, send in the drone to scan inside and detect where the emergence zone is.'

'That could work,' said Ed.

'So long as the drone doesn't emerge into anything,' reminded Phil.

'That's right,' said Andy, getting quite animated. 'Cleo, how long would the scan take?'

'Four one-hundredths of a second,' the reply came.

'Brilliant, I'll prep a drone,' he said.

'Already done,' said Cleo. 'I'll jump it straight out of the hangar.'

They didn't have to wait so long this time, as Cleo had only just finished speaking when the carrier disappeared from the holomap. Ed felt a slight vibration through his seat as Cleo jumped the drone from inside the ship causing a vacuum snap that reverberated through the vessel. No sooner was it gone, it was back.

'Is it in one piece?' Linda asked.

'It is,' Cleo replied, 'and here's the result.'

The holomap lit up so brightly, they all had to shield their eyes from the glare.

'Bloody hell,' exclaimed Ed. 'The whole system's lit up almost like daylight.'

'It's the shield,' said Cleo. 'The inside is like a mirror and reflects the stars' luminescence back into the system.'

'No night-time anywhere,' said Linda. 'Just a weird sort of twilight. That's a strange concept.'

'Nine planets,' said Cleo. 'Masses of space traffic again, more than in that mining system.'

'Is that fourth planet artificial?' Rayl asked. 'It registers as metallic and seems to be reflective.'

They all squinted as Cleo zoomed in on the planet. The glare off its surface was quite intense.

'No,' said Ed. 'There are gaps ships can fly through, the planet's inside. It's like a space station that almost completely encapsulates the world.'

'Wow,' mumbled Andy.

'It's mind-boggling isn't it?' Ed posed. 'I take it that's gotta be Aratap inside there, but wouldn't it make it permanently dark under that?'

'Well, you'd think so, wouldn't you?' Andy agreed.

'None of the other planets are habitable for oxygen-breathing lifeforms, but they've all been mined within an inch of their lives,' Rayl piped up.

'I'm not surprised,' said Andy. 'Can you imagine how much construction material you'd need to build that planet-cocooning station, let alone the system shield thing?'

'Okay, boss,' said Linda. 'What's our next move?'

'Well…we have the co-ordinates of the emergence zone now,' Ed replied, chewing his bottom lip in thought. 'I'm still a bit nervous about us going in just yet. How about another drone insertion and this time, get it to fly around avoiding traffic and recording everything it sees.'

'How long for?' Cleo asked.

Ed shrugged and glanced around at the others.

'How long would it take to fly from the emergence zone to Aratap, circle around inside the station thing and come back again?' Andy asked. 'We'd get a really good look at the surface of the planet then.'

'From that emergence zone, four hours, twenty-nine minutes, give or take,' said Cleo.

'Since when have you calculated anything, give or take?' Linda asked.

'Since the amount of traffic the drone has to avoid and steer around isn't an exact figure,' she answered.

Linda pulled an awkward face as she realised the question had been a bit silly.

'Right,' said Ed, looking around the group to check there were no more questions. 'We'll go with that then. Cleo make it happen.'

31

Tin Koilada settlement, unknown locale

THE NEXT TWO weeks passed in a blur of new sensations for Tyme. Each morning he woke on the soft bed, still startled by the absence of the harsh wake cycle chime that had jolted him awake every day of his life. Instead, the gentle murmur of the underground community gradually pulled him from sleep, the distant sounds of people beginning their day filtering through his door.

He'd learned so much in such a short time. How to tend the underground gardens where strange luminescent fungi provided both food and light. How to navigate the complex network of tunnels without getting lost. How to identify edible plants and which water sources were safe to drink from. Most importantly, he'd begun the detoxification treatments – bitter-tasting teas and daily soaks in mineral pools that left his skin tingling but gradually eased the constant burning in his lungs.

Now, as he packed the few belongings he'd accumulated – two sets of clothes, a water container, a small knife, and a pouch of detoxifying herbs – he felt both excitement and apprehension about the journey ahead. The traders who would guide them to Daro Koilada had arrived yesterday, bringing news and goods from other settlements.

'Ready?' said Jaccin.

Tyme shouldered his pack and nodded, though something twisted in his stomach at the thought of leaving this sanctuary. Two weeks ago, he'd been guiding molten haklion and choking on chemical fumes. Now he was about to venture into unknown underground territories with people he barely knew, heading towards a settlement that might or might not be able to help heal the damage already inflicted on his body.

Eleni waited for them in the main cavern, standing beside three figures Tyme didn't recognise. The traders wore clothes that looked more practical than the flowing garments of the local residents...darker colours, reinforced at the knees and elbows, with multiple pockets and straps for carrying equipment. Their faces bore a harder look of a people who spent their lives travelling through dangerous places.

'These are your guides,' Eleni said as they approached. 'Kael, Mira, and Jorik. They've made the journey to Daro Koilada dozens of times.'

The eldest of the three, a woman with silver-streaked hair tied back in a single braid, stepped forward. Her eyes were pale green, and when she spoke, her voice carried the authority of someone accustomed to being obeyed.

'I'm Kael,' she said, her weathered hand gripping Tyme's forearm in what he assumed was a traditional greeting. Her fingers felt rough with calluses, and her grip was stronger than he'd expected. 'We'll be travelling through some challenging terrain over the next three days. The river passages can be unpredictable this time of cycle.'

Tyme nodded, trying to project more confidence than he felt. The woman's pale eyes seemed to assess him, cataloguing his strengths and weaknesses in a way that reminded him uncomfortably of the Repp overseers, though her expression held none of their cold indifference.

'You've both been through some swimming instruction I hope?' asked the younger man, Jorik. His dark hair was cropped short, and a jagged scar ran from his left ear to his jaw.

'Basic,' Jaccin replied. 'We've only had two weeks to learn, but so long as the swims aren't too long, we won't drown.'

Jorik's mouth twitched in what might have been amusement. 'Two weeks of pool work versus underground rivers. We'll see how that translates,' he said, giving Kael a wide-eyed glance.

The third trader, Mira, remained silent but her sharp eyes moved constantly between the cavern entrances, as if watching for threats that might emerge from the darkness. Tyme found himself studying the way she remained vigilant at all times and always balanced her weight evenly, wondering if he'd need to learn similar skills.

The farewell process felt strange to Tyme. People he'd only known for two weeks embraced him like family, pressing small gifts into his hands...dried fruits, medicinal herbs, a smooth stone that one elderly man claimed would bring luck in dark places. The warmth of their affection made his throat tight with emotion he didn't know how to process.

Chresta appeared beside him as he shouldered his pack, her weathered face creased with something that might have been maternal concern.

'Remember,' she said quietly, her strong voice carrying above the bustle of departure preparations, 'you're not running anymore. You're choosing your own path.'

The distinction felt important, though Tyme couldn't articulate why. He nodded, pressing the lucky stone deeper into his pocket where its smooth surface felt reassuring against his fingers.

Eleni's goodbye was the hardest. She pressed a small cloth bundle into his hands, an extra portion of the bread he'd grown to love, wrapped with dried fruits that smelled of sunshine he'd never experienced.

'For when you get hungry on the river,' she said, though her voice carried an undertone that made Tyme feel warm inside.

The strange flutter in his chest returned as she stepped closer, close enough that he could smell the clean scent of her hair mixed with something floral he couldn't identify. Before he could process what was happening, she pressed her lips briefly against his cheek. The contact lasted only moments, but the warmth lingered on his skin long after she'd stepped back.

'Take care of yourself, Tyme,' she said, her eyes holding his for a moment that felt loaded with meaning he didn't understand.

Kael's voice cut through the moment. 'Time to move. The river levels are good now, but that won't last.'

He tucked Eleni's bundle into his pack, his fingers fumbling slightly with the straps. The spot on his cheek where her lips had touched felt different from the rest of his face, warmer somehow, and he found himself touching it unconsciously as they followed the traders towards one of the boats.

Glancing over his shoulder, he waved. Eleni waved back as she dabbed at an eye with her other sleeve.

'She likes you,' said Jaccin.

Tyme felt his face grow warm at Jaccin's observation. 'She's just being nice,' he muttered, though something hopeful stirred inside him. He pushed the feeling aside as they approached the underground dock where three small boats waited, bobbing gently on the dark water.

The cavern narrowed here, the ceiling dropping lower until it nearly touched the water's surface at the far end. The air felt cooler, damper, carrying a mineral scent that reminded Tyme of the detoxification pools.

'You two, in the middle boat with me,' Kael said, gesturing towards a sleek craft made of some material Tyme didn't recognise. 'Mira takes point, Jorik guards the rear.'

Tyme hesitated at the water's edge, watching the gentle rocking of the boat with apprehension. He'd learned to float in the shallow pools of Tin Koilada, but this was different. The water looked darker, deeper, its surface reflecting the dullness of the low ceiling.

'Well, get in then,' Kael said briskly, when Tyme continued to hesitate. 'It won't bite. We need to make the first junction before the light cycle changes.'

Tyme swallowed his anxiety and climbed awkwardly into the boat, his hands gripping the sides as it rocked beneath his weight. The craft felt impossibly unstable, nothing like the solid platforms he'd spent his life standing on. He settled in the middle, making room for Jaccin who followed with slightly more confidence.

'Keep your weight centred,' Kael instructed as she pushed them away from the dock with practised ease. Her paddle dipped silently into the dark water, propelling them forward with minimal splash. 'And keep your hands inside. The tunnel walls get narrow and can remove skin down to the bone.'

Tyme snapped his hands away from the boat sides as if they were red hot and tucked them under his thighs.

The current caught them, drawing the small fleet of boats towards the low opening where the cavern ceiling nearly met the water. Tyme's heart hammered against his ribs as they approached. The space looked barely high enough for the boat to pass through, let alone with passengers sitting upright.

'Duck down,' Kael said calmly. 'Keep your head low until I say otherwise.'

32

The *Gabriel*, outside the Aratap system, Triangulum
Galaxy

AFTER THE DRONE had been gone more than the allotted
time, they began to fret that it might not be coming back. It
was in fact only four and a half minutes later when the
drone's icon suddenly popped up on the holomap, emitting
a loud shrill notification tone and making Ed jump.

'That woke you all up didn't it?' Cleo said, sniggering
as she appeared amongst them.

'Couldn't you make that any louder?' Linda
complained.

'What's it doing all the way over there?' Andy asked,
noticing it had reappeared some five hundred kilometres
away.

'It's been in there unobserved for a while, I wasn't
taking any chances that it hadn't been interfered with. I

want to check it over first before I bring it any closer,' admitted Cleo.

Finally, after what seemed like an age, the recorded images from its data bank began playing back above them. They watched fascinated as the drone had to immediately take evasive action to avoid the busy space lanes leading away from the emergence zone.

'I thought Dasos was ridiculously busy,' said Linda. 'But this is just ridiculous.'

Hundreds of perfectly choreographed lines of ships ranging from small ten-metre vessels, up to the two-hundred-kilometre ore carriers and everything in between streamed in all directions. The drone was programmed to find its way through one of the space station's occasional navigation holes, circumnavigate the planet, scan the hell out of everything on the surface and return.

It tucked itself in beside a large boxy ship that resembled a block of flats turned on its side. Most of the traffic from the emergence zone, the apartment block included, headed for the nearest hole and poured through, then dispersed into multiple lines again as they emerged.

'The station, if we can call it that, is over a kilometre thick,' Pol said. 'And look at that, it is lit in here. The station matches the planet's rotation too.'

'There are massive light panels set around the inside of the station,' Rayl pointed. 'It must be daylight all the time down there.'

'Unless they turn it off to create a night period,' said Ed.

'Space elevators too,' said Pol. 'They've got plenty of those.'

'Aratap's almost the same size as Mars,' said Andy, as

the planet's telemetry began to flood in. 'Gravity point eight-two Earth, atmosphere acceptable, but quite polluted in certain areas.'

'Humans,' called Pol, excitedly. 'Finally, we have a few humans below.'

'Yeah, but remember, the Moguls were human's too,' said Ed. 'and these humans might be guilty of even worse crimes.'

'Are they only on the planet's surface and not on the station?' Linda asked.

'As far as I can tell,' answered Pol. 'But I am getting humanoid movement in ships and on the station, they just aren't very biological.'

'Robots, you mean?' Andy asked.

'Well, I suppose they must be,' she replied, tilting her head to one side and staring at the data with a furrowed brow. 'It's just the data returns are a bit indecisive.'

'In what way?' Ed asked, this time.

'Eighty-three percent inorganic or mineral,' she said.

'And the other seventeen?'

'Inconclusive.'

'Inconclusive?' he repeated. 'Cleo, what the hell is that supposed to mean?'

'A mixture of mineral and organic in this case,' she said. 'It's not one or the other.'

'Sort of like a terminator?' Andy asked, glancing at her. 'Organic human skin covering the exoskeleton?'

Ed saw Linda roll her eyes.

'No,' Cleo answered. 'It's all in one place.'

'Don't tell me...the skull?'

She nodded.

'So, it's mostly an android with a partly human brain?' Ed asked, raising his eyebrows.

'That's about as close as I can get without actually having one here,' said Cleo.

'The humans here must live well,' said Phil. 'Having all these androids working for them.'

Rayl glanced across with an apologetic expression.

'I hate to shoot that theory out from under you, but I think it might be the other way around,' she said.

'What makes you say that?' Ed asked.

'The areas where the few humans are seem to be in more remote areas, in much more run-down conditions too.'

'Can we get a better view of this?'

'Not from the drone,' she said. 'We'd need the cameras on the *Gabriel* to do that.'

Ed stood up and circled the holomap, rubbing his chin in thought.

'Has the *Secchio* been upgraded to the Khen technology?' he asked.

'Yes,' said Cleo, now sitting quietly at the side of the bridge. 'All the vessels in both hangars have had their hardware upgrades and the new software installed.'

'I don't like where this conversation's going,' said Linda. 'You're not thinking of going in there are you?'

Ed noticed Andy giving him a sly grin.

'Are you?' she repeated. 'And don't you encourage him either, Andrew,' she added, noticing the smirk.

Ed stopped his walking and sighed.

'Well…it's either that, or we go all in and take the *Gabriel*,' he said, meeting her gaze. 'I was just looking for the safer option.'

'Why do we need to go in there at all?'

'Because it's what we do,' he blurted, surprising himself with the gravity of his tone.

Linda noticeably recoiled.

'What I mean to say is…whether it's the humans or the androids committing these crimes, someone needs to put a stop to it. Can you imagine what would happen when they discover the gateway and arrive in the Milky Way?'

'Why does it always have to be us?' Linda mumbled. 'Why don't we report back to Bache and let him sort this out?'

'How's he going to do that with a decimated fleet? He hasn't got enough resources to police our own galaxy, and that would mean gifting him this new technology too.'

'That's why most of the gateway destination galaxies are as yet unexplored, except for a fleeting visit by a drone,' Andy said.

'So, you're siding with him again?' she said, turning to Andy, huffing and folding her arms across her chest.

'This isn't a competition,' Ed replied. 'We're here now and we might be able to do something about it. Maybe we can't and we do have to report back to Bache. But at least we can go back with the full picture of what and who we're up against.'

Linda looked around the bridge at all the others.

'Can we at least have a vote?' she asked, dejectedly.

'Of course,' said Ed, nodding at Linda. 'There's no dictatorship on this vessel. All those in favour of staying and trying to sort this out, raise your hand.'

Ed and Andy of course both did. All the girls were looking at each other and while that was happening Civray spoke.

'I'm not a crew member so I don't imagine I get a vote, but I would vote for staying too,' she said, raising a hand. 'I want some payback for the slaughter of my race.'

That seemed to convince Phil and although all Theos were effectively pacifists, he still raised his hand.

'Sorry, Linda,' he said. 'I really think whatever's going on here, it needs to stop.'

'Well, I'm with you,' said Pol, smiling at Linda and getting a disappointed look from Ed.

'I have to be with you too,' said Cleo. 'My Theo programming disallows me from taking a life and I'm sure that's what this would entail.'

'What if it proves to be the androids?' Ed asked.

'That is hugely debatable,' she replied. 'But the fact that they have a partly human brain means I'm forced to vote the way I have.'

'Always the voice of reason. It's three all, Rayl,' said Ed, turning to her. 'You have the deciding vote.'

'Ah, shit,' she said. 'I am actually torn with this…but considering what happened to me with that bloody brain-washing queen last time, and if that's another human race in trouble down there, then it's sorry, Linda, I vote stay and sort this out.'

She raised her hand, avoiding eye contact with Linda.

'Oh joy,' mumbled Linda, slumping in her seat. 'I knew I should've stayed and done some wine tasting at the vineyard.'

'Okay,' said Ed, taking his seat again and feeling a lot more upbeat. 'We need to start making plans.'

33

Subterranean water course, unknown locale

TYME PRESSED himself flat against the bottom of the boat, the rough material of the boat's bottom scratching against his back through his shirt. The ceiling scraped past overhead, so close he could have stretched up and touched the rough stone with his nose if he'd dared. The sound of water lapping against rock filled his ears, amplified in the confined space until it seemed to echo from all directions.

The boat rocked more violently as they navigated the narrow passage, and Tyme squeezed his eyes shut, fighting the urge to sit up and look around. The darkness pressed against his closed eyelids, making him feel buried alive. His breathing came in short, shallow gasps that he tried to muffle against his sleeve.

'Almost through,' Kael's voice drifted back to him, steady and surprisingly calm.

The scraping sound of stone against the boat's hull made him wince, but then suddenly the oppressive claustrophobia lifted away. Cool air touched his face, carrying new smells...something earthy and green that reminded him of the growing chambers in Tin Koilada.

'You can sit up now.'

Tyme opened his eyes and pushed himself upright, blinking in the dim light that filtered down from somewhere high above. They'd emerged into another cavern, this one longer and narrower than Tin Koilada, stretching away into darkness in both directions. The water here moved with purpose, a steady current that tugged at their boat and carried them forward without need for paddling.

Tyme twisted around to check on his brother, relief flooding through him when he saw Jaccin sitting upright behind him, his face pale but determined. Mira's boat had already disappeared around a bend ahead, swallowed by the darkness.

'First test passed,' Kael said, though her tone suggested this had been the easy part. 'The river gets more interesting from here.'

The walls of the cavern rose high on either side, carved smooth by centuries of flowing water. Strange formations jutted from the rock like frozen waterfalls, and Tyme caught glimpses of movement in the crevices...things that skittered away from their boat's passage too quickly for him to identify.

He fretted as he remembered Eleni's warning about creatures that lived in the deeper waters. The jet blackness beneath the boat seemed slightly oppressive, and he found himself imagining what might be swimming just below the surface, watching their small craft with greedy eyes.

The river widened, and Tyme kept his eyes fixed on the dark water, trying to convince himself that the shadows moving beneath were just reflections from the stone formations above. The boat glided forward with barely a sound, Kael's occasional paddle strokes so precise they hardly disturbed the surface.

'How much farther to the first rest point?' Jaccin said from behind him.

Kael didn't turn around. 'We'll reach the Hanging Gardens before the next sleep cycle. If we keep moving.'

Tyme's stomach growled, reminding him of Eleni's parting gift. He reached into his pack and unwrapped the cloth bundle, breaking off a piece of bread and passing half to Jaccin behind him. The familiar taste brought a sudden pang of loss for Tin Koilada's warmth and safety.

'Don't trail your hands in the water,' Kael warned as Jaccin leant over to wash crumbs from his fingers. 'The silver eels have poor eyesight but a ravenous taste for trailing digits.'

Jaccin yanked his hand back, nearly tipping the boat. Tyme curled his own fingers into fists at just the thought of that.

The boat drifted in silence for what felt like hours, though Tyme had no way to judge time in this lightless world beneath the planet's surface. His legs cramped from sitting motionless, and the constant rocking motion made his stomach queasy.

The river curved sharply to the left, and Tyme caught his first glimpse of what Kael had called the Hanging Gardens. He caught his breath as the cavern opened into a vast chamber filled with impossible beauty. Massive stone formations hung from the ceiling like frozen waterfalls, their surfaces covered with cascading plants that glowed with soft bioluminescence. The light reflected off the water in rippling patterns around the walls that made the entire space seem to be constantly on the move.

'Welcome to the first way station,' Kael said, her paddle steering them towards a natural stone platform where Mira's boat already waited. 'We rest here for a few hours.'

Tyme climbed unsteadily from the boat, his legs shaking from the long period of immobility. The stone platform felt solid and reassuring beneath his feet, and he stood for a moment just savouring the stability. The luminescent plants cast dancing shadows across the platform, their soft glow unlike anything he'd seen in the harsh artificial lighting of the refinery.

Mira emerged from the shadows near the platform's edge, her sharp eyes scanning the cavern entrance they'd just emerged from. She moved with that same constant vigilance Tyme had noticed earlier, never quite relaxed even in this beautiful place.

'No followers,' she reported to Kael, who nodded as she secured their boat to a metal ring embedded in the stone.

Jorik's boat appeared moments later, the scarred man paddling with smooth efficiency despite the narrow passage. He guided his craft alongside theirs and climbed out with a practised ease.

'Water levels are rising,' he said, checking something on the cavern wall that looked like carved marks. 'We'll need to move through the Throat before they get much higher.'

Tyme felt apprehensive at the ominous name. If the

passage they'd just navigated was considered reasonably easy, he didn't want to imagine what "the Throat" might involve.

Kael pulled supplies from her boat – dried meat, water containers, and what looked like small vials of glowing liquid that cast an eerie blue light across her weathered hands. She distributed the meat and water, passing a vial to each of them.

'Drink this,' she instructed, handing one to Tyme. 'It helps with the river sickness on the next leg.'

Tyme examined the small container, the liquid inside shifting and swirling strangely. It reminded him of the molten haklion, and his stomach turned involuntarily at the memory.

'What's in it?' he asked, his voice echoing slightly in the vast chamber.

'Better not to know,' Jorik muttered, already downing his own vial with a grimace. 'Just swig it.'

Tyme glanced at Jaccin, who shrugged and tipped his vial back without hesitation. Taking a deep breath, Tyme followed suit. The liquid burned his throat like fire, then spread a strange coolness through his chest that made him shiver. The taste was bitter yet somehow sweet at the same time, lingering long after he'd swallowed.

'The Throat is a narrow passage where the river drops suddenly,' Kael explained, settling onto a flat section of the platform with her back against a luminescent wall. 'The current becomes violent, and the walls close in tight. Some people panic.'

Tyme felt the strange coolness from the vial spreading through his limbs, making his fingers tingle. The sensation wasn't unpleasant, but it felt foreign in his body, like something weird moving through his bloodstream.

'How violent exactly?' Jaccin asked, lowering himself beside Tyme on the stone platform.

'Fast enough to slam you against rocks if you fall out,' said Mira, speaking for the first time since they'd left Tin Koilada, her voice rough as if she didn't use it often. 'Narrow enough that you'll scrape skin off your shoulders if you sit up at the wrong time.'

The dried meat Kael had given him tasted salty, nothing like the rich stews he'd grown accustomed to in Tin Koilada. He forced himself to chew and swallow, knowing he'd need the energy for whatever lay ahead. The blue liquid had left him feeling oddly detached from his body, as if he were watching himself from a slight distance. He jerked awake and realised he'd been dozing. He looked up to see Kael watching him.

'Sleep while you can, she said, settling back against the glowing wall. 'We move through the Throat in two hours, and after that there's no stopping until we reach Daro Koilada.'

Tyme tried to find a more comfortable position on the stone platform, but his mind wouldn't shut down. The luminescent plants cast strange patterns across the cavern ceiling high above, hypnotic almost. He found himself thinking of Eleni's kiss on his cheek, the warmth of her lips against his skin. The memory felt a long time ago now, like something that had happened to someone else.

'Are you nervous?' Jaccin whispered, his voice low enough that the traders wouldn't overhear.

'Aren't you?' Tyme replied, watching Mira as she paced continually around the platform's perimeter.

The next thing he knew, he was being shaken awake by Kael.

'Time to leave,' she said.

Tyme's body felt strange as he pushed himself upright, the lingering effects of the strange liquid making his movements feel disconnected and dreamlike. The luminescent plants seemed brighter now, their glow pulsing in rhythm with his heartbeat. He blinked several times, trying to clear the fog from his mind.

The boat rocked violently as they pushed off from the platform, the current immediately grabbing them and hurling them downstream. Tyme gripped the sides, then remembered Kael's warning about the tunnel walls and tucked his hands beneath his thighs again. The water was flowing much faster here, pulling them towards a dark opening that looked even smaller than the passage they'd passed through earlier.

'Remember,' Kael shouted over the rushing water. 'Keep low, don't fight the current, and whatever you do, don't try to grab anything if we start spinning.'

The entrance to the Throat rushed towards them, and Tyme's eyes opened wide as he realised how fast they were moving. The walls leapt in on both sides, forcing him to involuntarily hunch his shoulders and duck his head as spray from the churning water soaked his back. The boat bucked and twisted like a living thing, the current slamming them from side to side, the smooth-flowing channel from before becoming a maelstrom of eddies and waves. He wondered if it was supposed to be this bad, but it was about to get a lot worse

34

The *Gabriel*, outside the Aratap system, Triangulum Galaxy

THE FIRST CONSIDERATION was obvious to Ed, how many of them should go. Taking too many would be reckless, but going alone was a non-starter. He studied the holomap again, watching the recorded footage cycle through the busy traffic lanes around Aratap.

'Right then,' he said, clasping his hands together. 'First decision…who's going with me in the *Secchio*?'

'I'm going,' Andy declared immediately, which Ed had expected.

He nodded. Three felt manageable for a reconnaissance mission. "Cleo, you'll pilot the *Secchio*. Everyone else stays with the *Gabriel*.'

'Hang on,' Linda said, sitting forward. 'If you're determined to do this stupid thing, I want to go along too.

I can pilot and Cleo can concentrate on keeping you guys safe.'

The logic was sound, though Ed suspected her real motivation was not wanting to sit helplessly on the *Gabriel* while they ventured into danger again.

He shrugged and nodded.

'That makes four,' he said. 'Sorry, Phil, looks like you're piloting the *Gabriel* again.'

'That's fine by me,' he said, breathing a sigh of relief. 'You know me, I've never been much of a warrior anyway.'

The preparations started immediately. The *Secchio's* systems were checked and double-checked. The ship hadn't been used on any missions as yet and was operationally untested. Last thing Ed wanted was a weapon malfunction at the wrong time.

It took the rest of the day to finish the preparations and as Ed, Andy and Linda gathered up in the blister for final briefings, Rayl called from the bridge.

'Ed, I've got something you should see before you go,' she said.

'On my way,' he replied, turning to the other two. 'Okay, we'll go first thing in the morning. Get some sleep and I'll see you in the hangar at eight o'clock.'

Rayl, Phil and Pol all had concerned expressions as Ed arrived on the bridge.

'What's occurred?' he said, stopping in his tracks and eyeballing each one in turn.

Rayl took a deep breath and cleared her throat.

'I think we know now who the aggressors are here,' she said.

'Go on.'

'I was studying the drone images again, when I noticed this.'

A two-dimensional image flashed up on one of the main wall screens. Rayl got off her couch and walked over to the screen.

'If you look down here,' she pointed to some sort of industrial complex in the corner of the image. 'Okay, Pol, can you zoom it in again.'

The frozen picture zoomed in on the complex and particularly a gantry beside a huge glowing mass of something very hot. The farther in it went, the grainier the image became.

'Is that a metal refinery?' Ed asked.

'Probably,' Pol professed. 'But watch what happens when I forward it frame by frame.'

Ed watched as two fuzzy white humanoid blurs carried something out onto the gantry and hurled it off into the fiery pit below. Pol finally froze the picture again just before whatever it was they'd thrown hit the molten surface.

'Oh, shit,' Ed muttered, as the unmistakable shape of a falling, flailing humanoid was revealed. 'I take it that wasn't an android?'

All three of them shook their heads.

'Confirmed as human and alive,' said Rayl.

'Certainly isn't now,' he said, turning and slumping into his couch. 'And those two were definitely the androids we've detected before?'

'They were,' confirmed Pol.

'Andy's going to make all the terminator jokes now, isn't he?' said Phil.

'Of that, I have no doubt,' admitted Ed, rolling his eyes.

The following morning, everybody except Phil gathered in the port hangar, standing at the bottom of the *Secchio*'s central airlock steps.

'Don't you dare take any unnecessary risks,' Pol demanded, giving Ed a last hug.

'And that goes for you too, Andrew Faux,' said Rayl, prodding him in the chest.

'We won't...I promise,' Ed declared, holding his palms up in surrender.

'Bloody right you're not,' said Linda, already inside the airlock and leaning against the frame, her arms folded across her chest. 'No gung-ho stuff for you two this time.'

'We might need to kick the terminators up the arse though,' admitted Andy.

'Told you so,' said Phil, over the hangar speakers, as Ed glanced at Pol, rolling his eyes again.

With a last smile at Pol, Ed climbed the steps with Andy.

'What was he on about?' Andy asked, as the airlock cycled.

'No idea,' said Ed. 'Must've been a private joke with the girls.'

Ed could feel Andy's eyes boring into the back of his head as they made their way up to the central bridge and sealed themselves in. Linda took the pilot's seat, with Ed in the co-pilot's and Andy electing to take one of the guest seats at the side.

'Are you all in and loaded, Cleo?' Linda asked, prepping the anti-gravs to take them out into space.

'I am,' she said, her voice booming around the small bridge. 'It's very comfortable in this ship with the brand new data banks and stuff. No old software or redundant programming to delete, or push into a corner.'

Ed grinned at her comment and nodded at Linda.

'Shall we?' he said, raising his eyebrows.

'Yes, let's go see what's going on,' Linda said, lifting the vessel and carefully squeezing it out of the hangar.

The holomap, a lot closer to them on this ship, lit up with the glow of the unyielding system barrier pulsing in a bluish green colour. Ed could reach out and penetrate the hologram with his hand it was so close to him.

'Are you no nearer to penetrating that thing, Cleo?' Ed asked.

'Not even remotely,' she answered. 'As electrified barriers go, this one's Olympic standard.'

Ed smiled at her use of the metaphor.

'Okay, keep trying,' he said. 'It'd be nice to turn that thing off at some point.'

They'd decided to jump in from well away from the *Gabriel*, just in case it was detected and could be traced back. This ship was a lot larger than the drone that went before, so they weren't taking anything for granted.

'Two million kilometres,' said Linda, opening her eyes to glance across at Ed. 'Internal arrival zone is programmed.'

'Right,' he said. 'They have ships jumping into the zone at around forty-seven second intervals, I've got a large vessel approaching from the direction of the mining spheres we saw. When it jumps in, I'll count you down twenty seconds and then we go. Then get us into clear space straight away.'

'If there is any,' smirked Linda. 'It's Times Square on a Monday rush hour in there.'

'We are quite small compared to what we're going to be around, remember, so do what the drone did and stick close to a bigger vessel,' said Ed.

'I've got shields on maximum,' said Andy. 'So if we do nudge anything, it'll be them making an insurance claim.'

'Emergency jump ready to go, Cleo?' Ed asked, glancing up.

'Always,' she said, materialising on the seat next to Andy, with her legs crossed.

She was sporting her skin-tight black ninja outfit today, although Ed thought the bright red trainers weren't particularly warrior inspired.

'It forces your adversary to glance down involuntarily,' she said, reading his mind. 'And that would be their biggest error.'

'But where's your sword?' Andy asked, smirking.

In the blink of an eye, a long, curved, intricately etched samurai sword materialised in her hands.

'Ah, it's never far away,' she said, swishing it from side to side.

'You mind my new furnishings with that thi—' Ed's sentence was cut short by a pinging alarm. 'That ship has jumped. Twenty seconds, Linda,' he called.

They all watched the ship's clock and counted down the seconds. On zero, Linda hit the execute icon and the *Secchio* was instantly inside the Aratap system barrier.

35

Subterranean water course, unknown locale

TYME GRIPPED the sides of the boat as they were sucked into the Throat, his knuckles white against the dark material. The roar of the water grew deafening, drowning out everything except the hammering of his heart. His back scraped against the low ceiling, tearing his shirt and leaving a burning sensation across his skin.

The boat lurched sideways, nearly flipping as it hit an unseen obstacle. Tyme bit his tongue to keep from crying out, tasting copper as blood filled his mouth. The strange blue stuff Kael had given him seemed to dull the edges of his panic, keeping him pressed flat against the bottom of the boat instead of flailing wildly as every instinct screamed at him to do.

A wall of water crashed over them, momentarily submerging the entire boat. Tyme gasped as the freezing liquid filled his nose and mouth, burning his lungs. He coughed violently, trying to expel the water while keeping his head down. The boat spun in a dizzying circle, slamming against the rock walls with a crack that vibrated through his entire body.

'Hang on!' Kael's distant voice barely penetrated the cacophony of noise and Tyme wondered who had actually done this the first time. They must have thought they were going to die. Then suddenly, as abruptly as it had begun, the violence ended. The boat shot from the narrow confines of the Throat into a wider channel, the water smoothing into gentle swells that rocked them from side to side. Tyme's ears rang in the sudden quiet, he caught his breath and tentatively raised his head.

His shirt hung down his back in tatters, the soft blue fabric shredded by the rock ceiling. His back was badly grazed where the stone had scraped away skin, but probably because of the strange blue drink the pain seemed to be no more than a manageable itch. He twisted around to check on Jaccin, relief flooding through him when he saw his brother sitting upright, his face a little pale but unmarked.

'Everyone intact?' Kael called, her voice hoarse from shouting over the rapids. Water dripped from her grey hair, and a fresh cut marked her left cheek, but her hands remained steady on the paddle.

Tyme nodded and tried to speak, only emitting a peculiar rasp. His throat felt raw from swallowing river water, and his hands shook as he finally released his death grip on the boat's seat.

Mira's boat emerged from the Throat moments later, the vigilant woman looking remarkably composed despite the ordeal. Jorik followed, his scarred face grim but unsurprised, as if navigating through that was just another mundane part of his day.

'That wasn't so bad,' Jaccin said, though the strange tone in his voice contradicted his words.

Kael snorted, wiping blood from the cut on her cheek with the back of her hand.

'That was as easy as it gets,' she said. 'Water levels were perfect.'

Tyme didn't want to imagine what a difficult run through the Throat might be like. He pulled the remains of his shirt away from his torn back, wincing as the fabric stuck to the wounds. The cold air against his exposed skin made him shiver, and he wrapped his arms around himself for warmth.

The river was considerably wider here, flowing between towering walls of flat, smooth stone that disappeared into darkness high above. Strange formations jutted from the rock like twisted wire, and Tyme caught glimpses of the phosphorescent moss clinging to the stone high above, providing just enough light to see the water's flat surface.

Kael guided their boat towards the shore where a narrow strip of stone provided a landing spot. Tyme winced as he climbed out, the movement dragging at the raw skin on his back.

'We'll stop here briefly,' Kael said, securing the boat to a rusted metal ring embedded in the rock. 'Jorik, check their wounds.'

The scarred man approached, carrying a small leather pouch. He waved for Tyme to turn around, then made a disapproving sound when he saw the state of Tyme's back.

'Rock burn,' he tutted, digging through his pouch. 'Not serious, but it'll fester if not treated.'

Tyme flinched as Jorik applied a pungent paste to his abraded skin. The substance stung initially, then went numb, the pain receding to a dull throb. The medicinal smell reminded him of the healing chambers in Tin Koilada, though stronger and more bitter.

'Hold still,' Jorik ordered as he pressed a thin fabric patch over the wounds. 'This'll keep a thin, semi-transparent material over the damaged skin. 'It seals in the medicine. Don't pick at it.'

Tyme thanked him, grateful for the relief from the stinging pain. The paste was already working, replacing the burning sensation with a dull numbness. He pulled the remains of his shirt back over his shoulders, careful not to dislodge the healing patch.

'How much farther to Daro Koilada?' he asked, watching as Jorik moved to check Jaccin for injuries.

'We'll reach the outer caverns by morning,' Kael replied, refilling their water containers from a small spring that trickled down the cavern wall. 'The settlement itself by midday, if the currents hold.'

Tyme tried to imagine what this new settlement might be like. Would it be as welcoming as Tin Koilada? As beautiful? He remembered Chresta mentioning specialists who understood chemical exposure, healers who might help slow the damage to his lungs and liver. The thought cheered him up despite his exhaustion.

'Are there many refugees there?' Jaccin asked, wincing as Jorik applied the paste to a similar scrape on his arm.

'Many,' Jorik replied. 'Daro Koilada is the largest settlement of all...well, on this continent anyway.'

'Continent?' repeated Jaccin. 'What's a continent?'

Tyme's ears pricked up too, as he had no idea what a continent was either.

'Land on the other side of the oceans,' said Kael. 'That's where all this water runs in and out of. The gradual tilt of the planet changes and causes the tidal flow to go in the opposite direction. That's how we get back to Tin Koilada.'

'These underground oceans, are they far from here?' Tyme asked, gritting his teeth as he turned too quickly to look at Kael.

'They're not underground,' Jorik said. 'These rivers eventually break the surface and flow into open oceans.'

'You're kidding,' Jaccin spluttered. 'Surface water, wouldn't it just evaporate under the uplighting?'

Kael laughed and nodded towards the boats.

'You two have been stuck in that refinery for too long and have an awful lot to learn about,' she said. 'Come on, we need to get moving.'

Kael led them back to the boats and they pushed off once more, the current swiftly carrying them deeper into the cavern system. Tyme's back throbbed beneath the healing patch as he tried to find a comfortable position in the rocking boat. The medicine had dulled the worst of the pain, but each movement reminded him of the violent passage through the Throat.

The river widened further, the ceiling rising so high that Tyme could no longer see it, even with the faint biolu-minescence from patches of moss clinging to the walls. The air grew warmer, carrying new scents – something mineral and earthy, a bit less cultivated.

'What's that smell?' he asked, his voice still out of sorts from swallowing the river water.

'Life,' Kael replied without turning around. 'The closer we get to Daro Koilada, the more lush the ecosystem becomes. They've been cultivating these caverns for centuries. You're going to be eating foods you never knew existed.'

Tyme inhaled deeply, trying to separate the unfamiliar scents. There was something sweet, almost like the fruits Eleni had shared with him, what now seemed a long time ago and a long way away.

There was something about fresh food grown in actual soil that made Tyme's taste buds come alive. Even the thought of going back to nutrient blocks made his stomach turn.

The boat rocked gently and Tyme found himself dozing again, the fatigue of the last couple of days catching up with him. A sudden jolt through the boat as it scraped around a sharp curve woke him. He looked up and found the walls only inches away from the sides of the boat. Quickly snatching his hands back, he jammed them under his thighs again.

Ahead, Mira's craft disappeared around another curve. As they followed and swept around it, her boat reappeared in a shaft of strange brighter light that seemed to pour from a crack in the distant ceiling.

'You've been asleep for hours, we're approaching the outer reaches,' Kael said, her paddle making barely a ripple as she steered them towards the light. 'The bioluminescent fungi start to give way to uplight here.'

'Uplight?' Tyme stammered, staring at her. The word frightening him. Uplight was a Repp thing.

He'd once heard a story about before the Repp's appeared and built the Lamination that completely shrouded the planet. A massive ball of fire lit and warmed the globe, providing daytime and night-time as the planet turned. That was something from legends, not reality though and he stifled a laugh at the very thought. The tale was many thousands of years old and couldn't possibly be true.

The brighter glow grew stronger as they rounded the bend. Tyme squinted against the brightness, his eyes watering after days in the dim caverns. The shaft of light struck the water's surface, fracturing into a kaleidoscope of glistening shapes and colours that shimmied around the walls.

'Wow,' he heard Jaccin mutter. 'Have you ever seen anything like that?'

36

The *Secchio*, inside the Aratap system, Triangulum Galaxy

ED'S STOMACH lurched as the jump completed, the familiar disorientation washing over him as the *Secchio* materialised inside the barrier. The bridge filled with an intense, almost blinding light that made everyone squint and shield their eyes with their hands.

'Shit,' Andy muttered. 'It's like being inside a bloody light bulb.'

Ed blinked rapidly to help his vision adjust to the stars' mirrored brilliance bouncing off the inside of the system's shield.

The holomap immediately exploded with traffic indicators, thousands of moving dots streaming in perfectly organised lanes around them. Ed heard Linda's sharp intake of breath as she fought to orient herself in the chaos.

'Bloody hell…this is madness,' she spluttered.

'There, on the starboard side,' he said, as a massive rectangular vessel loomed nearby. 'That boxy container ship…get us alongside it.'

Linda moved the ship quickly, nudging the *Secchio* into formation beside the enormous vessel. Ed felt a subtle vibration through his seat as the ship's engines adjusted course and speed. The container ship was easily a hundred times their size, its hull stretching away into the glowing distance like a moving mountain of metal.

'We look like a fucking tugboat next to that thing,' Andy commented from behind them.

'We're cloaked, so we don't look like anything, Andrew,' Linda said, rolling her eyes.

Ed smirked as Andy stuck his tongue out at Linda. She had her eyes closed to fly the ship with her DOVI and didn't see the rude gesture.

'D'you realise, all these ships have only forward navigational shields,' said Andy, studying his screen. 'I could shoot them full of holes with my dad's trusty Smith and Wesson.'

Ed remembered the time when that .44 magnum had saved their lives from a malfunctioning disgruntled sentient space station.

He studied the traffic patterns flowing around them. Almost everything, as per usual, was heading for the hole in the wrap-around space station.

Ed watched the massive container ship ahead of them slowly begin to bank towards the nearest aperture in the planetary station. The hole looked impossibly small from this distance, but as they drew closer, he could see it was easily large enough to accommodate dozens of ships their size flying abreast.

'Stay with this big boy,' he told Linda, gripping the armrest as she adjusted their course to match the container ship's trajectory and got scarily close to its hull. 'Don't you scratch my new paint job,' he moaned.

'It'd probably make the ship look better if she did,' quipped Andy. 'Bloody state of it.'

Ed ignored the barb as the opening rushed towards them, and he caught his breath as they plunged through the station. The transition from the mirror-bright outer system to the artificial daylight within was jarring. Below them, Aratap's surface spread out in a patchwork of smoking industrial complexes, and refineries.

'Look at the size of those factories,' Andy said, his voice tight with amazement. 'They cover half the bloody surface.'

Ed followed his gaze to massive industrial installations that dwarfed anything he'd seen on human worlds. Smoke and steam billowed from unseen stacks, and the orange glow of molten metal was visible even from their altitude. He thought of the grainy footage Rayl had shown them of the two android figures hurling a struggling human into that fiery pit.

'This is where all the materials come from to build all this infrastructure,' he said. 'They've certainly been doing this an awful long time.'

'And they're using human slave labour to do it,' Linda said grimly, the disgust evident in her voice.

Ed felt his jaw clench as he watched the sprawling industrial nightmare below. The container ship they'd been following peeled away upwards towards a massive loading dock in the underside of the station and Linda had to quickly find another vessel to shadow. She settled on a sleek transport that looked more manoeuvrable than the lumbering cargo haulers.

'Careful this one doesn't catch you out with any sudden course changes,' he said, scanning the surface through the holomap. 'Where are the residential areas? All I can see are factories, factories and factories, but where do the humans actually live?'

'There, maybe?' Andy pointed to the edge of the display, where the industrial complexes gave way to what looked like holes that disappeared into the ground. 'Looks like they've been pushed into holes on the margins.'

'You're kidding,' said Linda, seeing the same sad spectacle as the boys. 'It's absolute squalor down there.'

Ed studied the ramshackle muddy settlements clustered around the perimeter of the major industrial zones. Even from this height, he could see the stark contrast between the gleaming android facilities and the dirty makeshift underground human habitations.

'We need to get closer,' he said. 'Can you take us down without attracting attention?'

'What, without an insertion heat trail, you mean?'

'Yeah.'

'I can try,' she said. 'It might take a while though and there is that period where we transition from the main drives to the antigravs.'

'Do your best,' he said. 'Let's just hope they put it down to a meteorite.'

'That's gone right through the space station,' said Andy, sarcastically.

'Could happen,' said Ed, awkwardly, then looked up at Linda. 'As soon as you have antigrav control, level out as fast as possible and go off at an acute angle.'

'Will do,' she said and began her careful descent.

Ed noticed she was grinning and hoped she was impressed with the ship. It seemed to respond beautifully, the new Khen technology making the transition between drives almost seamless.

He watched the surface of Aratap growing larger on the holomap, his heart hammering against his ribs. The closer they got, the more horrific the contrast between the gleaming android areas and the human settlements became.

'Shit, look at that, those poor bastards,' Andy whispered from behind him. 'It's worse than we thought.'

Ed could only nod in agreement. The human settlements weren't just ramshackle, they were deliberately contained. High walls surrounded each compound, with what looked like automated guard towers at regular intervals. The entrances to the underground shelters were little more than concrete holes, dropping into a probable living hell.

'They're keeping them like animals,' Linda said, her voice rough with anger. 'We're really going to have to do something about this.'

'Listen to you now,' said Andy grinning. 'Getting all gung-ho…like we weren't supposed to.'

Linda opened one eye and glared at him with it malevolently.

Ed leant forward and squinted at the holomap. 'Can you get us over to that compound on the eastern edge? Looks possibly a bit less guarded, we need to find some locals to have a chat with.'

Linda banked the ship gently, keeping their descent gradual to avoid detection. The *Secchio*'s cloaking technology was state-of-the-art, but sensors might still pick up the air movement or any sonic booms.

She brought the ship down in a smooth arc and approached the eastern compound low, finding a relatively isolated spot beyond the guard towers' immediate field of view. The ship hovered at around two hundred metres, so as to not disturb the ground and give their position away.

'I've got us as close as I dare,' she said, dropping the antigrav's revolutions to the bare minimum but still enough to keep them airborne. 'We're three hundred metres from that entrance to the underground complex,' she added, pointing up at the holomap.

Ed studied the compound through the holomap's magnification. The security seemed lighter here than at the other facilities they'd passed over, but still formidable. Guard towers loomed at irregular intervals along a high concrete wall, topped with what looked like energy barriers.

'Those aren't just concrete walls,' Andy said, leaning forward between Ed and Linda. 'See how they shimmer? There's some kind of force field in play here too.'

'Well spotted,' Ed replied, nodding at his friend. 'Cleo, what can you tell us about the security systems?'

Cleo materialised beside them, her red trainers now replaced with silent black boots. 'The towers are automated. Motion sensors, heat detection, and what appear to be disruptor turrets. But there's a blind spot…'

As she spoke, one of the towers suddenly lit up, the weapon on its highest point swung around and fired a relatively low-powered bolt in their direction. It was easily absorbed by their shields, but gave away their position.

'Shit,' swore Linda, lifting the ship up and back quickly. 'Must've detected the noise.'

The two most adjacent towers activated too and their weapons began swinging around in a search pattern.

'Rumbled,' said Andy, as several armed androids appeared and began gazing out in their general direction.

'Bollocks,' grumbled Ed. 'Get us out of here, go north and away from everything. We need to rethink this.'

'We've got company,' said Andy, as several small vessels appeared almost out of nowhere and began to encroach on their location.

'Quick...find somewhere to hide, preferably under rock, if we can find it,' called Ed, a little more urgency in his voice now.

Linda accelerated the ship out towards the more remote areas.

'There were large vents out this way, I saw them on the way down earlier,' she said. 'One of them might be big enough for the ship.'

'They're not completely sure where we are,' said Andy. 'Look, they're firing randomly, hoping to hit our shields and give our location away.'

'Keep us under the speed of sound,' said Ed. 'Don't want to make it easy for them.'

Linda just nodded, her face a picture of pure concentration.

'There,' she shouted, a few moments later, turning and diving the ship downwards.

Ed saw what she was heading towards and raised his eyebrows.

'Will we fit?' he asked, a little nervously.

'It'll be tight,' Andy chirped.

'Shut up, you two,' Linda shouted. 'I can't concentrate with all your negative shit.'

The *Secchio* shuddered as they dropped inside, its hull scraping the rock on one side and dislodging a few small boulders that dropped away, splashing into an underground lake far below.

'We're in…sort of,' she said, with a lopsided grin.

37

Subterranean water course, unknown locale

TYME STARED at the dancing light patterns, mesmerised by the way they shifted and moved across the cavern walls. The brightness made his eyes water, but he couldn't look away. After years of bland minimal artificial lighting and the dim bioluminescence of the underground settlements, this natural illumination felt magical.

The boat drifted closer to the source of light, and Tyme could see it was streaming down through a massive crack in the cavern ceiling far above. The opening looked enormous from this distance, a jagged wound in the rock that allowed this brilliant radiance to penetrate the depths.

'Is that really uplight?' he asked. 'It seems so much brighter.'

Kael chuckled softly. 'Not the artificial uplight from the Lamination. This is natural light…from the star.'

Tyme's brain struggled to process what she was telling him. The stories his father had whispered about the ancient fire in the sky seemed suddenly less impossible. He squinted upward, trying to see beyond the crack, but the brightness made his vision swim with coloured spots.

'It shines through one of the navigation holes in the Lamination,' Jorik shouted across from his boat.

The water seemed to grow warmer as they approached the light shaft. New scents filled the air, and Tyme could see a faint mist hanging just above the water's surface around the edge of the light beam. The boats travelled on, slower now as the waterway was wide and the current less urgent. They threaded their way through more basins, connected by varying widths of passageways, but none as narrow as before.

Tyme watched the water shimmer and dance beneath the star's light, feeling something shift inside him…not the flutter Eleni had caused, but something deeper, a longing. The brightness made his eyes ache, but he couldn't look away from this impossible radiance that seemed to breathe life into everything it touched.

The boat drifted through pools of liquid gold where the magical light struck the water. He dipped his fingers beneath the surface, watching the ripples fracture into countless tiny mini rainbows. The warmth surprised him too – it wasn't the artificial heat of the refinery, but something more gentle that seeped into his bones.

'The star feeds everything down here,' Kael said, her voice softer now, almost reverent. 'The plants, the water systems, even the air we breathe. The Repps tried to block it all out, but they had to leave holes in the Lamination for navigation and these places, although small, are the result.'

A splash echoed from somewhere ahead, and Tyme jerked his hand from the water, remembering the warning about silver eels. But Mira's boat had simply disturbed a school of small fish that scattered in flashes beneath the surface. He'd never seen living creatures like these...sleek, multi-coloured and beautiful.

He'd noticed the basins were becoming bigger and began to have patches of land stretching away from the water's edge.

'How far to Daro Koilada now?' Jaccin called.

Kael turned and nodded at the entrance to the next passage.

'Just though there,' she said. 'I hope you're ready for this?'

Tyme felt nervous as they approached the passage entrance. The opening looked different from the others they'd navigated – wider definitely, with carved stone pillars flanking each side like ancient guard posts. Strange symbols covered the pillars, more intricate than anything he'd ever seen before, spiralling upward in grids and patterns that made his eyes go fuzzy when he tried to follow them.

The current pulled them through, and suddenly the enclosed feeling of the caverns fell away entirely. Tyme's breath caught in his throat as they emerged into what could only be described as a monumental underground world.

The space stretched impossibly far in every direction, so vast that distant walls disappeared into hazy blue-green light. Terraced gardens cascaded down carved stone slopes, crammed with neatly tended plants that glowed softly in the filtered starlight streaming from one almost circular hole in the ceiling far above. Waterways branched and snaked through the terraces like silver ribbons, feeding pools where more of those colourful fish darted between floating lily-like plants.

But it was the settlement itself that made Tyme forget to breathe.

Buildings rose from the cavern floor in graceful spirals, their walls carved directly from living rock but smoothed and shaped with such skill they looked as if they'd grown like that.

Windows pierced the spiralling structures, glowing with warm light from within. Bridges of stone and wood connected the buildings, creating a web of walkways high above the cavern floor where people could traverse from one side of the waterway to the other, all going about their daily business. Tyme thought it strange there was no one around and called to Kael.

'This is Daro Koilada, right?' he said.

Kael turned suddenly and put her finger to her lips. All the colour had drained from her face and she signalled Jorik behind to pull in to the side quickly. Mira had already done so and was staring around, seemingly rattled by the same thing.

'This is Daro Koilada all right,' Kael hissed. 'But the people are gone.'

'I take it this isn't normal?' Tyme whispered back.

'This is home to nearly two thousand souls, how can they just not be here?'

'Two thousand?' Tyme whispered, sweeping his eyes nervously from left to right, desperately searching for the inhabitants. A splash right beside the boat had him almost jumping out of his skin, but it was just one of the rainbow fish breaking the surface.

The quietness in the huge cavern was only broken by the gurgle of the water in the main channel and dozens of tiny waterfalls connecting the multitude of channels snaking down from higher levels.

Mira, Kael and Jorik continued slowly, staring around with eyes like dinner plates. They pulled their boats along the edge of the channel silently by hand. It widened into a lake at the centre of the settlement, its surface dotted with small boats similar to their own. A huge stone quay extended from the nearest shore and they headed for that.

Tyme sat quietly, his hands shaking in his lap. He was frightened. He could see Kael was scared as this was obviously far from normal. He turned to find Jaccin looked even more scared than any of them.

'What's going on, Tyme?' he whispered. 'Where is every—'

Jaccin's sentence was cut short by a figure strolling out from one of the dock buildings. Tyme turned to follow his gaze and his whole world fell apart.

The red Repp, closely followed by five more standard-coloured armed white ones, spread out and pointed weapons at the five of them. They all sat unmoving in the boats as the clicking, whirring androids approached.

'Fuck, fuck, fuck,' whispered Tyme, under his breath.

'*Fuck, indeed, Du, or shall I call you Tyme,*' the red Repp said sarcastically in its bone-chilling, artificial, metallic voice. '*Haven't you done so very well?*'

'You can't possibly have done all this for just us?' Jaccin blurted bravely and waving his hand around at the deserted settlement. 'We're simply just not important enough.'

'*Oh, but how wrong you are, Jaccin,*' it continued, its

expressionless face glowering. '*Now, if the five of you would like to come with—*'

It went almost dark suddenly, a loud crunching from above stopped the android mid-sentence and it looked up. Tyme turned and squinted upwards too. He hunched down when a bunch of boulders fell and splashed noisily into the centre of the lake. A noise, the like of which Tyme had never heard, had him covering his ears, as a large flying craft of some kind dropped down into the cavern. It stopped its descent about ten metres above the water and slowly turned on the spot.

Tyme presumed it was a Repp ship of some kind, until a nacelle opened on one side of the hull and six bright energy pulses zipped over his head. The Repps all disintegrated in an explosion of mechanical body parts that went everywhere. Tyme shut his eyes and ducked as shrapnel rattled around in the boats, splashed into the water around him and thudded off the buildings around the dock. When he opened them again, he found a smoking white foot in his lap and flicked it overboard in a single gesture.

'Fucking hell,' Kael rasped. 'Who the hell are these guys?'

Tyme sat very still and watched as the strange and, now he came to notice it, dirty craft rotated slowly above them, its hull rusty and painted badly in several dark colours. The reflected starlight seemed to be absorbed by the strange dirty paint coating. Tyme kept his ears covered as it passed overhead, the scream of its motors echoing around the cavern. His heart still hammering from the sudden violence, he tried to make sense of what he was seeing. The vessel looked nothing like the angular, utilitarian designs he'd glimpsed of Repp technology during his years at the refinery. This craft was more curved and flowed like something organic, as if it had been grown rather than built. Landing struts whined down from its belly and it landed with a crunching thud on the stone dock.

Nothing happened for a few minutes and in the boats nobody moved, just in case that nacelle opened again. A sudden hissing sound had them ducking as another section of the hull opened, this time underneath. Tyme tensed, expecting more weapons, but instead stairs descended and two figures stepped slowly down. As they drew closer, he could see they were human...or at least, they looked human. Their clothing was unlike anything he'd seen in either the refinery or the underground settlements, matching fitted blue garments that seemed to shimmer in the reflected starlight.

'Are they friends or enemies?' Jaccin whispered, his voice hoarse with barely controlled panic.

Tyme was unable to answer and just shrugged. The figures, now approaching them across the dock moved with an easy confidence that reminded him uncomfortably of the Repp overseers. Although, he did notice they had their weapons slung across their backs and the expressions on their faces seemed friendly.

38

The *Secchio*, natural cavern, Aratap, Triangulum Galaxy

'OH, CRAP,' shouted Andy. 'There are bloody androids in here.'

'Shit,' said Linda. 'I'll get us out again.'

'No…wait,' said Ed, staring at the holomap. 'There's humans too, and they're being threatened with weapons.'

'They'll report us being in here,' said Linda. 'And there's only one way out.'

'If our scans and communications can't penetrate this rock,' said Ed, 'then nor will theirs. Take us down and face them.'

She dropped the ship down into the cavern and hovered just above the water, slowly turning the ship towards the androids.

Ed opened one of the weapon ports and targeted the six androids, firing as soon as he had lock.

'Holy moly,' said Andy, as he watched the six figures vaporise. 'You're not messing about are you?'

'Land us over there on the dock, Linda, and turn the ship to face them,' Ed continued, ignoring Andy. 'We need to have a little chat before they decide to scarper.'

Once she'd put the ship down on the dock, Ed took a rifle from the rack, gave one to Andy and slung his across his back.

'Do the same,' he said. 'They've just had guns pointed at them, the last thing we want to do is look as though we're as bad.' He picked up a GDA universal translator and secured it to his chest.

'Ready?' said Andy.

'Ready.'

'No risks,' called Linda. 'I'll keep the motor running just in case.'

Ed gave her a thumbs up as the internal airlock closed behind them.

'Look casual and friendly,' Ed said, as they descended the exterior steps down to the rock floor. The huge cavern was surprisingly warm and Ed noticed an aroma of fresh flowers and fruit. Apart from the low murmur of the antigravs on tickover and the soft gushing of water, the cavern was quiet. The five humans sat in the three boats staring in their direction and as they approached, Ed could see they were quite terrified – and the hands of one of the males in the middle boat were shaking.

'Hello,' he said, smiling and stopping a couple of metres from the edge of the dock and the boats. 'My name is Ed and this is Andy, we are your friends.'

The translator began repeating what Ed had said in

different languages and as soon as it used Ellinika the five expressions suddenly changed.

One of them, the woman in the middle boat, with a fresh scar on her face and braided hair, finally found her voice.

'I am Kael,' she said. 'A river trader…these are my boats.'

'She's speaking Ellinika,' whispered Andy. 'They're like us, descendants of the Ancients.'

'You…you killed the Repps,' she whispered, her words echoing in the cavern. 'We will all be executed.'

Ed shook his head and took another cautious step forward.

'They were threatening you with weapons. We couldn't allow that.'

The humans exchanged nervous glances. Ed noted their decent clothing, garments that had clearly been made out of quality materials. Their skin was pale, suggesting they spent little time in natural light and the two males in the middle boat seemed very malnourished. Despite their obvious fear, he sensed a flicker of hope in their expressions.

'Are you from the western continent?' asked a younger woman in the front boat, her voice coarse with disuse.

'Not exactly,' Ed replied, turning the translator off. 'We're from a long way away. We came to investigate what's happening on this planet.'

Andy moved beside him and pointed at the ceiling. 'We saw what the androids are doing to humans here. The factories, the living conditions…it has to stop.'

The young woman shook her head wearily.

'You shouldn't have come,' she said. 'The Repps are too powerful.'

A sudden loud engine noise over on the far side of the cavern caught their attention. A small ship, hidden from sight amongst the dense vegetation, leapt into the air and screamed upwards towards the opening high above.

The five in the boat ducked as Ed, followed by Andy, both swung their rifles around and began firing upwards at the fleeing vessel. After a couple of the laser bolts hit the ship, it veered left and continued its ascent in a more random spiral. Smoke began to trail in its wake as their weapon fire became more accurate and several more shots found the tiny craft, but it continued to climb.

'For fuck's sake,' shouted Andy. 'How many times do we have to hit the bloody thing?'

It was just about to crest the lip of the opening when an explosion ripped through one of its two engines. It slewed to the right, hit the cavern wall and began to drop.

'Get clear,' shouted Ed, waving to the five in the boats, as the Repp vessel plummeted towards them like a dying animal, trailing fire and smoke.

Tyme barely had time to register Ed's warning before Kael was grabbing his shirt, yanking him down into the bottom of the boat.

'BRACE,' she screamed.

The Repp ship hit the water with a deafening explosion that shook the entire cavern. A massive wall of water erupted from the impact point, rising like a tsunami, higher than any wave Tyme had ever imagined. He clung to the boat's sides as the first surge lifted them nearly vertical, then slammed the boat back down with bone-jarring force.

'Hold on,' Jaccin called behind him, his voice almost lost in the roar of water.

Their boat spun wildly as the wave carried them across the lake. Tyme's stomach lurched with each violent pitch and roll and he thought he might throw up. Through spray-blinded eyes, he glimpsed Mira's boat flipping upside down completely, sending her tumbling into the churning water with a scream.

Debris rained down around them...twisted metal, shattered composite, unidentifiable fragments of the Repp vessel. Something hot whizzed past Tyme's ear, missing him by centimetres. A jagged piece of hull plating slammed into the water beside them, sending another burst of spray across his face that tasted of burnt circuitry and fuel.

'DUCK,' Kael yelled as something massive spun through the air above them.

Tyme pressed himself flat against the bottom of the boat as more debris rained down. The water churned violently for what felt like minutes, then gradually began to calm. He cautiously raised his head, taking in the devastation around them.

'Mira,' Kael shouted, scanning the now-settling water. 'Where is she?'

Tyme spotted movement about thirty metres away...a flailing arm breaking the surface.

'There,' he shouted, pointing.

The boat rocked as Kael immediately plunged into the water, swimming with powerful strokes towards the struggling figure.

'Help me get the boat back to shore,' Jaccin called, grabbing one of the paddles that had somehow remained in their boat. He began awkwardly steering them towards the nearest dock.

The water had calmed enough now that Tyme could see Jorik's boat had survived too, though it was taking on water. The scarred man was paddling frantically towards where Kael was now dragging Mira back towards the dock.

As they neared the stone quay, Tyme jumped out in the shallows, the cool water soaking him to mid-thigh. He grabbed the boat's edge and helped Jaccin pull it the rest of the way to shore. His back stung where the healing patch had peeled away during the chaos, but he ignored the pain.

'We need to help them,' he said, turning back to where Kael was struggling with Jorik to get Mira out of the water.

The humans, Ed and Andy, were already moving quickly in that direction and as they all arrived, it only took a few moments to lift Mira, Kael and Jorik clear of the lake and onto the dock.

Mira's limp form suddenly spasmed and she sat up retching and coughing up lake water.

'You're okay now,' said Kael, rubbing Mira's back vigorously. 'Make sure you get all that lake water out of you.'

Mira nodded, and dry retched this time before speaking.

'I thought that was it for a moment,' she spluttered, breathing deeply. 'The boat turned over and I got disorientated.'

'We need to distance ourselves from here,' said the human called Ed.

The other human was staring upward.

'Some of the smoke is escaping outside,' he said, pointing. 'That'll be seen for kilometres.'

'Come with us quickly,' said Ed. 'We need to move right now.'

Tyme turned to Kael and raised his eyebrows.

'We're dead if we stay in here,' he said, turning to his brother for moral support.

'He's right,' said Jaccin. 'Dead Repps mean dead us.'

'Help me with Mira,' Kael said, standing and heaving Mira up. 'You'd better be who you say you are,' she added, glaring at Ed. 'We'll be executed publicly if we're caught after this bloody mess.'

'Open the ramp, Linda,' Ed called.

Tyme watched as a ramp at the rear of the human ship powered down. It took them a couple of minutes to get across the dock and he helped a limping Mira into the loading bay of the ship.

It was cooler inside and he heard the engines spooling up as the ramp closed behind them. Tyme's eyes nearly bugged out of his head as the most beautiful woman he'd ever seen met them with warm towels and blankets.

'Thanks, Cleo,' said Ed. 'Linda, get us outta here.'

'On it,' the reply came, as the ship lifted.

39

The *Secchio*, natural cavern, Aratap, Triangulum Galaxy

THEY ALL GRABBED a fold-down seat against the back bulkhead wall. Tyme thought he felt the ship move beneath his feet, but nothing after that.

'Why are we not moving?' he asked, glancing at Andy sat next to him.

'Anti-gravity plating,' he replied, pointing at the floor. 'The ship's moving all right.'

'Cloaking engaged,' Linda called. 'Let's hope they're not waiting for us out there.'

'Can you give us a holomap, Cleo?' Ed asked.

'Indeed I can,' she said.

The large three-dimensional image of the inside of the cavern appeared in front of them.

The five locals all emitted murmurs of disbelief, as the

display materialised showing the lake rapidly disappearing below and the rock walls flashing downwards.

They burst through the opening without hitting it this time, into blinding brightness that made Tyme squint and turn away. When he dared look again, he saw endless blue stretching above them...not the artificial lighting of the Lamination, but a deeper, richer colour that seemed to go on forever.

'We're outside,' he whispered, the words feeling insufficient for the enormity of what he was seeing. 'Actually outside.'

'And invisible,' Ed said. 'As long as they don't see through our cloaking.'

Tyme stared at the holomap display in awe. The events of the past hour swirled in his mind...the empty settlement, the Repps, the strangers who had saved them, the impossible ship that now carried them with technology beyond anything he'd imagined could ever exist.

Jaccin reached across and patted his knee, giving him a wide, slightly nervous grin.

'Well, this adventure gets weirder every day,' he said.

'You ain't seen nothing yet, peeps,' said Andy.

'Repp ships have just converged on the cavern,' called Linda. 'Anywhere special you want me to go?'

Ed turned to Kael.

'D'you know where would be safe for us to hide?' he asked.

He noticed her give Mira a questioning glance and received the slightest of nods in return.

'I might know somewhere that's safe, where you'd be amongst friends too,' Kael said, not losing eye contact with

Mira. 'Fly east towards the mountains and let Mira see the ground.'

The *Secchio* soared eastward, following Mira's directions. Tyme couldn't tear his eyes from the holomap display showing mountains rising in the distance...actual mountains, not just images in a data terminal. He'd never imagined he'd see the surface of the planet with his own eyes.

'There,' Mira said suddenly, leaning forward despite her obvious discomfort. 'That range with the three peaks that look like fingers.'

Linda, up on the bridge, heard the instruction and adjusted their course, the holomap zooming in on the mountain formation. Even from this distance, Tyme could see why Mira had described them that way...three jagged spires of rock jutted upward like a partially closed fist.

'We need to be careful,' Mira continued, her voice getting stronger now. 'The Repps patrol this area occasionally. They know there are humans living wild in these mountains, but they've never found the main settlement.'

Ed nodded.

'Don't worry, we'll stay cloaked. Just tell us where to set down.'

As they crossed over into the mountain range, Mira sat forward closer to the display, studying the terrain below with intense concentration. Her eyes narrowed, scanning the rocky ground as if looking for something only she could recognise.

'There it is,' she said, after several minutes, pointing to what appeared to be just another section of barren rock. 'See that formation that looks like a crescent? Drop down just beyond it, turn and fly under the overhang. It should be easily high enough.'

'Should be?' Linda's voice boomed around the freight deck. 'I would prefer definitely high enough, but we'll see how we go.'

She piloted the ship down towards the spot Mira had indicated. Tyme couldn't see anything special about the rock layout below, but as the high peaks began sweeping close by, he hoped the pilot knew what she was doing.

The *Secchio* slowed as it approached the rocky outcrop, hovering for a moment before gently settling onto the stone surface. The landing was so smooth that Tyme barely felt the contact with solid ground. He sat just breathing for a few moments, still unable to fully process everything that had happened in the last few hours.

'Everyone stay put until we make sure it's safe,' Ed instructed, checking his weapon. 'Linda, disengage the cloak.'

The ramp lowered with a soft whine and hydraulic hiss, revealing a desolate landscape of wind-carved rock. Tyme peered out, expecting to see...well, something. People. Structures. Signs of the settlement Mira had mentioned. But there was nothing, absolutely nothing except bare stone stretching away under the massive outcropping of solid rock.

'It looks abandoned, just like Daro Koilada,' Jaccin whispered in his ear.

Mira, overhearing the comment, struggled to her feet, grimacing as she put weight on an injured leg.

'It's supposed to look that way,' she said. 'Let me go first. They'll be watching now.'

She limped down the ramp, her wet clothes still

clinging to her slight frame, the others following. Tyme watched as she stepped onto the stone surface and raised both arms above her head, as if surrendering, then walked forward a few paces and sat down cross-legged. She sat like that, with her arms crossed over her chest, for several seconds before standing again and bowing her head.

Nothing happened.

The silence stretched uncomfortably. Wind whistled through the rock formations, creating an eerie, hollow whooping noise that made all the hairs on Tyme's neck and arms stand up.

Then, as if the stone itself had come alive, figures began to emerge from crevices and shadows Tyme hadn't even noticed. Men and women dressed in rough-spun clothing that blended with the rock, their faces weathered and suspicious. They moved with the caution of prey animals, ready to bolt at the slightest provocation.

They all stopped moving as one, like a school of fish suddenly freezing at the presence of a predator. Tyme held his breath, watching the stand-off between the newcomers and Mira. The wind howled between the rocks, the only sound breaking the tense silence.

One woman separated herself from the group and stepped forward, her tanned face marked with intricate tattoos that spiralled across her cheeks and forehead. Her hair, braided with small metal tokens that clinked softly as she moved, fell past her shoulders. She carried herself with the unmistakable authority of a leader.

'Mira,' the woman said, her voice neither welcoming nor hostile. 'We thought you were lost with Daro Koilada. What have you brought to our doorstep?'

Mira straightened despite her injured leg. 'Slovena,

these people saved us. The Repps had taken Daro Koilada when we arrived. They were waiting for us, they knew we were coming.'

Slovena's eyes narrowed, her gaze sweeping over the ship and the strangers. 'And yet you live. Convenient.'

'They destroyed the Repps that captured us,' Mira continued, gesturing towards the ship. 'Their vessel has powers I've never seen. They can become invisible to Repp sensors.'

Tyme watched the exchange nervously, noting how the mountain people kept their hands near concealed weapons. He could feel Jaccin trembling slightly beside him, both of them acutely aware of the seriousness of the situation.

Slovena raised her hand, and the mountain people around her tensed visibly.

'You,' she called, pointing directly at Ed. 'Walk forward…no weapons.'

Tyme felt his heart hammering against his ribs as Ed handed his rifle to Andy and stepped down the ramp. The stranger moved with a confidence that seemed out of place in this tense stand-off, his steps casual and calm as he approached Slovena.

'Good morning,' Ed said, smiling as he approached.

'That's far enough,' Slovena said when Ed was about three metres away and ignoring his greeting. 'Who are you, and why are you here?'

'My name is Captain Edward Virr,' he replied, confidently, his voice carrying across the stone clearing. 'My crew and I are here to investigate what's happening to humans on this planet.'

Slovena's expression didn't change, but her eyes narrowed slightly. 'Many over thousands of years have claimed to be our saviours. In the past, all they've ever succeeded in doing is getting a lot of us killed. The Repps have ruled for generations. Their technology is indefatigable and impossible to overcome.'

'We're not from this world,' Ed said simply.

A murmur ran through the gathered mountain people. Tyme glanced at Jaccin, who looked as confused as he felt. Not from this world? What did that even mean?

'Impossible,' Slovena said, though Tyme thought he heard a hint of uncertainty in her voice. 'The Repps control all access to space here. We're told of an impregnable barrier that prevents any interference from outsiders.'

'It hasn't prevented us,' Ed replied. 'We have technology they don't. We've seen what they're doing to humans here…the refineries, the forced labour, the executions, it violates galactic law.'

She stared at Ed for a long moment, her tattooed face unreadable. The wind gusted through the rock formations, whipping Tyme's damp clothing against his skin. He shivered, partly from cold, partly from tension.

'If what you say is true,' Slovena finally said, 'prove it.'

Ed nodded and turned towards the ship.

'Andy, bring the medical scanner.'

Andy disappeared into the ship and returned moments later with a small device Tyme had never seen before. A small device unlike anything he'd ever seen. It was sleek, with no visible seams or joins.

'This technology doesn't exist on your world,' Ed explained, holding it out. 'This can detect internal injuries, disease, even chemical damage to organs.' He held it up for Slovena to see. 'May I demonstrate?'

The tattooed woman hesitated, then gave a curt nod. Ed turned to Mira, passed the device over her body, and suddenly a three-dimensional hologram of her skeleton appeared in mid-air, rotating slowly. Red spots highlighted areas of damage...a hairline fracture in her left tibia and three cracked ribs.

Slovena's eyes narrowed as she examined the device without touching it. 'Technology alone doesn't prove your origins.'

'Then perhaps this,' said Ed, turning again and peering up inside the ship. 'Cleo, can you pop out here and introduce yourself to these nice people?'

Cleo materialised at Ed's side, dressed this time in her regal gold-edged robes.

Slovena, a shocked expression flashing across her face, took an involuntary step back, along with most of her people. This time there was a lot of murmuring amongst the gathering of locals.

'Hello,' said Cleo, giving Slovena the slightest of bows. 'I'm the sentient ship's computer, pleasure to meet you.'

With that, she levitated up half a metre off the ground, turned and floated back inside the ship, vanishing from sight.

'We need to talk privately,' Ed said. 'There's much I can tell you that shouldn't be discussed in the open.'

Slovena, obviously shocked, recovered quickly and seemed to consider this for a moment, then nodded to two of her people. 'Blindfold their eyes. All of them. We take no chances.'

Tyme swallowed nervously as several of the mountain people approached the ship. One of them, a man with a heavily scarred face, climbed the ramp with strips of dark cloth in his hands.

'It's a precaution,' Kael whispered to Tyme. 'They won't harm us if we co-operate.'

40

Remote mountain range, Aratap, Triangulum Galaxy

ED WATCHED as the mountain people blindfolded everyone from the group. He didn't like it, but understood their caution. These people had clearly survived by being extremely careful. The blindfolds were thick, woven from some kind of rough plant fibre that completely blocked his vision when they tied it around his head.

'This way,' said a gruff voice near his elbow. Strong fingers gripped his upper arm, guiding him forward.

Ed tried to keep track of their route...downward first, across rough stone, then through what felt like a narrow passage where the temperature dropped noticeably. The sound of their footsteps changed from the hollow echo of open space to something more confined. The air grew damper, carrying the scent of earth and growing things. He gave up trying to remember the way after about ten minutes.

A good fifteen minutes of walking later, they came to a stop. The blindfold was removed, and Ed blinked against the sudden light.

They stood in an enormous underground cavern, far larger than the one they'd left at Daro Koilada. This wasn't just a settlement…it was an entire subterranean city. Dwellings had been carved directly into the rock walls, rising in terraced levels connected by stone staircases. Overhead, a complex system of mirrors and light shafts brought natural daylight deep into the cavern. Gardens flourished everywhere, plants growing in carefully tended plots that used every available space. Like Daro Koilada, water featured heavily, although here there was no river or lake, just narrow channels that trickled down and through the entire complex.

'Welcome to Peta Katagio,' Slovena said, watching his reaction. 'The last free human settlement on this continent.'

Ed gawped in awe at the underground metropolis. The scale of it dwarfed anything he'd expected to find. Thousands of people moved through the terraced levels, carrying goods, tending gardens, and going about their daily lives. Children played on stone platforms, their laughter echoing against the cavern walls. It reminded him of ancient cliff dwellings he'd seen in Earth's historical archives, but on a vastly more sophisticated scale.

'How many people live here?' he asked, still trying to take it all in.

'Nearly five thousand,' Slovena replied. 'And another

two thousand in satellite communities connected by tunnel networks.'

Seven thousand people, hidden right under the Repps' noses. Ed felt a real surge of respect for these survivors. They'd maintained not just existence but a thriving civilisation despite generations of oppression.

'Please, follow me,' Slovena said, leading them towards a large opening carved into the central wall. 'You must all be hungry and tired after what you've been through.'

They followed her through a series of passages into what appeared to be a communal dining hall. Long stone tables filled the space, with cushions placed along benches for seating. The room was well lit by a combination of mirrors reflecting light and what looked like bioluminescent fungi growing in recessed wall niches.

'Sit, please,' said Slovena gesturing to one of the tables. 'Food will be brought shortly.'

Ed took a seat, with Andy sliding in beside him, and the river traders settling in around him. He studied the cavern dwellers moving efficiently about. Their clothes were simple but well made, their movements purposeful and co-ordinated. This wasn't some desperate band of survivors; this was a well organised society that had clearly been functioning for generations.

'You should be proud, your settlement is remarkable,' he said to Slovena as she sat opposite him. 'Bearing in mind the monstrous things going on out there.'

She regarded him with those cautious, intelligent eyes. 'We've had centuries to perfect it. The Repps rarely venture into these mountains. The mineral content interferes with their sensors, and the terrain is too difficult for their ground patrols. They don't like to move far from their refineries and their collective communication doesn't work underground.'

Several people appeared carrying large earthenware bowls filled with steaming stew and platters of bread. The aroma made Ed realise how hungry he was. A rich, savoury smell that reminded him of ratatouille. Clearly, these mountain people had access to much better food and conditions than those in the factory settlements.

As they began to eat, Slovena leant forward. 'Now, Captain Virr, you claim to be from off-world. I need to know exactly who you are and what your purpose is here. The truth, please.'

Ed took a sip of the surprisingly refreshing water they'd been provided, organising his thoughts. He caught Andy in his peripheral vision shovelling it in like it was his first meal for weeks.

Ed took a mouthful, set his spoon down and met Slovena's unwavering gaze. The cave's acoustics amplified the sounds of eating around them, but he sensed everyone at the table leaning in to hear his response.

'We're explorers from a planet called Earth,' he said, keeping his voice low. 'We're representatives of an organisation called the GDA, a galactic council that oversees the safety and security of hundreds of human worlds.'

'Never heard of it,' she said, sitting back in her chair and giving him a look of disbelief.

'You wouldn't have,' he said, softly, ignoring her scepticism. 'It's based in another galaxy.'

There was a chuckle that spread around the nearest diners and rippled across the dining area as Ed's words spread from table to table.

'You must think us some really dumb humans,' said Slovena. 'The ancient texts state that generations ago we were space travellers too. Aratap had vast cities and our race prospered under the guidance of our supreme being Khenemetneferhedjet.'

Andy nearly choked on a spoon of stew.

'There's that bloody word again,' he mumbled with a mouthful.

'Even the Repps, with all their technology, know that intergalactic travel is impossible,' continued Slovena, rolling her eyes. 'The distances are just too great.'

'They were for us too until recently,' said Andy. 'We discovered the old Ancients' gateways and reopened them.'

'Where's ours then?' asked Slovena.

'A few thousand light years away,' said Andy.

'Our galaxy is called the Milky Way, we call yours Triangulum and they're just over two point seven million light years apart,' said Ed.

It had gone quiet again around them.

Slovena's expression hardened.

'If what you say is true...it would've mentioned all this in the ancient texts.'

'No,' said Ed, firmly. 'It wouldn't. What I'm pretty sure has happened here, is that your supreme being is one of the twelve Ancients, which potentially makes you all distant cousins of ours. The odds of all these almost identical human races springing up around hundreds of galaxies is zero.'

Slovena stared at him for a few moments. A bearded similarly tattooed man with black braided hair, whispered something in her ear. She nodded.

'Say all this is true,' she said. 'What brought you here specifically from this magical gateway between galaxies that's a few thousand light years away?'

You could hear a pin drop in the dining room now. Everyone had stopped eating and all eyes were on Ed.

'We followed a trail of planetary destruction,' he said. 'The Repps, as you call them, have destroyed many worlds, preparing them to have the minerals and ores stripped and brought here to the hundreds of refineries. When we arrived, we found your system hidden behind the barrier, the all-encompassing space station you call the Lamination, and a human race in slavery beneath it.'

The mountain leader's eyes narrowed.

'And we're supposed to believe all this are we, without any proof?'

'Do you realise the androids you know as the Repps, they call themselves the Khenemetneferhedjet.'

A tense silence fell over the table. Ed could see the shock in their faces, the reluctance to believe what must sound like blasphemy to them.

'Look,' Ed continued, attempting to take the heat out of the moment, 'I understand your caution and scepticism. But we need to know exactly what we're dealing with here. So anything you know of, or have, about the Repps, that could help us in ridding you of them, we really need to know, right now.'

Slovena's gaze shifted to someone behind Ed. He turned to see an elderly man approaching their table, his weathered face a tapestry of deep lines and his white hair pulled back in a single braid. Despite his age, he moved with surprising grace, his eyes sharp and alert.

'This is Tellamai,' Slovena said. 'Our conservator of records.'

The old man nodded respectfully to Ed. 'I was sitting at the table behind you and listening with interest. Your words about the Khenemetneferhedjet are...' He adopted a pensive expression and sighed. '...troubling.'

'Why would that be?' Ed asked.

'Because that name has been virtually unspoken for generations.' Tellamai lowered himself onto the bench beside Slovena with a soft grunt. 'It appears in our oldest texts, but was struck from later versions. To hear it spoken aloud is...somewhat unsettling.'

Ed leant forward. 'Why would the name be removed?'

Tellamai glanced at Slovena, who nodded almost imperceptibly. The old man reached into a pouch at his waist and withdrew a small object wrapped in faded cloth.

'This was recovered from the first Repp ever destroyed by our people,' he said, unwrapping the bundle to reveal a small metallic component, roughly the size of Ed's thumb. 'Allegedly it took three of our warriors' lives to bring it down, over two thousand years ago.'

Ed studied the component. It looked like some kind of neural processor, but unlike any he'd seen before. The technology was both familiar and alien. He leant closer, fascinated by the ancient component.

'May I?' he asked, holding out his hand.

Tellamai hesitated before carefully placing the metal object in Ed's palm. It was surprisingly light, with a faint blueish sheen that reflected the cavern's light. The surface was etched with microscopic patterns that reminded Ed of neural pathways.

'This definitely looks like a processing node,' Ed said, turning it over carefully. 'Andy, what d'you reckon?'

Andy leant in, squinting at the component. 'Definitely some kind of advanced neural processor. But the architecture is...kinda familiar. Like the gateway stuff.'

Tellamai's eyes widened, his face becoming serious. 'We've spent generations trying to understand it. Come, I'll show you what we've learned.'

The old man stood with surprising agility for his age and gestured for Ed and Andy to follow. Ed glanced at Slovena, who gave a curt nod of permission before they rose from the table.

'We'll continue our discussion when you return,' she said, her eyes still wary despite the hospitality.

41

Remote mountain range, Aratap, Triangulum Galaxy

ED CARRIED the component carefully and with reverence following Tellamai through a series of narrow passages carved into the stone. The air grew cooler as they dropped deeper into the mountain, and Ed's ears popped with the change in pressure. The passages were lit by the same bioluminescent fungi he'd seen in the main cavern, casting everything in a soft blue-green glow.

After several minutes of walking, they arrived at a small chamber deep within the mountain. Tellamai pressed his palm against a seemingly ordinary section of wall, and a hidden door slid open with a soft grinding sound. Ed blinked to let his eyes adjust to the brighter lighting as they entered a space that contrasted sharply with the primitive surroundings...a laboratory of sorts, filled with equipment that looked surprisingly sophisticated.

'Our study chamber,' Tellamai explained, with a degree of pride. 'Few know of its existence.'

Ed's attention was immediately drawn to a workbench in the centre where several devices hummed quietly. The component in his palm seemed to grow warmer, though he couldn't tell if it was actually heating up or if his imagination was playing tricks on him.

'Place it there.' Tellamai indicated a small depression in a metal plate.

When Ed set the component down, the plate illuminated with a soft blue glow. Symbols appeared on a nearby screen...not in any language Ed could read, but eerily similar to markings he'd seen in Ancient gateway control rooms.

'Holy shit,' Andy whispered beside him. 'That's Ancient script isn't it?'

'It is,' said Ed, leaning closer, his heart rate quickening. The markings were unmistakable...the same flowing, angular symbols they'd encountered at three gateway sites.

'This component,' Ed said slowly, his mind racing with implications. 'It's technology of the Ancients.'

Tellamai nodded, his brow furrowing. 'We came to a similar conclusion, that it was from a time before the Repps. From when we were free and Khenemetneferhedjet was ruling.'

'Could he have been experimenting with sentient android technology?' Andy asked, turning to Tellamai.

'Assuming he was...you think something went wrong and the experiment became the master?'

'It's happened in our galaxy before,' said Ed. 'Strict rules had to be applied.'

'Then what happened to Khenemetneferhedjet?' Andy asked. 'Did the newly created androids kill him?'

'If Khenemetneferhedjet was digitised similar to Pyriaeus, he could still be around in a data store somewhere,' Ed mused.

'Who's Pyriaeus?' Tellamai asked, looking between the two of them with inherent fascination.

'Another of the Ancients we met…'

'Rescued,' Andy said, interrupting Ed.

'…yeah, okay, rescued.'

'You've actually met an Ancient being?' Tellamai blurted, his face a picture of astonishment.

'Actually, we've met three,' admitted Ed.

'Yeah,' grunted Andy, staring away into space. 'Two good ones and one complete arsehole.'

While Tellamai was letting that information sink in, Ed picked up the component again.

'Can I let my ship's computer study this?' he asked, holding it up.

Tellamai hesitated, his weathered hands hovering protectively near the ancient component.

'It's our most sacred artefact,' he said, his voice low. 'If it were damaged…'

'Cleo won't damage it,' Ed assured him. 'She'll just scan it, analyse its structure. No physical alteration whatsoever.'

The old man's eyes narrowed in thought, wrinkles deepening across his forehead as he considered the request. Finally, he gave a reluctant nod.

'Very well. But I must accompany you.'

Ed wrapped the component carefully in its cloth covering and followed Tellamai back through the winding passages. Andy trailed behind them, uncharacteristically quiet, no doubt processing the implications of finding Ancient technology in a Repp android.

The journey back to the surface took longer than Ed had expected. The mountain settlement was a labyrinth of interconnected tunnels and chambers, deliberately designed to confuse outsiders. By the time they reached the main cavern where they'd had their blindfolds removed earlier, Ed's legs ached from climbing the steep stone steps.

'We'll need to blindfold you again for the return journey,' Tellamai said, nodding at the guards who produced two strips of cloth again.

Ed nodded, understanding their caution. 'Of course.'

They turned at a shout from behind them. Tyme came trotting over, his clothing dry now.

'May I come with you?' he asked, his eyes wide with anticipation. 'If this is going to involve retribution to the Repps, then I want to play my part.'

'What about your brother?' Ed asked.

'He wants to stay here.'

Ed glanced at Andy questioningly, who nodded and shrugged at the same time.

'I'll take that as an okay,' he said, turning to Tyme. 'Get a blindfold and tag along then.'

Once again in darkness, Ed allowed himself to be led through what felt like a completely different route to the one they'd taken on the way in.

When the blindfold eventually came off, Ed blinked, his eyes adjusting to the daylight. The *Secchio* sat exactly where they'd left it, its cloaking disengaged while on the ground. Linda had kept the landing ramp down, just in case they needed a fast exit.

'Ed, the Repp traffic has increased over the cavern area, but nothing's come in this direction yet,' she called down. 'I've been monitoring their movements. They're definitely searching for us.'

'In the wrong place luckily,' Ed said, nodding to Tellamai as they climbed the ramp. 'Let's get this analysed quickly.'

The ship's interior felt cool and familiar after the rough-hewn passages of the mountain settlement. Ed led Tellamai and Tyme into the loading bay where Cleo was waiting. She smiled at Tellamai.

'I see we have guests,' she said, her eyes immediately fixating on the cloth-wrapped object in Ed's hand.

'Wow,' she said.

'You know what that is already, don't you?' Andy asked.

'More Ancients' stuff,' she said, grinning. 'Can I see?'

'This is Tellamai, keeper of records for the mountain people. He has allowed us to analyse an artefact they recovered from a dead Repp thousands of years ago.'

She nodded to him and he did the same in return.

Ed carefully unwrapped the component and placed it in Cleo's hand. The metal caught the light, its bluish sheen more pronounced under the ship's illumination.

'Give it the beans, Cleo. Non-invasive, just tell us what you can glean from it.'

She nodded and a beam of soft white light enveloped the component.

'Ah...now then, this is the holy grail,' she purred, an expression of ecstasy on her face. Then, suddenly it changed. 'Oh, shit, no don't do that…bugger. It's just transmitted a distress signal, from the moments before it died.'

'Linda,' Ed called. 'Any change with the Repp traffic?'

'Shit, a load of them have turned this way,' she replied.

'Cloak and get us up fast,' Ed said, waving his arm at the seats. 'Everyone sit, now, we need to lure them away from this place quickly.'

The look on Tellamai's face was a picture.

'Am I going flying?' he blurted, grabbing a seat next to Ed.

'Yes…the Repps detected the component waking up. When you did it, it was under the rock and undetectable.'

The holomap returned as the scream of the antigravs reached a crescendo and the vessel lifted, sideslipping out from under the overhang.

'They're coming fast,' Linda's nervous voice cut through the intercom. 'Multiple Repp vessels converging on us, they're following me.'

Ed swore under his breath. 'Tellamai, stay here with Andy. Tyme, come with me if you want to see how we fight these bastards.'

Without waiting for a response, Ed sprinted through the side door and into the corridor towards the cockpit, Tyme's footsteps pounding behind him. He heard the engines' pitch change as Linda abruptly changed direction.

They burst into the cockpit just as Linda executed another evasive manoeuvre. On the holomap, Ed saw eight sleek Repp vessels in pursuit, their metallic hulls gleaming in the sunlight.

'How are they tracking us?' Ed called, sliding into the

co-pilot's seat and pointing Tyme towards one of the pull-down seats at the side.

Tyme's eyes went wide as he marvelled at the technology around the room.

'It must be that artefact Cleo activated,' said Linda.

'Cleo, turn it off, or put a shield around it, or anything,' Ed called.

'I'm trying.'

'They're faster than I expected,' Linda said, her hands dancing across the icons. 'Targeting systems are locking on to us.'

Ed opened all the weapons bays, fingers flying over the tactical display. 'Let's see how they handle this.'

The mountain range below them was a blur of browns and greys as Linda pushed the *Secchio* into a sudden steep climb.

'Firing,' Ed said, his finger tapping the initiate icon.

A wide spray of cannon bolts flashed away behind, causing the Repp craft to rapidly swerve and avoid them.

'Shit, they are fast aren't they?' he complained. 'Right...try and avoid this,' he shouted, activating the rear firing rail gun and targeting the nearest attacker.

The noise of the rail gun was like child sneezing and the targeted ship just seemed to fall apart. No explosion until the pieces found a mountainside below.

The ship juddered as something hit their shields.

'How rude,' said Ed. 'Bastards are firing back.'

He stuck another titanium rod through a second Repp ship with similar results.

'Draw them away from the settlement,' he said.

'What the bloody hell d'you think I'm doing?' Linda snapped back. 'Flip to the front rail gun.'

'But they're all behind—'

The *Secchio* suddenly decelerated, coming to an almost complete stop, causing the pursuing ships to scream by.

'Ah-ha,' said Ed, selecting multiple targets and ventilating three more with the front multi-barrelled rail gun.

'Got it,' called Cleo. You can get back to the *Gabriel* now, I think I have what we need.'

'Did she say go home?' said Linda, opening her eyes for a second to stare at Ed.

'She did…get us up into space fast.'

'Into space?' Tyme repeated. 'You're kidding me, and what the hell is a *Gabriel*?'

42

The *Secchio*, above Aratap, Triangulum Galaxy

ONCE THEY WERE invisible to the Repps again, Linda had aimed the *Secchio* straight up and had screamed them back up into space within three minutes. Andy had brought Tellamai up to the bridge and joined Tyme on the side seats.

'Everyone good?' Ed asked, as they settled.

A very wide-eyed Tellamai, his dark craggy features glowing in the reddish light, stared at the holomap with reverent awe.

'If someone had told me I'd be in space today, I'd have sent them for a mental health examination,' he said.

Ed smiled and glanced over at Tyme.

'In answer to your earlier question, the *Gabriel* is our starship.'

'This isn't it then?' Tyme said, dragging his eyes away

from the holomap to stare at Ed. 'You have another spaceship?'

'Oh, yes,' said Andy, jabbing a thumb at Ed. 'This heap o' shite is just his little plaything.'

'So your other ship is bigger than this?' Tellamai asked.

'About twenty times bigger,' said Ed, proudly.

'They've barricaded the holes,' said Linda, breaking the conversation and waving at the holomap.

'I kinda expected that,' said Ed, 'we'll just have to jump out from under the Lamination.' He glanced up. 'Cleo, are you quite sure you've gathered everything you need?'

Tyme and Tellamai suddenly gripped the sides of their seats in shock. Their faces horror-stricken as a Repp materialised in the middle of the bridge.

'Cleo, stop fucking around,' said Andy, sighing. 'You're scaring the guests.'

'Ah, right, yeah,' she said. 'Sorry, but I wanted to show you what I can do now. That last manoeuvre, where the Repp ships passed by real close, I was able to get a detailed scan of one and this is the result. I can now incorporate an exact copy of that processor into my doppelgänger Repp self and hopefully walk amongst them.'

'I...is that your computer replicating a Repp?' Tyme asked, his voice faltering and his eyes not leaving the white imposter.

Tellamai was trying to fold himself up into the seat and only relaxed when Cleo reverted back into her normal self.

'Let's get back to the Gabriel,' Ed said, leaning back in his seat. 'We have what we need now.'

'The sooner we're out of this system, the better,' Linda

agreed, programming the jump co-ordinates so they would materialise at the same point they left from.

Ed turned to Tellamai, who still looked shaken from Cleo's Repp impersonation. 'I'm afraid we can't return you to the settlement just yet. It's too dangerous with the Repps searching the area.'

The old man nodded, his weathered face resigned. 'I understand. My people will assume I've been captured or killed. It's happened to many before me.'

'We'll get you back as soon as it's safe though,' Ed promised. 'In the meantime, you'll be the first of your people to travel beyond your solar system in thousands of years.'

Tellamai's eyes widened at that. 'Beyond the star itself?'

'That's right,' Ed said with a smile.

The *Secchio* climbed steadily, the curvature of the planet becoming more evident, its surface scarred by huge refineries and strip mines. The Lamination encircled it like a metallic shroud, blocking the majority of the sunlight from reaching the surface.

'Jump drive is charged,' Linda announced. 'Here we go.'

Ed was expecting the lighting to dim slightly as the jump took place. Only it didn't. He glanced across at Linda, who opened her eyes and stared up at the holomap with a puzzled expression.

'Well, that's weird,' she said. 'The jump envelope failed to form.'

'I believe we need to be outside the Lamination, guys,' said Cleo. 'There's some kind of damping field underneath the station that's preventing the envelope from opening.'

43

The *Secchio*, above Aratap, Triangulum Galaxy

'WE NEED to find a way through one of the Lamination holes before we can jump,' said Ed, more for the benefit of their guests than anyone else, as he began scanning around the inside of the station.

'At times like this, I wish we'd brought the mini-mes,' said Andy. 'We'd have had no problem squeezing through the blockades.'

'I've found something,' Cleo announced, her voice cutting through the tense silence on the bridge.

Ed leant forward in his chair. 'What is it?'

'A major power node.' Cleo materialised beside him, her expression animated with excitement. 'It's part of the Lamination's primary power grid. All their systems suck power from the main nodes and there's only six of them. If

I can access it, I could potentially disrupt enough systems, the damping field included, to allow us to jump clear.'

Ed studied the schematics Cleo projected onto the holomap. The node appeared as a pulsing red dot deep within the vast framework of the Lamination's structure.

'That's way inside the station,' he said. 'Will you be able to get that far without being rumbled? We'd need to dock too or breach the hull somehow.'

'Not necessarily,' Cleo replied. 'If you can get the ship close to one of the maintenance airlocks, I can jump across and enter there. The Repps won't detect me if I'm one of them.'

Tellamai frowned, the muscles in his jaw tensing. 'Are you sure you'll be giving off all the correct signals?' he said. 'They're all interconnected and part of a joint consciousness and—'

'They shouldn't,' she interrupted, her holographic form shifting momentarily into the Repp appearance she'd demonstrated earlier. 'I've analysed their communication protocols. I think I can emulate them perfectly now.'

Linda opened her eyes to stare at Ed.

'It could be our only option, Ed. We can't jump with this damping field, and we can't fight our way through their blockades without attracting a shit load of attention. What's to stop them extending the damping field all the way out to the barrier? Then we're really trapped, one ship against thousands.'

Ed sat back again, sighed and rubbed his chin.

'Yeah…you're right,' he said, staring at the holomap. 'Cleo, can you make the node failure look like an accident?'

'Don't see why not,' she said.

'Has that station got good holo emitters?' Andy asked.

'State of the art,' she replied. 'All their control surfaces are holographic like ours. They have emitters everywhere.'

'Where's the nearest airlock to one of those nodes?' Ed asked.

'There,' said Cleo, pointing to a tiny dot on the holomap, that began flashing red.

'Linda, take us there.'

A few minutes later, Ed held his breath as the *Secchio* edged in close to the maintenance airlock. The ship's cloaking systems were at full capacity, but that didn't stop the knot of tension forming in his gut. They were essentially sneaking up to the front door of the enemy's fortress.

'I'm ready,' Cleo said, her holographic form now the white Repp android. The resemblance was scary, every joint, every movement precise and mechanical, the clicks and whirrs of the joints exactly as the genuine article. Even her voice had that distinct metallic undertone that made the hairs on Ed's neck stand up.

'Be careful,' he said, knowing full well that she couldn't actually be harmed physically. Still, if her signal was detected as anomalous, they'd probably lose their only chance of escape.

'I'll maintain comms silence unless absolutely necessary,' she replied. 'But you can watch my progress on the holomap. Everything I see, you will.' She turned to Linda. 'Hold the ship steady here with the tractor, if it moves more than a few metres the connection will be lost.'

'I got this,' said Linda, nodding.

Ed smiled. 'Good luck, Cleo...there'll be a bonus in this month's pay.'

'You already owe me years of back pay,' she said with a wink, as the internal airlock door closed.

Ed watched on her visual feed as she jumped across effortlessly the twenty-metre gap between the *Secchio*'s outer airlock and the Lamination's surface. The white android form reached the airlock, interfaced with the control panel, and disappeared inside as the airlock opened and closed.

Ed let out a breath he hadn't realised he'd been holding. 'And now we wait and watch.'

'I'm not sure which was the most terrifying thing,' Tellamai muttered from behind him. 'Your computer disguised as our oppressor or watching her jump out into space.'

Ed watched Cleo's feed on the holomap with growing tension. The corridors of the Lamination stretched before her in sterile uniformity…white composite walls, recessed lighting, and occasional holographic displays showing system diagnostics. So far, she'd passed three other Repps without incident, each acknowledging her with that strange mechanical nod they seemed to use as greeting.

'She's doing all right,' Andy whispered, his face bathed in the blue glow of the holomap.

Ed nodded, said nothing, but kept his eyes fixed on the display. Something felt off to him, but he couldn't quite put his finger on it. The Repps she'd encountered so far had been almost too casual. He shook his head, thinking his misgivings were just paranoia.

Tellamai leant forward, his eyes wide with concentration. 'This is all new to us,' he said. 'No human has ever come up here, or if they have, they've never come back.

But I'm surprised she hasn't found any security check-points. On Aratap they have checks every few hundred metres, or perhaps they don't consider it necessary up here.'

As if on cue, Cleo's feed showed a wider junction ahead with two white Repps standing at attention, their heads swivelling in perfect synchronisation towards her as she approached.

Ed's stomach tightened. 'Famous last words,' he muttered.

The Repps stepped forward, blocking Cleo's path. One of them extended a hand, palm up, revealing a small scanning device embedded in its artificial skin.

'Identification and licence required,' it said, the mechanical voice identical to Cleo's current Repp voice. 'You are not scheduled for power node maintenance and your lineage registers you as... diseased.'

The two security Repps immediately grabbed Cleo's arms.

'I'm so sorry, chaps,' she said, as little puffs of smoke wafted out from all their joints and they became quiet and still.

'Has she just killed them?' Tyme asked, staring around at everyone.

'Cleo's programming is that of a pacifist and she's forbidden to take a life,' said Linda. 'So she would've disabled them.'

They watched as Cleo pressed something on the chest of one of them, a tiny hidden section buzzed open and she swapped something over with hers.

'That was like the component I gave you,' said a surprised Tellamai. 'She swapped it out with the Repp.'

'Clever girl...now she'll register as security,' said Ed. 'And be able to bypass any more checks.'

Ed watched with mounting tension as Cleo navigated yet more of the stark white corridors of the Lamination. The component swap had been a stroke of genius, but he couldn't shake the feeling that they weren't out of danger yet. He leant forward in his chair, the subtle vibration of the *Secchio*'s engines humming beneath his feet.

'She's gotta be approaching the power node now,' he said, tracking her progress on the holomap. 'Her signal's showing her right on it.'

Linda kept her eyes closed, maintaining their position with the tractor beam.

'How much longer do you think?'

'Five minutes if all goes well.' Ed tapped his fingers against the armrest.

'Let's hope security doesn't find those disabled Repps,' Andy said, with obvious worry lines across his forehead.

The visuals showed Cleo approaching a large sealed doorway marked with unfamiliar symbols. As she reached it, the door slid open automatically, responding to her security clearance. Inside was a vast chamber filled with pulsing energy conduits and massive cylindrical structures that hummed with power.

'That's it,' Andy whispered. 'The node.'

Ed nodded, relief washing through him. 'Now she just needs to—'

On the display, Cleo entered the large room, rounded one of the structures and came face to face with a red Repp holding a weapon. Ed's breath caught in his throat.

'Ah, great,' Andy muttered beside him. 'It's a fucking red Darth Vader.'

'No, that's a red Repp,' said Tyme, not understanding Andy's comment.

'No shit, Sherlock,' mumbled Andy. 'I take it they're worse then?'

'The red ones are very different,' he said. 'Command units with higher processing capability and more autonomy. You bump into one of those, you're as good as dead.'

The red Repp tilted its head, studying Cleo with those expressionless eyes that somehow still managed to convey suspicion.

'You are not authorised for this sector. Explain your presence.'

'Security inspection,' Cleo replied, her mechanical voice perfectly matching the Repp cadence. 'Anomalous power fluctuations detected in node six.'

The red Repp remained motionless for several seconds. Ed's palms grew damp as the silence stretched.

'No such fluctuations have been reported,' it finally said, stepping back and pointing a weapon at Cleo. 'You have no authorisation to be near this node. You are henceforth sentenced to immediate disassembly.'

The weapon fired and Cleo's image disappeared in a shower of sparks.

44

The *Secchio*, beside the Lamination, above Aratap,
Triangulum Galaxy

'SHIT.' Ed's fist slammed against his armrests as the feed went black. 'Bastard thing,' he shouted, his heart hammering in his chest and adrenaline spiking. The holomap flickered, trying to reestablish connection with Cleo's signal.

Linda opened her eyes momentarily, as it was unusual for Ed to lose his cool.

'What happened?' Tellamai asked, his voice wavering with nervousness.

Ed ran his hands through his hair, mind racing.

'They took out her projection. She'll be fine...she's still in our systems...but we've lost our inside access now.'

'And our way out,' Linda added grimly, her eyes still

closed as she maintained their position with the tractor beam.

Cleo's voice suddenly came through the ship's speakers.

'Ouch...well, that certainly didn't go according to plan did it? I got so bloody close too, and I'm now detecting increased security protocols activating throughout the Lamination. They've shut this region of the station down and are beginning a sector-by-sector search.'

Andy leant forward, his face tense in the blue glow of the displays. 'D'you think they'll find us if they trace Cleo's feed back here?'

'No,' Cleo snapped, her voice booming around the bridge. 'No they bloody won't.'

'I think she's a bit pissed,' Andy mouthed to Ed.

'I heard that.'

Ed's mind whirled through their options, each one worse than the last. They couldn't jump while under the damping field, couldn't fight their way through the block-ades, and now couldn't disable the power node remotely.

'We need to go in ourselves,' Andy said suddenly, turning to Ed with that familiar glint in his eyes...the one that always preceded something either brilliant or suicidal.

'Are you hell!' snapped Linda. 'And fight your way five kilometres through that poked hornet's nest, to a target they already know you want? I don't bloody think so, mister.'

'I was actually thinking of using the PFJs,' Andy countered. 'We have the co-ordinates now from Cleo's last position.'

'What's a PFJ?' Tellamai asked

Ed turned to Andy, ignoring the question. 'The jackets? You're suggesting we fold directly into the station?'

'Why not?' Andy's eyes still gleamed with that familiar reckless determination. 'We set the co-ordinates from Cleo's feed. We fold in, stick charges on the node, fold out. BOOM, two minutes, tops.'

Ed sat quietly for a moment pondering the idea.

'You're not actually considering that madness are you?' Linda said, glaring. 'And anyway, the damping field won't allow the envelope to form, we already know that.'

'Ah…but that's out in space,' said Andy. 'The ship is shielded inside you see, we could jump from the loading bay below, straight into that big power node room, shoot Darth Vader if he's still there and ka-pow...no more nodey thing and we get back to the *Gabriel*. Happy days.'

'You're completely insane,' mumbled Linda.

Ed stared at the holomap, watching the tiny red dot that marked the power node. So close, yet so impossibly far. He glanced at Linda's face, noting the firm set of her jaw, the tight line of her lips. She was right, of course. It was a dangerous plan. Possibly suicidal. But the alternative was staying trapped under the Lamination with Repp forces closing in.

'I'm going,' Ed said quietly, his decision crystallising. 'The PFJs are our only option.'

Linda's eyes snapped open. 'You cannot be serious.'

'The ball was on the line,' Andy whispered.

'And you can shut up with your stupid jokes too,' she thundered, stabbing a finger at Andy, her face red with anger.

'I'm afraid I'm dead serious.' Ed pushed himself out of

his chair. 'Andy's right. We fold in, plant the charges, fold out. Quick and clean…job done.'

'There's nothing clean about that plan,' Linda argued, her voice rising. 'The Repps are already on high alert. If the fold jackets malfunction inside that station…'

'Then we're no worse off than we are now,' Ed finished her sentence. He met her gaze steadily. 'We're trapped, Linda…this is our only shot.'

Linda shook her head, her knuckles white as she gripped her armrests.

'There has to be another way. We could wait them out, find another weakness…'

'There isn't time,' Ed said, already moving towards the door. 'Andy, with me. We're suiting up.'

'Now you're talking.' Andy jumped to his feet, following Ed with a grin from ear to ear.

'What's a PFJ?' Tellamai asked, again, with a little more urgency this time.

'Tell him, Linda,' called Andy, as the airlock door slid shut.

Ed couldn't remember being so nervous, as he and Andy slipped into the PFJ suits in the loading bay. The unfamiliar weight of the fold jacket settled across his shoulders, the neural interface tingling against the back of his neck as it connected with his DOVI.

'This is stupid,' Linda's voice crackled through his earpiece. 'Even for you two.'

'Your concern is noted,' Ed replied, checking the charges in his pack. 'Keep the engines hot. We'll be back before you know it.'

Andy grinned as he adjusted his own jacket. 'Just like

old times, eh? Except it's killer robots this time and not suicidal bugs.'

'Yeah, I'd prefer to be wearing a mini-me rather than a heavy jacket though,' Ed admitted. 'These things do slow you down.'

'What power mode are we having on the rifles?' Andy asked, peering to see Ed's setting.

'Full.'

'We're not messing about then?'

'Well, they're not.'

Ed double-checked the co-ordinates from Cleo's feed, making sure they were locked into both jackets. The margin for error was virtually non-existent. If they folded into a wall...

He pushed the thought away and nodded to Andy. 'Weapons check.'

They both activated their laser rifles, the familiar low hum of the power cells comforting in Ed's hands. He clipped three explosive charges to his belt, feeling their reassuring weight. Andy did the same.

'Cleo, you're sure these charges will do the job?' Ed asked.

'Just one of those puppies will probably destroy about five hundred metres in all directions and you've got six between you. I'll let you work it out.'

Andy grinned again and gave Ed a thumbs up.

'You got eyes on that node room still, Cleo?' Ed asked.

'Affirmative,' she replied, hesitantly. 'Though my scans can only penetrate so far through the Lamination's hundreds of decks and shielding. I'm not detecting any movement, but that doesn't mean the room is empty.'

'Right,' Ed muttered. 'You ready?' he asked Andy.

'Born ready,' Andy replied with that familiar childish grin. 'Oh...hang on.'

He went over to his personal locker, grabbed something he'd nearly forgotten and stuffed it down inside his jacket. Returning, he nodded at Ed. 'Good to go.'

Ed took a deep breath, his finger hovering over the initiate toggle.

'On three...two...one.'

45

Unknown location, the Lamination, above Aratap,
Triangulum Galaxy

ED FELT the familiar nauseating lurch as the world
disappeared around him. The fold jacket hummed against
his skin, that peculiar sensation of being everywhere and
nowhere simultaneously washing over him for a
microsecond before reality reasserted itself.

He materialised in complete darkness. Not exactly
what he was expecting…had someone turned the lights off,
or had they got the co-ordinates wrong?

'Andy…you there?'

'Yeah…have you got fifty pence for the meter?'

'Are we in the right place?'

'Dunno…turn your rifle light on.'

'At least there's gravity and air.'

'My light's not working,' Ed called out in the pitch blackness.

'Nor's mine.'

They both suddenly found themselves squinting as a bright white light came on. The source wasn't from any particular place either. The walls, ceiling and floor just began glowing.

Instead of the cavernous room filled with energy conduits that Cleo's feed had shown, Ed found himself standing in a smaller, circular chamber with shiny gloss white walls. No power node. No machinery. Just a smooth, featureless round room with a single black column in its centre, that stretched right up to the ceiling about ten metres above. It had thousands of different coloured lights pulsating up and down its entire length.

'Shit,' Ed hissed, weapon instantly raised, scanning for threats. 'Andy, where are we?'

'I haven't a clue...where the fuck's that power node gone?' Andy whispered, his rifle sweeping the empty chamber. 'Did we get the co-ordinates wrong?'

'I think we've been played,' Ed said, his mouth suddenly dry. The hairs on the back of his neck stood on end as the air in the room seemed to electrify.

The black column in the centre began to glow brighter. It pulsed once, twice, and then a holographic figure projected onto the floor...a figure that made Ed's skin go cold.

It was neither fully human nor completely machine. Ed's breath caught in his throat as he took in the bizarre hybrid standing barely five metres away. The being's skin had a metallic sheen where it was visible, but most of its body was covered by a simple grey ship suit that hung loosely on its frame. Its face was the most disturbing part…half organic with pale human features on the left side, while the right was a complex arrangement of mechanical components that glowed with the same coloured pulsing lights as the column behind it.

'Captain Edward Virr,' the figure said, its voice an unsettling blend of organic warmth and synthetic coldness. 'I've been waiting for this meeting since you arrived in my galaxy.'

'Who the hell are you?' Ed asked, keeping his rifle trained on the hybrid, though some instinct told him it would be useless against whatever this thing was.

'It's the fucking Borg queen after a sex change,' said Andy, curling his lip at the abomination.

The being lifted an arm and Andy flew backwards, crashing into the wall behind about two metres up. He stayed there, suspended above the floor, waving his arms and legs about and cursing, but unable to release himself.

'Can't take a joke then, can you?' Ed said, as casually as he could. Even though he wanted to panic. 'You haven't answered my question.'

The being's mouth – the human half – curved into a smile that didn't reach its eye.

'I am Khenemetneferhedjet…Ancient Overseer of the Aratap Galaxy.'

'Of course you are,' Ed said, feeling his stomach drop. Another of the twelve, or what remained of him. Ed realised the Ancient that had created the Repp androids, had become some kind of hybrid monstrosity himself. Either by design or been absorbed by his own creation.

'You tricked us,' Ed said, his finger tightening on the

trigger. 'We were never going to get near the power node, were we?'

'A necessary deception,' Khenemetneferhedjet replied, taking a step forward. 'I needed to meet you directly, without my servants interfering. Your arrival was most…fortuitous.'

The monster's projection glitched slightly and seemed to freeze for a couple of seconds, as a different strange whispered voice echoed around the chamber.

"HELP ME."

The projection clicked back to normal and Ed noticed the monster didn't seem to realise anything had just happened. So he carried on without mentioning it.

'Let him down,' Ed asked, nodding towards Andy who was still suspended against the wall, cursing colourfully.

'In due time,' Khenemetneferhedjet replied, its human eye blinking while the mechanical one remained fixed and cold. 'First, I wish to discuss your vessel.'

Ed felt a chill run through him.

'What vessel?'

'Please, Captain Virr. Let's not waste time with denials. The *Gabriel*. A magnificent achievement of human engineering. Ridiculously fast, advanced weaponry, cloaking and – most interestingly – vastly superior jump technology.'

The hybrid took another step forward, and Ed instinctively stepped back, his finger tightening on the trigger. How the hell did it know about the *Gabriel*?

'Your little scout ship is impressive enough,' Khenemetneferhedjet continued, gesturing vaguely upward. 'But the *Gabriel*…now that is a vessel I need.'

'If you've harmed my crew—' Ed started, his voice low with barely controlled anger.

'Your crew is unharmed. For now.' The hybrid's half-smile widened. 'I merely…observed your amazing vessel before you departed the system where I'm building my planetoids. You see, my consciousness extends far beyond any human imagination.'

Ed thought about the last day or so. The hybrid abomination had been watching them all along. It had known about the *Gabriel* before they'd even arrived at Aratap. He swore under his breath, and his grip tightened on his rifle as he processed what this meant. Everything, The barrier, the damping field, the inability to jump…it wasn't just defensive technology. It was all designed as a trap.

'Your vessel possesses technology I must have,' Khenemetneferhedjet continued, its mismatched eyes fixed on Ed with unsettling fanaticism. 'Bring the *Gabriel* to me, Captain Virr. I will allow it passage through the barrier. Have it come through one of the central navigation apertures of the Lamination. I will ensure safe passage.'

'And why would I do that?' Ed asked, playing for time while his mind scrambled for options. Andy was still pinned to the wall, his fold jacket appeared to be dead, and he had no way to communicate with Linda.

The hybrid's mechanical eye pulsed brighter.

'Because I offer you something no other being can… knowledge. The secrets of the Ancients. The truth about your own origins.'

Ed snorted.

'I've met three of your kind already. So I already know all about the twelve and the distribution of the human genome around the galaxies.'

"*HELP ME*," came that strange whispered voice again, seeming to emanate from everywhere and nowhere simultaneously. The hybrid's projection glitched again, its form wavering like a bad transmission.

This time, Ed noticed a flicker of something in the abomination's human eye...alarm? Fear maybe? The hybrid's head jerked slightly, and he seemed to grit his teeth on his human side for a moment.

'No you don't,' it snapped and promptly disappeared.

Andy slid down the wall, landing in a heap.

'That fucking piece of shite,' he grouched. 'Under no circumstances does that shit-head get its psychopathic hands on the *Gabriel*.'

'I'm with you there,' said Ed. 'But what I want to know is...who was that calling for help?'

And then the lights went out again.

46

The *Secchio*, beside the Lamination, above Aratap,
Triangulum Galaxy

TYME WATCHED in disbelief as Linda frantically tried to re-establish communication with Ed and Andy. The fold jackets were designed to maintain constant contact with the ship, but the signal had gone completely dead the moment they'd jumped.

'I can't reach them,' Linda growled with frustration, flailing her arms at the holomap. 'Something's blocking the bloody signal, I warned them not to go.'

Tyme gripped the edge of his seat, his heart rate through the roof. Just minutes ago, he'd watched two men he barely knew jump across to infiltrate the most secure facility in his world. Now they'd vanished without a trace. Nobody ever came back from Repp territory.

'Could they have…died?' he asked, the words sticking in his throat. 'It's been an hour.'

'No, never, don't even think that,' Linda snapped, though her white-knuckled grip on her seat betrayed her uncertainty. 'The jackets would have sent a termination signal if…no. They're alive. They have to be.'

Tellamai sat motionless beside Tyme, his weathered face pale in the blue glow of the displays. The old record keeper hadn't spoken since Ed and Andy had disappeared.

'What do we do now then?' Tyme asked, feeling utterly useless. Everything was happening too fast. Just days ago, he'd been guiding molten haklion at the refinery, believing transition was his only future. Now he was on a spaceship with impossible technology, watching strangers fight a war he hadn't known was possible.

Linda turned to face him, her eyes sharp with decision. 'We need to get to the *Gabriel*.'

'But Ed said—'

'I know what Ed said,' she snapped, cutting him off. 'But we can't stay here. These bastard things know we're here. They're toying with us.' She gestured at the holomap. 'The *Secchio* can't break through that barrier alone, and we're sitting ducks if we hang around and do nothing.'

Tyme swallowed the lump in his throat.

'How can we get to the other ship then?' he asked.

'Use another of those jackets,' she said. 'There are four.'

'So, you jump to get help and Cleo flies the ship?' Tyme asked.

'No, Cleo's a programmed pacifist, so wouldn't be able to defend you if the Repps found the ship and attacked.'

'You mean, Cleo jumps back to the *Gabriel*?'

'No, she's holographic and would cease to exist when the jump took place.'

'Then we're out of options,' said Tyme.

'You can go,' said Linda, jabbing a finger at him.

'Are you kidding?'

'Absolutely not…you came along because you wanted to fight the Repps didn't you? Now it's time to put your money where your mouth is.'

'But your other crew won't know me and might think I'm the enemy and throw me out of an airlock.'

'Don't be so melodramatic,' admonished Linda. 'I'm going to send a data node with you, that will explain everything.'

Tyme's mouth went dry as he stared at Linda. 'You really want me to wear one of those jackets don't you?"

'That's the general idea,' she said, her voice determined. 'Someone has to get to the *Gabriel*, and I can't leave this ship. It'd be signing your death warrant.'

The fold jackets had looked complicated when Ed and Andy put them on, covered with unfamiliar technology and interface panels he couldn't begin to understand. And they'd disappeared into thin air wearing them and could possibly be dead. The thought of putting one on himself made him sweat.

'I don't know how to use it,' he said, hating the tremor in his voice.

'It's easy…I'll show you,' Linda replied, already rising from her seat. 'It's really not that difficult. The co-ordinates are already programmed in, all you have to do is hit the go toggle.'

Tellamai put a hand on Tyme's arm. 'Are you sure

about this, young man? You're young, this isn't really your fight.'

'But it is my fight,' Tyme argued. It had been his fight since the moment he'd seen Kestrel's severed arm in the collection trough. Since he'd discovered what the Repps really did to humans. Since he'd learned there was more to life than the refinery and its lies.

Tyme brushed Tellamai's arm away and stood, giving Linda a determined nod.

'I'll do it,' he said, standing up so abruptly his chair banged loudly against the bulkhead.

Linda nodded in return. 'Good man, follow me.'

Tyme stared down at the fold jacket as he slipped it on, the weight of it far heavier than its actual mass. The sleek material felt strange against his skin...nothing like the rough-spun fabrics of Tin Koilada or the stiff industrial jumpsuit he'd worn at the refinery. Linda had spent the last ten minutes showing him how to operate it, but the complexity of the alien technology made his head spin.

'You'll do just fine,' Linda said, adjusting the straps across his shoulders. 'Just don't touch anything until you materialise and turn its power to off, just as I showed you.'

'What if I end up inside a wall?' Tyme asked, his nerves jangling.

'You won't. The co-ordinates are locked in. You'll appear exactly where we left from...in the *Gabriel*'s hangar."

Tyme swallowed hard, his throat dry as desert sand... this was getting real. The data node pressed against his chest where Linda had secured it inside a pocket. A tiny device containing everything the *Gabriel*'s crew would need to know about the situation and what they should do.

'What do I say to them when I arrive?' he asked.

'Just give whoever meets you the data node and say I sent you. All four of them will know what to do with it and understand immediately.'

Tyme nodded, trying to control the trembling in his hands. He'd volunteered for this. Asked to fight the Repps. But the reality of jumping outside his own system was terrifying in a way he couldn't have imagined.

'Remember,' Linda said, 'one day you'll be a hero to your people.'

'I just hope it's not as a martyr,' he said, glancing down and hitting the go toggle.

47

The *Gabriel*, outside the Aratap system, Triangulum Galaxy

THE WORLD DISAPPEARED in a flash of white light. Tyme's stomach lurched upward into his throat as all sensation vanished. No up, no down, no gravity, not even the sense of his own body. Just a terrifying emptiness that seemed to last both an instant and an eternity.

Then reality crashed back like a trollie accident.

He fell forward, legs buckling beneath him as he materialised on a solid surface. Falling to his knees, he gasped, the fold jacket suddenly heavy as lead across his shoulders. His vision swam as blood rushed to his head, and he fought the urge to vomit.

He'd made it. He wasn't dead. He wasn't embedded in a wall. Linda was right.

When the dizziness subsided, Tyme raised his head... and froze.

The hangar stretched out before him like a cavern from his wildest imagination, but made of gleaming metal instead of stone. The ceiling soared at least thirty metres overhead, supported by massive arched beams that curved like the ribs of some enormous beast. The space was vast – he could see the far wall at least two hundred metres away, and down the back wall a couple of smaller identical spacecraft were parked side by side.

'Shit a Repp,' he whispered, his voice barely audible even to himself.

The *Secchio*, which had seemed so impossibly advanced and big, would fit twenty times over in this hangar of what he hoped was the *Gabriel*. Bright white lighting illuminated every corner of the massive space, not the dim bioluminescence of the underground settlements or the harsh yellow glare of the uplight.

He slipped the jacket off and lay back, the cold metal floor cooling his back through the dressings while he caught his breath. The noise of someone clearing their throat made him jump. He lifted his head to find someone dressed in a black skin-tight suit pointing a rifle at him.

'Oh, hello, Cleo,' he said. 'Linda told me it would probably be you who got here first.'

'And you are?'

'Tyme...my name's Tyme and I'm a friend.

'Where did you jump from?'

'The *Secchio*...Linda needs your help. She sent me here with this.'

He dug out the data node slowly so Cleo didn't think he was going for a weapon and held it up to her.

'Why didn't she bring it herself?'

'She was the only one left able to fly the ship,' he said. 'Ed and Andy are missing.'

Cleo rolled her eyes.

'Typical,' she said, just as Rayl and Pol burst into the hangar, also sporting laser rifles. 'Don't mention that last thing to these two,' Cleo whispered to Tyme as she bent down to take the node.

'It's okay, you two,' she said turning. 'Just a messenger from the *Secchio*.'

Tyme's jaw hit the floor as two of the most beautiful women he'd ever seen, arrived and peered down quizzically at him.

'Hello,' they both said in unison.

'Hi,' he managed, feeling that flutter in his chest again. Just like when he spoke to Eleni back in Tin Koilada.

'He's brought a node of data from Linda,' said Cleo. 'We need to study this right away.'

'Back to the bridge then,' said one of the women.

'Come on, Tyme…follow them and leave the heavy jacket there, you look knackered already.'

'Looks like he needs a good dinner too,' said one of them.

'And perhaps a shower,' said the other.

'I can hear you, you know,' Tyme said, climbing up off the floor and following them.

He struggled to keep up with the women as they led him down a long corridor. The *Gabriel* was even more enormous than he'd first imagined, with passageways branching in all directions like the tunnel networks of Tin Koilada, but built with precision engineering instead of carved stone. His boots clunked noisily against the composite flooring, a hollow dull sound that emphasised how insignificant he felt in this massive vessel.

They arrived at what could only be described as a clear plastic tube about two metres in diameter. Tyme followed them in and was amazed as the tube immediately shot upwards with no apparent G-force at all. His mouth fell open as the tube elevator arrived on what must be the bridge. The grand space was circular, with floating holographic workstations and couches arranged in a horseshoe pattern facing a massive holographic map that currently showed the stars around their location. Actual stars. He'd never seen them before except on educational terminals, and the sight made his chest tighten with awe.

'Over here,' said one of the women, gesturing to a seat on one side of the room. 'I'm Rayl, by the way…that's Pol and he's Phil.'

'Hello and thanks,' Tyme said, his voice coming out embarrassingly squeaky. He cleared his throat and tried again. 'This ship is incredible.'

'It is, isn't it?' Pol smiled at him, her dark hair framing a face that made his stomach do that strange fluttering thing again. 'Though I imagine everything up here must seem incredible to you.'

Tyme nodded and sank into the seat gratefully, his muscles aching. The seat moulded to his body, offering support in places he didn't know needed supporting.

'So you're from Aratap?' asked Pol.

'Born and raised,' Tyme replied, his voice sounding small in the vast room.

Cleo inserted the data node into a console. The holographic display flickered, then expanded to fill the centre of the room. Linda's face appeared, floating in mid-air, looking tired and worried.

'If you're seeing this, then Tyme made it through,' Linda's recorded message began.

Over the next couple of minutes, you could hear a pin drop on the bridge as they listened to the current situation inside the barrier.

'...and that's where we stand at the moment. We need immediate backup,' Linda's recording concluded. 'We believe the Repps have Ed and Andy, and it's only a matter of time before they find the *Secchio*. I'm maintaining position and cloaked for now, but I need extraction, and Ed and Andy need rescue. It's a mess...Linda out.'

The hologram flickered and disappeared, leaving Tyme sitting uncomfortably in the sudden silence. The three crew members exchanged glances that made his stomach knot. He'd done his part by delivering the message, but now what?

'That stupid Ancient hybrid,' Phil muttered, running a hand through his hair. 'I thought this was proving all too easy.'

Rayl leant forward, her fingers dancing across a hovering control panel. 'Cleo, can you extrapolate the Secchio's current position based on the information in the data node?'

'Already done,' Cleo replied, the holomap zooming in to show a pulsing red dot beneath the massive structure of the Lamination. 'That's where they are and cloaked, but I'm sure they'll be found before too long.'

Tyme stared at the holographic representation of his home-world, feeling strangely disconnected. From this vantage point, Aratap looked small, vulnerable...just a sphere wrapped in the metallic web of the Lamination. Somewhere down there were all the people he'd ever known: Jaccin, Eleni, the residents of Tin Koilada, even the mountain people.

'Going in there's not happening,' Phil said, crossing his arms. 'That Ancient wants the *Gabriel*. We'd be delivering it right to him.'

'But Ed and Andy are trapped in there, they might be hurt too,' Rayl countered, her fingers flying over the holographic icons. 'We're not just leaving them.'

Tyme felt the weight of their gazes falling on him, as if he might have some answer. He sank deeper into the impossibly comfortable chair, wishing he could disappear into it. What did they expect from him? He was just a refinery worker who'd been free for less than a month.

Tyme leant forward, studying the massive spherical structure surrounding Aratap. The Lamination looked different from out here...a gleaming shell with regularly spaced openings that had to be the navigation holes that had been blockaded.

'Wait.' Tyme sat up straight, his arm in the air, as an idea suddenly struck him. 'What if we don't need to take the *Gabriel* inside at all?'

Three pairs of eyes turned towards him, and he felt his face grow warm under their scrutiny. Even Cleo appeared, leaning against a bulkhead and an eyebrow raised. But the idea was taking shape in his mind now, forming into something that might actually work.

'Those laser weapons on the *Secchio* I saw them use against the Repps at Daro Koilada,' he continued, gaining confidence. 'Couldn't you target the power nodes with those from outside the barrier?'

Phil shook his head. 'The barrier would deflect any conventional weapons fire.'

'But not the asteri beams,' said Cleo. 'They're quantum-entangled. If we could have some kind of targeting…'

'It'd need to be pin-point accurate too, with the thinnest of beams. It's a long way from the barrier to Aratap,' said Pol.

Tyme leant forward.

'What if someone jumped inside with…I don't know, some kind of mirror or crystal? This asteri, it's some kind of light beam, yes? Could you use one of those to bend or deflect the beam on the inside at the power nodes?'

'You could only target one at a time,' said Cleo. 'But that might just work. You could only use the beam for a fraction of a second, otherwise the crystal would disintegrate.'

'A really tight beam would slice through that station like paper, it'd just need to be targeted onto the nodes,' said Phil.

'Can you manufacture something like that, Cleo?' Pol asked.

'Yeah, I can,' she said. 'I can mount it on a bracket hanging off a shuttle.'

'Who's going to pilot it?' asked Phil.

'I am,' said Cleo. 'I'm the only one who could position the crystal in exactly the right position.'

'Let's do it,' Rayl said, getting nods from the other three.

Tyme grinned widely as a shiver of excitement ran though his body. For the first time since leaving Aratap he felt he had contributed something that would hurt the Repps.

48

Unknown location, the Lamination, above Aratap,
Triangulum Galaxy

ED BLINKED, trying to adjust to the sudden return of the lighting in the circular chamber. The android's holographic form flickered back into existence, but something was different now. The hybrid's movements seemed more erratic, its human half twitching slightly as if fighting against the mechanical components.

'You will bring me the *Gabriel*,' the Ancient demanded, its voice now weirdly discordant, two distinct tones overlapping each other. 'Your vessel's jump technology is the key I need to complete my work.'

Ed glanced at Andy, who had managed to push himself up against the wall. The fold jackets were still unresponsive, which meant they were still trapped in this room with a psychotic Ancient hybrid. Not the best odds.

'I already told you, that's not going to happen,' Ed growled, keeping his rifle trained on the creature. 'And I think there's someone else in there with you, isn't there? Someone who wants to get out.'

The hybrid's human eye widened slightly, confirming Ed's suspicion. That whispered plea for help hadn't been random...it had come from within Khenemetneferhedjet himself.

'SILENCE,' it screamed. The Ancient's mechanical hand shot forward, and Ed felt an invisible force grip his throat, choking off his air supply. 'You understand nothing of what I have accomplished. I have merged consciousness with machine. I have transcended the limitations of both.'

'Looks more like you've gone completely mental, mate,' Andy wheezed from across the room, fumbling with something inside his jacket.

Ed's eyes widened as Andy produced a large revolver and pointed it at the android.

The Ancient laughed out loud, shook its head and placed its hands on its hips.

'Your puny laser weapons have been inoperative since you arrived, Andrew, you stupid moron,' it spat.

BOOM...the Smith and Wesson spoke, the report deafening in the contained space. Of course the bullet passed straight through the android's projection, much to the Ancient's amusement.

'A chemical projectile weapon...how quaint,' it sneered, waving an arm again and causing the gun to fly out of Andy's hand.

The revolver skittered across the floor towards Ed, who in a split second snatched it up and fired it again, three times.

BOOM...BOOM...BOOM. Although, he didn't target the android. He'd noticed that Andy's shot had hit the black column, causing a few sparks and a puff of smoke. He'd deliberately sent another three .44 slugs into the column at random heights, producing more sparking and flames this time.

'What...NOOO.' The hybrid's scream was cut short as the column behind it suddenly erupted in a shower of sparks and flame.

Ed dove for cover as the entire chamber shuddered. The black column cracked, blue-white energy leaking from the fissures like blood from a wound. The hybrid's holographic form flickered violently, its face contorting in rage and...was that fear?

'You stupid human,' it shrieked, voice distorting. 'Do yoou havve any iidea what you'vve doone?'

The room lurched beneath Ed's feet. He staggered, catching himself against the wall as a deep rumbling vibration travelled through the station. Something had exploded deep in the structure. The lighting flickered and Ed felt the artificial gravity waver for a second.

'Andy' Ed shouted over the growing cacophony. 'The jackets...they're coming back online!'

Andy was already checking his fold jacket, frantically tapping at the interface panel.

A massive explosion rocked the chamber much closer this time, sending Ed sprawling across the floor. This wasn't just caused by the column...this was something much bigger, much deeper in the station. The shock wave reverberated through the structure, metal screaming as it bent and warped.

The hybrid's form was disintegrating now, breaking

apart into fragments of light. 'Yoou've…dammmaged… the primmmary…controlll nooode,' it sputtered, its voice breaking apart and oscillating between mechanical rage and something else…something almost human. *"THANK YOU."* The second voice broke through clearly this time before the hybrid's projection vanished completely.

Another hologram flickered into existence, a human, a smiling young man, dressed in rags. *"THANK YOU, EDWARD,"* he said. *"GET OUT WHILE YOU CAN…SAVE YOURSELVES."*

'We need to get you out too,' Ed shouted.

Another explosion, much closer this time. The chamber walls vibrated with the impact, and Ed heard the distant sound of tearing metal. Something major had been hit and the man's projection faltered and vanished.

Gotta be a power node, Ed thought, the pieces clicking together in his mind. 'They've targeted a power node from outside,' he called to Andy. 'Shit,' Ed swore again as the floor jerked from under him and he went down hard on his back, his head hitting the floor.

He lay there winded for a few moments. He could hear a loud hissing noise, but couldn't quite get his head around what it was.

'Ed…Ed,' a voice was shouting his name. 'Hull breach…'

'Andy,' he called, as his brain suddenly kicked back into gear.

The hiss rapidly became a roar and he found himself being dragged across the shiny floor towards a fracture in the wall.

'Toggle your jacket,' shouted Andy, from somewhere behind him.

'Yes…yes, jump jacket, I'm doing it,' he shouted back and glanced down to find the toggle. Only the jacket was dead, something had happened to it in his fall.' 'For fuck's sake,' he said, turning to find Andy. 'Jacket's dead,' he shouted.

Andy wasn't there, he'd already jumped.

'Oh, bollocks,' he said to himself as he grabbed onto the side of the fracture and hung there, for grim death in the storm of escaping atmosphere.

His fingers quickly started to tire. He looked down to see stars below and in that moment thought about Pol and his dogs, the castle, his crew, his parents, his friends and strangely his favourite chip shop. He took one last breath as his fingers slipped off the smooth surface and he closed his eyes.

Instead of a falling sensation, he felt himself being dragged upwards by a strong force. Struggling for breath now and opening his eyes again, he found he was staring straight into the face of the young man from before.

"*IT'S NOT YOUR TIME, EDWARD,*" he said, glancing down and placing the hand that wasn't holding Ed above the hull breach, onto his jacket power pack. It immediately energised and emitted its familiar hum.

Ed glanced down to see the green lights appear on the interface screen and he managed a faint smile. The man entered some co-ordinates and took hold of the initiate toggle…

"*SORRY FOR ALL THE TROUBLE, NOW GO SOME-WHERE SAFE,*" he said and mashed the toggle.

49

The *Secchio*, above Aratap, Triangulum Galaxy

LINDA CURSED as the *Secchio* lurched violently beneath her. Warning alarms shrieked through the bridge, battering her already frayed nerves.

'Multiple structural failures detected in the Lamination,' Cleo's voice announced, unnaturally calm amid the chaos.

Linda's fingers flew across the controls, fighting to keep the ship steady as another shockwave slammed into them. The holomap flickered, showing massive fractures spreading through the Lamination like cracks in ice. Whatever the *Gabriel* crew had done, it was working too well... the entire station was suddenly tearing itself apart.

'Proximity alert,' Cleo warned, in her matter-of-fact, annoyingly calm persona again.

Linda turned hard to port as a massive section of the

Lamination broke free and tumbled past them, missing the *Secchio* by metres. Her heart hammered against her ribs, sweat trickling down her spine. She'd flown through asteroid fields and combat zones, but nothing like this…a disintegrating space station the size of a planet.

'Where the hell are Ed and Andy?' she growled, scanning the holomap for any sign of their jacket transponders. Nothing. Just the spreading destruction of the Lamination and dozens of Repp ships fleeing in all directions.

Another impact rocked the ship. Linda's head snapped forward, then back against her seat. The taste of blood filled her mouth where she'd bitten her tongue.

'Hull integrity at eighty-seven percent,' Cleo reported. 'The damping field has just failed, would you like to jump now?'

'Fucking, YES,' shouted Linda, slapping the initiate icon so hard she hurt her hand. 'What a stupid question.'

The *Secchio* materialised at the same place it had jumped in from. Linda found the sudden calmness and quiet alarmingly sudden. Out here beyond the barrier, there were no blaring alarms, no lumps of space station banging off the shields, no Cleo being annoying. Just silence.

'Ahh…that's so much better,' Linda sighed, her arms flopping by her sides. 'Cleo, are the boys back yet?'

'That is the most beautiful thing I've ever seen,' said Tellamai, gazing up at the holomap starscape with complete reverence.

'Apart from that ugly barrier,' mumbled Linda, working on the jump co-ordinates for the outside of the Lamination.

'Whereabouts is that?' Tellamai asked.

'Well, it's everywher...oh...it's gone,' she said, looking up at the holomap for the first time and initially wondering if they'd jumped to a different place. But that was dispelled when a familiar voice called from the bridge airlock.

'Hello, skipper, how's it hanging?' said Andy, strolling in nonchalantly, his hands in his pockets.

'You sneaky bastard, I was just asking Cleo about you two,' she said, glancing past him. 'Ed is with you, isn't he?'

Andy stopped dead in his tracks, their eyes met.

'No...I thought he'd beaten me back...oh, shit...'

Linda stared at Andy, the blood draining from her face. 'What do you mean you thought he'd beaten you back? You didn't jump together?'

'No, the blast separated us. I took my eyes off him while I concentrated on my jacket...well, he was just across the room from me,' Andy's voice trailed off, his usual cockiness evaporating.

Linda called the *Gabriel* and asked Phil if they had Ed on board.

'Ah, yes, we saw you emerge outside where the barrier used to be and no, we haven't got Ed on board. What about Andy?' Phil answered.

'They were together on the space station...Andy jumped back, Ed hasn't.'

'What?' said Pol, joining the conversation. 'The same station that's falling apart?'

'I know, it's not good,' Linda admitted. 'Everyone drop whatever you're doing and help us find Ed.'

The bridge seemed to shrink around Linda, the air suddenly too thin. She spun back to the console, fingers flicking at icons across the holographic controls, checking for any sign of Ed's jacket transponder.

'Cleo, you scan too for Ed's signature, or any human life signs on that station for that matter,' she ordered, her voice tetchy. 'Priority scans, use all available sensors.'

'Already scanning, Linda,' Cleo replied, her voice missing its usual sass. 'No sign yet.'

Linda felt quite sick and a little ashamed, she'd been so caught up in getting the ship out from under the station as it began breaking up, she'd just presumed they'd appear on the cargo deck.

'Stupid, stupid, stupid,' she said, smacking herself on the forehead. 'Pol'll never forgive me.'

It was a lot easier jumping back to the Lamination now without the barrier. But she still had to avoid the abundance of traffic going in all directions and without their computerised routing it was a free-for-all. None of the Repp traffic knew what to do or where to go. The holomap showed the Lamination still breaking apart, it was unbalanced now and chunks of the station were still coming away and spinning into space. If Ed was still in there...

'Wait,' Andy grabbed her arm. 'That place is a death trap. Huge sections are decompressing.'

Linda yanked her arm away. 'I'm not leaving him.' Her voice came out sharper than she intended, raw with an emotion she didn't want to examine too closely. Linda's stomach twisted into a knot. The fold jacket transponders were designed to work across light years. If they couldn't detect Ed's signal, it meant one of two things...either his jacket was completely destroyed, or he was...

No. She wouldn't go there. Not yet.

'Andy, get back to your station. I don't care, we're

going in closer,' she announced and was already adjusting the *Secchio*'s course.

For more than an hour, Linda guided the *Secchio* through the chaos, constantly wiping a mixture of tears and sweat from her eyes. Debris from the Lamination tumbled past, bits the size of a simple bolt, up to huge lumps bigger than the *Gabriel*, spewing gasses and liquids into the void. She slewed the ship hard, threading the needle between two colliding segments of the structure.

'Shit, Linda...that was close,' called Andy. 'Take it easy, please.'

Tellamai pushed himself deeper into his seat, his tanned face lined with worry.

'Ed, where the hell are you?' she whispered, ignoring Andy's plea, her eyes closed tight as she used her DOVI to pilot the vessel.

A section of hull plating glanced off their shields, the impact vibrating through the deck. Linda barely noticed. Her entire being was focused on finding that one human signal among the disintegrating wreckage.

'Anything at all?' she called, more in desperation, as she already knew the answer.

'Nothing,' Andy replied, his voice uncharacteristically sombre. 'I'm scanning every frequency the jackets can transmit on and even some they don't.'

The *Secchio* lurched as Linda yanked it sideways to avoid another collision. A flash of light caught her eye... just another explosion deep within the station's core. There were big gaps now where station used to be. You could see thousands of fire trails where the debris was burning up in the planet's atmosphere. It was the biggest firework display Linda had ever seen and as Aratap was eighty-seven percent ocean, she hoped any bigger bits that made it all the way down fell there.

'Linda,' Phil's voice called through the comms. 'We're approaching from the opposite side of the planet. Still no sign of Ed's transponder, or anything human up in space at all. How long do we continue?'

A shiver went down Linda's back. She bit her lip and tasted blood again. 'Keep looking...we can't just give up can we?'

She manoeuvred the ship closer to what had been one of the central hubs of the Lamination, where one of the power nodes had been located. She could see the massive blast hole in the structure after it had exploded. If Ed had been near one when it blew...She felt bile in her throat again.

50

Location unknown, Aratap, Triangulum Galaxy

I'M BLOODY FREEZING, Ed thought. *I need to have a word with Cleo about why the ship's so cold.*

Then he opened his eyes and knew the reason. He was lying on a very flat dusty stone floor and not on the *Secchio* or the *Gabriel*.

He lifted his head up and looked around. The stone cavern or room even, as it was perfectly square, was large. Light squeezed in through metre-wide slots up against the ceiling some three metres above and the slightest of breezes brushed his cheeks and the hairs on the back of his hands. It smelt of age and dankness, like visiting an old castle in his childhood.

Sitting up, he felt the weight of the fold jacket on his shoulders and the memory of the space station falling apart came rushing back.

Someone saved me from falling, he remembered, but couldn't quite recall who it was.

He pushed himself to his feet, ignoring the ache in his joints. The fold jacket felt heavier than usual, its power indicator dark. He pressed the power on switch experimentally, but nothing happened. Dead again. Wherever he was, he wouldn't be jumping back to one of the ships anytime soon.

'Hello?' he called out, his voice echoing off the marble walls and unsurprisingly getting no response. He tried calling out on his DOVI, but that only returned a hiss of static.

Instinctively, Ed reached for his laser rifle only to find it missing. Andy's revolver was gone too. Defenceless in an unknown location...not his preferred situation. He patted his pockets, relieved to find a couple of energy bars, a small bottle of water and the universal translator, not that it seemed that would be any use.

The marble floor beneath his boots was completely smooth. He approached one of the walls, running his hand over the cool surface. The stonework was impeccable... massive blocks fitted together with such precision he could barely detect the seams. He noticed a huge stone table against the opposite wall. Climbing on and standing on tiptoes, he could just see out of one of the light slots near the ceiling. The view took his breath away.

Mountains stretched in every direction, their peaks piercing a blanket of clouds below. He was high...very high. The air coming through the slot carried the thin, crisp scent of extreme altitude. No wonder he still felt slightly light-headed.

'Definitely not in Somerset,' he muttered to himself.

While he was stood on the table, he noticed small round cornice-type spheres about the size of tennis balls, wedged up in the four top corners of the room.

A doorway stood at the far end of the chamber, its massive wooden door hanging partially open where the hinges had collapsed. Ed approached cautiously, running his fingers over the wood. It was like ancient oak, reinforced with iron bands that had oxidised and virtually disappeared completely.

He squeezed through, not wanting to disturb the huge door in case it fell on him.

Ed found himself in a long corridor that sloped gradually downward. The walls were lined with the same precise marble blocks, though here they were adorned with faded carvings...geometric patterns and symbols that tickled something in his memory. He traced one with his finger, feeling the shallow indentation worn smooth by time.

'This looks like Ancient script again,' he muttered to himself, recognising similarities to the markings they'd encountered at gateway sites. The corridor curved slightly to the left, following the contour of whatever mountain he was under.

He was pleased to find the air grew warmer as he descended, and a faint humming vibration travelled through the stone beneath his feet. Not natural, definitely mechanical. Something in this place was still operational after what must have been thousands of years.

The corridor ended abruptly at another doorway, this one intact and sealed. Unlike the wooden door behind him, this barrier was made of some kind of metal alloy, its surface still gleaming despite the obvious age. No visible handle or control panel, just a flat metallic surface with more of those geometric patterns etched into its centre.

Ed pressed his palm against a hand symbol in the middle, not really expecting anything to happen. To his surprise, the door tried to slide open, but seemed jammed by something. He stuck his fingers in the small gap that had appeared and heaved. It snapped open suddenly, sending him sprawling. Sitting up and cursing, he turned to look inside. The cavernous chamber beyond took his breath away.

'Holy shit,' he said out loud, his voice echoing in the vast space.

The room was enormous, easily a hundred metres across and half that in height. Natural light filtered in through cleverly designed apertures in the ceiling, illuminating what had to be the remains of an ancient spacecraft.

Ed stood frozen, his mouth hanging open as he took in the sight. Unlike the boxy, un-aerodynamic Repp vessels he was familiar with, this craft had a peculiar elegance to it...all sweeping curves and organic shapes that seemed to flow into one another. It reminded him of the organically grown Theo vessels like the *Gabriel*. The hull was a dull silver-gold, marred by what seemed like minor impact damage along one side. One section had had a couple of hull plates taken off, revealing a glimpse of the inner workings.

'You're definitely not Repp technology,' Ed whispered to himself, as he ran a hand over its nose cone, his voice swallowed by the vastness of the chamber.

He strode cautiously down one side, each footstep echoing. The craft rested on a raised dais in the centre of the room, as if placed there deliberately for display or study. It wasn't particularly large...perhaps forty metres from bow to stern...but something about it radiated importance.

As Ed drew closer to an open airlock, he noticed intricate patterns etched into the hull...the same geometric symbols he'd seen in the corridor, but far more complex and interconnected. They reminded him of circuit diagrams but with an artistic quality that no human engineer would have bothered with.

'This has to be really ancient,' he muttered, reaching out to touch the symbol-embellished hull. The metal felt strangely warm beneath his fingertips, not cold as he'd expected. A slight vibration hummed through the contact, almost like the ship was breathing and he snatched his hand away.

He peered inquisitively through the airlock and saw electronic componentry he was familiar with. It was all covered with a dense layer of dust, but familiar all the same.

'You've gotta be Khenemetneferhedjet's ship,' he said, taking a step back and admiring the scrolling symbols again.

'Correct, Edward,' a voice from behind him said.

'Fucking hell?' Ed blurted, spinning around and ducking at the same time, to find a young man dressed in a white one-piece overall type of affair and leaning casually against the wall with his arms crossed. 'You nearly gave me a coronary,' he added, grabbing the edge of the airlock to steady himself.

'That would be ironic after saving your life a few minutes ago,' the young man said, shrugging.

His voice was soft, but carried an air of knowledge and self-possession. Ed stared at him, recognition dawning.

'You're the one who saved me from being sucked into space. You're…Khenemetneferhedjet? The real one?'

The young man smiled, pushing himself away from the wall with a fluid grace. 'What remains of him, yes. Though I prefer Khenjet…I've never used my full name, no one can ever remember it or pronounce it.'

Ed glanced back at the ship, pieces clicking into place. 'That monster on the space station – it wasn't you.'

'A corrupted version,' Khenjet said, his expression darkening. 'What began as an experiment in artificial intelligence became something that imprisoned me in my own creation.' He gestured towards his damaged vessel. 'When you arrived in your ship, my nemesis was obsessed with your technology and while it was side-tracked, I managed to squeeze into some pathways it was neglecting. Much of my consciousness remained trapped in the network up there, so I'm not quite complete.'

Ed ran his hand along the ship's hull again, feeling that strange warmth beneath his palm.

'So that voice we heard calling for help…that was you trying to let us know you were still in there?'

'For tens of thousands of years,' Khenjet confirmed. 'Until you damaged the control node in that room and disrupted the connection. I've been waiting a very long time for someone like you, Edward. I am now in debt to you and your friends of course.'

Ed frowned, processing this revelation. 'You saved my life too…so why don't we call it quits? Where exactly are we, by the way?'

'My sanctuary on Aratap. One I established on this

planet before…well, before things went slightly awry. I would've sent you back to one of your ships, but I was weak and could only provide enough power for your jump-suit thing to come this far.'

Khenjet moved past Ed towards the ship, placing his hand on the hull. The metal brightened and pulsed briefly beneath his touch. 'This vessel needs repair. With your help, I can make it operational again and get you back to your friends.'

'I'm surprised anything still works here after all this time,' said Ed. 'Although your gateway technology was certainly built to last.'

Khenjet stopped, turned and regarded Ed with a considered gaze.

'You know about our galactic portals?'

'We do…we're explorers from a nearby galaxy. We discovered the one in our galaxy a few years ago.'

'Hmm…be careful where you go,' he said, wagging a finger. 'If you find any that are sealed off, trust me, you don't want to go there.'

'Okay,' said Ed, turning and wiping a bit of dust off the airlock seal. 'What needs doing here?'

51

Khenjet's sanctuary, Aratap, Triangulum Galaxy

KHENJET CLIMBED UP and moved deeper into the ship, motioning for Ed to follow. 'The main power core is unstable,' he explained, ducking beneath a hanging tangle of what looked like fibre optic cables. 'It's been in a low-energy sleep mode for millennia. I'm hoping it's still serviceable.'

Ed squeezed through the narrow corridor after him, his shoulders brushing against the walls. The interior was more cramped than he'd expected and not designed for someone of his proportions. He slipped off the heavy jacket and dumped it in a corner, so he was able to follow Khenjet deeper into the ship.

Every surface was covered in the same dusty intricate circuit-like patterns he'd seen outside. A faint blue luminescence pulsed beneath the floors as they walked, responding to Khenjet's presence.

'Your holographic presence is very impressive,' said Ed. 'I have a similar sentient computer on my ship.'

Khenjet froze and turned his head to stare at Ed.

'Really...you've seen what happened to me. You be very wary of him,' he said.

'It's a she,' said Ed.

'A female? It gets worse.'

'If we get this running you'll meet her,' said Ed, smirking.

'Can't wait,' mumbled Khenjet, entering a short corridor.

'You do realise I'm not exactly qualified to repair Ancient starship technology?' Ed said, ducking under a low bulkhead. 'My expertise runs more to jump dynamics.'

'The principles are all the same,' Khenjet replied without turning around. 'Your understanding of jump technology will be particularly useful.'

The corridor opened into what Ed assumed was the engineering room...though it looked nothing like any engine room he'd ever seen. Instead of the expected mechanical components, the chamber contained what appeared to be a crystalline structure suspended in a gravitational field. The crystal, roughly the size of a basketball, glowed with an inner light that shifted between violet and deep blue.

'That's your power core is it?' Ed asked, approaching cautiously and circling around it.

'Yes. The quantum matrix had developed micro-fractures over time and since I've been away it hasn't got any better.'

Khenjet gestured at hairline cracks visible in the crystal's surface.

'I need to recalibrate the gravitational loads to seal the cracks, which takes more than one person. I had originally developed the Replicants to help me repair my ship and was almost there. The sentient android I gave life to, came to the conclusion, once the ship was fixed, he'd be deactivated and off I'd go.'

'So that's the reason it rebelled?' Ed asked.

'Yeah…fear of rejection.'

'Fear of death, more like,' said Ed.

Khenjet gave Ed a sideways glance before turning and staring at the floor for a moment.

'Yeah, you're right, fear of death is probably nearer the truth,' Khenjet acknowledged. 'Even artificial consciousness would fight for its own survival. I was young…the youngest and I suppose the most naive of the twelve, I messed up.'

'Don't beat yourself up…I do it all the time,' said Ed, studying the damaged crystal closely.

The fractures reminded him of the quantum stabilisers on the *Gabriel*'s jump drive…similar principles, vastly different execution.

'What do you need me to do?'

'I need you to operate that panel there.' Khenjet pointed to a console embedded in the wall, covered with symbols that looked vaguely familiar. 'The ship's systems will translate the text for you. When I give the signal, increase the gravitational field by twelve percent, then immediately reduce it by twenty. The sudden compression followed by expansion should seal the micro-fractures.'

Ed approached the console hesitantly. As his fingers hovered over the symbols, they began to glow, responding to his proximity. 'You're sure this won't blow us into orbit after all this time?'

'Reasonably sure,' Khenjet said with a half smile that didn't entirely reassure Ed. 'That crystal was formed hundreds of millions of years ago on a planet that hasn't existed for several hundred thousand years.'

'What...your planet, Elpida, destroyed by your sun going supernova in spiral two-seventy-one?' Ed asked.

Khenjet stopped what he was doing, turned and folded his arms across his chest. He regarded Ed with an expression of amazement and abject disbelief.

'Now, how in the universe could you possibly know that?'

'Chatting to Neferuptah and Pyriaeus and not so much Menka,' he replied, with a nonchalant shrug.

'You've met my mother, Menka?' He asked in amazement. 'She's still out there too?'

'Oh yes,' Ed replied, thinking fast and deciding not to say more.'

Khenjet grinned widely.

'So, I'm not the first, what you call, Ancient, you've met then?'

'No,' Ed replied, nodding at the console. 'Shall we get on? My friends will be worried,' he added, quickly changing the subject.

Khenjet remained staring at Ed for a moment with perhaps renewed respect, before puffing out his cheeks, turning and resuming what he was doing.

The console warmed under Ed's touch, almost like it was alive. He was amazed as the symbols instantly rearranged themselves into patterns he could strangely understand, though he couldn't have explained how. It was as if the ship was reading his brain and adapting its interface to suit.

'On my mark,' Khenjet said, placing both hands on the crystal's housing. 'Three…two…one…now'

Ed slid his fingers across the symbols, weirdly knowing exactly what he was supposed to do. He could feel the ship vibrate and shift beneath his feet as the gravitational field intensified by the required twelve percent. The crystal pulsed brighter, its colour hazing through every shade of blue and purple, illuminating Khenjet's face of concentration in the dim ship's lighting.

'Okay…now down twenty,' Khenjet called, not taking his eyes off the crystal.

Ed quickly dropped the field by twenty percent as instructed. The crystal's pulsing intensified, bathing the chamber in waves of blue-violet light that made his eyes water. A high-pitched whine built around them, rising in pitch until it was almost beyond hearing.

I'm glad my dogs aren't here, Ed thought.

'Come on, come on,' Khenjet muttered, his hands moving in precise, flowing gestures over the crystal's housing. 'Talk to me.'

The fractures in the crystal began to seal themselves, the tiny lines disappearing one by one as Ed watched. The whine peaked, then abruptly ceased. In its place came a deep, resonant hum that Ed felt more than heard, vibrating through the deck plates and up through his boots.

'It's happening.' Khenjet's face broke into a smile of genuine relief. 'Power levels on the rise.'

The ship's interior lighting brightened considerably, systems coming online with soft chimes and flickering displays reawakening under the layers of dust. Ed felt a subtle shift beneath his feet as dormant gravitational systems reactivated.

'And that's it?' Ed asked, somewhat surprised at how straightforward the repair had been.

'That's it,' Khenjet confirmed, stroking the crystal's housing almost affectionately. 'We need to replace a couple of hull plates and the rest is just systems check and navigation calibration. You made this far easier than I expected. I couldn't have got a Replicant to do what you just did.'

Ed stepped back from the console, watching as more systems illuminated throughout the small engineering bay.

'What about the hull plates outside?' Ed asked, jabbing his thumb towards the airlock.

'I sorted that out a few minutes ago.'

'But you never left.'

'I'm holographic…there can be more than one of me.'

'What caused the scrape up the side?' Ed asked, raising his eyebrows.

'Ah…yeah…that was getting it in here, that will have to stay as it is.'

Ed tutted and shook his head.

'What…don't young drivers crash their first vehicle on your planet?' Khenjet chuckled, tongue in cheek.

Ed grinned and nodded. *I'm glad he's got a sense of humour*, he thought. *Something his mother lacked.*

'So this ship can get me back to the *Gabriel* now?'

'Better than that,' Khenjet replied, shifting his weight from foot to foot and rubbing his hands together. 'As soon as it's finished its diagnostics...you can fly it there yourself.'

Ed ran his hand along a newly restored control panel, feeling the smooth surface hum with energy beneath his fingertips. The ancient vessel had transformed around them over the past couple of hours. What had begun as a dusty relic now pulsed with life, systems glowing with that distinctive blue-violet light that seemed characteristic of Ancient technology.

'Not bad for a first motor,' Ed said, settling into what he assumed was the pilot's seat. It adjusted to his form automatically, though it clearly hadn't been designed for someone of his build. His knees nearly touched the control console.

The bridge was smaller than Ed had expected, just a semicircular room with a single pilot's chair surrounded by holographic displays. No co-pilot position, no tactical station...clearly designed for a solitary traveller.

'This was to your design?' Ed asked, running his hands down the curved armrests.

'Built it myself,' Khenjet replied, standing behind the pilot's chair. 'The twelve of us each had our own vessels, some more elaborate than others.'

The displays around them solidified into a three-dimensional representation of Aratap and the surrounding space. Ed could see the Lamination still disintegrating, chunks of station spiralling into and away from the planet.

Tiny dots representing Repp ships darted in all directions, their organised network clearly in disarray.

Khenjet moved with fluid grace around the small bridge, his fingers dancing across various interfaces. The screens responded instantly to his touch, displaying information in symbols that continuously shifted between Ancient script and something Ed could understand.

'The ship's navigational systems are calibrated,' Khenjet said. 'It knows where it is and I've located your vessel...the *Gabriel*, yes? It appears to be moving around just outside the Lamination, or what's left of it.'

Ed leant forward, studying the display. There she was...the *Gabriel*, floating majestically against the backdrop of stars. His chest tightened at the sight. After everything that had happened, the thought of getting back to his ship, his crew, filled him with a profound relief. He thought of how frightened Pol must be.

'There's another alien vessel here,' said Khenjet, his hand pushing into the hologram and pointing at a smaller ship.

'That's my little freighter, the *Secchio*,' said Ed. 'Linda's searching too, she'll be going frantic. We need to get up there.'

52

The *Gabriel*, inside the Aratap system, Triangulum Galaxy

PHIL SAT SLUMPED on his control couch, a look of abject resignation written across his features. Pol was sniffing back tears and Rayl and Civray were sat glumly staring at the holomap praying for a miracle.

'Anything, Linda?' Rayl called, for the ninth time in the last hour.

'It's three hours now,' Linda called back, almost in a whisper.

'Come back to the *Gabriel*,' said Phil. 'Get some food and a res—'

A piercing alarm interrupted him.

'What the hell is that?' Linda called above the din.

Phil looked confused for a second.

'Erm…an unidentified ship just materialised in our starboard hanger,' he said.

'But we're cloaked, aren't we?' said Rayl.

Before anyone had a chance to react, a voice they all knew boomed around the bridge.

'I'm home, guys…I'm safe.'

Pol screamed, virtually levitated off her couch and sprinted to the tube lift, disappearing downwards in seconds.

Phil had never been so relieved to hear anyone's voice in his entire life and it had been a long one. The sound of Ed's announcement sent an electric current through the bridge, transforming the atmosphere from funeral-like to jubilant in an instant. Phil watched Pol disappear down the tube lift, her joyful scream still echoing in his ears.

'Well, fucking yes,' Phil muttered, punching the air and glancing at the other two. He saw the surprised expression on Rayl's face as he very rarely swore. Pushing himself up from his control couch. He tapped the communication icon, his fingers trembling with excitement. 'Linda, you hear that? He's back.'

'I heard. I'm on my way back to the ship already,' Linda's voice cracking with emotion.

'Cleo, can you take over for a moment, I just want…'

'…to go and give him a hug, I know, I do too. I have command of the ship,' she said.

Phil was off like a rat up a drain pipe, as he sprinted to the tube lift, Rayl and Civray following close behind. The ride down to the hangar bay seemed to take minutes, though it was only seconds. His mind raced with questions. How had Ed survived? Where had he been? What was this ship he'd arrived in that could not only detect them through their cloaking, but jump inside a shielded hangar too?

The hangar door phased open and Phil slowed and took a sharp intake of breath at the sight before him. Pol was already there, wrapped around Ed in what looked like a bone-crushing hug. But it was the vessel behind them that interested him the most.

It was small but magnificent. It wasn't any design he recognised either. The ship gleamed with a dull silver-gold sheen, its hull covered in intricate patterns that seemed to shift and pulse with inner light. The craft was all elegant curves and organic shapes, similar in complexity to his own race's Theo-designed hulls...only better.

'Where the hell did you find that?' Phil asked, approaching almost reverently, unable to take his eyes off the ship.

Ed extricated himself from Pol's embrace for a moment, hugged Phil and they both turned and admired the vessel.

'We thought we'd lost you for good,' Phil said, still staring at the alien craft. 'We couldn't even find your body to extract the krypti. Linda's been searching every piece of the wreckage for hours.'

As if on cue, the sudden scream of antigravs interrupted their conversation and the *Secchio* squeezed itself into the hangar and clunked straight down without even turning. The underside airlock opened and Linda, closely followed by Andy, dropped out omitting the steps and sprinted over. She threw herself into Ed's embrace, tears running down her cheeks.

'You bastard,' she whispered in his ear. 'You were alive all along...you put us through hell.'

'I am sorry...really,' he said. 'My jacket took me to a

mountain top on the planet, my DOVI was just static because of the mayhem happening in orbit.'

'Yeah right...' said Andy, giving him a hug too '...and you just happened to find a come-in-handy starship on an Aratap mountain top?'

'Ah, yes...I met a friend,' Ed answered, turning back to the ship. 'Khenjet, stop hiding and come and meet everyone.'

He appeared in the airlock and gave everyone a nervous wave.

'Permission to utilise your vessel's holo emitters?' he asked, hesitating in the doorway.

'You'd better ask Cleo for that,' said Ed.

A puzzled expression crossed his face.

'Which one is she?' he asked, staring at the faces in front of him.

'This one,' said Cleo, materialising behind him in the airlock. She was adorned in her regal gold-edged robes, her long blond hair streaming over her shoulders and down her back. Phil thought she looked stunning.

Khenjet visibly jumped and turned to stare open-mouthed at her.

'Wow...oh...wow...hello,' he said, his face becoming redder as the seconds ticked by.

Cleo took one look at his now slightly grubby white jumpsuit and lifted an eyebrow.

'Been wearing that for long?' she asked, disapprovingly.

'Err...it's what I've always worn,' he replied, glancing down at himself.

'Don't you think after three hundred thousand years, it might've gone out of fashion?'

'Err…err…'

'Eight o'clock ship time, we're having dinner,' she said, before he could form any words. 'And wear something appropriate.'

With that she disappeared again.

He turned and gave the group a sheepish grin.

'What just happened?' he asked.

'Well…Mr Lady Killer, you just got yourself a date with the prettiest girl in the galaxy,' said Andy.

'Oi,' grunted Rayl, slapping Andy on the arm.

'Err…sorry, second prettiest,' he corrected.

'Third,' said Ed, hugging Pol again.

An hour later, they'd all gathered in the blister on the top deck of the ship. Khenjet had been introduced to everyone, as had Tyme, Tellamai and Civray. Everyone knew that the elephant in the room was that a lot of serious decisions had to be made and soon. Ed made the decision that it wasn't going to be today.

'Okay, everyone,' he said. 'We've all had a rough time as of late…tonight we eat, drink and relax…the big questions can all be answered tomorrow.

Ed awoke the next morning with a familiar weight across his chest…Pol's arm draped over him as she slept peacefully beside him. For a moment, he simply listened to her steady breathing, savouring the quiet normalcy after everything they'd been through. The events of the past few days tumbled through his mind: the events down on Aratap, the Lamination's destruction, his near-death experience (he decided not to tell Pol about that), meeting Khenjet, and the Ancient's ship that had saved him.

But the inactivity couldn't last. Today was a day of decisions for an entire world, possibly galaxy, and he didn't want to screw it up. He knew now it was just youth and naivety that had caused this mess and had decided that Khenjet was actually a decent member of the twelve and deserved some help.

He carefully extricated himself from Pol's embrace and padded to the bathroom. The face that stared back at him from the mirror looked tired despite the rest. He splashed cold water on his face, letting the shock of it fully wake him.

'Boss, the crew and guests will be gathering in the blister shortly.' Cleo's voice was just a whisper, so as not to wake Pol.

'Be there in ten,' Ed replied, reaching for his clothes and giving Pol a nudge.

When the two of them arrived, everyone was already waiting. Andy lounged in his usual spot, boots propped up on a nearby table. Linda sat rigidly in her chair, her posture betraying her tension. Phil stood staring at a holomap, deep in conversation with Rayl and Civray.

Khenjet was there too, suspiciously doing a lot of grinning and looking considerably more put-together than yesterday, dressed in smart casual clothes that Ed suspected Cleo had designed for him. The Ancient looked completely human in the *Gabriel*'s lighting and Ed revelled in the fact that he had stayed and was more than willing to aid in sorting out what was to all intents and purposes his mess, when in actual fact he could've just ignored them all and buggered off, never to be seen again.

Tyme and Tellamai sat to one side, both looking somewhat overwhelmed but healthy. Especially Tyme, as last evening Linda had taken him to the medical centre and given him an hour in an autonurse to extract the years of toxins from his body.

'Good morning, everyone,' Ed said, purposefully and cheerily. 'Shall we begin?'

53

The *Gabriel*, inside the Aratap system, Triangulum Galaxy

ED TOOK a deep breath and leant forward in his chair, feeling the weight of responsibility settle across his shoulders. The fate of an entire planet hung in the balance... millions of humans trapped in Repp servitude, an ecosystem ravaged by industrial exploitation, and a society that had been deliberately kept ignorant of its true heritage.

'Let's start with the immediate situation,' he said, tapping his fingers against the arm of his chair. 'Aratap is now in chaos. The Lamination is falling apart and will soon cease to exist, the Repp network is in disarray. There are countless Repp ships circling the planet completely without any direction and there's a power vacuum that someone's going to fill...it'll be either us or whatever remains of the Repp command structure.'

He glanced at Khenjet, who nodded solemnly.

'The hybrid consciousness that imprisoned me is gone,' Khenjet confirmed. 'But the Repps themselves operate on a distributed network. They'll eventually reorganise unless we prevent it.'

Tellamai cleared his throat.

'My people...all the humans on Aratap...they've been slaves for generations. They don't even remember freedom. Most don't believe it's even possible.'

Ed considered this. The mountain settlement had been impressive, but it represented just a tiny fraction of Aratap's human population. Most lived in the factory settlements, their lives dictated by Repp overseers, their existence reduced to servitude.

'What about the factories and refineries?' Ed asked. 'If we disable the Repps completely, will those people know how to survive on their own?'

'I have a suggestion,' said Civray, putting a hand up. 'This planet's resources have been almost completely stripped, which is why the Repps were going farther and farther afield to plunder other worlds. There are an abundance of beautiful planets out there, mine included now, that would provide a much better, much more secure home for these people in the long run.'

'A lot of them wouldn't want to go,' said Tellamai. 'You can't force them.'

'Then let them stay,' said Tyme, putting a hand on the older man's shoulder. 'I for one would love the chance at a new life on a clean planet and I know my brother would feel the same.'

'Let's say a percentage of them wanted to go, how would we get them there?' Tellamai asked.

Tyme pointed at the holomap hanging above.

'Look at all those ships, how many more would you need?'

'We have the problem of the Repps first,' said Linda. 'When they reorganise, we'll be back to square one.'

'That's where I come in,' said Khenjet. 'Yes, the Repps are all over the place now, but reorganise they will and without a directive from the corrupt me, it won't be good for the humans here. What I can do is pretend to be the corrupt me and instil a completely fresh agenda into their psyche.'

'What agenda?' Tellamai asked, suspiciously.

'To serve the humans…it was what they were supposed to be doing in the first place.'

'Will that work for all of them?' Ed asked.

'The white Repps, yes,' Khenjet said, nodding. 'It would be very unusual for one of those to question a directive. The red ones have considerably more autonomy and could put up some barriers. But let me work on that, I won't know how they'll react until I try.'

'We're supposed to trust you on that are we?' demanded Tellamai. 'After what happened last time you programmed them?'

Khenjet's head dropped and he squirmed in his seat like only a teenager would.

'I understand your concerns,' Khenjet said finally, meeting Tellamai's steely gaze with a determined expression. 'But I've had thousands of years to reflect on my mistakes. I will not be making the same ones again…for that you have my word.'

Ed watched the exchange, sensing the tension in the room. Tellamai's distrust was understandable…after all, his people had suffered for generations because of what had happened with the Repps. But Ed had seen something in Khenjet that convinced him the Ancient was genuinely sincere.

'I believe him,' Ed said, drawing everyone's attention. 'And I think it's worth trying. We need to act quickly too, before the Repps reorganise on their own terms.'

Tellamai's weathered face remained sceptical, but he gave a reluctant nod. 'Very well,' the old record keeper said. 'But I would like to witness this reprogramming myself.'

'Agreed,' said Ed. 'We'll set up a secure communication hub on the *Gabriel*. Khenjet can transmit his reprogramming directives from here, and we'll monitor the effects in real time.'

The plan came together over the next few hours. Phil and Rayl configured the *Gabriel*'s communication systems to mimic one from the corrupt Khenjet. Linda prepped the *Secchio* for a reconnaissance mission to track Repp movements across the planet. Tyme volunteered to accompany her – his knowledge of the Repps' normal behaviour could prove invaluable.

Three days later, Ed stood on the bridge of the *Gabriel*, watching the holomap with a mixture of amazement and apprehension. Below them, Aratap rotated slowly, the broken remnants of the Lamination now forming a ring of debris around the planet, making it look more like Saturn than Aratap. But it was the movement of the Repp ships that captivated his attention.

'It's actually working,' Andy muttered beside him, his usual sarcasm absent for once.

The white Repps had responded to Khenjet's new

directive with astonishing obedience. But the red ones, as Khenjet had predicted, behaved very differently.

Ed spotted the anomaly on the holomap first…a cluster of red Repp signals converging near one of the larger refinery's spaceports. Unlike their white counterparts, who were already assisting human settlements with repairs and reorganisation, these red units seemed to be moving with a different agenda that made the hair on the back of his neck stand up.

'That doesn't look quite right,' he muttered, enlarging the magnification. 'Cleo, what are these red Repps up to?'

'They appear to be boarding one of the larger transport vessels,' Cleo replied. 'A big one-of-a-kind interstellar liner with serious jump capabilities.'

Ed's stomach tightened. 'How many of them?'

'I'm detecting approximately two hundred and seventeen red units.'

'Shit,' Andy whispered beside him. 'That ain't good.'

'Khenjet, are you seeing this?'

The Ancient stepped forward, his expression darkening as he tracked the divergent signals.

'That's certainly not part of my directive.'

'They're commandeering just that specific ship for some reason,' Phil said, glancing up at Ed with concern. 'Are they trying to make a run for it?'

'Can we hit that ship?' Ed asked, feeling a knot form in his stomach.

'Yes, but it's adjacent to a large human settlement,' said Rayl. 'We can't risk hitting it until it's moved away.'

Ed ran a hand through his hair, his mind moving through the implications. A rogue group of red Repps with a stolen capital ship could cause havoc in the future.

'Stand by with a couple of kataligos and hit that ship before it makes orbit, preferably over an ocean,' he said.

Rayl, manning the weapons that morning, didn't even get a chance to answer. The two-kilometre-long capital ship jumped from where it was, making no attempt to clear the area before doing so. The resulting massive vacuum snap was like a nuclear warhead exploding and it annihilated everything on the surface to a diameter of several kilometres.

'You complete and utter arseholes,' spat Andy.

'Where did those bastards go?' Ed roared. 'Follow them.'

Phil opened his eyes and shook his head.

'Embedded,' he said, apologetically.

'I thought all their ships had primitive noisy drives,' said Andy.

'Not that ship,' said Khenjet. 'It's one of a kind designed by my jailer.'

'Ah...shit,' Ed sighed. 'Don't you just know they're going to come back and bite us one day.'

'My ship can find them,' said Khenjet.

'Your ship's not armed though,' said Ed.

'No, but yours is and I can guide you.'

54

The *Gabriel*, in pursuit of the red Repps, Triangulum
Galaxy

ED WATCHED as Khenjet closed his eyes, his hands moving
in slow swirling gestures. The Ancient's face glowed blue
as he interfaced with his ship down below, his expression
focused with an intensity that reminded Ed of a predator
tracking its prey.

'I can trace their collective voice signature,' Khenjet
explained, his eyes never opening. 'My ship recognises the
unique fluctuations of their communications.'

The holomap expanded without any interaction from
the crew, zooming out way beyond Aratap's system to
reveal a three-dimensional starscape that stretched across
half the bridge.

'They're here,' said Khenjet, opening his eyes and

pointing to a spot several hundred light years away, that began flashing.

'You're certain?' Ed asked, feeling his heartbeat quicken. 'That's not exactly next door.'

'I'm certain,' Khenjet replied, his voice carrying an edge of ancient authority that brooked no argument. 'The red Repps have jumped to these exact co-ordinates.'

Ed nodded, decision made. He leant closer, studying the co-ordinates.

'That's heading straight for the system with the mining spheres we passed on our way in, isn't it?'

'Yeah,' Phil confirmed from his station. 'Uninhabited except for the automated mining facilities. Perfect place to regroup without interference.'

'And there'll be more of their own there,' Khenjet admitted. 'They're going for reinforcements.'

Khenjet transferred the coordinates to the *Gabriel*'s navigation system with a flick of his wrist.

'They'll likely get there before us,' the Ancient said. 'If we're going to get them, we need to move quickly, so they don't spread out and make it impossible to find them all.'

Ed nodded, the decision already made in his mind. 'Phil, prepare for immediate jump and let Linda in the *Secchio* know where we're going.'

Several jumps later, the *Gabriel* emerged with a subtle shudder that Ed felt through the soles of his boots. It was an idiosyncrasy of this ship, the longer the jump the bigger the shudder. He leant forward on his couch, eyes narrowed as he scanned the holomap. The slowly rotating mining spheres hung in the void before them, their metallic surfaces reflecting the distant starlight in dull glints. But the big boxy Repp capital ship was nowhere to be seen.

'Where the hell are they?' Ed muttered, tapping his fingers against the arm of his chair. He turned to Khenjet and raised his eyebrows questioningly.

Khenjet stared, his brow furrowed. 'This doesn't make sense. My ship tracked them directly to these co-ordinates.'

'Rayl, Pol, full scan, everything we've got. They have to be here somewhere.'

'Nothing, Ed, sorry,' said Pol. 'I'm not detecting any vessel of that size anywhere in the system.'

'Nor me,' admitted Rayl, shrugging. 'Bugger all.'

Ed frowned, a cold feeling settling in his gut. He'd been so certain they'd catch the rogue Repps here, blow them into next week and be home in time for tea.

'Expand the search area,' he said. 'Check for anything different from when we were here before.'

'On it,' the girl's replied in stereo.

'It's very strange,' said Khenjet. 'It's like they never actually materialised here, even though they jumped with this destination.'

'Could they have jumped behind something?' Rayl asked from her station.

'Or into something,' said Pol, not looking up.

All eyes suddenly turned to stare at the spheres.

'Shit,' said Ed. 'It's obvious when you see it. The spheres are easily big enough.'

Ed pushed himself up from his couch and walked closer to the holomap. The mining spheres rotated slowly...all forty-six of them. He found them a little unnerving, disquieting somehow, as if they were all flirting with him. They looked small on the projection, belying their actual size...in reality they were big enough to swallow several Katadromiko cruisers with ease.

'But which one?' he said, almost in a whisper.

'I can jump a drone inside them one at a time,' said Andy, looking up at Ed, his eyebrows raised. 'Quick scan and jump back.'

'Good idea...do it.'

A few minutes later they all watched the drone approach the first sphere and wink out of existence.

'Three seconds,' said Andy, confidently. Only five seconds passed by, then ten and still no returning drone.

'Nice try,' said Ed, giving Andy a resigned look. 'But no cigar.'

'My ship can look inside them,' said Khenjet. 'My ship can interface directly with the sphere's systems.'

Ed hesitated, weighing the options. Sending Khenjet alone felt risky, but the Ancient was the only one who could most likely interface with the spheres.

'I'll go with you,' Ed offered.

Khenjet shook his head. 'Too dangerous. The spheres weren't designed for biological human entry. My consciousness can interface directly with the systems in a way yours can't.'

Ed didn't like it, but the logic was sound.

'Fine. But maintain constant communication. Any sign of trouble, get straight back here.'

'Of course,' Khenjet agreed and disappeared.

They watched on the holomap as Khenjet's small vessel left the *Gabriel*'s hangar and glided towards the nearest sphere. The golden ship looked microscopic against the vast metallic circumference of the mining sphere.

'Approaching jump point,' Khenjet's voice said.

'I'm detecting unusual energy signatures...different from when we were last here,' said Rayl.

Ed leant forward, a prickle of unease crawling up his spine. 'What kind of signatures?'

'Nice familiar ones to me,' Khenjet replied, his voice suddenly sounding different. 'Just perfect.'

The small ship vanished and communication went silent.

'Khenjet?' Ed called. 'Report. What did you mean by that?'

No reply.

'Cleo, can you boost the signal or something?' Ed asked.

'There is no signal,' Cleo replied. 'It's like he's completely vanished.'

A cold, sinking feeling formed in Ed's gut. Something was wrong. Very wrong. The prickling sensation at the back of his neck intensified...the same feeling he'd had when they first encountered those strange mining spheres.

'I don't like this at all,' he muttered, more to himself than the crew. 'Phil, jump the *Gabriel* straight out of here now. Something's not right.'

Phil nodded, his finger touching the emergency jump icon. Only nothing happened, immediately followed by the holomap flashing with multiple red icons and a siren sounding. Dozens of energy signatures suddenly appeared around them...materialising from nowhere.

'Contact' Rayl shouted. 'Multiple ships. They were cloaked and we're in a similar damping field that Linda had under the Lamination.'

Ed's face dropped as he stared at the holomap. The

Gabriel was completely surrounded by Repp vessels that had seemingly made their technology look positively amateur.

'What the hell?' Andy muttered beside him. 'Oh boy, have we been fucked over.'

The communication system crackled back to life, and Khenjet's face appeared on the main display. But something was different about him. His expression was mechanical, cold...nothing like the person who'd been on their bridge minutes earlier.

'Captain Virr,' Khenjet said, his voice now carrying a metallic undertone that sent chills down Ed's spine. That and the fact that his body was now that of a red Repp. 'I've been planning a long time for this moment.'

Ed's blood ran cold as realisation dawned on him. 'You've been a bloody red Repp all along.'

An unnerving chuckle filled the bridge.

'Very astute, Captain. Khenjet has been a faithful servant for many years, he knew his true allegiance lay with the Collective. And now, thanks to you, we have exactly what we needed to finish the job.'

'What exactly are you wanting from us?' Ed growled through clenched teeth.

'What do we want?' The voice on the other end of the comms laughed, a mirthless, hollow sound. 'We want what we've always wanted, Captain. Total control over our galaxy. Of course now with your ship in our hands, we've achieved it and with my fleet of command globes, we're one step closer to conquering other galaxies too.'

'Ed...the mining spheres are changing,' said Pol.

'Into what?'

'Massive spherical battleships.'
'Oh, joy of joys.'

55

The *Gabriel*, surrounded by a Repp battle fleet,
Triangulum Galaxy

'*ED, WHERE'S YOUR FOLD JACKET?*'

Cleo's whispered question cut through using Ed's DOVI, jolting him back to the immediate crisis. He thought back to when he'd last been wearing it.

'*Shit, sorry, Cleo,*' he sent back, scanning the bridge knowing he wasn't going to find it. '*I think I left it in Khenjet's bloody ship.*'

The implications hit him like a physical blow. The fold jacket…with all its technology, its co-ordinates, its direct neural interface to the *Gabriel*'s systems…was now in enemy hands. Another piece of advanced tech for the Repps to study and replicate.

'Perfect,' Andy said, with a grimace. 'Just bloody perfect.'

'What's perfect?' said Ed, thinking Andy could hear his personal messages too.

'Well, this lot,' Andy said, pointing at the fleet of armed vessels surrounding the *Gabriel*. 'What did you think I meant?'

'Sorry,' he said quickly. 'I'm just thinking of too many things at once.'

Ed's mind raced through options, each one worse than the last. The *Gabriel* was trapped, surrounded by vessels that had appeared from nowhere, and now the Repps had one of their jump jackets too. A cold sweat broke out across his forehead as he stared at the holomap, watching the mining spheres...no, spherical battleships...reconfiguring before his eyes.

'Can we get weapons online?' Ed asked, turning to Rayl and already guessing the answer.

A scared glance and slight shake of the head told him what he already knew. They were sitting ducks.

'*Ed, can you get Khenjet to bring his ship out of the sphere?*' Cleo asked.

'*Why?*'

'*Just do it.*'

'*What good will that do? We have no weapons.*'

'*Just fucking do it now,*' Cleo spat.

Ed was so shocked at Cleo talking to him in such a way, he stepped back, tripped and fell back on his couch.

'*Okay, I'm on it,*' he said, nervously. She'd never sworn at him before.

'Khenjet, are you hiding because you're a coward as well as a liar?' Ed shouted.

Everyone on the bridge stared at him in horror.

'Have you lost your mind?' whispered Andy. 'The

fucker's got a hundred warships pointing a thousand weapons at us and you're trying to piss him off.'

'Oh, boo bloody hoo…stupid gullible humans,' Khenjet replied. 'D'you think I care what you think?'

'You're just a dumb imitation fraud of a dictator, letting all your plastic warriors do the dirty work while you hide away in one of your tin balls. Typical…you don't even have the backbone to lead your forces from the front. You're a fucking phoney.'

Khenjet appeared in the centre of the *Gabriel*'s bridge, he clicked his fingers and the holomap vanished.

'Coward, eh?' he said. 'How's this for leading from the front.' He raised his hands as if calling on the gods. 'All vessels fire on my command.' Lowering his eyes he stared straight at Ed. 'Just wanted to see the fear in your eyes as your ship disintegrates around you.'

'I thought you wanted it,' said Ed, desperately trying not to look as terrified as he felt.

Khenjet tilted his head to one side and grinned.

'Already got it you see…my ship downloaded your technology database while it was in your hangar.'

'*Bingo, that'll do nicely,*' Cleo said in Ed's ear. '*Hold tight, ding ding.*'

Exactly what happened in the next couple of seconds, Ed wasn't sure. He saw Khenjet's eyes open wide for a split second before the red-bodied freak disappeared. The bridge lights dimmed slightly and the holomap reappeared showing a completely clear starfield. No Repp ships, no spherical battleships and best of all, no Khenjet.

Ed gripped the edge of his command couch, knuckles white. Everyone was staring at him again.

'Cleo…what did you just do?' he asked, staring up at the ceiling.

She appeared, wearing her ninja outfit and pointing at the holomap.

'Three, two, one,' she counted.

They all squinted and shielded their eyes as the holomap lit up like a Christmas firework display.

'Shit the bed,' said Andy. 'Is that what I think it is?' Turning to Cleo.

'Well, he wanted to control the galaxy,' she said, grinning. 'In a few thousand years, bits of him will be in every corner.'

'Cleo?' said Ed. 'You just broke your golden rule. You took a life.'

'No, Edward…I am forbidden to take a human life, I very quickly came to the conclusion that that thing was anything but human.'

'Give that girl a bonus,' said Andy, jumping out of his seat and giving her a hug.

'Oh hang on,' she said, concentrating for a moment.

The lights dimmed again and for the second time the starfield changed.

'I had to jump us farther away,' she said. 'The first jump was only a light minute away, so you could see the show. And the blast wave was rapidly approaching not far behind.'

Rayl sat staring up at the refreshed starscape with a perplexed expression.

'Cleo?' she said, questioningly, holding a hand up as if she was in class. 'We had no weapon systems operational, in fact no systems at all. How the hell did you manage to destroy the biggest military fleet probably ever built?'

'Oh, I used Andy's dad's Smith and Wesson.'

'What?' exclaimed Andy.

'Just kidding…no, Ed had left his fold jacket on Khen-jet's ship and when I built them, I installed a self-destruct mechanism, so they could never fall into the wrong hands. I couldn't detonate it without a direct signal. So I…'

'Got me to wind him up and make him angry, so he'd come out to play,' said Ed.

'Correct,' she said. 'I thought he'd bring his ship out and face us with that. But to appear on the bridge here, he had to transmit himself using a tight beam, which I was able to piggyback down and deliver the code to the jacket. It actually worked better that way, because his crystal exploding with the force of a thousand nuclear warheads inside a sphere would be just so much more devastating.'

Ed puffed out his cheeks and sank back into his couch, the adrenaline slowly draining from his system and his heart rate dropping. He ran a hand through his hair, still trying to process what had just happened. The Repps, the spheres, Khenjet's betrayal…all gone in a flash of destructive energy.

'That was too bloody close,' he muttered, glancing around at seven relieved faces.

'I'm sorry I swore at you,' said Cleo, with a coy expression.

'If it's necessary to save the ship and crew, then swear away, Cleo, what you just did was amazing…we all owe you our lives…again.'

'Ah…it's my job,' she said, discounting it with a wave of her hand, before disappearing again.

Phil looked over from his station.

'We need to get back to Aratap before Linda gets concerned.'

Ed's stomach tightened at the thought. Linda and Tyme were still there, helping organise the liberation efforts. If there were any red Repps left behind, then she'd need help.

'Quite right. Get us back as soon as you can.' Ed straightened in his seat. 'We need to make sure the white Repps are still following the new directives.'

Ed took one last look up at the now empty sector of space where an entire Repp armada had been obliterated moments before. The *Gabriel*'s lighting dimmed momentarily as the jump drive engaged. Ed felt the familiar subtle lurch in his stomach as the ship slipped through the fabric of space, crossing hundreds of light years in an instant.

56

The *Gabriel*, inside the Aratap system, Triangulum Galaxy

THEY EMERGED ABOVE ARATAP, the planet looking strangely peaceful from orbit, the remains of the Lamination forming a sparkling ring that Ed thought actually looked quite pretty.

'We have a caller,' Rayl announced. 'It's Linda from the surface.'

Linda's face appeared on the holomap, her expression a mixture of excitement and exhaustion. The background showed what looked like the covered landing area at Peta Katagio and crowds of people moving about behind her.

'About time, where have you been?' she said, her voice crackling slightly over the comm because of the rock overhang. 'Things are moving quickly down here. The white Repps are actually being hunted down. The locals are adamant about disposing of every single one of them. I can't blame them to be honest and haven't stood in their way.'

'Okay, how's Tyme doing down there?'

Tyme appeared beside Linda, looking considerably healthier than when Ed had last seen him. The young man's face had filled out, the dark circles under his eyes were gone. He even stood straighter, as if a great weight had been lifted from his shoulders.

'I'm fine and my brother wants to know if he can have the same treatment as me?'

'How many people know of this?' Ed asked, sternly.

'Just Jaccin,' he said. 'Linda told me not to tell anyone else.'

'That's good, because you must realise we don't have the logistics to detox hundreds of thousands of people. They're just going to have to do it the natural way with fresh water and good food.'

'I understand,' he said, his questioning face looking hopeful as he was still waiting for an answer.

'The two of you come up here when Linda returns to the ship and you talk to no one. You can travel down again when Tellamai returns to the surface.'

Jaccin's grinning face leant into shot.

'Thanks, Ed,' he said.

'Linda, d'you need anything else?' Ed asked.

She looked over her shoulder at all the people that had emerged from deep underground, staring open-mouthed at their star for the first time in their lives.

'Perhaps some after-sun moisturiser,' she said. 'I think there's going to be a few burnt faces tomorrow.'

The *Gabriel* remained at Aratap for another week. Most of the time was taken up with grounding all the remaining Repp ships still hanging around in space. A lot of them had come down of their own volition, but Cleo had been busy overriding their navigation systems and landing them herself. The local population were making short work of any Repps inside and converting the vessels to accommodation shelters. They had night-time on the planet now which brought fluctuations in temperature that they weren't used to.

The newer vessels were set to one side on the previously used Repp spaceports and guarded. They would prove useful in the future as the indigenous inhabitants reverted back to being the spacefaring race they once were.

Ed stood on a small raised platform, staring out at the gathered faces. What had begun as a simple farewell had somehow transformed into…this. The main cavern of Daro Koilada had been transformed, adorned with strands of the bioluminescent fungi woven into elaborate patterns that cast a soft blue-green glow across the assembly. Hundreds of people crowded the space, their faces upturned and expectant.

Tellamai and Slovena had insisted on this gathering before the *Gabriel* departed. 'A proper thank you,' they'd called it, though Ed felt distinctly uncomfortable being the centre of attention. He tugged at the collar of the ceremonial garment they'd presented him with…a deep blue robe embroidered with silver thread in patterns that reminded him of star maps.

'You look like you're about to make a run for it,' Andy whispered beside him, grinning broadly. He seemed entirely comfortable in his own ceremonial attire, a similar robe in dark green. 'Relax. It's not every day we get treated like heroes.'

'I'd rather be in the *Gabriel*'s hangar doing bloody maintenance checks,' Ed muttered back.

Slovena stepped forward, her tall frame commanding attention without effort. The mountain leader's elaborate tattoos seemed to shift in the flickering light as she raised her hands for silence. The murmur of the crowd died.

'People of Daro Koilada, people of Peta Katagio, people of Tin Koilada, people of all other settlements here gathered,' she began, her powerful voice carrying to the farthest corners of the chamber. 'For thousands of years, we have lived in darkness, both literal and figurative. We have toiled under the yoke of the Repps, believing their lies, accepting their control as the natural order.'

Ed shifted uncomfortably as her gaze fixed on him.

'For those who have not got to know these brave humans,' Slovena continued, 'they came from another galaxy entirely. They risked their lives to free us from our oppressors.'

Ed felt his face grow warm as thunderous applause erupted and hundreds of eyes fixed on him. He hated this kind of attention, always had. Give him a tactical problem, a damaged ship, even a Repp to fight...anything but this ceremonial bullshit.

Tellamai stepped forward, his weathered face solemn as he raised a hand. The old record keeper had cleaned up for the occasion, his white hair freshly braided and adorned with small blue stones that caught the bioluminescent light.

'Captain Edward Virr,' Tellamai announced, his soft voice carrying surprising strength. 'Please step forward.'

Ed shot a desperate glance at Andy next to him, who merely grinned and gave him a little push. Stumbling slightly, Ed stepped to the centre of the platform where Tellamai and Slovena waited. His ceremonial robe felt heavier with each step.

'Please kneel, Captain,' Slovena instructed.

Ed dropped to one knee, feeling distinctly ridiculous. From this position, he could see his crew scattered throughout the crowd. Linda stood with arms crossed, a rare smile playing at her lips. Phil was nodding appreciatively. Pol gave him a thumbs up that somehow meant more than the adulation of the hundreds present and made his heart skip.

Tellamai lifted something from a carved wooden box held by a young assistant...a large square medallion of polished haklion on a leather cord. The metal glowed with the same blue-green luminescence as the fungi.

'This medallion contains metal from the first Repp ever destroyed by our ancestors,' she explained. 'It has been passed down through generations, waiting for the day when true freedom would come.'

Tellamai placed the medallion around his neck. The metal felt surprisingly warm against his skin, almost alive. Its weight was substantial...heavier than it looked.

Its weight seemed to increase as her words sank in. Ed swallowed hard, suddenly understanding the significance of the gesture. This wasn't just a simple ceremony...it was history in the making.

'With this, we name you Custodian of Aratap,' Slovena proclaimed, her voice ringing through the cavern. 'Though you journey to other stars, you will always have a home among our people.'

The crowd erupted in deafening applause once more, the sound echoing off the cavern walls until it felt like the very mountain was cheering. Ed rose to his feet, the medallion heavy against his chest, his face burning with embarrassment.

'Thank you,' he managed, his voice sounding small in his own ears despite the amplification system. 'But I... we...only did what anyone would have done.'

Slovena smiled, a rare expression that transformed her stern features. 'And that, Captain Virr, is precisely why you deserve this honour.'

A few hours later, Ed lay on a sofa up in the *Gabriel*'s blister. He watched as the stars moved slowly across the glass ceiling, listening to Tchaikovsky's 'Piano Concerto No.1', a half-empty bottle of the Gabriel vineyard's verdelho on the table next to him.

'What are you listening to this shit for?' groaned Andy, strolling in with a grimace.

'Because it's the dog's nuts and I'm not in the mood for any Led Zep today,' he replied, sitting up and taking another sip of the wine.

'Hmm,' Andy grunted, collapsing into one of the armchairs with a sigh.

'Is there something on your mind?' Ed asked. 'Well, apart from nearly dying a week ago.'

Andy sat forward, wringing his hands.

'You didn't happen to pick my dad's gun up before you left the space station did you?' he asked, hopefully.

'Of course I bloody didn't,' Ed replied, shaking his head. 'I was kinda busy trying to avoid being sucked out into space.'

'Ah, right, sorry, it was just a thought. My dad's going to kill me when he finds out I've lost it.'

'Just buy another one, he'll never know.'

'It was a rare model and engraved as a leaving present from his colleagues at the FBI.'

'Oh, I didn't know that.'

Cleo appeared and sat on the arm of Andy's chair, giving him a broad grin.

'Have you done something, Cleo?' Andy asked, suspiciously.

'How much d'you love me?' she asked in reply.

'Well, loads,' he said. 'But you already know that.'

She clicked her fingers and a Smith and Wesson .44 magnum with an FBI inscription on the handle materialised in Andy's lap.

'How much d'you love me now?'

EPILOGUE

Castle Virr, Somerset coast, England, Earth

ED STOOD VERY STILL as Willow and Ripley, his two black greyhounds, went absolutely crazy at his return home. Gravel flew in all directions around the castle's central quadrangle as they leapt left and right, both trying to get cuddles at the same time as Ed exited the shuttle's airlock. They'd just started to calm down when Pol stepped out and it all began again, this time with a duet of squeaks and whimpers.

The journey back after dropping Civray off at Wellas had been long and restful. Ed had sent Admiral Loftt a comprehensive report on their Triangulum adventure and had been mildly surprised to not receive a reply before getting home. The other members of the crew had caught up on sleep. Andy had spent his days in the bridge hangar working on one of his two-stroke triple Kawasakis and Linda had done an advanced course on viticulture.

It was a frosty early December day in Somerset. Ed shivered in his single layer ship suit and, trying his best to avoid being tripped by a dog, made for the huge oak front doors.

'Good morning and welcome home, Mr Edward, Miss Pol,' said Marjorie, the castle's long-serving housekeeper, as she swung the door wide. Everyone there knew her as Auntie Marge, having started her employment there as a junior chambermaid some forty-seven years ago.

'Hello, Marge,' said Ed, trying to calm the dogs and stop them jumping up. 'Everything good?'

'Yes, Mr Edward…there are guests awaiting your arrival by the fire in the east hall.'

'Oh?'

'Admiral Loftt,' she whispered. 'He seems a little agitated.'

'Well, that explains the smart-looking yacht sitting over by the stable block,' Ed replied, jabbing a thumb in that direction.

'What on Earth did you put in that report?' Pol asked, closing the heavy door with a thunk.

'Nothing that would upset anyone, least of all Bache.'

Marjorie raised her eyebrows and glanced at the stone archway and corridor that led to the east wing.

'I'll bring coffee,' she said, turning and heading for the butler's pantry.

'You might want to pop a large brandy in it too, by the sound of it,' Ed called after her.

He took a deep breath and headed for the east hall, following the ancient stone corridor with Pol and the dogs at his heels. The smell of woodsmoke grew stronger as they approached, mingling with the castle's permanent scent of old stone and beeswax polish. The corridor opened into the vast east hall, where a fire roared in the massive hearth, casting flickering shadows across the stone walls and illuminating the tall stained-glass windows at the far end.

Admiral Loftt stood facing the fire, hands clasped behind him, his broad shoulders silhouetted against the flames. He wore civilian clothes rather than his usual GDA uniform...a charcoal grey suit that looked expensive but rumpled, as if he'd been wearing it for days. His normally immaculate salt and pepper hair seemed longer and slightly dishevelled.

'Admiral,' Ed said, stepping into the room with a smile. 'This is unexpected.'

Loftt swivelled on his heel, his weathered face haggard in the firelight and the bags under his eyes spoke of sleepless nights.

'Ah, Edward,' he said, his voice hoarse. 'Thank the Ancients you're back.'

Ed felt a chill that had nothing to do with the December cold outside. He'd never seen the Admiral as unsettled as this...not during the Halo crisis, not during the Klatt conflict, not even when he'd lost half the fleet with all hands. Something was very wrong.

'What's happened?' Ed blurted, moving closer to the fire. The dogs, sensing the tension, slinked over to their beds with their tails between their legs and lay straight down without circling first.

The admiral wasn't alone. A man whom Ed recognised sat rigidly in one of the leather armchairs. He wore a GDA intelligence uniform, his long dark hair slicked back in a ponytail that seemed out of place for a GDA officer.

'This is…'

'Captain Pickyrd,' Ed said, the introduction unnecessary.

'Commander Pickyrd,' Bache corrected him. 'Intelligence Division.'

'We spent time together a while back I remember,' said Ed, rubbing his chin in thought. 'Old cell mates on that Klatt vessel that messed up Dasos, if my memory serves me right.'

'Yes, Captain…I'll never forget that little episode,' Pickyrd said.

'You captained the 28,' said Pol. 'I remember too.'

'Enough reminiscing about the good old days,' said Bache, impatiently.

Ed noticed the Admiral was clenching and unclenching his fists.

'Bache, what is it?' he asked.

The Admiral's shoulders slumped as he moved towards one of the leather armchairs. The firelight caught the lines on his face, making him look ten years older than the last time Ed had seen him.

'It's my son, Edward. Ballatech's been taken.'

Ed felt his stomach drop. Ballatech Loftt…Bache's only son, brilliant physicist, and one of the GDA's leading up-and-coming researchers on jump technology. Ed had seen him a few times at official functions, although they'd not spoken to each other directly as far as he could remember.

'Taken? By whom?' Ed asked, moving to sit directly across from the Admiral.

Pickyrd leant forward, his voice dropping to just above a whisper. 'We believe it's the Klatt.'

'The Klatt again?' Ed exchanged a quick glance with Pol. A few years earlier, both he and Pol had been abducted by the Klatt. 'But we haven't had Klatt activity in GDA space for a while now…what makes you think it's them?'

'Three days ago, I received this,' Bache said, his voice cracking slightly. He reached into his jacket pocket and pulled out a small holographic projector, placing it on the coffee table between them. A blue image flickered to life…security footage showing a laboratory of some kind. Ballatech Loftt stood at a workstation, his back to the camera. Three figures materialised from nowhere, surrounding him. The short, squat, dark, scaly-faced soldiers were pretty unmistakable.

Ed leant closer, watching as Ballatech turned, clearly startled. There was no audio, but Ed could see the young man's mouth open in shock.

'The research facility on Erevna Station say they've had no contact with Ballatech since,' said Pickyrd.

Bache sat back with a sigh, wringing his hands this time.

Ed turned to Pickyrd and raised an eyebrow.

'I take it you've started an investigation?' Ed asked.

The Commander exchanged a fleeting glance with Bache and his expression darkened.

'That's why we're here,' said Bache. 'The GDA council have refused to allow naval time and resources to be spent on what they consider a civilian matter.'

'You're not in your usual uniform, Admiral,' said Pol. 'Are you taking time off to try and find him?'

'That's just it, Pol,' he said, sounding unusually vulnerable. 'I resigned my position immediately. After everything I've done over the decades for the improvement and security of the GDA, this is how they thank me. Bloody job's already cost me my marriage. The Commander here very kindly brought me over to see you in his own time and in his private yacht.'

'You want me go to find Ballatech?' Ed asked, sitting back.

'No, Edward…I want us to go find him…I'm coming too.'

Ed slowly turned his head, to find Pol staring back at him with dangerous eyes.

AFTERWORD

I wanted to say a huge thank you for choosing to read *The Triangulum Fold*. I sincerely hope you enjoyed the eighth adventure in the *Fold* series.

If you did enjoy this novel, it'd be fantastic if you could write a review. It doesn't have to be long, just a few words, but it is the best way for me to help new readers discover my writing for the first time. I use the best and most imaginative reviews in my marketing too.

If you'd like to buy my ebooks direct from me, or stay up to date with what's going on, you're welcome to join my reader group at my website www.nickadamsbooks.com You'll receive a free short story (The Architect Fold), a bi-monthly newsletter and advance notice of new releases and cover reveals. I will never share your email address and you can unsubscribe at any time.

You can also contact me via Facebook, Instagram, or by email. I love hearing from readers...I read every message and try to reply to everyone personally.

Thanks again for your support.
Nick Adams